Bread and Swans

♋

"Erwin, this is no time for off-color humor."

"How the devil can you even say that? After what I just saw?"

"You saw nothing, unless it was in your own imagination." Pfirsich settled his rumpled jacket back into place. "Now come. You're making a public spectacle of yourself." He turned away.

"Where do you think you're going?" demanded Erwin.

Pfirsich turned back, stooped down and put his face right into Erwin's. When his pretty features stiffened with anger, his cheekbones protruded like Erwin's, and in everything but height the Rommel brothers could have been twins.

"I'm going into the library," he snapped. "Where you will be forced to keep your voice down."

Erwin plunged right after him. "If you don't think I can tell you off in a whisper -- you just try me!"

Bread and Swans

Donna Barr

AFLP
A Fine Line Press

For information regarding fair use, review copies, wholesale, bulk or retail
purchases, or negotiations for re-publication, please contact A Fine Line Press
at barr@stinz.com

Arch and Bruce Brown Foundation Grant awarded for the short story "A Good
Example," later expanded.

Library of Congress Cataloging-in-Publication Data

Barr, Donna   Bread And Swans

Fiction: Historical
History: Germany
Humor: Political
Social Science: Gay studies/gender studies.

Library of Congress Control Number: 2005934000

ISBN: 1-892253-22-4
EAN: 978-1-892253-22-4

Printed as POD and electronic book at Booksurge.com
Available wholesale at: www.booksurgedirect.com

1 2 3 4 5 6 7 8 9 0

Cover photography: Eric Schneider

To

Robert Drake.

T. Brian and Mike.

Barb Rausch. For Venice.

John, who knew the Captain.

Eric Schneider, for making me learn the basics of InDesign.

And all my readers, their knowledge, and their inspiration.

For clarity and spelling, and for the bad French.

And for the patience of the Germans.

But Karl May
did it
to us.

First.

♋

Note to the reader:

Some of this is History.

Some of it is Reality.

Some of it is still happening.

All of it is True

♋

Those who know history
are condemned to repeat it —
just in different clothes.

1. Bread and Swans

The White Bear hung his head and sighed.

The boy was just a bark-brown lump of school jacket and shorts and despair. His thin white legs dangled forlornly against the dank mossy stone wall paralleling the unpaved road to the medieval town of Heidenheim an der Brenz. Far above drowsed Hellenstein Castle, its sunlit white walls and red tile roof stretching along the shadowy forested ridge like the loins and limbs of a dozing lion. To the boy it was as though the castle had reached down and set a paw upon his shoulders. That's how he felt: crushed.

He was trying not to weep – but not from fear.

Even as a toddler the boy, whom his family had nicknamed for his pale hair, had been startlingly fearless. He'd been known to solemnly shake hands with the wirey sooty chimney sweeps that so terrified the other children. It was as though the part of his mind that generated Fear had never been properly wired.

But he'd been sickly all his short life. Illness made everything very serious for him. Any faint incidence of dishonesty, any lack of character in those around him, at least as he perceived it, made him insecure and unhappy in his world. He needed to be able to count on people. He was so dependent on the truth he didn't even know what a lie was.

Invalids are often lazy, even after they've recovered. The boy wasn't applying himself in the elementary classes. No remarks by his impatient exacting father could convince the boy to attempt anything in a life he'd barely been able to hold onto.

Only two days before, his teacher -- frustrated by yet another of this boy's inattentive papers, with its usual wander of drawings in the margins – had made an announcement to his class.

"If our Erwin ever turns in a perfect paper," harrumphed the man. "We shall hire a brass band, and go out for a day in the country."

Erwin's slanted blue eyes opened wide. There was nothing he loved more than a romp alone in the woods. Never thinking that a class full of children would accompany him, he buckled down and wrote a wondrously standardized essay. The margins were impeccable. *Herr Lehrer* would surely be pleased.

Herr Lehrer was pleased, but the only reward the boy received was a pat on his head and the pronouncement that the paper was "Very good, Erwin. I knew you could do it, if you just applied yourself."

Erwin stood there, all faith in promises frozen, heart bruised.

Now he sat hunched on the wall, too childishly bitter to go home, and trying not to cry.

"Erwin!"

A voice like a *Rotweiler* puppy. Erwin looked up to see his youngest brother Pfirsich come pelting down the dusty road, his wiry little form silhouetted against the modest brick-built medieval town where they'd both been born.

Nothing could overshadow this vibration of childish rage. The boy's blue sailor suit was dusty from his latest street-side squabble, his white stockings falling down around his brown buckle shoes. Under his arm was his beloved blue-and-white toy tugboat that Erwin had knocked together for him from wood scraps and leftover paint. Pfirsich used it for everything from a boat to a hammer, and it looked it.

Erwin was used to seeing him in this rumpled state, and didn't even look up, sitting there on the wall like a cracked egg.

"Erwin!"

Pfirsich was a tiny personification of Mad Mad Mad. He plummeted to an indignant stop right in front of his brother.

"The spelling, the punctuation -- perfect," mourned Erwin, studying his paper. "Look at the handwriting."

"Erwin, they bite-ed me!" howled the little terror, jumping up and down.

"It's not right," said Erwin.

2

"Bullies! Ganging up on me!"

"I don't know why I bother," Erwin sighed again, and dropped down off the wall into the road.

Pfirsich smacked him in the arm with the tugboat. "Oh, pfui on your ol' paper! Them swans bite-ed me!"

"Au!" protested Erwin, and dropped his paper, scattering the three pages on the ground. He was twice as big as Pfirsich, but that didn't keep the little bully from bruising him.

Rubbing his arm, he said, "Pfirsich, were you sailing your boat in the pond again?"

"Yes! And they bite-ed me! Look!" He pulled up his sleeve. "Bruises!"

Erwin only squatted down to pick up his papers. "Then find another pond. Why are you being so stubborn?"

Pfirsich plumped down in front of his brother, and held out his arm, whimpering, "Er-win -- Loook. They *bite*-ed me. Erwin? Look --."

"Then bite them back," snapped Erwin. He stood up, dusting off his papers. "Stop attacking everything, Pfirsich. Life isn't a war." He turned and walked off, sliding the papers into his school bag. "You're going to get hurt one of these days."

"Am not! Am NOT!" yapped Pfirsich the invincible child. "If you don't help me -- you're a sissy! A sissy a sissy a sissy!"

Erwin just shook his head and kept walking.

"Come home, Pfirsich. Mama will wonder where you are."

"Erwin, you're a GIRL!"

"You have beautiful manners, Pfirsich," said Erwin, without looking back.

"I'm gonna show you!" yelled Pfirsich, and raced past him, heading into town.

"Very good. Let me know when you do."

Was gilt, thought Erwin. What do you want to bet, he's going right back to that pond, because he has no sense. Those swans will teach him a lesson. Make him pull his horns in short. *Wer hört nicht, muß fühlen.* _Erwin sniffed. Don't listen, and you'll hurt. They'll hold him under water until he comes to terms, and goes crying home to Mama.

He stopped. Under water?

The next moment, he was flying down the road after his brother,

3

screaming, "Pfirsich! Leave the swans alone! They're dangerous!"

Erwin was fast for his size. He arrived at the pond in town in time to catch his baby brother doing a passable military low-crawl through the long grass on the bank. The brat's target was a big Mute Swan cob.

The bird's neck bent in a snaky militant curve. The black knob on the hot-orange bill shone like a helmet crest, and the long wide snowy wings were hunched in challenging display. It was capable of drowning a man if it caught him in the water, and on dry land of breaking his knees with those huge bony wrist joints. And inclined to do it.

To oppose the great cob Pfirsich clutched only a sappy little stick in his little hand. With this primitive armament he imagined he was about to equally oppose the avian world's equivalent of an English Dreadnought. But before he could make his rush forward, he felt himself whipped into the air, an arm across his chest, a hand struggling to wrest the stick from his grip.

"*Nein!*" yelled Erwin. "Put it down! Pfirsich!"

Pfirsich only growled and kicked like a bad-tempered kitten.

"Ow!" cried Erwin. "Don't bite! Stop it."

The small child's three weapons are biting, kicking and spitting. The first two hadn't worked, so the brat turned and spat right into his brother's face. It was only spittle, but Erwin was a decent child, and decently clean, and he released the brat in disgust.

"You horrible little monster!" he said, wiping the saliva from his lips and cheeks. "Pfirsich!"

He cried out in terror to see Pfirsich on direct course for the big cob. The creature saw him coming, and lowered its neck from its dominating curve, grunting nearly inaudibly, its only voice. It made up in size and attitude what it lacked in noise.

Pfirsich wasn't intimidated. He raced right into the shallows, oblivious of his shoes, waving his stick, determined to have at the cob. And then it stood up on its thick black legs in the shallows and spread its wings.

They spanned more than two meters, and the black knob ranged upward on the white neck like the head of a cobra; a big water-bird had become a snake-headed warrior archangel, an angel with a feathered sword, and mean with it.

Pfirsich only had a moment to squeak in fear; the next moment the bird's wrist joint had swung down and bashed him in the temple.

In another moment Erwin's school bag, swung at the full extent of its straps, caught the cob in the head. The bird hissed and nearly fell over backwards into the water. Righting itself with a tremendous explosive slap of wings on water, it came after Erwin, determined to break something. Erwin hit the bird again, then repeatedly; he could think fast when he had to, and he knew he hadn't a hope of killing the angry brute, that he had to drive it away without further resistance. His brother was lying facedown in the water, and couldn't be dragged out until that cob was gone.

The cob wasn't prepared for such a furious schoolboy tornado. It fled grunting out into the pond, swollen with anger, but not daring to return. It had won its share of fights in its warlike life, and like any experienced *Krieger*, recognized a beating when it got one. It could only take out its feelings on the other swans in the pond.

Erwin would never gloat over an enemy's defeat. But he would take advantage of its retreat, as he did now, to drag Pfirsich out of the pond and onto the bank, without so much as hearing the wings of the squabbling swans singing and splashing behind him. An instinct told him the swan wasn't coming back.

"Pfirsich?" he muttered, kneading his brother's back. "Pfirsich? *Oh, Gott,* they can kill little kids. Pfirsich, please."

Pfirsich was pretty, but he was tough, like a Persian kitten. He moaned, and rolled over. Erwin was quick to prop him up against his own body.

"Komm doch, Kind," he encouraged him. "I'll take you home."

"Ooh," moaned the little battered hooligan. "Mama.... Rotten swans," he snuffled.

Erwin gathered him up in his arms; he could still carry him easily. "Promise me, Pfirsich, you'll never, *ever* go near those birds again."

"Won't," gulped Pfirsich, rubbing his sore head. "Hurt-ed me." He squinted, and began to sob. "Ooh... Erwin... my head hurts.... so *bad.* It hurts, it hurts. It hurts."

Before continuing on his way, Erwin threw a glance over his shoulder at the hissing swans. He had the high cheekbones and slanted eyes of the Mongol horsemen who had invaded Swabia so many centuries ago. In that moment, his eyes, blue as they were, looked as black as the eyes of any of his steppe-racing ancestors.

5

* * * * *

"He'll be all right, *Frau* Rommel," said the doctor, moving a finger back and forth before Pfirsich's bright blue tearful eyes. "No concussion, but those birds gave him a good hard knock."

"Gott sei Dank."

"Just some scrapes. I see you've already applied plenty of Merbromin."

"We can't have infection, *Herr Doktor.*"

"Good, because I didn't bring any. I've never seen a good German household without it -- or a bad one, for that matter. I'm perfectly happy to miss all the crying and squirming."

"Well, if it didn't sting -- "

"It Wouldn't Be Any Good," grinned the doctor, recognizing a stolid German belief. "Now, rest is the best medicine. Perhaps this will cure him of taking on everything bigger than himself."

"I hope so, *Herr* Doktor."

"Your Pfirsich has too much courage for his own good. Perhaps he'll grow up to be a soldier."

"I wish he were more like our Erwin."

"Our Erwin" was listening at the door of the room little wounded Pfirsich shared with their elder sister. Helene was wringing out cool cloths over a basin, then handing them to their mother, and looking very stern and nurselike through her spectacles. Helene didn't imagine that she looked grown up yet, but she was searching for the impression. Erwin shared the other room with the middle brothers, Karl and Gerhard, and all the boys were peeping in at the door.

"Erwin will be a quiet, sensible man, *Frau* Rommel," continued the doctor. "Perhaps he will take after his mother in his temper."

"We can hope," *Frau* Rommel said dryly.

The doctor bowed and clicked his heels. *Frau* Rommel had been born an aristocrat, and the doctor always remembered, and found a way to compliment little Erwin. The boy looked just like his Mama, and the doctor assumed he was the favorite.

The doctor tucked away his stethoscope into his brown leather bag. "You'll always be able to depend on Erwin to use his head." he said,

6

and gently patted the whimpering Pfirsich's little clenched fist. "And with this little wild animal on your hands, you'll need someone like Erwin to keep him out of trouble."

Erwin missed all the compliments. He had withdrawn from the little crowd of rubbernecking brothers, and retreated back down the hallway, toward the kitchen. Even as the adults expressed their hopes for his future, he was carefully and silently digging through the cupboards, with thoughts developing in his mind that would have raised his noble-blooded upright mother's hair, not to say her hackles.

"It's not the swan's fault," he thought, rummaging into the pantry, properly assigning responsibility as Mama had taught him. "It was Pfirsich's. He deserved what he got. But I'm his brother, and those swans are a lot bigger than him."

Erwin collected what he had found into his cap, and tiptoed down the back stairs.

The little personification of Biblical Justice didn't run to the swan pond; he walked, with solemn determination. On the bank of the pond, he put down his cap, and set out its contents upon the grass: a hank of bread and a pepper grinder. An eye for an eye.

The swans were used to being fed by people. While they watched, Erwin crumbled up the piece of bread on the grass. Pepper was expensive, but he.ground the fresh pricey condiment lavishly over the breadcrumbs. Mama was going to swat him good, but those were the Necessary Consequences.

The swans came grunting and snaking their necks from the water, their thick black legs glistening with wet. They didn't rush, like ducks -- they were too big -- instead wobbling forward with dignity, like parade float towers. They ducked their heads and began to greedily gobble up the proffered crumbs. Erwin, as grave as they, stood back and watched.

As the swans began to gag and hiss, thundering and whistling with their regal white wings, in a royal explosion of indignity and pain, Erwin was glad Pfirsich wasn't there. This was a very, very bad example.

* * * * *

Pfirsich, unaware of the Acts of Revenge that had been going forward in his name, opened his eyes in the dark room when he heard his brother's voice.

"Hullo, Pfirsich. How are you feeling?"

"Erwin?"

"You'll be all right, now," Erwin reassured him. "You can go to the pond any time you like. I took care of it for you. "

He leaned over to kiss his brother on his bandaged forehead.

"Erwin!" barked <u>Frau</u> Rommel from the hall, and both brothers jumped.

"*Ja*, Mama?" Erwin came cautiously out into the hallway to find his mother staring intently into his cap.

"What is this in your cap?" she demanded, and then started in horror. "Heavens! It looks like -- " She swung around and took him by the ear. "Let me see your head."

"Au!" yelped the future General. "Mama!"

"Oh! Have you been playing with that Schmoren boy again? Look at you! You're infested! To the bathroom, young man."

Erwin, as a Swabian the child of a cleanly people, realized with horror what she must be thinking. "No, Mama, it's not lice. It's just -- "

She'd been picking bits of the offending vermin out of his white hair, and didn't give him a chance to explain. "Bread crumbs!" she said. "Bread crumbs and black pepper."

Erwin had managed to get loose from her short strong fingers, and stood vigorously scrubbing his own fingers through his hair, scattering breadcrumbs all over the hall carpet runner.

"Erwin!" his mother demanded.

"Um," he hesitated. "I was feeding the swans."

"With black pepper?"

Mama was shaken to the root of her careful householding soul. She might have been a *von* herself, and brought her own fortune and gems to her marriage into a family of schoolteachers and minor bureaucrats, but rich people don't get or stay rich by being spendthrifts. Pepper was still very expensive, and not to be squandered on pranks.

"They hurt Pfirsich," exculpated Erwin. "They hurt my little brother."

"Wasteful *and* cruel!" came the short swift judgment, and just as swiftly followed the punishment. SWATT! came her firm hard hand across Erwin's small shrinking bottom, just as he'd expected.

"Au!" he squeaked in hurt and humiliation, but he stood still for it. He knew he deserved it, but it didn't make it any easier to take. He was just happy she hadn't gone to fetch that chastising weapon of a German mama, a wooden spoon. As angry as she was, she would have broken it on his butt.

"You know better than that!" SWATSWATSWAT

Pfirsich lay in the semidarkness of his room, listening to Erwin take punishment for protecting him. He put his little damp fists to his eyes and snuffled with gratitude and guilt. And sorrow that he hadn't been there to see the swans get theirs.

"I'm very disappointed, Erwin." he heard their mother say, "Now, have you learned your lesson?"

"*Ja*, Mama," whispered Erwin, slinking head-hung by the bedroom door.

"Me too," sobbed Pfirsich, sitting up in bed and hawling out the door way. "I learnded, too -- don't go near the swans. You get hurted."

Bread and Swans

2. Life in Venice

The Rommel family was staying on the third floor of an unpretentious Venice hotel, a few narrow twisting waterways from the palaces of the Grand Canal. The hotel was close enough to share in the atmosphere of the princely neighborhood, and far enough removed for quiet, modesty and moderation. The soft blue shadows along the little canal glowed with the pots of red begonias balanced on the broad limestone windowsills, their bright petals reflected in the dark water below like little spots of fire.

The only drawback was the city's distinctive version of street sanitation. True, the canals didn't need to be swept of horse leavings, but the low marshland tide was never strong enough to flush the main waterways completely clean, much less the minor channels, and in the backwaters the garbage washed tranquilly back and forth between the city pilings. Middle-class tourists risked cholera, the high-collared aristocrats on the Grand Canal cholera and heat stroke. Everyone braved disease for the art and the society. And the sunshine.

"Stay away from the back windows," *Frau* Rommel told her children. "If you fall into the canal, you don't know what you can catch. If you don't break your little necks, it's so far down. And we're not paying for those flowers if you knock them off."

"Ignore the smell," said *Herr* Rommel, when his daughter Helene turned up her nose as they stepped into the street. "We'll buy nose-gays at the flower market."

"Cinnamon and lavender," said her mother. "Strong but subtle."

"Oh, Mama," said Helene. "That's from the old days."

"It smelled like this in the old days," said her father. "Welcome to history."

"History smells!" said Pfirsich.

"There aren't any elevators," whined Karl.

11

"Good exercise," boomed Erwin Senior. He spread out his arms, took a deep breath, and had a coughing fit.

They'd put Helene in charge of the four boys, as usual, on the trip from Germany on the train, as usual indulging her yearning for adulthood. But even on the train there had been the first simmerings of discontent. Helene spent much time polishing her glasses, her lips pursed in concentration, and Erwin sat silent in the corner of his seat, his arms crossed and his chin set, frowning out window at the swoop of the telegraph wires.

Upon achieving Venice and their hotel rooms, *Herr* and *Frau* Rommel strengthened their resolve and went forth to enjoy their first superb sun-drenched Italian day, Helene marshaling the boys behind them. The family wandered the canals and piazzas, looked up at the statues, studied the mosaics that glimmered in color underfoot and the towers that shimmered in light above. The parents Rommel spent the day delightedly matching up what they saw with around them with what they found listed in the Baedecker Guide, worrying less about their sons than they might usually have, serene in the maturity of their eldest child. They wandered the canals and piazzas, took notes about the statues, studied the mosaic that glimmered in color underfoot and admired the towers.

They went to bed tired and content, and awoke to find an open rebellion on their hands.

"They're completely out of hand," reported Helene in the breakfast hall. "I don't want to spend the rest of my whole vacation trying to make them behave."

"We've been studying the maps of Venice, just for this trip," said *Frau* Rommel. "Don't you boys enjoy seeing what you've been studying?"

"Ach, Mama," said Karl. "Do we have to be in school here too?"

"You're not Red Indians," said their father. "You just don't put your brains aside, simply because you're away from home."

"We want to rest our brains!" whined Gerhard, and pressed his hands to his forehead as though it were bursting with all that knowledge.

"Ja!" repeated Pfirsich, imitating him, and crossing his eyes.

"Boys!" said *Frau* Rommel, glacing around at the other tables.

"They won't obey me," protested Helene. "Especially Erwin."

"Erwin?" said her mother.

Erwin was sitting at the end of the table, chin on his hand, staring out the hotel window this time. He didn't respond beyond a one-shouldered shrug.

"Erwin, answer your mother!" commanded *Herr* Rommel.

"And elbow off the table," said Helene.

Erwin turned around and sat up and left his elbow where it was. "I don't need to obey her. I'm too old."

Herr Rommel half stood up. "Young man! You'll watch your mouth at this table."

"You certainly will," said *Frau* Rommel. "What's wrong with you, child?" She pointed at his elbow.

"Not a child," muttered Erwin, looking down at his breakfast and slipping his elbow under the table where it belonged.

"Ha!" said Pfirsich, and then, because Gerhard pinched him under the table, "Ow!"

"Very well," *Herr* Rommel said. "If you're not a child, you can watch the other children. Helene can go with us to the museum today."

"Thank you," said Helene, adjusting her spectacles.

"Papa!" protested Erwin. "I don't want to watch these three."

"You'll watch them and like it. Now eat your breakfast."

"Especially Pfirsich," said his mother, and pointed meaningfully at the wild youngling.

"Ow!" said Pfirsich, again.

Frau Rommel reached out and shook Gerhard. She knew perfectly well who did the pinching at table. Karl giggled and blew out his cheeks, then ducked when Mama turned and glared hard at him.

"They don't need me," protested Erwin. "Let them go out by themselves. Nothing could stand up to the three of them when they're together."

His mother's look silenced him. "This is Italy, dear," she said.

That day, Helene sailed out into the streets and canals in the company of her parents, pointedly walking beside them as an equal. Behind them straggled Erwin, sullen and feeling sorely mishandled, leashed by his new authority to his trio of younger brothers.

It wasn't long before their giggling and shoving infringed upon his sense of responsibility. If he was going to be in charge, with or without his choice, then his charges were going to get in line, like it or not. He turned on them like an old wolf. They yipped and protested like pack pups for a little while, before they gave in and followed him as they were used to follow Helene. Erwin put his head in the air and after that, his mere glare was enough to reduce them to obedient silence.

The Rommels and their children toured until they were tired, then stopped for tea and lightly sugared *cenci* in a shady narrow street behind the bell tower of St. Mark's basilica. *Cenci* fritters were more a Florentine sweet than Venetian, but an easy compromise to be offered the taste of a tourist, and northern Europeans liked cookies with their coffee. The younger boys were finished first, and begged to be let go on their own.

"We got Erwin to go with us!" said Gerhard, wiping the powdered sugar off his face before speaking up. "He's a grownup, now."

"Yes, Erwin," said *Frau* Rommel. "You go with the boys, now. Make sure they're safe, and don't get into any trouble. And don't let Gerhard spend all his money the first minute."

"Aw, Mama," said Gerhard.

"Mama," said Erwin.

"Do as your mother says," said *Herr* Rommel.

Erwin got up in silence and obeyed, stalking off with his burdensome brothers, trying to maintain his newfound dignity while they chattered and clattered down the street around him. The three elder Rommels sipped their steaming cups of coffee in peace.

It had recently become apparent that Erwin was in possession of a remarkable sense of direction, and Karl and Gerhard and Pfirsich had often tested it back home by blindfolding him, leading him along alleys and bridges, to spin him around several times before they freed him to guide them back to more familiar streets. Venice's unknown sunlit byways and gloomy covered alleys would pose an even greater challenge. Erwin didn't seem all that excited by the concept, but they kept at him until he agreed to being blindfolded and led away. They had some thrilling moments while he stared up at the towering medieval walls, and they were all atremble that they might be picked up as vagrant boys by the police and led over the Bridge of Sighs into a real royal Italian dungeon.

It wasn't long before Erwin tired of the game, and to teach the boys a lesson he pretended he was really lost, and put his hands over his mouth, looking around with very realistic confusion in his eyes. Gerhard screamed, and Karl and Pfirsich both hit him, before Erwin relented and led them all back to the hotel, stopping to carefully wash everybody's face in a fountain, so Mama wouldn't find out the children had been crying and hold him responsible for their distress. .

Pfirsich wasn't distressed for long, and he didn't want to play the Lost game any more. When he plunged out into the city with his brothers the next time, he did it on the run, and he was on the lookout for elevators. There were no elevators in the little back canal hotel the Rommels were occupying, no elevators back home, at least none a small boy would be allowed to ride loose with. And the exceptionally ornate mirror-faceted and iron-filigreed confections that moved people in the most sumptuous glittering hotels and palaces were one in grace with the gondolas that moved people in the waters of the canals. A body didn't ride them but rather soared as royalty.

They fascinated Pfirsich, and his enthusiasm was catching. All Erwin could do was try to keep the boys leashed in. He didn't yet possess Helene's complete grown-up authority, and they were taking full advantage before he found it.

The Rommel boys crowded gracelessly into a high-class hotel elevator, Karl and Gerhard giggling, Erwin frowning at Pfirsich, who was punching all the elevator buttons.

"Stop that!" snapped Erwin. "You'll have us stopping at all the floors."

"That's the idea," chortled Karl, as Pfirsich kept poking the buttons.

On every floor, the ingenious doors came open and closed, and Gerhard clapped his hands in delight. On the sixth floor, a woman and boy stepped aboard. The two of them looked Slavic, probably Polish or Ukrainian. The woman was fat, irritable, and resentful, sweating in the southern heat; this was probably not her choice as a vacation resort. The child, her son, was a sallow fat dark boy with oddly transparent, fragile teeth. She turned her own dark eyes upon the four German boys, and the three young gigglers became as silent as their elder brother. Erwin looked sternly at the son, and bowed solemnly and politely to the mother. He was startled when the boy stuck out his tongue at him.

"Dahtzyo!" snapped the woman, in the exact tone that Erwin had used toward Pfirsich, and smacked her son. The doors of the elevator drew open one floor up, and the Slavs stepped off, the woman pushing the boy ahead of her.

"Dahtzyo!" hooted Pfirsich after them, and Erwin smacked him.

After her first pronouncement of the name, the Slav mother's impatient repetition of her son's moniker seemed intent upon following the Rommel boys around the streets and plazas. "Dahtzyo," or so his name sounded to them each time it was repeated, was a perverse stubborn child, constantly running away and hiding and almost falling into the canal. Karl and Gerhard began to admire his rebellion, but Erwin and Pfirsich, for once in agreement, stood firm and consorted in an effort to avoid his company.

Soon Karl and Gerhard openly took Dahtzyo's part, and accused their brothers of snobbery. Erwin said, "He is spoiled and stupid." Pfirsich said, "His teeth are ugly." Nothing is more unrelenting than the prejudice of children.

While his mother hunted her fat son, the German boys went around in circles through the city, two and two, half of them siding with the boy from the East, and even assisting him in fleeing his mother, and half of them trying to glare or intimidate him away or terrify him back to mama. Gerhard would show off by buying his new friend sweets and fruit, if he could do it before Erwin caught him. Karl would keep a lookout. Pfirsich called named and tattled. Erwin tried to break up the resulting battles. Dahtzyo wasn't the first to come up against inconsistencies among the Germans.

Erwin sniffed. "That woman's voice! She shrieks like a *Rohrspatz.*"

He meant the noisy reedbird that matches the English fishwife for a harsh voice, and Pfirsich took it up with such a nasty glee that Erwin immediately denied him any further use of the word.

"Don't tell me what to say!" yelped Pfirsich. "I saw you creeping up on him by a canal, once."

"I was not!"

"You meant to push him in."

"I did not!" Erwin was aghast. "I wouldn't push anybody into those filthy canals. That water is diseased."

He realized that siding with Pfirsich was the worst thing he could do, and he finally reported Pfirsich's bad manners to their mother. She was very familiar with the reports of her boys' misbehavior in their home town, their flying about where they pleased -- the brainless Pfirsich at their head -- with no concern where they went, or whom they might encounter. When Erwin came in with his misbehaving flock, red in the face with frustration and anger and accused Pfirsich of harassing the neighbors, *Herr* Rommel wanted to take a strap to all four of them. Gerhard almost squawked "Tattletale!" but Karl put his hand over his mouth.

"It's not Erwin's fault," said his mother.

"Then he'd better take care of all of them. *Mein Gott,* this is Italy, boy!" said Erwin's father. "Don't you know any better?"

"Yes, sir, I do," said Erwin. "It won't happen again."

If he thought the look he gave Pfirsich was going to make the little blond hellion stay in line, then Erwin didn't know as much about as his brother as he flattered himself that he did. He did know enough to stay right on Pfirsich's heels, and even keep his hand in his most of the time. This meant he had either to haul Pfirsich painfully along behind him, or to follow him reluctantly on his forays into the streets.

"Keep it up, *Bursch,*" he threatened. "And I'll put you on a leash."

"Like a dog!" said Gerhard. "Let's buy a dog. One of those little Italian greyhounds – "

"It's just what he deserves," said Karl. "He even smells like a dog."

"One more word out of either one of you, and I'll get three leashes!" threatened Erwin, hauling back on Pfirsich's hand before the boy could lunge forward and kick Karl.

Pfirsich headed right to where he had last seen his favorite prey, Dahtzyo, and now he stood watching the dark boy in the shining middle distance of the *Plaza di San Marco*, hiding as he so often did behind a handy column, the yelling Slav woman in the background.

Pfirsich was so intent on watching them that he didn't know that someone was observing him. In his neat sailor suit Pfirsich looked very young, and angelically pretty, even when he frowned childishly at the dark Slavic boy. He didn't know a tall angular middle-aged man was contemplating him. The well-dressed gentleman with a neat moustache stood in the dappled shade of an acacia tree, under a tower that flew one bright red-and-yellow medieval pennant. Erwin saw him, and observed him with fierce ignorant suspicion. He took a tighter grip on Pfirsich's hand, and stepped between his brother and the gentleman, with the first

17

burgeoning of an intense guardianship. In that moment, Erwin stopped looking like child.

The gentleman took out a small yellow-bound notebook and began to make what appeared even from a distance to be scrupulous little notes, with a tiny gold-bound pen that sparkled in the sunshine filtering through the acacia. He was an author, and while here in the watery city he had begun to write another of the finely crafted *Novellen* that had been so well received in recent years, in his home country, and even in England.

At the moment he wasn't looking at the architecture around him, or the picturesque gondoliers or the shadow of the floating pennant. He was looking at Pfirsich, and only stopped taking notes when he realized he was being watched himself. All his attention had been on the vibrating bundle of blond energy in the sailor suit, and he was startled by his own lack of attention when he found himself fixed by Erwin's piercing blue glare, directed right at him over one sharp adolescent shoulder. Pfirsich felt his brother stand up straight, pulling on his wrist.

"Erwin, don't!" he snapped, and then saw the look on his big brother's face. If Erwin could have put his ears back, they'd have been pinned to his skull.

Nasty spaghetti eater, he thought. Papa was right.

That was the end of Pfirsich's bratty cockiness, at least for the afternoon. Something was out there that the elder brother felt was a threat, and it was only natural that the little brother whimper and hunch behind him in fear.

The tall gentleman had an excellent imagination.

"That very protective young man over there," he thought, "Is possessed of all of the fierceness of the Northern Italian. The ancient Gothic blood flows pure in him."

Erwin threw up his chin, signaling the man away. The man nodded in satisfaction.

"And its ideals of chivalry," he mused. "He looks as though he were perfectly capable of flying at a gentleman and kicking him, or at least putting some very vicious pointed questions." He scanned his notebook. "These moments of adversity make for very piquant source material."

The gentleman was irresistibly tempted to prompt a confrontation. He lifted his elegant glazed straw hat with just that shadow of unnecessary provocation. He smiled politely, just a hair too politely. He got the desired

18

original result, but not as expected. The young blonde man bared his snaggled little teeth at him, exactly like a wolf cub, even to the sudden flip of the tongue against the top incisors. The gentleman fancied he could hear the moist smack of the retracted lips. Pfirsich yipped and closed his eyes, hiding his face in his brother's back, and shivering.

Some Germans have disturbingly bestial teeth; too many migratory bloodlines over too many centuries cramming the wrong size teeth into the wrong jawbones. A taste for sugar, honey, dried fruit and coffee doesn't help. Erwin knew he had unattractive teeth. He never smiled for photographs -- but the gentleman didn't have a camera. He lifted his chin and sneered again.

Erwin saw the man pull back his own chin and blow out his lips lightly, in a puff of disgust, and in the same moment he and the gentleman recognized each other as fellow Germans. Humiliation! It was one thing to disgust or tease an Italian. Who cared about strangers or foreigners? Who would ever know? But to disgust a fellow countryman --! They both blushed and looked away.

The man recovered first. He observed that the young man was still very pink, and had to struggle to raise his eyes again. The man saw the clear look of recognition in those young pure eyes, and made another careful little note. Then he doffed his hat again.

This time Erwin returned the gesture, eager to be polite to his own kind, and watched the man stride away on his long lanky legs. Then he patted his brother on the back. The poor mite was quivering with a timidity very unlike him.

"Pfirsich?" said Erwin, and bending down, he took his baby brother's face in his hands. The blue eyes were big with uncertainty. "What's wrong?"

"Hm-m!" protested Pfirsich and rubbed his mouth.

"Well, what are you scared of?"

"What are you scared of?"

"I'm not scared. *Himmel,* you're shivering. Are you sick?"

"I wanna go home," whimpered Pfirsich.

"You want to go back to the hotel room."

"Home."

"All right," said Erwin. "You've worn yourself out."

He put his arm around Pfirsich's shoulders and led him back along

19

the canals. He'd never seen his little brother this subdued. He hoped he'd not kept him out in the sun too long; heat exhaustion could be dangerous for such a young child.

The tall gentleman was contentedly patting his breast pocket, where he'd stored his little notebook. When he passed the far side of the Plaza, he heard the woman again bawling "Dahtzyo!"

He looked up and nodded; he'd already taken down that name in his book.

3. Growing Pains

"Mettez hautes fos mains! Et pas de bouffonnerie."

Erwin Rommel had outgrown his diffidence. When he hit – very nearly literally hit – puberty, all meekness had simply slipped away from him, like the soft inoffensive chrysalis splitting open to reveal a hornet. He was grown and an officer in the German Army, accepted for induction after an operation for a hernia that he didn't even know he had, in plenty of time for the war with the French.

Now *Leutnant* Rommel, he stood abroad in his muddy soldier's greatcoat, flat officer's cap and wispy attempt at a boar's-tusk moustache, holding a *Kar. 98 Mauser* carbine on his prisoners. Three French *Poilus,* all that remained of the unit he and his men had attacked.

"Ah -- les prissonniers restent zages ou les prissonniers -- uh -- defiennent MORTS."

Rommel pronounced his bad French with great vigor and confidence. Despite the French reputation for linguistic snobbery, he knew that *Le Populace* respected anyone who at least tried to speak their language, no matter how badly. Besides, he had the gun.

They didn't need to know he'd run out of ammunition. He'd shot two of their fellows in the preliminary skirmish, and if this particular trio wasn't going to cooperate, then he'd use the bayonet. Now would be a good time to pull it from its scabbard and fix it on the bayonet lug at the muzzle end of the barrel. He would make the action of attachment look threatening.

The prisoners didn't seem to be impressed. They were moving away, sideways, with their eyes fixed on him to catch their moment of opportunity.

The little German officer had hardly fixed the blade and charged at the disappearing prisoners when he was struck by a bullet in the left thigh. He spun over backwards like a cartwheel toy, with a dry squeal of breathless surprise, his carbine flying from his hands.

He found himself sitting disoriented on his butt in the mud, his weapon flung on the ground halfway between himself and his erstwhile prisoners. They didn't miss the chance.

"Il est blessé!" cried one of the *Poilus.* *"Vite, prenez son fusil."*

"Oh, put it down, it's not loaded," snarled Rommel, trying to struggle to his feet. *"Verdammt und verhaut,"* he groaned. "Sniper -- and a good one."_

He couldn't get his feet under him, and collapsed, like a day-old puppy in a puddle. The French soldiers laughed at him, and waved the point of his own bayonet in his face. They even clucked their tongues in sympathy at his wail of despair.

"I don't want to spend the war in a prison camp," he cried. "I'll miss all the fun!"

* * * * *

In a hallway of a military German hospital, a blond youth sat alone on the edge of an empty wooden bench.

He was engaged in a recently developed habit, nervously rubbing his jaw, where a little white mole had lately arisen, marring an otherwise unusually pure complexion. The mole had been declared medically benign but it disturbed him, and it had become a symbol for anything that bothered or simply embarrassed him. He was reminding himself not to pick at it when a nurse put her head out of a door farther down the high white hallway.

"Herr Rommel? I've changed your brother's bandage. You may see him now."

Pfirsich stood up nervously. *"Oh. Vielen Dank, Schwester."*

When Pfirsich's voice had changed it had gone the wrong way. The donkey bray was gone. It was so quiet and soft he was never sure if people even heard him.

"Are you sure I couldn't have been of assistance?"

"No, no, young man. Your brother was being very brave. When young officers are being very brave they don't want their family to see them biting their lips."

Pfirsich put his head in at the sickbay door. It was an officer's ward,

22

and there were pale green curtains dividing it into private compartments.

"Erwin?" he barely whispered.

Erwin, without his moustache, was sitting up in bed, in the eternal institutional striped pajamas of Germany. With his hairless face, pale skin and eyes big and deep with the alert vulnerable look -- part hunting eagle, part hunted deer -- that comes to men in war, he so resembled their mother that Pfirsich felt a clench in his chest. Pfirsich put his hat to his mouth and set his perfect white teeth in the brim.

"Come in, Pfirsich. Come in, come in! *Ach Gott,* if my men had stood and stared sheep- eyed the way you do, I'd be on the French ration lists by now." The *Leutnant* motioned his timorously hovering brother to the chair by bed. "Sit down, *Knabe.* I'm not going to bleed on your shoes."

"Lucie says she'll be in on the next train." Pfirsich hesitated. "She said she knows you'll be up dancing soon."

"That's my girl!"

Lucie Rommel, *nee'* Molin, a dark Polish/Italian spark with her own real diamonds, had been a Tango champion when Erwin met her before the war. She married him because he was just like her -- bright, well educated and pretty. His military and aristocratic relations and his adoration for her weren't a blemish, either. Especially not for a woman with her own money, who could marry for love.

"And she'll see me like this?" moaned Erwin. "*Schande!* Look at my lip. First they drowned me in chloroform and then they snuck in and shaved off my moustache. Vandals. It took me months to grow that."

"Ah, dear, you don't have to try to be brave with me."

"Brave? Brave for what?" Erwin snorted. "I'm just shot in the leg. Nothing but punctured meat. Look!"

He threw back the covers and slapped his leg. Pfirsich winced and looked away.

"It hurt worse when I broke my anklebone as a kid. Took out a chunk the size of a fist, but I'll be up and marching in two weeks."

"Is that what the doctor said?"

Erwin threw his legs out of the bed. "Doctors! Help me get up, will you?"

Pfirsich tried to press him back down. *"Ach, sachte, Lieber,* you don't have to prove yourself to me. You'll just start bleeding again."

23

"I'll start leaking somewhere else if I can't get out of this bed."

"Well, there's the bed pan, right beside the bed."

"I don't want a pisspot. Allow a man a little modesty."

"What did you do in the trenches?"

"Didn't piss with an audience, I'll tell you that! I want my crutch. There's a toilet down the hall, and I mean to walk there. *Verdammt!* They've purposely put my crutch out of my reach."

"Oh, Erwin, but you're so pale and weak."

"Look who's talking. About as robust as a white rosebud." Erwin gave him a couple of friendly slaps. *"Gott,* Pfirsich, what's happened to you?"

"Me? What's wrong with me?"

Erwin rolled his eyes. "You were such an energetic brat." He stuck out his arm, and Pfirsich took it. "It seems the closer you get to being a man, the less you act like one."

Pfirsich put his hand to the mole on his face. "Well, you've changed, too. I think it must be the army."

"If it helped me, it would do wonders for you. I don't understand it; you've got as timid as a deer. Stop rubbing that!" snapped Erwin. "You're going to make it go bad."

Pfirsich dropped his hand. "Sorry."

"So can I have my crutch?"

Pfirsich obeyed, maneuvering him up out of the bed.

"Na, I'll have to do my general service too, someday," he said. "But the war will be over by then."

Erwin snorted. *"Meinst du, Brüderchen?* It's early days, yet. I'm sure there will be plenty of war left for you, too."

"Oh, *bitte,* Erwin. It's not a second helping of *Linzertorte;* I'm not worried about not getting my little piece." Pfirsich set the crutch under his brother's arm. "The Kaiser and all our generals will have it all sorted out by next spring."

"Ganz recht. We'll have the Tommys on their knees before the cherries bloom."

"The Emperor won't let it become so bitter, not against the English." Pfirsich drew back the curtain. "Our own *Kaiser* Wilhelm is Queen Victoria's eldest grandson. She died in his arms. The whole of Germany went down on their knees with England in mourning."

"*Stimmt!* He's related to 'em, he knows how to make 'em jump."

Pfirsich put an arm around his brother's shoulders. "It will be easier if you stand up straight, and lean against the crutch. "

"If I stand up any straighter, I'll be on tiptoe."

They'd finally progressed to the doorway, and Pfirsich came to a full stop. Erwin looked up irritably, to see the shock and confusion on his brother's face.

Pfirsich put his hand on his brother's head. "You've --." He put a hand on each of Erwin's shoulders and stood back to look at him. "They've --."

"What!?"

Pfirsich set his hand upon his own head, then drew it away and held it over Erwin's, measuring their heights.

"Oh no!" he wailed. "Oh dear!"

"What what what?"

Pfirsich realized that the other patients didn't need to hear this, and quickly pulled Erwin out into the hallway. There he put his hands gently about his brother's face, peering earnestly into it.

"What have they done to you?"

Erwin twisted loose as Pfirsich had done when they were children and Mama had been checking them for dirt.

"What? Did they do something to me when I was out cold? Have I got stitches on my scalp? Did I get it in the head?" He scrabbled at his scalp with all his fingers, trying to locate the scraps of surgical gut he feared he'd find. "Why didn't they tell me?"

"It's not your head! It's your legs! They're shorter!"

Erwin panicked. Hospitals scared everyone witless anyway. It's where you went to die, and the great terror of the hospitalized trench soldier was the loss of a leg in surgery. He ran his hands over his thighs and twisted out his feet, trying to see the amputation he dreaded.

"Damn doctors! If I find out they've been playing knife games with me, the Fatherland's going to be short some surgeons."

Pfirsich gazed down sorrowfully at this elder brother who had become so small, so suddenly. He protectively clasped Erwin's stiff narrow shoulders in his hands. Pfirsich could feel the very faint restrained trembling in his brother's body, and the narrow eyes staring up at him widened until they were as vulnerable and pure as his own. Erwin was

25

scared.

Pfirsich murmured sorrowfully, "I - I used to look up to you. You were my hero. When you went away, you were so strong and tall, and now -- you've shrunk."

Erwin's jaw dropped. He was so relieved, he sobbed out loud. Then he forced a stiff grin, and ruffled Pfirsich's silky hair.

"Nein, nein, nein, Dümmling. I haven't shrunk, you've just grown. Good God." He leaned back on his crutches and stared up at his brother. "How you have grown. Look at you!"

High and pale and tasseled as a cornstalk. Erwin wondered where in their ancestry had the Danes married in? A Viking blood, this shy tentative brother, who could have worn the iron helmet and raided down the German coasts in the raven ships. Instead here he was in his neat modern wool-blend suit, forever worrying over the shine on his shoes and the pleats in his trousers.

Pfirsich's long black lashes dropped in embarrassment. "Oh, course I've grown. It was only your being hurt that confused me."

Erwin, balancing bravely on the crutch under his armpit, caught his brother's hand in both of his, and looked him up and down.

"If this is how they're feeding up our next generation, Lord! What would you look like in a *Fähnrich's* uniform?"

"Erwin." Pfirsich made a grab for his brother as Erwin wobbled on his crutch. "I'm not of an age for call-up. Oh -- your crutches -- "

Erwin and his crutches dropped flat onto the polished hardwood floor. He sat flat on his butt, and couldn't help but yelp. The mud had been a lot softer.

"Damn leg," he moaned, and held a rueful hand up to his brother. "Give me a hand, Pfirsich before I find myself sitting in a puddle."

Pfirsich put his hands to his own face. "Oh, you poor thing, you're hurt so badly."

"Honorable wounds. Got me another medal, and a wound badge this time, too! Come on, come on, and help me up. I don't want to miss using a decent indoor toilet for a change. Having to piss where I sleep was getting old."

Pfirsich took his brother's proffered hands and easily drew him to his feet; he was so naturally strong he even had to be careful not to lift Erwin right up into the air. Pfirsich was startled at his own strength, and he put a supportive arm around the small man's shoulders.

"Komm, Lieber, careful; don't strain yourself."

Even while limping down the corridor toward the toilet, Erwin managed to look up at him, grinning. "I guess you'll just have to join the army to care for your poor little big brother, eh?"

Pfirsich started. Erwin had read his mind. Erwin sized him up with an expert recruiting officer's admiration.

"We need officers like you'd make, *Knabe."*

"Oh, so now I'm to be an officer? Thank you, but two years' enlisted service will be plenty for me."

"Pfirsich, I need an officer like I know you'll be."

"You? How do you propose to guarantee I'll be serving with you?"

"That's how much you know about the German army. We keep the family together, the captain as papa, the first sergeant as mama, *die Kompagniemutter,* and all the little soldiers together at the table. You'll train with my home garrison, of course. The 124th Infantry Regiment, *Koenig* Wilhelm I, 6th *Württemberg.* We'll serve arm-in-arm, literally as brothers-in-arms. We'll be *Kameraden!"*

Pfirsich nudged Erwin into the door of the toilet. "You have hundreds of braver and better officers than I'll ever be."

"Don't sell yourself short, Pfirsich! It takes a special man to be a first-class German officer, and you're that kind of man."

"Oh, I'm special, all right."

He was still bothered about the way he'd nearly bounced Erwin right up off his feet. It made him feel giddy and out-of-control. He tried to close the door of the toilet, but Erwin's sudden energetic push defeated him, and the little intent face thrust out at him.

"I'll teach you to ride a horse, Pfirsich. You'll love it. Once you start flying over jumps. Believe me, you'll love it."

Pfirsich pushed his brother into the toilet. "Our family is all schoolteachers, Erwin, not soldiers. They've got you; what more could the army desire?"

"I'm not as good as I was, Pfirsich. Not with this leg." Even as the door closed upon him, he begged, "Come stand by me, for Germany."

"Not here. You do that by yourself."

The door closed, and Pfirsich stepped away, to allow his brother

27

auditory privacy. He was left leaning against the opposite wall, eyes closed, fine forehead wrinkled, face flushed.

"He's so small and thin, now," Pfirsich thought. "With that smooth shaved face and big blue eyes, he looks like a little boy." Pfirsich's face crumpled in denial. "He's going to make me ache with such pity for him that I won't be able to help it. I'll join the army, I know I will. *Oh, über ihn!*"

* * * * *

As an officer candidate, *Avantageur* Manfred Pfirsich Marie Rommel stood silent and stiff and upright in full army uniform. He was so mad he could have bitten a radiator and made it sorry, if he hadn't been standing in the full sun in the middle of the parade square formed by four two-story brick barracks, trapped by vows and promises as much as he was trapped by masonry, and boiling over with silent curses.

Über ihn! thought Pfirsich. The wretched little brute! Was I wrong? Look what he's done to me. Look what I've done to me."

The helpless officer recruit stood silently, buttoned up in *Feldgra.* "Field Gray," the warm green-gray of the German uniform, was the symbol of its soldiery, as dark Prussian Blue had symbolized the King Friedrich's army. His chin was properly up and in like a well-dressaged colt's, uncommitted blue eyes shaded beneath the shining black leather visor of his cap, quiet gloved hands, nowhere near his face, clasped in front of his genitals in the best ladylike style of an old-fashioned officer. But the glare he sent after his brother was far from ladylike.

Erwin was over there, out of the sun, strutting around his comrades, grinning and chattering. Pfirsich could see his teeth even in the shade. Lousy rotten snaggly little teeth, what was he doing smiling like that? Some of the officers' uniforms showed an ironed perfection of line that hinted they were wearing the plain cotton corsets that could be ordered from any of a number of uniform-supply books, and that were a affectation of the aristocracy. Pfirsich wasn't corseted – he was very slender – but Erwin's stockier silhouette was imperfect enough for Pfirsich to suspect he wasn't wearing one either.

"Bourgeois," muttered Pfirsich.

Once the newly graduated recruits had been dismissed, they'd been shunted across the parade square into the shade like a shoal of herring, taken off their caps, and begun fanning themselves.

But not Pfirsich. He was still out in the sun. Standing in the hot light just made him even angrier, and he wanted to feel angry. The glare he could send after Erwin would grow even hotter as a consequence.

Leutnant Erwin Johannes Eugen Rommel, sleek and tight and happily at home in his own dress uniform, was overjoyed nearly to the point of bouncing. His was descended from teachers, all right, and he honored his heritage by believing there could be no more noble a calling than to be the guide of young willing boys, to turn them into good students, good citizens, good fathers and workers and soldiers. And here he'd got his two hands on the young unwilling boy he wanted to guide and train most of all.

Erwin swaggered over to his brother, slapped him on his shoulder, and held out his own little gray-gloved hand.

"gratuliere, Soldat," he almost cheered. "Basic training wasn't so bad, was it?"

Pfirsich saw him look over his shoulder at his comrades. *Gott,* he thought. I'm a prize. I'll be lucky if he doesn't shrink me in hot water to wear on his medal bar.

"Hardened you up," continued Erwin, "Put some weight on you. You performed magnificently. It's a good sign."

Pfirsich answered meekly, first exchanging salutes, then properly shaking his brother's hand.

"Thank you, Erwin. I tried my best."

Erwin turned to salute and shake hands with fellow officers, then salute them again, in the complicated social hand jive of his army, never aware of the look in his brother's blue visored eyes. Erwin was back to his old self, thought Pfirsich. With that precious moustache of his grown out, all nurtured back to its full vigor, or as vigorous as that little string of fluff could ever be. Other than his attempt to grow that thing, there was nothing pitiful about him now. Well, unless shaming his own brother into his precious army could be counted.

Making me feel sorry for him, thought Pfirsich. If that's not pitiful then what is?

He watched Erwin floating around the parade field, flicking his

29

riding crop as though he were still on his horse and the flies were thick. Pfirsich's blue eyes narrowed, sending predator looks after his happy sibling.

Keep it up, Erwin, he thought. Just keep gloating, and I'll tell you and all your fellow officers exactly why I joined.

4. A Good Example

By the window in the barracks room that he shared with three other cadets, Pfirsich sat at the desk, bent over against the high stiff collar of his stiff gray uniform, writing a letter. Before him lay an envelope, neatly addressed to his brother, who had been transferred to Italy.

"Lieber Erwin!" he began. *"Pardon me for writing so seldom, but we've been very busy in the triangulation classes this week. You'll be pleased to know that I'm really beginning to enjoy mathematics as you do. It means more when you see it actually knock a target into the dust!"*

He paused, and smiled tenderly at a little silver-framed photograph sitting on the desk, then continued.

"Our training officer is very pleased with my projections. He says that someone so clever with numbers should train to be an engineer. I hadn't thought of it, but I place a lot of faith in what he says. How could he have guessed you had thought about being an engineer, too?"

The photo was of a superbly handsome officer, with a calm, good-natured face.

"Leutnant Kurt Stiefler is a very upright and able man, and he never loses his temper with us, no matter how silly we can be."

Pfirsich closed his eyes in a poignant surge of hero worship, and saw Stiefler standing nobly upright, looking more impossibly magnificent in his worshiping imagination than he did in the photo. But the boy's imagination added a beautifully carved ornate cane in Stiefler's hand; he wasn't leaning on it, merely posing with it. Its silver head was in the form of a swan.

"He's a very brave man, too. He has a cane, and limps, but he never shows he's in pain."

He saw Stiefler beside an artillery piece, thrown romantically backwards by an explosion, head thrown up, exposing his powerful gleaming white throat.

"The reason he's here with us instead of at the front is because he was hurt in

31

the very first week of the war. He was an artillery officer, and while he was heroically standing to his guns, his right hip was smashed by a mortar shell."

Stiefler lying in bed, gazing with noble loyalty at a large framed picture of the Kaiser gleaming on the hospital wall.

"But he never gave up hope of returning to his country's service."

Stiefler blowing away target after target with a tooled ivory-handled pistol.

"You should see him at target practice. He never misses! The French and English can thank God they managed to cripple a man like him, because otherwise he would be a terror on the battlefield."

Stiefler with his immaculately white-gloved hand on Pfirsich's shoulder. Pfirsich looking up at him as though he were God.

"He reserves extra time to train students who show promise. I'm one of those. He says I have a hunter's eye for shooting -- just like you, Erwin! But it took this man to bring it out in me."

Stiefler nonchalantly taking a 'magnificent black stallion' over a very high gate.

"You should see him ride! He's a centaur, Erwin, just a pure classical centaur. They say you can't make a horse jump unless you throw your heart over the barrier for the horse to follow. Stiefler throws everyone's hearts!"

Pfirsich in the saddle, looking down at Stiefler, who is looking up proudly but sternly at him.

"I hope to be able to earn private instruction with him in riding, too. If I ever have a seat half as good as his, I could ride lions!"

Stiefler, with his romantic Byronesque limp, patrolling the halls of the barracks, keeping eagle-like watch over his sleeping trainees.

"Sometimes I hear him walking the halls in the night. He always has our welfare in his mind; to the point it makes him wakeful. I'd like to get up and walk with him, and respectfully assure him he has nothing to worry about, not from us, so he could go back to sleep."

* * * * *

Erwin Rommel stood in a trench in Italy, reading the letter, lips moving, grinning.

"I know that someday, with his help, I'll be able to join you as an officer worthy of his name -- and yours. Deiner -- Pfirsich."

Erwin folded up the letter, slipped it into his uniform breast, and patted it fondly. He turned to another officer, who was leaning against the parapet, smoking a little clay pipe.

"Heia, Werner, I think my little brother has a crush."

"Does he? Is she pretty?"

"No, on his training officer."

"When's the wedding? Are we invited?"

"Don't be smutty, Werner. You know what I mean, how kids get to admiring an older fellow, wanting to be just like him."

"This is good?"

"Don't be such a *Gerneweis*. It *is* good. Especially in my little brother's case. He's changed, lately. He'd taken to hanging on me, like a lost ship on a polar star; hardly even speaks to the rest of the family. I thought he was angry with me, but now I can't tell. I have to admit he's had me worried. He's the kind of tender child who needs someone to look up to. I'm glad he's found another guide, instead of just me."

"*Ich meine,*" agreed Werner. "When they're young like that, they can get too intent on their own tight little circle of friends."

"Or their own thoughts, if they haven't got friends. Pfirsich's become such a loner."

"It'll be good for him to learn to think outside of his group. Especially if growing up is scaring him."

Erwin patted his breast again. "And from the sound of his letter, his training officer, a *Leutnant* Stiefler, is the right man for the job. Upright, honest, strong and able."

Werner said suspiciously, "What's he doing training kids? There's a war on!"

"Pfirsich says he's crippled. A mortar shell crushed his hip, only a week into the war. "

"Oh, that's different. No desk driver. A hamstrung warhorse, who can tell them what it's like out here."

"That's what I thought."

"Too bad about his hip," said Werner. "He sounds competent. If he can't walk, his career won't, either."

"Ach, it's an ill wind," shrugged Erwin. "We'll always need good training officers, and the best would be out fighting if at least some of them weren't hurt in action. Sounds like this one's got himself maimed into an honorable retirement. I hope he's tough on my brother. Pfirsich really needs shaking up out of himself. And if he's fawning on Stiefler, it wouldn't be bad if his limping hero surprised him and took a swift rattling kick at him with his good foot."

"I've seen your picture of that brother of yours. Kid's a water-blue-eyed baby. And too pretty for a boy. The storks that flew him in got their orders mixed up."

"Not Pfirsich," said Erwin." I know him, better than anybody. You watch; he may have lost his way for the moment, but you could pour bullets out of what he's made of. Someday he's going to surprise us all."

"*Ja?* And someday you'll be a General."

"Of course! We're all shooting for General, aren't we?"

"Shoot for the moon, Erwin. Try 'Field Marshal' while you're dreaming."

* * * * *

Pfirsich was standing in the garrison yard, explaining things to a grown colt. Part of a German officer's job was to train the horses of the nation in his spare time. It was a tradition that united Germany had taken over from the Prussians. Any horse not needed immediately by the army, an officer was free to sell for a tidy little profit. Pfirsich liked horses anyway, and as any young cadet, he needed the money. This rangy young bay was only one of three he'd been taking pains with.

"No, no, no. Stand still," he said, and pulled firmly on the bridle. "I'm training you to go to the front. Do you want to embarrass yourself and me! In front of the Frenchies?"

The horse butted him, first knocking off his cap, then pretending to be afraid of it.

"*Brrr! Böse Blage!*" scolded Pfirsich, and bent down to retrieve his cap. The buckled leather shin wraps he wore for riding still made him feel constricted and stiff in the knees. With the willowy thoughtless resilience of a strong young man, he bent right straight over from his hips.

"Hey, Rommel! Nice butt!"

Pfirsich whipped upright to glare at another cadet, who was slouching toward him across the yard. A dainty fair narrow lad, with a pretty mouse like face, and malicious eyes.

34

The cadet yelled, "Quit kissing the horsie and get your butt up to see *Herr Piphacken!* He wants you!"

"Don't call him that, Jakob!"

With Jakob, Pfirsich lost all his shyness, and just felt a good old childish urge to poke him in the nose. It was a mean thing to call the crippled man, the Low German word for a horse with narrow faulty hocks.

"*Leutnant* Stiefler can't help it if his leg's ruined. He didn't do it to himself."

Jakob rocked on his heels, enjoying himself. "What should I call him? *Engelsdrescher?*"

Angel thrasher. Flailer of innocent flesh. Not just a mean word, but dirty and low class. Pfirsich pointedly turned to lead the dancing bay colt into the stables. He was disappointed in his hope that Jakob wouldn't follow; the mouse-faced boy tailed him right into the colt's stall. Pfirsich glared back at him over the bay's high clean-cut rump.

"With your name, you better watch whom you accuse of wrestling angels. Remember what happened to Jacob in the Bible."

"Jacob beat the angel he wrestled. If *Leutnant* Stiefler tried wrestling anybody, he couldn't even walk away on a bet!"

"*Leutnant* Stiefler wouldn't wrestle. Wrestling is for low street fighters."

"I think Stiefler is just made for wrestling, with the right pretty little wrestler."

"Pfui! You can be so disgusting!"

"Ach, dearie, dearie me. Have I insulted your grand handsome lover?"

Pfirsich whirled around, his face hot. "My what!"

"Oh, come off it, Pfirschen." Jakob righteously put his hands on his hips. "Everybody's seen you mooning around after him. You act like a love-struck farm girl."

"You have a dirty mind, Jakob Prässelmeier. Everybody knows it; our chaplain himself wouldn't be safe from your nasty crawling innuendoes."

"You keep *Piphacken's* picture on your desk! Do you wear a locket for him too, dear?"

"Don't be sordid!"

35

"Me? I've seen how you turn your nose up at the girls in town. Better things in mind?"

Pfirsich's hands were shaking so that he dropped the lead twice, trying to tie the colt into his stall.

"I don't give in to my animal urges, if you want to know. My respect for women makes me respect myself."

"These girls aren't respectable."

"All the more reason," said Pfirsich, stroking the colt and shushing him.

"You training that colt for *Piphacken?*"

"I am not. The *Herr Leutnant* trains his own horses."

"Didn't think so; that colt still has his balls. Old Scuttlebutt can't get on top of anything that ain't gelded. Like that dumpy lazy yellow brute he has to ride now."

"The *Leutnant* doesn't care about appearances. His 'Aldair' is an intelligent, gentlemanly animal. He's very steady, and experienced in combat. And he's not yellow, he's apple gold."

"Old as dirt, and about as much fire as a lady's butt-worn velvet sewing chair."

The knot in the lead finally took. Pfirsich turned his back and stalked off, but he could hear Prässelmeier eagerly trailing him out of the stable and into the yard. He sniffed and held his head higher, and Jakob couldn't stand it.

"Beeil' dich, Bühlchen! He's fluffing up the pillows! Why else would he want to see a snooty pale bean pole like you?"

Pfirsich spun around. "Because I forgot myself yesterday during drill and used your kind of vocabulary toward *Schütze* Brusawski. That's why!"

"Ha! I heard about that. I'll bet *Piphacken* got wet over that one. His best dewy-lipped little *Arschkriecher,* hawking up curses like a raunchy old sailor!"

Pfirsich went pale. "I would hope *Leutnant* Stiefler is very disappointed in me. *Leutnant* Stiefler is a gentleman. And gentlemen don't curse at their men. That is properly left to the sergeants." He raised his head on high like one of his colts. "Perhaps you would be more suited to become a sergeant? Wouldn't you feel more at home?"

This time Jakob went red. Sergeants still didn't come from the gentle classes. Pfirsich's father was a respectable teacher, and his mother a propertied noblewoman. Jakob's father hauled cement. Pfirsich hoped Jakob didn't know that Erwin had spent time as a sergeant major. The rodent-faced boy clenched his fists.

"At least sergeants have to sleep in the barracks at night, and in their own beds. The Devil knows where the officers end up when it gets dark."

"Then you'll be much happier when you don't manage to become one," sniffed Pfirsich, and stalked off.

"Give him a big deep kiss for me, *Süßerling!*" choked Jakob. "Soften him up for the night!"

* * * * *

A door slammed in the battalion barracks.

Pfirsich, standing in the white-stuccoed hall with his eyes closed, breathing hard, tried to control himself. Breathe deep, practice practice practice self control. "The temper is a stallion, born to be bitted." That's what the *Leutnant* said.

He removed his cap and brushed back his hair. Jakob couldn't help himself. Jakob had had an uneasy childhood; his mother used to beat his father. And there was a possibility his father was entirely too personally close to Jakob.

Pfirsich tucked the cap under his arm and headed up the heavy square polished stairs. The *Leutnant* had said they were to gentle Jakob down like any other mismanaged colt. Someday Jakob would be a good officer, if no one gave in to his prodding, and they allowed the *Leutnant's* good influences to work upon him. Someday Pfirsich would remind Jakob how very painfully lucky he was to be rescued from living at home.

Pfirsich topped the stairs, and stood leaning on the massive balustrade. Stiefler's office was at the far end of the hallway, and Pfirsich had to spiritually whip himself like a bad colt to continue to stride briskly, as he'd been taught, down the whole polished length of the floor. Stiefler always praised a cadet in public, at parades or in classes, to reward him and mark him for emulation. Private interviews were reserved only for reprimands. It was the proper way of doing it, public humiliation being a man's punishment, deemed too severe for anything a young recruit could commit, but it had turned the harmless phrase "Stiefler wants to see you" into a thing of horror to the nervous young cadets.

This nervous young cadet stopped outside the door, brushing himself down before knocking. He hadn't meant to say what he did to Brusawski during drill. Who was hurt when the man misheard *Avantageur* Rommel's command and took a wrong turn face-first into the flagpole? Just him! Pfirsich didn't get the bloody nose, and yet he cursed him so viciously. The way the sergeants had stared. Pfirsich was so ashamed.

He polished his buttons. It wasn't his people's kind of language. He'd picked up every word of it since he'd been in the army, from poor children like Jakob. How could he help using what he'd learned? He bent over to flick off a speck of dust from his leather shin wraps. It was no excuse. He must never forget, that an officer was not a Non-commissioned Officer. N.C.O.s pushed troops, so N.C.O.s must curse. But not an officer. 'Officers must set standards!' "

Pfirsich stood looking down at himself. He'd run out of things to polish. Maybe he should polish the door latch.

A voice from the other side of the door startled him. *"Nur herein, Avantageur* Rommel."

Pfirsich took a deep breath, opened the door, and timidly peered in.

The *Leutnant* said, "I'd have to be deaf to miss all your shuffling around out there. Na? *Berichtet, Knabe."*

Pfirsich strode forward, came to attention with a ferocious heel click, and a sword-swift salute, stood himself ramrod-straight before the desk, and reported as instructed.

"Bitte Herr Leutnant, gestatten zu berichten Avantageur Rommel, *wie befehlt!"*

"Very good, Rommel. *Bitte,* sit down."

"Thank you, *Herr Leutnant,"* said Pfirsich, and sat down. But he was thinking, uh-oh. "Sit down." He was in trouble, now. He was going to get his butt chewed so badly he have to find a cushion for his naked tailbone.

Leutnant Kurt Stiefler sat with his hands folded on the desk. In Pfirsich's fawning eyes, he remained the avatar of a god, magnificent and faultless. But had anyone with less hunger for a hero looked upon him, all they would have seen was merely a man, a thin, worn-down and failing man. The only touch of immortality that remained to him was the unsullied uncomplicated honesty of those preoccupied brown eyes. His face was reserved and sympathetic, but its once superior beauty had been gnawed away by unremitting pain.

His uniform was unadorned; he didn't even wear his silver wound decoration, let alone his First and Second Class Iron Crosses. He sat very upright; he always wore a plain corset, even in field uniform, but it was to support his back, not improve his line. Hanging on the coat hook behind him was a worn gray greatcoat and a worn gray cap; peeping from a pocket was a pair of regulation gray gloves, smelling of the benzene used to scrub their frayed tips. Propped in a corner was a plain durable wooden cane. *Leutnant* Kurt Stiefler received only basic officer's pay, and saved every penny he could spare. In another month he would be downright shabby.

Usually the man would have been quietly and patiently plugging away at a stack of battalion documents, but today he was just as quietly cleaning a pistol. On a much-washed kerchief on the desk lay a cleaning kit and the fieldstripped pistol, everything as neat and careful as his paperwork. The pistol was an ordinary featureless *Luger .09 mm. Parabellum.* It disjointed insides gleamed as matte black and precise as the pieces of a Japanese lacquered box-puzzle. As was usual with him, Stiefler had put aside his own business, even the care of his faithful pistol, to concentrate on the needs of one of his trainees.

"Ah, *Avantageur,*" he said. "Do you know why I've summoned you?"

Pfirsich would have wriggled if it hadn't been trained out of him.

"Oh, yes, Herr *Leutnant,* and I'm very sorry. That of course was not the way for an officer to act, and I'm ready to take my punishment."

Stiefler grimaced. "I wasn't so much thinking of punishment."

Pfirsich leaned forward eagerly. *"Bitte, Herr Leutnant,* I know I did wrong. Please; I'm in your hands, as I should be."

Stiefler cleared his throat uneasily. "It's not something you can be punished for, *Avantageur,* without repercussions."

"Does *Herr Leutnant* mean, without it impinging upon my career? Or my family being informed?"

"Among others," Stiefler said, nervously.

"It's that serious?"

Stiefler didn't say anything. He just looked at Pfirsich, perplexed, as though to ask, What planet did you fall from?

"Oh. I knew it was wrong," blurted the boy. "But is it viewed as even more unseemly in a cadet than in the officers?"

Stiefler stared at him in undisguised shock. "What officers?"

Pfirsich said uneasily, "Na, like *Hauptmann* Briesemann. He's always doing it; right up on horseback, where nobody can miss it. I could see it in *Oberfeldwebel* Steinkirk; that's part of his training and duty, and is expected of him."

Stiefler's mouth fell open. Then he sat right back and rolled his eyes in relief.

"Oh, heavens, we're talking at cross-purposes!"

"Men Herr?"

"What did you think I called you up here for?"

Pfirsich shrank. "My -- my horrible cursing at one of the enlisted men, *Herr Leutnant?"*

"Oh, der liebe Herr, Kind."

Stiefler laughed out loud and rose clumsily from his chair. He couldn't stay put for pure amusement and relief. Without thinking, Pfirsich jumped up and put out his hands to assist him.

"Please, *mein Herr!* Let me help you!"

Stiefler hated to be touched. Not from shame that he was twisted and scarred -- he'd gotten over that long ago -- but because it just plain hurt. The nerve-damage from his badly-healed hip-wound would set off little sympathetic explosions of suffering all over his body, and he never knew when the simple kindly pressure of a human hand would make him break down and weep. Conscious overdoses of pain-killers had led first to addiction, and then to the inability to foresee the reactions of his abused nervous system, until he and what had once been his own body had become separated and estranged from one another, spirit versus meat, unceasingly aware of their mutual weary hostility. Stiefler had poured out all his energy controlling his reactions to his body's lashing attacks of unpredictable pain. It had become so easy to make him cry.

Crippled as he was, Stiefler lost his balance and fell, one arm swinging over and scattering the kit and the pistol parts, before he went down face-first and struck his mouth on the corner of the desk. He didn't even try to hold back the tears. He collapsed right down on his twisted butt, put his hands over his bleeding mouth, and began to sob.

Pfirsich didn't know what to do. His hero was crying! Not weeping strongly with fine manly emotion, but howling snot and water, like a hurt child. And blood. It was dripping like watercolor through his fingers. The man had really busted his lip.

"*Herr Leutnant!*" the boy gasped at last.   "*Mein Herr,* are you all right?"

Stiefler mumbled through the red-dripping fingers clamped over his mouth, "Han' off, 'ou 'iddow 'ool!!"

Hurt and confused, Pfirsich knelt down to pick up the pistol parts. "I didn't mean to hurt you."

Stiefler struggled to rise, shaking with misery. "Would you stop it, *Knabe?*" he snapped. "You hang over me like a lover, and that's one thing I don't plan to be!"

Still picking up parts, Pfirsich knelt bolt upright. "*Mein Herr?*" he gasped.

Stiefler grappled his way grotesquely to the window. His painful limp was not the dainty accustomed tiptoe of a congenital clubfoot, but the horrible, dipping, straddling lurch of a ruined major joint.

"Take your affections someplace else," he snarled. "I'm too old for you."

Pfirsich's mouth dropped open. "'Too old?' For what?"

Stiefler pulled a thin gray handkerchief out of his sleeve and stood leaning against the windowsill, swabbing his broken mouth.   He glanced irritably at the boy.

"What do you mean, 'for what?' You're too young to play these games with me. And this is a game that could hurt us both worse than you'll ever understand -- unless it happens."

Pfirsich, nearly in tears himself, jumped up and threw the last of the pistol parts onto the desk.

"I don't understand, *Herr Leutnant!* I really, really don't know what you mean."

The pain had stopped dancing around in blue flashes before Stiefler's eyes, and he could attempt to regain his self-control, or at least make a temporary pact with his body. He took up his cane, and gingerly leaned himself upon it. He wiped the handkerchief over his face, rubbing away all the dribbled secretions, and dabbed at his uniform, before tucking the handkerchief back into his sleeve. Then he smiled tightly at Pfirsich,

41

with as much kindness as he could muster with a split lip.

"There, there, *Knabe*. I'm not going to force it out of you. And I'm genuinely flattered that you admire me. I had hoped it meant you wanted to be a good officer, as I try to be, with occasional success. But when you keep my picture on your desk, and gush over my eyes and hands, what can anyone finally assume about the two of us?"

He leaned forward on the cane. "If you're going to be like me then you have to learn to be subtle."

"'Like *Herr Leutnant?*"

Pfirsich stared at Stiefler, who was obviously waiting for him to stop pretending. Pretending what? How did Stiefler mean they were alike? What did that have to do with the photograph on the desk? And that's when Pfirsich remembered what Jakob had said. He gasped, and put his hand to his own mouth. Stiefler rolled up his eyes.

"Don't be shocked, *Knabe*." the *Leutnant* reassured him. "It's not so hard to see. You're just lucky that I'm in the same position as you are. I can sympathize. I used to have crushes when I was your age, and I was fortunate I had good officers. They didn't pretend they couldn't see what boys would get up to when the lights went out. Boys get urges and give in to all of them, if they're not controlled. I can help you learn to control and conceal yours."

Pfirsich was staring at him. Then he blushed. "I'm not -- not one of those! What do you think?"

Stiefler started. "Oh. What did I say? "

"And what do you mean, 'the same position'?" Pfirsich's eyes bulged like blue glass marbles. "You're not --?"

Stiefler closed his eyes. Lord, what had he said, out loud to this child? Where was his brain? Rotted with hurt, as usual, liable to betray him with every word it let loose. He hated the rotten thing. He thought about what he could say to reverse the effect of what he had just said, but out was out. He opened his eyes and stared directly into the boy's huge blue trusting eyes.

Firmly he said, "I was." Then, "I am."

Pfirsich put his hand over his mouth, and said, in a wretched little voice, "No. Not you."

"Well, yes, me. And now you know. What will you do, *Knabe?*"

Pfirsich put his face in his hands, trying not to weep. "I don't

42

know."

Stiefler was rearranging the black pistol parts on the cloth; some of them were very small, and easily misplaced. The extractor-spring was there, but the tiny extractor-pin was missing; the part they called the "mouse-turd." Once lost, the pins were impossible to find, and he knew better than to waste his time and his temper looking. First Sergeants in the trenches usually kept a little box of them, in case of cleaning mishaps.

"You lost the mouse-turd," he said.

"Mein Herr?" said Pfirsich, and looked down at the floor. "Oh, I'm sorry."

"Don't bother looking, they seem to disintegrate. When we get done here, you'll go get me another one from supply."

"Jawohl, mein Herr! But what are we going to do now?"

Stiefler glanced up "Wouldn't it be safer for both of us, if you didn't do anything?"

Pfirsich looked up. "Safer for both? *Herr Leutnant,* I'm not that way."

Stiefler stopped playing with the parts. "What?" He carefully lowered himself into his chair, and put his face in his hands, asking his body to please please behave. When he had its promise, for what that was worth, he looked up.

"Of course you're not."

"No, *mein Herr!"* moaned Pfirsich.

"Boys aren't one way or the other. They'll try anything once, and more if they like it."

"I haven't!"

"Well, good, because I thought you did. Everyone probably thinks so, too."

"No, no, never!"

"Fine. You're too young for any of it, the usual way or my way."

"Oh!" squeaked the boy in protest. "I haven't. I just admired you."

"And showed your admiration. Every chance you got."

"But, all the boys look up to their --." Pfirsich blushed. "Their heroes."

"Thank you, I'm flattered."

"What did I do?"

"You're an enthusiast, Pfirsich. You have spirit. You go overboard. Remember what I've told you about moderation and balance? I had my reasons for emphasizing them, especially with you."

Pfirsich looked down in shame.

Stiefler said, "I don't know if you know who you are, yet, or if you really are 'like me.' But you're going to have to watch yourself from now on. You had me fooled." He shook his head. "And now I've gone and given myself away to a scared kid. Pretty swift, Kurt."

Pfirsich hung his head even lower. "I'm sorry. I'm so ashamed. I never meant to do any of this to you. I did this all wrong."

"You're sixteen years old," said Stiefler, gingerly fingering his mouth. "I didn't expect you to do it 'right.' "

Pfirsich looked up, his eyes big and confused. "What's the right way?"

"'The right ' --? *Ach, lieber Gott.* There's no 'right way.' What a stupid thing for me to say." He shook his head at the boy. "People are weak, Pfirsich. And they're weakest if they've just been whacked in the mouth with a desk."

"Oh, I'm so sorry."

"The mouth is made for the soft things. It eats, it speaks and it kisses. It doesn't pound nails; it doesn't go for route marches. It never gets tough. If you ever want to really hurt someone, *Knabe,* take it from me, go for the mouth."

Pfirsich nodded meekly. *"Jawohl, Herr Leutnant."*

"You can still say, *'Jawohl, Herr Leutnant,'* to me? After what you've just discovered?"

"I have to."

"You're supposed to report me."

"It's none of my business!"

"If you start saying that now, you'll have to say it all your life."

"'It's none of my business."

"All right. But remember, you'll have to be careful, very careful, from now on."

Pfirsich's eyes hardened. *"Jawohl, Herr Leutnant."*

"This is dangerous knowledge, *Avantageur.* It can hurt you worse than a kick in the mouth."

"Jawohl, Herr Leutnant."

"You can't use *'Jawohl, Herr Leutnant,'* forever."

"I'll use it as long as it works, then I'll use something else."

"You have a hard streak in you, don't you, *Avantageur?*"

"Jawohl, Herr Leutnant. All the Rommels do."

"I hope I never have to meet your family, then." Stiefler abruptly sat up and saluted him. *"Abgetreten.* Back to duty, boy. Watch yourself, and watch your mouth. And get my photograph off your desk."

Pfirsich saluted. *"Jawohl, Herr Leutnant."*

As he strode stiffly away down the corridor, he heard Stiefler call after him:

"Don't forget my mouse-turd!"

* * * * *

That night, in the barracks, Stiefler's silhouette limped crookedly down the hallways. Pfirsich, lying in bed in his bay, heard the *Leutnant's* uncertain footsteps, and the faithful click of the cane.

He sat up carefully in his bed. "That poor man," he thought. "No wonder he can't sleep. I thought he was watching over us, but he's eaten up with guilt."

Stiefler, in a worn set of hospital pajamas and a hospital robe and a pair of thin old toweling sandals, scuffed out onto the cement balcony that ran the length of each floor of the barracks. He was exceeding cautious; smoothly puddled cement, polished and waxed daily by over-driven trainees, develops a surface like ice. Once he'd reached the safety of the balcony, he propped himself against it and stood muttering into the dark sky, kneading his throbbing hip.

He'd been down in the latrine, having a quiet little vomit from sheer nervous exhaustion. It hurt like hell, but it took his mind off his hip, and he'd hoped it would wear him out enough to let him sleep. Sometimes he could purge himself into a nice refreshing coma.

Fat chance; his body was getting back at him for that stunt in the office this afternoon.

"Himmelsgötter, make up your mind!" he moaned to the night. "Either rain, or don't rain. When you're pushing dry clouds around like this, it hurts."

45

* * * * *

Pfirsich lay back against his pillow. Poor Stiefler, knowing what he knew about himself. Why did he do it? It was sordid. Pfirsich didn't even want to think about what -- what people like that did.

He curled up in the rough blanket, even covering his head. And why would a man like him choose to be that nasty way? It would ruin him if it got out. Why choose ruin? Pfirsich uncovered his head. What if the man doesn't have any choice? he thought.

The boy sat straight up. What if there was something wrong with Stiefler? What if he was cursed from birth? What if it was something that just happened to you?

The boy's eyes were wide in the dark. Could it happen to anybody? Could it -- happen to me? Is that why he said he thought I was -- that way? Pfirsich put his fist in his mouth. Was he trying to lure me into being what he is? Or does he need to lure me? Did he just see what was already there?

Whacking his pillow a few times, Pfirsich whispered to himself. "I'm not that way! I'm not!"

A pillow hit him out of the dark. "Rommel! Go to sleep. Quit jumping up and down like a bedwetting kid."

"Shut up!" hissed Pfirsich. "Or you'll have Stiefler in here."

He returned the pillow, as hard as he could, then threw himself down with his hands over his face. As though he's not in here already, he thought. He lay in the dark, breathing as Stiefler had taught him to breathe while taking aim, trying not to hyperventilate.

It took a while before he began to dream. A dream of his favored officer, as beautiful and heroic as Pfirsich had ever imagined him in his daydreams. There was no trace of the distressing image of Stiefler as he had seen him that day, or the truth of his torn exhausted humanity.

The boy didn't picture what he'd really seen of naked male flesh. Most of that had been in the showers in the barracks, most of it unattractively young, and pale, or pimply, or pudgy. Dangly. The liaisons Stiefler had been worried about weren't common, and didn't go far.

Instead, Pfirsich could take advantage of an education in classical art, that lent him a mental gallery from which he could choose the most beautiful and desirable forms of the human body, detailed and accurate particularly in the depictions of the male. Beautifully muscled, strong-throated, stallion-hipped, proud-nippled, glossy-genitaled males, portrayed in a thousand statues and paintings of and by a sex in love with itself.

So he couldn't help but imagine the man, this man, his man, classically naked, a delicate fan-brushed silver fog curling modestly about his delectable spare hips, his scars glowing faintly like pink jewels obscured by mist, standing strong and languid as a saint or a hero in a Mannerist painting.

The boy imagined none of the real man's ugly real scars; this was a warm smooth lithograph by Blake, not the tortured green church-triptychs of Grünewald. Not a St. Sebastian sweating, trembling full of arrows, or a rotting eye-rolling Christ of The Slivers, but a Christ of polished white virgin marble, in a drapery of clouds, long-lashed eyes glimmering half-closed in sacred traditional desire and sacrifice, a droplet of blood, drawn by the softly-gleaming Crown of Thorns, glimmering ruby-like on the smooth forehead, the Caste-mark of the Glorious Victim, mouth pink-gaping and moist with the devoted breathlessness of prayer.

Without being able to help himself, the boy murmurs, "Oh, how beautiful."

The man holds out his lithe strong luminescent arms and speaks.

"Come, *Kind*. I'm not angry with you. Fear not. Be of good cheer."

Forgiveness!

Naked as a soul, the boy rises toward him, as a released spirit toward an angel, as on a breeze through the glowing rolling pink-and-purple clouds, Ganymede in the baroque talons of the Jovian eagle, and murmurs, "Forgive me, I know not what I am."

"I know," says the angel.

They kiss, in a sacred melting, a holy oneness, the two sliced soul-halves finding one another again, the anatomies of their beings seizing together, penetrating into one another, hearts beating like wings, in true physical agapè.

And Pfirsich awakens with a gasp, lying trembling on his back, truly prepared to receive his love, spiritually and bodily capable, a living picture of Egyptian Osiris in his winding-sheets, lying in erect posthumous godhood to impregnate the soaring vulture-winged sister goddess Isis.

If his noble propertied mother could have had any idea how he'd just used her art education!

* * * * *

Outside, on the balcony, Stiefler turned his haggard pale face to the moon and whimpered.

"*Liebe Mutter,* strength for one more day. I swear, I won't come whining to you again, at least until tomorrow night."

He bowed his sweating head down upon the cool smooth railing, and held one hand up to the sky. "Honest to God, I promise. I SWEAR."

"*Herr Leutnant?*"

Stiefler lifted his gray damp face from the railing, amazed.

"Rommel? What are you doing out of bed?"

Pfirsich was standing behind him in the doorway, arms clutched across his chest. Stiefler almost gasped with pity. The boy, trembling and pale, looked as though he'd been blown up, and come down conscious.

"Child, what's wrong?"

"*Herr Leutnant* -- oh, God -- you're right."

"You baffle me, child. Right about what?"

"I -- I'm like you. I know it now."

"Like me? Like me?"

All Stiefler could think of was his hip; at the moment it was his whole universe. He was confused. He hadn't heard any explosion; why did this silly insistent boy look like he needed a transfusion? When had he been bleeding?

Pfirsich whimpered, "Like -- like you said I shouldn't tell anyone you are."

Stiefler realized what he meant, and said wearily, "How did you find this out?"

Pfirsich blushed. "I imagined -- it. I imagined it with -- another person. With somebody else. With -- a man."

"You imagined it? 'It?'"

Pfirsich hung his head and whispered, "Yes. With -- *Us.* "

"What do you mean by 'Us?'" "Stiefler frowned. "Don't tell me -- ?"

Pfirsich whispered, "*Jawohl, Herr Leutnant.* I couldn't help it. You

48

just came to me, in my mind -- I was completely unable to defend against it -- and there you were!" He held out his hands, imploring and helpless.

"Well, did we enjoy it?"

"Mein Herr, bitte!" Pfirsich was scandalized. "This is serious. Life-and-death serious!"

"It's not serious, *Avantageur.*"

"But it is!" insisted Pfirsich. "It -- it excited me!"

"Excited you?" Stiefler snorted. "You're sixteen years old. You're lust with legs. You could imagine doing it with a hedgehog and it'd bring your little joystick there to attention."

Stiefler pointed. Pfirsich put both hands over his crotch.

"Mein Herr!"

"What you have is a crush," Stiefler said bitterly. "A normal *Backfisch* crush, like homesick boys get on their training officers. I don't want to hear the details of your imagination; I've heard them before, and probably in the same order. The silly little twits actually imagine they're in love with us and with each other. They start Grande Passions behind the barracks, and have little love-spats. It's all very boring; kids aren't very original." Stiefler shrugged. "Now go to the latrine and run some cold water over your wrists, and then go back to bed."

"It's not a crush, *mein Herr!* It's serious!"

"You have a crush. You have a crush, and my career is on the line. My entire reputation is about to slide into the mud, because of your overheated young loins and your *verdammte* imagination. If you're going to fall in love, fall in love with one of the other boys."

"I'm sorry, *Herr Leutnant.*"

Stiefler eased the angle of his hip against the railing. "I have four more years left in the army, Rommel. I want those four years. I want my pension. I need that pension. Do you know why?"

"Na, Herr Leutnant --."

"I'm glad you don't know. I hope -- I pray -- you never know. Child, I have a hip full of pins. I walk funny; the trainees call me *'Piphacken'* behind my back -- I've heard 'em -- and with good reason. A horse in my condition would have been sausages as soon as they could get me near the grinder. I couldn't begin to satisfy your imagination, even if I wanted to, because I hurt so much. I don't even think about my groin any more. All I think about is my hip. At this point it's my entire body, and gets all my attention. I'm completely self-centered. A pension will feed me and house me, so I don't have to think about anything else, and perhaps the money will occasionally allow me to stew the pain out of my hip at a mineral spa. Understand?"

Pfirsich hung his head, and said sorrowfully, *"Jawohl, Herr Leutnant."*

"This isn't right." Stiefler grabbed his forehead; he felt completely out of control. "I'm not supposed to be doing this to you." For the life of him, he couldn't stop talking. "I'm supposed to be steeling you for war, teaching you to die, not teaching you what happens if you don't. Not showing you what can become of you if you're a poor weak swine like me."

"'Weak!'" protested Pfirsich.

Stiefler slapped his hand over his mouth so hard it stung. Shut up, he told himself. Shut up! What are you trying to do to this boy? *Jesus Christus, Mann!*

They stood there, in silence except for Stiefler's sniffling and counted breathing. At last, the *Leutnant* wiped his nose on his sleeve.

"You know, " he paused. "If you're really worried about what you and I are to each other, you can do my reputation a priceless service."

Pfirsich stood with his head hanging. "I understand, *Herr Leutnant*. I will no longer expect private shooting instruction from you."

"You can keep an ear out at night, in case you hear a pistol shot."

"Mein Herr!"

Stiefler said absently, "It's worst for me at night. If you ever hear a shot, make sure you're the first one down there; I'll leave the door unlocked. You'll come in to find my cleaning kit scattered across the desk. Do me the kindness of moving my hand and my pistol away from my temple. Make it look like a cleaning accident."

Pfirsich gasped.

"If you can't do that, swear to the board of inquiry that I'd scheduled you for shooting practice that day. Convince them that a punctual man like myself would never purposely miss an appointment. Make it plausible."

"But how? But why?"

"I'm not trying to win your sympathy; I simply suspect the limits of my strength. You saw yourself how small my remaining reserves can be. This may teach you to be a better officer. There are always weak links in a command, and you have to learn how to deal with them. I'm the weak link."

"No!"

Stiefler held up his hand. "So like a good officer, you have to watch out for me. Consider this a permanent honor assignment, awarded you in consideration of your feelings for me. Now go back to bed and go to sleep."

Pfirsich could hardly breathe. "After this? How can I sleep knowing this?"

Stiefler shrugged. "Well, if your imagination impinges upon your rest, this will induce you to curb it. If you really can't sleep, you can do what the entire German army does when it can't do something. You can pretend."

"But --."

Stiefler rubbed his eyes, then leaned forward and said, "Go - to - bed. That's an order."

"Jawohl, Herr Leutnant!"

* * * * *

Alone on the balcony, Stiefler stood peacefully smoking. The evening's crises had exhausted his ability to fully feel the pain, and he was almost content. He happily puffed on the cigarette, and blew the smoke out his nose, enjoying it more than he'd enjoyed anything in a long time.

That'll take care of the kid's crush, he thought. Bet it never came into his busy little head again. Imagine that silly skinny kid, running in and getting me so upset that I blurted out what I've been hiding all these years! He shook me right up out of myself. I didn't think it was still possible.

Stiefler smiled, and took another drag on the cigarette. Perhaps he was still able to react to beauty -- to lose his head over it. To get honest-to-god manly urges. Wouldn't that be something? He's a toothsome child, thought Stiefler, I'll give him that. Give him another five years, and some young lady is going to get herself candy from heaven. The man grinned. Another five years, and I wouldn't be able to resist. That kind just gets prettier as they get older.

A ruminating look came over the *Leutnant's* face; he was indulging himself in a harmless fantasy of a future decade. His eyebrows rose. He looked down at his groin.

"Well, I'll be damned. Twinges. The thing still works."

Stiefler looked up at the moon, and for the first time in a long time, he truly didn't hurt, not badly enough to center his whole self on it.

Maybe he should look up some old friends. A pension could keep two warm as one.

Stiefler wiped away a tear, and for once it was one of happiness. That kid's an angel, he thought. A goddamn goading silly little angel.

He gave me back my heart.

* * * * *

The boy lay flat on his back in bed, eyes wide and dry, his mind running out of control.

How the hell did he expect me to ever go to sleep again? Every time I get up, I'll have to race down to his office, knowing any day I could find him with -- with his brains all over his desk.

The boy flung himself over on his face and moaned. Oh, the rotten heartless bastard!

5. Why Was He Born So Beautiful?

In 1917, the Austrians were bombing Venice from airplanes. They aimed for the railway station, missed, and hit the church of *Chiesa degli Scalzi,* on the Grand Canal, completely blowing out the roof and vault, along with its magnificent ceiling by Tiepolo.

Stationed out in the Carnic Mountains, high in the Italian Alps, where the line of battle ran down the middle of the peaks, Pfirsich, now serving with his brother and commanding officer, heard of the thoughtless desecration and used very bad language.

"Austrians. Careless flyers and worse aim," was all Erwin said.

* * * * *

By 1917, *Fähnrich* Pfirsich Rommel thought he was tough.

He marched down a shattered street in a deserted village, wrapped in a huge greatcoat, its dusty skirts whirling fiercely around his neatly booted legs. A cigarette was cocked up martially at one corner of his pretty mouth. *Mann,* he knew he looked good.

Now and again dust arose from an artillery shell that couldn't quite lob itself over the rocks and exploded against the cliffside. He ignored it.

Brother Erwin was trying to win the *Pour le Mérite,* and complaining when he didn't, so he wanted Pfirsich to be a war hero. Erwin was unbearable now; he'd be worse with the Blue Max banging on a ribbon around his neck. Pfirsich blew smoke out his nostrils like a war hero should, and got a memory of a real war hero right between his martially narrowed eyes. He gulped and blinked, feeling his eyes go wet.

After pawing his gloved hand all over his face, he stood up straight, puffed manfully at the cigarette and took a violent coughing fit. He dug a grimy handkerchief from his breast pocket, tears tracking the patina of dirt he couldn't keep off his pink cheeks. He recovered at last and stood gasping and spitting, wiping his mouth with the handkerchief.

53

"Pfui!" he spat at the cigarette in his free hand. When were these nasty things going to stop surprising him? They were filthy, they didn't calm his nerves -- he flicked the cigarette over the cliff -- and they stank.

He dusted the ashes from his uniform, wiped his gray gloves and wrinkled his nose. His nose felt crusted; it always seemed to be full of black snot, from the smoke of campfires, and ill trimmed kerosene lanterns. He sniffed the tips of his gloves and grimaced.

The coffin nails weren't the only things that stunk. These wool gloves were positively rancid. He sniffed the knuckles, then the bare inside of his wrist, fascinated by the reek. When he was growing up he'd always thought that adults stank. And men were the worst. They smelled hot and musky, animal. Sweet and salty, like a tide pool. And cream. Seaweed and fresh goat cheese. Pfirsich sniffed his sleeve in the crook of his elbow, taking two or three long breaths, as humans will do now and then when they know they shouldn't be smelling of themselves, and unable to help it.

He shook his head and dropped his arm, and when it slapped against his coat, it raised a cloud of dust. Well, he certainly smelled like a man now! He didn't believe he'd had a bath in three weeks. But neither had anyone else, so he shouldn't feel he stood out. He scratched daintily under one arm. He could endure the apish smell; he was even getting used to it. But he could not get used to this intolerable itching!

Looking over his shoulder, he assured himself no one would see him trying to scratch between his legs. It was amazing how crowded a war could get, and the intolerably private places it made a body itch. The other lads might have thought it manly to scrub away at their privates in public, but it wasn't his cup of tea. He'd have given up his hope of salvation for a bath, but there wasn't a hatful of water to spare for cleanliness up there on those dry plateaus.

He left the trail and pushed through the trees, and peered down through the branches at a powerful river boiling through the narrow canyon, far below. All the water was down there in the river, with the Germans and Austrians holding this bank and the Italians on the other. The officers of both sides had forbidden their men to go into the canyon unless during an attack. So there they both sat, in sight of a clear surging river, and all the water either side could get had to be hauled up the cliffs in barrels. On muleback.

Pfirsich squealed and slapped the back of his neck, then examined what he'd caught in his fingers. He knew what it was; he'd caught them before, but he still winced when he saw it was a flea. Pah! *Ungeheuere Ungeziefier!*

All of us have fleas, he thought, using his fingernails to crack the obnoxious bug. The Austrians have fleas. The Italians are sitting over there with their own private insects.

Pfirsich gazed down wistfully at the river. If he didn't get to bathe soon the winter cold would set in and by spring he'd have to scrape his uniform off. God knew what he'd have to excavate from between his toes. And the summer weather has already been holding longer than it should. He ran a finger under his collar and shuddered.

Erwin would be furious if he got anywhere near that river. Pfirsich had already tried arguing that cleanliness was necessary for unit health. Erwin shot back that there were other duties beyond mere hygiene, and if anyone became a casualty for a bath – even younger brothers – his commander would be within his rights to leave him in the river. With a boulder on top of him.

Pfirsich peered down the trail. He wondered if it would even be possible to get down to the river from there while crawling under the branches. Since it would be against orders and he had no time, he wouldn't attempt it even if it were possible. He backed along under a dry crumbling overhang in the cliff face, that he was sure he hadn't seen on any of the maps. If he were to follow it, if he kept back against this cliff wall, the Italians shouldn't have a chance of seeing him and sniping him and leaving him to rot in a hole in the rocks where no one would ever think of looking for him.

Lieber Gott, Erwin would have a fit. And think what their mother would do to *Herr* Commander, losing his little brother and not even finding the body: *War Hero Earns Silver Wound Badge: Beaten black and blue with wooden spoon.*

After enjoying the image for a few moments, and looking around to see if he were really alone, Pfirsich began inching his way along a very narrow shelf in the cliff face.

No wonder no one had been down there. You'd have to have feet like a forest fairy to find purchase here. Pfirsich's feet were tiny for his size, but small-footed people seldom think about their feet. Little Erwin was the one with the big feet. He obviously didn't think so, the way he kept his boots polished.

The shelf and the overhang spread out to form a partially open gallery, and then a darkening tunnel. Pfirsich hunched over, lower and lower, until he was compelled to crawl. If it got any narrower, he'd have to buttock out backwards. How undignified.

If Erwin caught him, he could always tell him that he'd been trying to find a better route for the water to come up the cliff, but this way wouldn't be any better than with the mules. The only way to carry water would be to cover a man with canteens and allow him a comrade with a rope to help him scramble his burden back up the cliff. But it would be an option. Erwin liked options.

Pfirsich stopped foursquare and stared like a suspicious pony. He heard water, right in front of him. He crawled forward and then cringed in amazement.

The tunnel opened out above a disturbed underground pool, illuminated by bands of light passing through long fissures in the natural vault ceiling. To the left was a smaller and much darker tunnel , and from it a glittering arch of waterfall crashed into the pool far below.

Over the narrower end of the pool before the waterfall ranged a precarious natural stone bridge, sunset-colored in the columns of soft light. The water sent up undulating gold and purple reflections over all the surfaces of the cave. The waterfall had acted as a natural drill bit and pile driver, the bright hurling drops like so many diamond bits, digging out the bridge and the deep pool below it.

Pfirsich rose slowly to his feet, gazing down into the black lapping water. He glanced up toward the ceiling. This stream wasn't on any of the maps, either. It must run underground right down from the heart of the glacier; his breath formed in clouds from the chill in the vault. He'd only been ordered to stay away from the river, but he didn't need orders to stay out of this icy pit. Even if he could swim it, he could imagine what Erwin would say if he caught pneumonia and used up the scarce medical supplies.

"Heilige Sankt Peter," Pfirsich murmured. "Look at that."

At its far end, the water discharged into a morning-glory whirlpool so deep it didn't throw foam. A beam of light from the cracked ceiling illuminated the ripples around the suction tunnel's perfectly glassy black sides. It was a throat waiting to be fed.

Pfirsich put his collar up around his chin. It looked as though there were light farther on over the bridge. He edged bravely but cautiously onto the stone expanse, standing upright. He wouldn't crawl across. Erwin wouldn't have. Erwin? Erwin wouldn't have had the sense to crawl across. He'd march, head up, *ein zwei, ein zwei.* Erwin thought he'd been put on earth to see what he could get away with. Pfirsich tried not to look down into the evil black whirlpool.

Pfirsich sensibly crawled out onto the bridge, clutching hard with his fingers. It was no use showing off when there wasn't even anybody to see. Bravery should keep for when it was needed.

The other side of the bridge led into a brightly-lit gallery. Pfirsich, emerging suddenly into the sunlight, threw his hand up over his face. The shadows were very sharp, the harsh high-altitude autumn sun reflecting from the brilliant pale walls of the enclosing cliffs. The light stabbed like an arc lamp. He rubbed his shoulders, squinting around and smiling. It seemed so nice and warm after that icebox in there.

At his feet a trickle of clear water flowed between the stones and collected in a bowl crevice carved out by the stream when it fresheted in the spring. Such a tame little burble, compared to its big brother in the cave. Farther down the stream a tiny pool glinted deep blue in the white stones, a dear little puddle hardly bigger than a bathtub.

Pfirsich was soon squatting over the pool with one glove removed, slipping his fingers into the water, sun-warmed to the temperature of a pleasantly tepid bath. There wouldn't be time to dry his uniform if he washed it, would there? Of course not. But he could wash his underwear and socks. He looked up toward the flesh-smooth limestone cliffs standing chaperone. Just a quick dip. He was needed elsewhere. He'd be dressed almost before he was undressed.

In certain fastidious souls, the drive to decency can outstrip all discretion. Some people would insist on soap and showers in Hell. Some people, with the enemy possibly lining them up for sniping range, would still strip naked in literally under the gun. They would figure that snipers would be too shocked to shoot bare people.

In a moment, Pfirsich was no longer a sturdy German *Fähnrich,* but just another endearing slender half-grown boy, his allegiance only to the sunshine on his back, busily scrubbing his soapy underwear and socks on a rock, his pale skin and golden hair gleaming in the hot white light. Now he knew why old soldiers always carried a sliver of soap, just for the chance of clean water. He laid the wet undergarments out on a sun-baked rock, looking eagerly back over his shoulder at the pool. He wouldn't bathe a moment longer than it took for his underwear and socks to dry. As thin as they'd worn, he wouldn't be a minute. And this scabrous handkerchief. He shook it out, grimacing.

He sat right down into the water with a happy gasp and began scrubbing his hair and spitting soap, smug as a cat in the noonday sun. He'd make sure he was dried off afterwards; wouldn't want to go back into that icy cave with a wet head.

Behind him, up the short trail into the cave gallery, the dark side tunnel vomited out a man. He came tumbling into the limestone vault, shooting out with the waterfall and under the narrow stone bridge, heavy military coat tails flinging spray. In his moment in the air, the lost soldier managed one high-pitched despairing cry.

Bouncing along the gallery and outside into the sunshine, the cry was translated into an unearthly echoing scream. Pfirsich jumped to his feet, flinging soapsuds from his hair, desperately trying to scrape the soap out of his eyes.

"Ein Gespenst!" he gasped. A ghost! He'd been startled out of his wits and most of his reassuring modern education

"Ai--glrrg --uto!" gurgled the voice, now recognizably human in its distress.

Pfirsich grabbed for his gun belt; that was no ghost. He scrambled naked into the gallery, still dripping globs of soapsuds, strapping the gun belt around his waist as he ran.

In the cave pool, clinging precariously to the stone bridge was a young soldier, his wet dark hair hanging in his face. He was struggling desperately to keep his head above water against the undertow.

"Oh Cara mia -- no, no -- NO!" he wailed.

Pfirsich ran thoughtlessly upright right out onto the bridge. "Hang on! Don't let go! It will pull you under!"

The spent young man turned his eyes up toward Pfirsich. The naked boy came to a precarious stop above on the narrow bridge, and seen from below, shining pale gold in the beams of light, he became an unclothed, unhampered image of release and finality to the victim of the

58

stream.

"An angel." thought the young soldier. "I'm dying." His head ducked under the water again. An angel had come to fetch him. He might as well sink and submit.

He went all the way under but for the last flying locks of his hair. Pfirsich, without a thought for his own safety, flung himself flat onto the bridge and, clasping the rock as much by the friction of his own bare skin as with the strength of his fingers and toes, and thrust his arm into the water, grabbing fiercely after the soldier. He reared back, hauling the startled youth by his hair up out of the pool.

"Hang on. Help me. Fight!"

He dragged the young man, who was weakly kicking in an attempt to assist, right up onto the bridge, where he drooped him across the narrow stone crawlway like a landed salmon. The boy couldn't even sit up or make himself more secure, but only hung in shuddering exhaustion above the pool, kept there by little more than the weight of water in his clothes.

Pfirsich squatted over him, peering into his face.

"Are you all right? Did you follow me down here? It's against orders."

The young man, lying on his back, gasped up at his rescuer, "Oh, thank God. Thank you. I was almost a goner!"

Then both of them said, "I don't understand you. Why don't I understand you?"

Then: *"Lieber Dio mio Gott!* You're one of them."

"Don't try anything," ordered Pfirsich, grabbing for his pistol. "I'm armed."

The young Italian reached for him, and fainted.

* * * * *

The young soldier lay on his back in the full sun, his eyes closed. He was warm and dry. He opened his eyes and he heard a voice say, "Are you all right? Do you speak German?"

He looked up to see a well-made, slender young blond, wearing nothing but a German pistol belt, smoking a cigarette with a careful reserve.

"You look like you've been beaten half to death," said Pfirsich.

"You didn't come rolling down the underground river, did you? You must have fallen in, where the that smaller stream runs above ground."

"Excuse me?" said the young man. He sat up and looked down at himself. He was naked.

The young German said, pointing, "Your clothes were wet, and cold as a shroud. That's them drying over there, in the sun."

"Do you mean my clothes were wet?"

"You don't understand a word of German, do you?" Pfirsich slipped a pack out of his own uniform and offered it.

"Want one? Cigarette? Ah -- *Zigaretto?*"

"Oh. Yes, please. That I understand."

He took a cigarette, and lighting up, looked into Pfirsich's face, trying to smile in the most grateful manner.

He thought, Ah, it's true. Look at the color of his eyes. They have eyes like little fallen bits of heaven. Isn't he pale, though? Like he's molded of fine milled soap. Don't they ever get any sun up there in the German lands? The Italian blushed and said to himself, Ah, Felice, they didn't tell you what to do if you met the enemy *naked*.

Felice sat up, to cover himself. He really did feel naked in front of the other soldier. Felice didn't feel like this in front of the rest of the fellows. But this was the enemy, and the one with the pistol. They were naked; the German was armed and could hurt him. It was like being a girl.

Pfirsich was trying to look tough, but he was bothered. He'd never seen one of the enemy naked. He couldn't keep his eyes off the Italian's body; it was as though he were searching for something that was different from his own people. The Italian was so small and smooth and young it was like looking at a girl. What great dark eyes; like a roe fawn. Was he as curious about Pfirsich as Pfirsich was about him?

He saved my life, thought Felice. And he didn't have to.

Of course, thought Pfirsich, he'd have to take the soldier prisoner. This valley was the back door to the German position, and the Italian had seen it. But how was he going to explain where he'd captured an enemy? He wasn't even supposed to be down here. Could he say he'd been making a reconnaissance detour?

"Ah! No you don't!"

Felice was reaching for Pfirsich's free hand, smiling nervously, making soothing, submissive gestures. "No no no no. I only want to thank you. You saved my life."

Pfirsich frowned, confused, cautious, the pistol wavering around by his ear. What did he want? He was courting and cooing like a pigeon. Pfirsich didn't like it.

Felice knelt up, carefully taking Pfirsich's hand. "Thank you. Thank you. See? I'm grateful. I take your hand."

Pfirsich blushed. "What? Oh. You're thanking me. What a warm hand. I'd heard that southern people are warm."

"I thank you, I'm grateful. But I won't be your prisoner. Do you understand?"

Pfirsich brought the pistol down upon him. "I don't speak Italian. What do you want? Stop it. You're making me very uncomfortable."

"I know where they send Italian freedom fighters. Into the mountains, into Moldavia -- to Fortress Spielberg. They work on your mind there; they take yourself from you. I won't go."

"I don't understand. Don't talk to me."

Felice made a sudden leap for the pistol, knocking Pfirsich over backwards into the pool. They landed in a leg-lined splash, and began to struggle in the shallow water, kicking and twisting.

"Laß das los! Nein!"

"Ma, Cretino! Give it to me!"

Four young hands, trying to twist the pistol into their grip and away from themselves sent the weapon spinning. It landed out in the sunshine in a puff of dust. Felice, snorting, wet black hair hanging in his face, lip bleeding, tried to snake after it over the slippery wet margin of the pool.

Pfirsich grabbed him by the ankles. "Leave it alone!"

Felice made a vicious backhand grab at Pfirsich. "Let me go -- *Tuder!"*

Kraut! So he was calling names, was he? When he put his mind to it, Pfirsich could be a regular heroic little Siegfried. He grabbed Felice's clawing arm and flipped him right over onto his back. Then he sat on him, his hard little haunches driving the air out of Felice's hard little belly.

"You sneaking macaroni hound!" Pfirsich rose up and sat back down, like a lithe pink pile driver. "Give up or get a beating!"

"Oww!" gasped Felice, and then, when he'd got his breath back, "Brutal German bastard!"

61

"Call me names? I'll beat you 'till you won't fit in a coffin!"

Pfirsich didn't punch, he grabbed, sinking his fingers into Felice's warm flesh, and the Italian twisted under the predatory grip. Pfirsich grimly wrestled Felice down onto the edge of the pond, and pinned him hard with his whole body, like a swan on a head in the water. Their faces were very close. Pfirsich grappled close on top of Felice, his legs wrapped around his body, firmly controlling him, at least for the moment.

"Give up, you're my prisoner now, if you weren't before!"

If they could have only seen themselves; wet, squirming, their infuriated pretty faces glaring in charming boyish hate at one another, pale furious Pfirsich gripping swarthy Felice's tender wrists over his dark gleaming head, Felice struggling fiercely and admirably between the legs of his handsome captor. Full of victory and malice and intimidation, Pfirsich thrust his face right down before Felice's, believing his mouth set like a fighting dog's, and unaware that all he was achieving was a little moist pink pout.

"Ha! Now what are you going to do?"

Unlike Pfirsich, Felice could see that pout, and his warlike urges to bruise and break and bring blood were distracted by such pink vulnerable lips. He thought himself more ferocious than his German captor, but he chose a childish weapon, from a childhood not far in his past. With his own softest weapon, made for the soft things of life, he kissed Pfirsich fiercely, right on the mouth.

"Take that, *Tuder!*"

Pfirsich froze; he looked as though he'd been bitten. Kissing had been a means of teasing intimate intimidation when he was a child, a cousin to tickling, and could be just as intrusive. Had he been younger -- only a little younger -- he might have simply punched his antagonist in the face, and everyone would have gone home bawling and bruised, to be punished for fighting. Instead he tried to sit up, so shaken he felt emptied. Felice wouldn't let him get away. Having found the enemy's weak spot, he gripped the struggling German in his arms and continued to pop kisses across his face.

Didn't expect that, hah! thought Felice, and smacked him again.

"Don't! Don't!" sputtered Pfirsich, turning his face desperately right and left. Felice energetically kissed the squinting blond on the alternate presentation of his pure pale temples.

"Don't."

Pfirsich's struggles grew weaker, until he lay stiff and still, head bowed, eyes shut, an expression of pain on his face, as Felice pressed a firm kiss on his forehead.

"Don't," he begged.

Felice's lips brushed his cheeks like stray breezeblown petals. Pfirsich relaxed, empty of protest. The Italian boy closed his eyes and breathed a tender kiss into the blond hair. He raised his hands and held the golden head to his face, whispering. Pfirsich leaned into his touch.

"Oh, don't you smell good…" murmured Felice.

A young boy isn't much different from a young girl, slender and warm-hued in that first endearing sexual bloom. Presented with only a smooth bud-nippled breast, how does the yearning youthful soul resist its perfect altar?

Pfirsich lowered his head and gently kissed Felice's musky bosom.

"It must be you," breathed Felice, sniffing in wonder. "No soap smells so good."

I shouldn't do this, thought Pfirsich, and began to helplessly kiss the delicate olive throat. Felice as helplessly leaned back to receive it.

"Oh, you should stop," he crooned.

Pfirsich's lips butterflied along Felice's cheek. Neither of them had the power to open his eyes.

"Bello Tedesco. You must stop."

"I can't stop," whispered Pfirsich, who didn't need to understand his trembling enemy's language to know what he meant.

"Oh, your lovely wounded mouth." Pfirsich's lips closed over his enemy's bleeding lips.

"Cara mia, if only you understood me."

They put their arms around one another. Still, neither of them dared open his eyes. They moved against one another, oblivious of everything but one another's bodies, Pfirsich's legs still wrapped around Felice's hips, still in a pressure of capture. But what sort of captivity was this?

Oh, Gott, I've got to have you, thought Pfirsich, who had never had anyone in his life.

And then Felice threw back his head and Pfirsich gasped and stiffened. What was that? No – he wasn't? This was far more intrusive than any kiss. Felice arched in ecstasy, holding firmly to the gun belt, while Pfirsich strained to pull up and away

"No, no -- don't! Get out!"

"*Oh, bellisimo --.*"

The dark boy thrust up and savagely consolidated his capture. The fair boy, conquered, leaned back, no longer struggling, thighs tense, toes clenched, lips barely parted, surrendering. The dark boy raised a hand and began to gently rub one of his enemy's shining pink nipples.

"*Bellisimo.*"

Pfirsich arched back against Felice's hips, hands desperately gripping his beloved enemy's shoulders, face beatific.

"I love you. I love you!"

Both hands kneading Pfirsich's breast, Felice moaned, "*Oh, bellisimo Tuder.*"

Digging his fingers into Pfirsich's hips, he writhed with his climax; Pfirsich drove his hand between his own legs, clutching himself, gasping, as he consummated an alliance with his conqueror.

Then they were still, exhausted, Felice lying with one arm over his eyes, the other thrown back above his head, Pfirsich still straddling him, head bowed, golden hair brushing over his eyes, hands limp across Felice's shuddering breast.

The poor kids didn't dare move. Pfirsich dazedly brought his hand away from his body, not daring to look it, shocked and repulsed. His teeth bared, he crept backwards off Felice into the shallow water, not daring to look at him, holding his hand out where he wouldn't have to look at it, either.

He squatted hunched over in the water, nearly in tears, washing his hands as if in recognition of murder. All the black soaps of Spain could not cleanse this little soul. Behind him, Felice lurched up with his eyes still closed. Eyes averted from his recent conquest, the trembling boy crept into the water, biting back his own tears. Each of them behaved as though the other didn't exist, two frightened children bowing down away from their sin.

The two of them sat with their backs turned toward one another, at a conspicuous distance, grimly washing everything they had. Baptized, they both crept out of their opposite sides of the pool. And to themselves they wept Oh, sordid! Sordid!

Both of them dressed as quickly as they could, huddling on their uniforms any which way, missing half the buttoning, stuffing their socks into their pockets. Neither of them cared that their underwear and clothes were still wet. Without looking up, eyes turned away so obliquely that they kept falling over their own boots, they made the most desperately quick mutually compacted retreat in history.

* * * * *

Two German officers stood at the edge of a cliff. Between them they gripped a map. One was *Oberleutnant* Erwin Rommel, energetically stabbing a gloved finger out over the chasm. Beside him, *Fähnrich* Rommel wasn't being much more than an inattentive paper clamp.

"You see that tongue of stone, Pfirsich? We'll haul six men and a machine gun right up there!" Erwin slashed the air with his little hand. "We'll put the first bursts right over the top of their heads; they'll be running in circles, scared witless. Why haul up enough ammunition to murder 'em, when we only need to make 'em hold up their hands and squeal, *'mika Froynta!'* in bad German? We'll never need to harm 'em; we can just herd 'em out like cows. It will be fun!"

Pfirsich wasn't looking at the map; he was staring off over the chasm, towards the Italian side of the river.

"Pfirsich!" barked Erwin. "Pay attention! What's wrong with you, you stuffed dummy? You haven't said a word all afternoon." He grasped his brother's chin in his hand and peered up sharply into his face. "You don't look right. You getting sick on me?"

Pfirsich reared back, eyes terrified and ill. "No, no. I'm fine." He jerked away his head and burst into tears. "I'm fine."

"Pfirsich? If you're sick, you'd better not try to hide it."

Pfirsich angrily wiped his face. "Don't pay any attention to me," he snuffled. "It's nerves."

"Oh. Scared, eh?"

Erwin roughly patted him on the shoulder; Pfirsich held himself very stiffly, as though barely enduring his touch. Erwin thought he recognized the frightened pride of the virgin soldier.

"I understand. First time I went into a fight, I hadn't slept in two days. I paid for it, too."

"I don't have your bad stomach," gritted Pfirsich.

Erwin glared at him. He wished he'd never told Pfirsich about the food poisoning.

"The first fight's hard, boy. But if you worry about it too much, you'll make yourself even sicker, at the worst time to be sick."

"I'm not scared, Erwin. I'm --." Looking down at his brother's brave, simple face, Pfirsich could only mutter, "Just nerves."

He pulled his freshly washed handkerchief from his sleeve, where Japanese ladies and German officers kept kerchiefs and letters. He neatly wiped his eyes, delicately blew his nose, and took the little traditional glance at the contents. Nice clean snot. Then he as neatly folded the handkerchief, carefully tucked it back into his sleeve, turned to his brother, who had been eyeing him, and said, in the most proper ladylike military manner,

"Herr Oberleutnant."

Erwin cocked his head up at him.

Pfirsich took his side of the map. *"Herr Oberleutnant* was saying?"

Erwin still didn't speak, and continued to look up at him. There had been some kind of disturbing change in his little brother, worse than whatever had made him so withdrawn and shy in the first place, and Erwin was beginning to think he didn't like it. The next moment Pfirsich dropped his eyes and began to study the map.

What's happened to him? thought Erwin. He's put up a wall.

"Pfir-sich! Look at me! What have you been up to?"

The boy looked up, his face white. "None of your business. And my name is 'Manfred'."

Erwin stiffened with indignation. *'Bitte!* Watch your tone, *Fähnrich."*

"'Manfred'," insisted the boy.

"One of your names is Manfred."

"Well, that's the one I want you to use."

"But -- the other name, it's our mother's favorite name," tendered the elder brother.

"I don't like it now."

"But why not?"

Manfred dropped his eyes back to the map. Erwin was insulted as an officer, but more than that, he was hurt and confused and shaken.

66

And there went another wall, that Erwin could feel, slammed shut as if journeled on hinges of steel. Against him! Something had happened to Pfirsich -- or Manfred, if he insisted. *Mein Gott,* he didn't even stand the same. And he wasn't going to reveal why. Even a direct order couldn't get it out of him. Erwin knew him. Torture couldn't have made him tell what he didn't want to.

In Erwin's moment of disorientation, Manfred had regained his composure, and now stood as alert and proper as a well-trained secretary.

"Herr Oberleutnant? Could we continue?"

"Yes," said the *Oberleutnant,* recomposing himself and giving the map a sharp shake.

"Yes, of course."

* * * * *

In an Italian stone trench, the boy Felice was a sad damp lump squatting on a firing step, hiding under his helmet, rifle clutched across his shoulder, staring at nothing.

He wouldn't look up; he knew that to look up was to see the other side of the river, where the Germans were. Where one German was. He put his head in his arms, and whispered,

"Oh, mio bello, bello Tuder..."

Bread and Swans

6. When I Look At You

"Manfred" followed Erwin dutifully from campaign to campaign. But the day he found the recommendation that he be awarded The Iron Cross, Second Class, lying on a stack of papers on the rickety field table in Erwin's entrenched quarters, he stamped and swore and then looked over his shoulder.

He was named on the paper as "Pfirsich Rommel," and his mouth tightened as he read the name and the report of his own behavior. Yes, he'd done his duty. Yes, he could triangulate artillery and lead a charge and direct reconnaissance as well as any officer in the army. A flesh wound in the arm had earned him the Wound Badge, Third Class, and he'd had no choice but to take it and wear it. It was only a nondescript black metal ellipse, not like the silver Second Class, or gold First Class, that in any case would have been accompanied by crippling injuries. But the red-white-and-black ribbon of the Iron Cross, that he would have had no choice but to wear in his second buttonhole, would create unwanted attachments and expectations by the military.

The fox that lived under Erwin's cot watched with cruel bright eyes as the young man slipped the recommendation into the bottom of the stack, where it would simply go missing. Nobody ever got to the bottom of the stack, least of all Erwin, who didn't like paperwork. Probably just as well he'd never ended up as a teacher.

* * * * *

When the Kaiser abdicated and the war ended, the Versailles Treaty demanded that the German Army be compressed into a minor defense force. The German Army responded to the pressure like coal. What remained would have to be a small bright perfection, diamond-hard. The army would have to sieve for men with medals. Manfred didn't have any medals, and Manfred's reaction was Hurrah for the French -- he was free!

69

Hauptmann Erwin Rommel, on the other hand, with enough medals and wounds to get him portrayed on Sanka coffee trading cards, was overjoyed to be selected to remain in the army as one of a very choice cadre. Erwin pitied Manfred, and Manfred was just happy to get away clean, with a pale small scar, and all his limbs.

After a very pleasant reunion party with the family, in his almost-new three-piece suit, Manfred signed up on a program to find work for returning veterans and obtained a place as a teacher's assistant near Berlin. It suited him. He wanted to be somewhere away from people he knew, for a while at least, if only to be able to sit by himself of evenings in his own quiet little flat, where he could have tea or a short pitcher of beer and read the papers without being inspected by anybody, officers or relatives.

Erwin had been assigned to Berlin, but he hardly knew Manfred was in town. He hadn't been long mourning over the end of the war; his army was still there, and he was still part of it and all its plans for the future.

The little *Hauptmann* went out to walk off his spirits one evening, down Berlin's bright-lit *Kurfürstendamm,* stopping to pet the horses and dogs. He was twirling a riding crop like a baton, throwing it up high in the air, until he missed the catch, so that it landed at the feet of an officer of the Allied Occupation. The officer quickly snatched up the crop and gallantly returned it.

"Oh," said Erwin. He'd never had a social conversation with the Enemy. Then he saluted and held out his hand. "Rommel. *Hauptmann* Rommel."

"Leftenant Harrington." The man returned the gestures. "Australian Expeditionary Force. Call me John."

"Chohn," said Erwin, and grinned, bad teeth and all. "Komm -- ve go to Press Clubb. Ve hafe -- I buy -- *Wein?*" It always took him about an hour to warm up to a language he hadn't been using.

"*I* buy vine," laughed John in delight. Erwin's thrifty Swabian soul expanded in sympathy.

Everyone went to Berlin's Press Club. Erwin had been too busy polishing the German Army's diamond to join in. Now, with the excuse of an interest in the Enemy's military, he claimed social duty to bring his wife to dance. Lucie was sharp, in many ways sharper than her husband. She could keep up with and even lead the steps in the politically charged

70

society of the Press Club, and Erwin valued her for it.

The Occupation officers who patronized the Club had their own stock of phonograph records, the hottest Jazz and Foxtrots. Erwin had never had an observation post so close to the enemy, and he got closer by borrowing the records. His favorite was the immensely popular *Oh, Johnny, Oh Johnny, Oh!* His Australian friend John never danced to any of the records; he'd been out on a wiring party and his own Captain neglected to inform the artillery, and John had nearly had a leg blown off by English shells. But if he couldn't dance he could still sing, and Erwin got a big kick out of urging him to sing along with the song that bore his name:

> *Please tell me dear.*
> *What makes me love you so?*
> *You're not handsome, it's true,*
> *But when I look at you,*
> *I just, Oh, Johnny!*
> *Oh, Johnny! Oh!*

John never failed to give it the archly naughty twist it demanded — sometimes even, on particularly alcoholic evenings, vamping it with an effeminacy that made everybody giggle. Rommel grinned like a badger. He began to bring his violin along just to accompany the Australian. The pair of them were a sissy hit. Rommel didn't sing, himself; he left that to his younger brother Gerhard, who was studying opera. Lucie hid her face in her handkerchief and gasped with laughter.

The musical duo involved another of the anomalies of personality that made it impossible for Harrington to know what to make of this Rommel person. Everybody called the little officer "The Fox" because he kept pet foxes. The one he had now he called "Baby Fox," in English. But he was as elusive as any of his pets.

When Rommel was in uniform, he was a proper German Officer, full of himself and his Fatherland, even in defeat. On the one rare occasion John had met him wearing civilian clothes, Rommel was a different person, introspective, modest and confiding. He had shown John photos of his wife, and his own son, and a wartime photo of himself in an underground bunker with a young big-eyed fox snuggled up safely in his lap. Out of

71

uniform, he seemed so gentle. In uniform, he was a spitfire. To John, talking to Rommel was like dealing with twins, one who wore the uniform, and one who didn't.

If he'd ever met Manfred, he would have seen the concept of multiple sartorial personalities made literal flesh.

* * * * *

"Proper demeanor, *Kinder!*"

The Fox was promenading with two young *Reichswehr* officers who had left the Press Club with him and joined him in a stroll down the springtime streets of Berlin. They were all the servants of a Republic now, but that didn't keep Erwin from swinging that riding crop.

"Erwin, will you put that under your arm?" One of his companions said, looking around nervously. "You'll get the cockade pulled off your cap."

"Pft!" said Erwin. "I'd like to see 'em try, Arnold."

"You were in Italy," said Arnold. "You didn't see how the war ended here, with Communists in the streets, and revolutionaries attacking us when we came home."

"That's not the German people."

"What were they then – cows?"

Rommel stepped aside to let a middle-aged woman walk past. She turned and gave him an approving look, then extended it to his two comrades. Rommel beamed, and saluted. She nodded and smiled at him, before going on her way.

Rommel pointed after her and demanded, "You see? That's what our people think of us. They trust in us. We're their soldiers."

"She just likes our looks," said Arnold, and polished a breast-button with the back of his glove.

"They're counting on us to come back and protect them."

"No," said the other young officer. "We're just a token army, *meine Herren.*"

They sighed, and shrugged all together. Germany's short day was over; she was as weak as though Bismarck had never unified her. Germans would be fortunate to have a say in their own sham government. So what else was new? As for the Army --

"We'll just be glorified police all our lives."

"Ach, pfui, Michael." spat Rommel. "If it takes a hundred years, Germany always comes back."

"Wonderful," said Michael. "A hundred years. Do you think we'll be retired by then?"

"Germany will be back, and it won't take any hundred years. The lower Germany falls, the higher and faster she bounces back. Sooner or later, we will have our day. Big things are happening."

"Thugs and riots, that's what's happening," said Michael. "Not our people; foreigners and radicals."

They knew what he meant. Communists and Trade Unions and Jews and cashiered Corporals, beating each other up in the street and getting themselves thrown in jail. When they weren't outright shooting at each other from the rooftops. The government had been forced to build new prison camps just to hold them all. If they were all going to kill each other in their own streets, the soldiers could have stayed home and done that, instead of wasting an entire generation on that miserably mismanaged war.

Michael growled, "Good riddance if they just wipe each other out."

"Why ever did they pick you to stay in the army?" wondered Arnold.

"What's left of it."

"You are so well-named."

Arnold meant *Deutscher Michel*, the sad little comic figure in a nightshirt, nightcap, and the slippers evocative of timidity, sloth and ignorance, who had long been Germany's humble long-suffering equivalent of Uncle Sam, or Britain's Bulldog. Anybody who thought the Germans weren't willing to laugh at themselves had only to see poor fingernail-chewing German Michael being confused by the politics of the day in dozens of German editorial cartoons. His countrymen were very fond of him, but he made them shrug and sigh. Germans have a very deep and finely-pointed sense of irony.

Michael stabbed at the marksman's medal on his chest. "I'm still an officer because of this. And my record as a sniper. If nothing else, they'll need me to teach our young men to pick off the thugs on the roofs. And not care about 'em when we do it."

"You're a cold-blooded bastard," said Arnold.

"I have my reasons," muttered Michael.

"Let the thugs butt heads," retorted Rommel. "The Army can take care of them when the time comes. I trust my country, she'll come out all right in the end."

Michael was in a mood. He paused before a door on the sidewalk, a polished door painted dull Chinese red, inset with a leaded fan of beveled glass. To the right of the door was a row of five high narrow windows, veiled by hand-made lace curtains. It was all very pristine, countrified in a delicately artificial and cosmopolitan manner, and very very private, as only an exclusive commercial address in a city can be. It had the appearance of a club, the sort you had to know someone in order to enter, discreetly, politely, as a mature understanding among gentlemen. Not ladies. A breath of refined masculinity hinted Ladies Requested Not to Attend. At that door, nothing so tacky as a password would have been accepted; everything would be communicated by the eyebrows.

The lights were on, but the blinds were drawn. Rommel sniffed archly as they walked by. Michael thrust a thumb back over his shoulder.

"Want to get a cup of tea, Arnold?"

"Tea?"

"Michael!" snapped Rommel. "Don't be tasteless."

"What?" said Arnold.

"Michael's just being nasty, Arnold. Don't mind him."

"Is it a brothel?" said Arnold.

Rommel said, "It's a known hangout for --." He lowered his voice and made a dismissive gesture. "Oh, you know, Arnold."

"You know -- the Hirschfeld boys," said Michael, held up a hand, and let the wrist fall limp.

"Oh," said Arnold, looking back at the door with a tourist's interest. "Is that where the local queers get together?"

"Erwin," said Michael. "You're blushing."

"Ridiculous." said Rommel, and covered a flaming cheek with one gloved hand.

"What's brought this on? You're as red as a virgin."

"Don't, Michael," said Arnold. "You know Erwin doesn't like smutty jokes."

"Pfui! Maybe we're cutting too close to the bone. I've heard about those Press Club duets."

Rommel just about choked. "How dare you even intimate that?"

"Go on," said Michael. "Go in and tell 'em you want a tea-cake. I dare you."

"Michael," said Arnold. "For Heaven's sake. That's nasty. Don't tease him about such things. Erwin really hates to be teased."

"I'm sorry, Erwin," teased Michael. "I would never have known you were so delicate."

"I'm not delicate like them, if that's what you're trying to say," grumbled Rommel. "You're just damn' lucky we aren't allowed to duel any more."

"Forget dueling," said Arnold. "You can't handle a sword, Erwin. And you're not stupid enough to duel with a pistol, not with Michael. He's even better than you are."

"Only with his own pistol."

"You have me there," agreed Michael.

Erwin had the gift of being able to pick up any old weapon that was lying around, and hit what he aimed at, or rather anything he just threw a bullet at, without squinting or holding his breath, more as a woman shoots, as easy and natural as breathing, unlike the painful schooled care of a man. When a woman did it it was sniffed at as ignorant. When a man did it, as Rommel did, it was remarked upon with admiration, as a talent or a gift. Michael was usually just outrightly jealous, but even he would never have dared say that Rommel shot like a girl.

"Thank you," said Rommel, his ruffled feathers settling.

"How about that tall blond?" said Michael, pointing to a man leaving the front of the cafe. "Isn't he winking at you?"

If Rommel had actually had feathers they would have just flown loose; as it was, he stood naked down to his lesser emotions. He glared along Michael's directional arm, trying to decide whether to bite the arm, or the disgusting unnatural creature it was accusing. He shuddered to see it. The monster was actually looking at him, focusing its unclean pale eyes upon him! He cringed, as though its gaze could soil him, and then its clear silvery voice reached right out and took hold of him, right in broad daylight, where everyone could see his contamination.

"Erwin?" it said.

Erwin froze.

75

"Uh, Peter," it said quietly to its companion. "Could I meet you later? I need to -- speak to someone first."

"What?" said Peter, a nice-looking young man, in a modestly-tailored suit, and a natty snap-brim hat. The Monster was tall, a slender blue-eyed blond, handsome in a used black suit that would have been dowdy on anyone else, and a plain gray much-brushed Homburg that couldn't help, on him, to be the peak of fashion. On one side of his jaw was a little brown mole.

"Meet you where, Pfirsich?"

"I'll meet you back here, in about an hour," whispered Pfirsich Rommel, then turned and walked past three officers who were standing on the pavement, staring at Peter and him. As he passed the little indignant knot of *Feldgrau* that was his eldest brother, he spoke pointedly to Peter over his shoulder.

"I need to go to the library. I have a book overdue."

Peter was a little miffed. He wasn't in a good mood, anyway; Pfirsich still demurred from introducing him to the family, even though he had a brother stationed in the town. Peter hadn't asked that the family be informed of his relationship with their son; far from it. He preferred his privacy. He'd only wanted to shake the brother's hand. *Mach freundlich.* And Pfirsich had promised him a pleasant -- a very pleasant -- evening. As the majestic broad-shouldered blond pulled away from him and their plans for the night, Peter's eye focused upon the little officer who was standing revolving like a compass around one point on the sidewalk, facing always toward the true north that was Pfirsich, his slanted eyes as wide as his horrified mouth.

Peter didn't like uniformed officers and the way they gazed down, like highbred horses, from under their cap visors. His experience with them, as a sergeant during the war, had not been generally friendly. There had been a lot of arguments, especially about command stupidity, unnecessary deaths, and ill-placed loyalties to thoughtless provincial royalty. Peter had spent a lot of time not being a sergeant any more, and sometimes behind bars. When the war ended and the uprisings started Peter had done a little cockade ripping himself.

Now there was this shrunken booted visored stupid cockaded cane-carrying lump of military arrogance staring after his dear desirable friend. It made the air choke off in his throat. Peter didn't know who the little uniformed man was, but he felt a very peculiar disorder, part jealousy, part indignation at being inconvenienced, mostly plain mean fury at being infringed upon, and it all welled up burning and came out like vomit at his mouth.

"Na? Surprised? We look like everybody else, no horns, no hooves, no pink ribbons stuffed up our butts!"

Erwin spun around and stared back at Peter, with such an appalled stupid look that Peter couldn't help himself. He pointed after the swiftly-disappearing Pfirsich and snapped:

"We even have library cards."

Then he turned on his heel and left the little officer standing among his friends, with his stomach churning down around his boots.

"Erwin?" said Michael. "Erwin, you're as white as a sheet."

"Oh, leave him alone, Michael."

"Excuse me," murmured Erwin. *"Bitte,* excuse me. I just remembered. I -- I have to -- do something --."

"Certainly," said Arnold. "Are you all right?"

"You really look terrible," said Michael. "Are you sick?"

Erwin was clutching his belly. "My -- my old wound." He gulped. "I need to lie down."

As the little captain hurried off down the sidewalk, directly opposite the direction taken by the tall man in black, his two friends stood and clucked their tongues in sympathy.

"Poor thing," said Arnold. "Those old wounds never leave you alone."

"He was wounded in the thigh," said Michael. "Why is he holding his stomach?"

Arnold sniffed. "Na, he always did have a delicate stomach. And I can't think of anything more stomach-turning than running head-on into a hunting couple of -- those."

Coming to an alley down the street, Rommel took a sudden turn into it, raced along its length, and dashed out the other side, nearly running down an elderly lady.

"Excuse me," he coughed, and ducked around her.

"Pushy *protzig* officer," she snapped, glaring after him as he headed back up the sidewalk, in the same direction as his brother, but on a parallel street. His two companions, strolling on their street and passing the alley, saw the swift shadow of someone run by at the opposite end, but having last seen their friend staggering along with gippy tummy, didn't think to equate it with him. They continued on, commiserating with a man who didn't need it.

Erwin raced through the well-known streets, just as his brother's hinted comment had directed him. Straight ahead of him was the library, and here were the stairs, and standing there in the dark cool arched doorway above him was --

"Manfred!" yelped Erwin, and slammed to a stop at the bottom of the stairs.

"Hello, Erwin," said Pfirsich, and removed his plain gray Homburg. "I'm sorry I haven't seen more of you."

"No! You'd rather meet with your -- your friends," choked Erwin. His heart was going so fast he couldn't breathe, and it wasn't from running.

"There's nothing wrong with my friends," said Pfirsich.

"How could you!" demanded Erwin, and came up the stairs like a fighting bantam. "You - - you --."

"Now, Erwin --."

Pfirsich quickly replaced his Homburg, and held out his gloved hands, stiffening his arms. He knew what was coming. He braced himself for a shock, and Erwin, in an uncaring fury, swinging that vicious little crop, ran right into his hands. Pfirsich held him back with all his strength; the smaller older brother could be frighteningly strong.

"*Bitte,* Erwin," he pleaded.

"You --," scrabbled Erwin, witless with anger.

"Erwin, I'm taller than you, with a longer reach. You can't get to me."

Erwin butted against the arms; he was going to By God try.

"Erwin, good heavens! Think how this looks. You're an officer, think of your position."

"I'm thinking of yours," snarled Erwin.

Pfirsich dropped his arms, and Erwin almost fell on his face.

"Erwin, this is no time for off-color humor."

"How the devil can you even say that? After what I just saw?"

"You saw nothing, unless it was in your own imagination." Pfirsich settled his rumpled jacket back into place. "Now come. You're making a public spectacle of yourself." He turned away.

"Where do you think you're going?" demanded Erwin.

Pfirsich turned back, stooped down and put his face right into Erwin's. When his pretty features stiffened with anger, his cheekbones protruded like Erwin's, and in everything but height, the Rommel brothers could have been twins.

"I'm going into the library," he snapped. "Where you will be forced to keep your voice down."

Erwin plunged right after him. "If you don't think I can tell you off in a whisper -- you just try me!"

Pfirsich strode through the door and into the foyer, whipping his hat off his head like a flag. Erwin came growling along right behind him, like an insulted terrier, and almost had to be reminded to get his cap off his head. He opened his mouth, and the audible indrawn preparatory breath brought Pfirsich's face back into his.

"Bst, Bst!" whispered Pfirsich. "Just keep your hair on -- at least until we get back into the stacks."

They managed to reach the still, musty privacy of the high-shelved books, without Erwin losing his hold on himself, although the energy of fury in him was so palpable that some quietly- reading patrons looked up in alarm at his mere passage. Pfirsich hustled his brewing brother back between the high shelves. There, in the sweet musty pineapple-and-ammonia odor of old books, Pfirsich stopped, took a breath, and whispered:

"I appreciate your coming back here with me, dear."

"You should thank me for even speaking to you," Erwin stage-whispered back.

Pfirsich shook his head. "You're only upset because you're with those two soldiers, and they were teasing you. Otherwise, you'd be perfectly reasonable about it."

"Don't tell me what I'd do!"

"Well, then, if you don't want to accept it -- it's just none of your business."

"That thing called you 'Pfirsich!' "

"Well, it is Pfirsich now, Erwin," Pfirsich whispered to the books. "I've changed back."

"What were you before? How did you change? Why, why, *why?*"

79

Erwin said it in a sob. Pfirsich turned back to see his brother, one hand over his forehead, trembling, eyes shut tight, little mouth pursed up against a wail, looking as small and pitiful as that day Pfirsich had seen him in hospital, that time he was wounded.

"Oh, Erwin."

"Why!" came the harsh whisper.

"Oh, dear, I'm sorry, if I could only tell you."

"Don't try. I don't want to hear."

"No, I mean, I don't know why." He stopped. "Erwin?"

Erwin was beginning to cry, miserably, silently, against his will, the tears squeezing out like drops from a lemon.

"Oh, *Gott,*" said Pfirsich, his throat catching. "I'm so sorry."

He held out his hands, and put them on his small brother's narrow shaking shoulders.

"Oh, stop it!" hissed Erwin, and threw them off.

"You're crying --."

"So what? A tear from me means nothing; it's my nervous eyes, that's all." Erwin scrubbed furiously at his wet eyes with one hand, and loudly sniffled his voice back. "And the nerves come from *anger,* my fine lad. How could you do this to me?"

"I didn't do a thing to you."

"You lied to me!"

"How?"

"You pretended!"

"I didn't want you to find out," said Pfirsich.

"Find out what? Find out you're -- were you afraid I'd stop you?"

"It wasn't fear. Never fear."

"*Why* is there anything for me to find out?"

"I told you, Erwin, I don't know. It just seemed to happen." Pfirsich hesitated. "I know how lame that sounds."

"He seduced you, didn't he?"

"Erwin. I'm not your sister."

"He must have. It's the only thing makes any sense. I understand, it's the nerves, the loneliness, from the war. You're still hurting, you're confused --."

"I'm not confused. And listen to yourself. How can you seduce someone if they didn't find what they were being offered -- pleasing in the

80

first place?"

Erwin choked. "So you find these stiff-collared young men to be 'pleasing'?"

"Helene does," smiled Pfirsich. "And so does Lucie."

"Don't you dare bring our sister or my wife into something like this."

"No, no, Erwin. I mean that Helene and Lucie know that young men are as pretty as young women. Lucie has told me how pretty you are."

"'Pretty'!" gasped Erwin. "Me!"

"Bst!" Pfirsich reminded him. "Keep your voice down. Of course the women find us lovely. I know that and I sympathize because it's a beauty I can see with my own eyes."

Erwin backed right into the stacks.

"Don't be disgusting!" snapped Pfirsich. "You're my brother!"

"Your brother?" came a pointed female whisper.

Both brothers turned quickly, to see the librarian looking at them over her reading-spectacles.

"I haven't heard the details, gentlemen," she said, her educated accent layered over the nasal twang of Jewish Berlin. "But I take it this is a family matter. And those seldom grow more restrained in the course of the conversation. For the benefit of our other patrons, would you mind discussing your family business outside?"

Both brothers looked down at their toes.

"Perhaps in the park, where you can raise your voices?"

The Rommel brothers slunk red-faced back down the stacks, and out through the library, feeling the eyes of many indignant distracted readers upon them, and even worse, the supercilious autocratic glare of a Keeper Of The Books, disturbed in her silent kingdom.

As they hurried out blinking into the sunshine, Pfirsich asked, "Why is it always so embarrassing to be reprimanded by a librarian? It's worse than being thrown out at church."

"'Pretty?' "said Erwin, starting down the steps, biting his lip. "That's what Lucie said?"

"You were handsome in a girlish way, when you were sixteen," said Pfirsich, following him down. "Do you remember your cadet commander? The one so set upon amateur theatricals? In *La Belle Helene* you played a

81

ballerina."

"Because I could dance."

"In a shell-pink frock."

"I was the only one who could stay up on point!" Erwin was proud of that.

"You were radiant."

"Pfirsich," gritted Erwin.

"I was just reminding you that pretty is pretty."

"I may have been pretty then, but I'm not pretty now."

"In Lucie's eyes? You haven't heard what she tells me."

Erwin gasped, and almost choked trying to hide it.

"She adores you," said Pfirsich. "She loves your looks. She's never told you?"

"That's none of your business!"

"But perhaps not," mused Pfirsich. "It goes to a man's head, you know, and that's never good."

Erwin planted himself wide-legged at the base of the steps, but he was still blushing.

"Since when are you such an expert about women?" he demanded.

"Na, I've always been able to talk to them. They seem to trust me."

"Why not? It seems there's nothing they had to worry about around you."

"I think that has less to do with my being 'this way' and more to do with my being a *gentleman.*"

Pfirsich actually used the English "Gentleman," because there was no such concept in German; *"Herr"* was the highhanded old word for "Lord," "Master," and had only within the last century become a common form of address, gradually coming to resemble the English "Mister."

Erwin put his hands behind his back, gripping his riding crop, and stalked away, looking at his feet, still blushing, and Pfirsich followed along, strolling to match Erwin's stride, his hands in his pockets. Erwin was completely at a loss what to say next. He finally looked up, and then he saw an opening.

"What's that on your face?" he demanded

Pfirsich's hand went to it immediately. "It's that little pink mole I had."

"It's changing color," said Erwin. "That's not a good sign."

"I know. It has me worried."

"Because of your looks?" sniffed Erwin.

"No, of course not. Na, I can't say that, either; nobody's unconcerned with his own looks."

"I'm not!"

"You used to wear a monocle."

"I was young," sniffed Erwin. "But a changing mole can be malignant. It's a sign of corruption in the flesh."

Erwin hadn't meant it that way, but it was enough to shut them both up until the end of the street, while Erwin figured out what to say next. He knew he'd have to be the one to speak. Pfirsich was doing his imitation of a clam.

Pfirsich was a talker. Sometimes Erwin wondered if there was any way to shut him up. But when he was angry, he could keep his mouth shut all day and night too, if that's what it took. The family had given up trying to shake, spank, tickle, cajole, reward, fool, command, beg, wheedle, hug, blame or shame a word out of him when he didn't want to speak; it was easier getting apple-butter from a rock. The only way to get him to talk, short of breaking his leg, was to give in and say the first word.

Erwin finally said, "I was wondering why you were so long becoming involved with someone."

"I was wondering myself. I guess I was just looking in the wrong cupboard."

"Well, at least -- if you must -- you're seeing --." Erwin gulped. "Someone your own age."

"Excuse me?" Pfirsich frowned. "I may have gone to the other bank of the river, but I am not a pederast."

"Don't." Erwin hunched his shoulders and squinted. "Don't use that word. The sergeants had to sleep in the barracks with the cadets, to protect the younger ones."

"Children should be protected," Pfirsich agreed stiffly. "Especially from one another. What I've found has nothing to do with that."

Erwin pulled out a handkerchief and blew his nose. "Well, at least that's a relief."

"You're adapting very readily. I'd be surprised, but I remember the way you tumbled headfirst into the army, with no background, and no family military tradition, and found a second home."

"Excuse me!" cried Erwin. "The German Army is an old, respectable institution. What you're doing is not."

"Right now the German Army is anything but respectable. We lost the war, dear, and armies that don't win are despised."

"Don't try to bring my Army down to your level."

"That's not what I meant, dear."

Erwin knew what he meant. Less than a century ago, what was called the 'German Army' hadn't existed, and wouldn't exist, until the French Army, making one of its traditional happy incursions onto German territory, got the shock of its life at the Rhine when it was met for the first time by the combined German Armies, and was driven back into the English Channel. Before that there had been the Prussian Army, admittedly, but the rest were nothing more than a lot of little play-pretty comedy armies, each belonging to a little German king, some of whom sold their peasants to wars in the new World, and many who went off to Moscow with Napoleon and back to Paris with the Russians. Even the fairy-tale started: "Once upon a time, a thousand years ago, when there was nothing in Germany but little kings..."

"I know my history," Erwin said in exasperation. "Stop being a teacher."

"I am a teacher."

"Don't play teacher to me!"

"Among the ancient classical Greeks, homosexuals were allowed an honored public presence."

"Ha! 'Honored.' I've read those plays; don't pretend to be the only educated one in our family. I'm warning you."

"Well, they were allowed their public, as well as their private lives. Things change, Erwin. Your army, my way of life, they could exchange places."

Erwin exploded. "The day ho-mo-sexuals can stage parades with flags in the street, and the German Army has to hide in shame, I hope I am dead!"

"Don't be silly, Erwin. You're exaggerating. My sort of people is discreet. It's the womanly side of our nature. 'Parades.' Oh, please."

Erwin had started sniffling again, and hid his nose in his

handkerchief. *"Gott.* That I would hear a brother of mine call himself 'womanish.' "

"'Womanly,' my dear. There is a great distinction."

"There's a distinction between 'infamous' and 'notorious' -- but they're both bad."

"My dear! Women are not 'bad'. Nor 'infamous,' nor 'notorious'."

"I didn't say that."

"They are lovely, worthy people. I can think of worse models."

Erwin's eyes narrowed. "I know this one, Pfirsich. You've used it before. We are not talking about 'women.' But then, they're not your favorite subject, are they? Shall we spare you?"

"You can be an awful little *Rotzlöffel,* did you know that?"

Erwin glared at him.

"Go ahead, Erwin. I can say that. I'm not in the army any more, not even in the reserve. Germany doesn't have one, or not one worth mentioning."

Erwin shook a finger right up in his face. "If we ever have that reserve, if we ever re- instate the draft, I'll get you back into the army, right where I can keep an eye on you!"

"But Erwin, then it would be true, that there would be homosexuals in the German Army." Pfirsich pointed archly at himself. "Or at least one."

"No, there wouldn't."

"If you are implying I could be coerced into redirecting my affections --."

"The army can be a powerful persuader."

"Then I would merely be forced to do what gentlemen like myself have done so often before," Pfirsich said coldly. "And pretend that I had changed."

"Ganz gut. It's an old rule that cowards need only pretend to be brave until they really become heroes."

"Fool the audience until you fool yourself?"

"Yes," said Erwin, not in the least put off. "I don't see why it wouldn't work with you."

"Do you want to put money on that? Or is the only thing you ever bet with your own life?"

Erwin just stood there and hated him.

"Erwin," Pleaded Pfirsich. "We're brothers. You know I do love you."

"Do you? I think you've got it backwards. The real question here is what I feel about you."

Pfirsich hung his head. "I'm sorry. I was trying to use 'love' as an emotional crowbar."

"I'm done with this discussion. I'm done with you."

"You can't be. For Mama's sake, we must remain on speaking terms."

"I bet you haven't told Mother."

Pfirsich just looked up at the sky.

"You hypocrite."

"It's not hypocrisy," began Pfirsich.

"I dare you to continue out of decency to hide something like this from our mother."

"I dare you to tell her."

"I've never told on you," snapped Erwin.

"Then it's my business. And in the meantime, we really must pretend we're still brothers. Whether we want to or not."

"You don't want to? Good!"

"*Gott, nein,* Erwin. I love you. I admire you. I --."

"That again!"

Pfirsich said through his teeth, "I will meet you for dinner tomorrow night, as planned. Give me a hug."

"And have my friends see me? The ones who saw you come out of that cafe?"

"I'm your brother, you twit! You can hug your brother."

"But still --."

"Tell them I'm from out of town. Tell them I didn't know. The food is good."

"Why didn't you tell me that in the first place?"

"I can't lie to my brother."

"It would be nice if you'd show the same consideration to family you show to perfect strangers." Erwin threw up his chin. "Besides, your darling boyfriend mouthed off in front of them. How am I going to explain that?"

Pfirsich went white. "Peter?"

86

"He lost his stupid temper and gave away everything."

Pfirsich slapped his forehead. "He told me he knew enough to keep his mouth shut!"

"Well, it must be that 'womanly' side of his nature. Can't keep a secret." Erwin sharply tapped Pfirsich in the chest with the riding-crop. "If I were you, I'd get another boyfriend -- one you can damn-well depend on in a tight spot. One you can trust."

Pfirsich stared at him. Then he burst out in an incredulous titter. Ten minutes ago, Erwin had wanted to smother him in mud under a stile, like an ancient Teuton symbolically executing sodomites -- and now he was advising him on the choice of his boyfriends.

He began to laugh outright, in wonderful relief. He threw his arms around his brother, so hard that Erwin almost fainted from the sudden grip of the strong affectionate arms.

"I love you, Erwin, I absolutely adore you. And don't you dare tell me I can't!"

And then Pfirsich kissed his brother, with honest love, right on the mouth, right there in the street. He opened his arms and Erwin leapt backwards, spitting and rubbing his mouth with both hands. Pfirsich turned on his heel and strode off down the street, laughing like a free man. Behind him, he could hear the pressurized little volcano go up in an explosion.

"That does it! I'm getting you back into the Army. You'll be back in the service if I have to sell my soul and honor to the devil to do it!"

"I believe it!" said Pfirsich, delightedly waving his hat and walking backwards. "You only have my good at heart. See you at dinner tomorrow."

Bread and Swans

7. Basket Case.

On a fine unruffled Saturday morning, *Hauptmann* Erwin Rommel, *gestriegelt und gebügelt,* clattered up the stairs to his brother's flat, sword clinking, spurs ringing. He looked even smaller in his pale sage-green dress uniform, fit and tight without a corset, his riding boots polished 'till the rag took a hole.

"Pfirsich!" he yelled. "Ready? Perfect day for it. We've got ten minutes until the next trolley – plenty of time to trot ourselves down to the stop."

The officer leaped over the last two steps onto the flat landing, and banged on the door with the hilt of his sword.

"raus, Pfirsich! Anna's already there. Come on out and face the music!"

"Erwin, I don't need this now."

Pfirsich had come out the door so suddenly he almost flipped Erwin backwards down the stairs, like a living *Max und Moritz* comic strip. Erwin didn't care. He was so happy this morning he could have rolled down, broken his neck, and been found by the police in the evening, smiling, with his fingers linked on his chest.

He whipped off his cap and bounced into the room, trotting jingling like an hussar pony after the fuming Pfirsich. The taller brother had retreated into his bedroom. He stopped before his dresser mirror, and reengaged his duel with his necktie. He was still in his shirt, a particularly snowy and slick-starched shirt, and his braces kept slipping off his shoulders.

"Look at this tie!" he snarled. "It won't tie. And the color – pink! It looks like it's been kept in an ice-cream cart. Who bought this thing?"

"I did, and you know I did. Don't be snotty."

Still desperately trying to get his tie into order, Pfirsich glanced at Erwin.

"Ach, Gott, you're wearing boots and breeches; are we going to the

party on a horse?"

"They look better on me than slacks and shoes." Erwin was screwing a shiny new monocle into his left eye. "Civilian clothes make me look dumpy."

"And a monocle? A monocle, Erwin? You remember what happened last time."

"I was disciplined because I was a poor little cadet and didn't have any rights. Now I'm a captain and I can wear what I please. Besides, it's practical; you know my eyes aren't equal."

"You still don't have any rights. You can't vote."

"That's a considered decision of the Army. We leave the politics to the civilians."

"Stop playing Prussian fashion-plate and help me tie my TIE!"

Erwin fluttered an impeccably-gloved hand over his shoulder at his sweating brother.

"I'm in dress gala. I don't know how."

"Ooh, you shirty little --."

"What is wrong with you?" demanded Erwin, sitting himself down on Pfirsich's bed, and cheerily crossing one leg over the other, then bouncing his boot so both the leather and the spurs glittered. Erwin was so happy he could have burst. His difficult vacillating baby brother had finally, finally made up his mind to get himself married. Erwin and Lucie had made Pfirsich an uncle in 1928, when another little Manfred was born. Now the prospect of having Pfirsich return the favor made the future *Onkel* Erwin itch to teach his impending nephew – or niece – mathematics and horsemanship and engine-repair. Erwin grinned up at Pfirsich with a heart full of loving kindness, and said:

"You're shaking like a new recruit with an unmade bed." He stood up and took Pfirsich's elbows, and whirled him around like a dance-partner to face him. "Come here. It's just your engagement party, not your execution. Hold still."

He quickly tied Pfirsich's tie, and tucked it into place. "How are you going to act for the wedding, if just the engagement party is doing this to you?"

"I know, I know, but I'm worried about Anna --."

"What's wrong with Anna? She's a lovely girl. The whole family adores her."

"I like her." Protested Pfirsich.

"You *like* her?" said Erwin, taking up Pfirsich's jacket by the shoulders from the chair and giving it a sharp shake. "You just *like* your own fiancée?"

"No, not 'just like'," moaned Pfirsich, and put his arms behind his back, in preparation for the jacket, but looking more like he expected handcuffs. "I like her. I like her – a lot. That's why I keep asking myself, am I doing the right thing by her?"

"Oh, there's no question. You're marrying her, aren't you? You're making a gift of yourself forever, aren't you? The girl worships you, and her family thinks you hung the moon."

Pfirsich stood disconsolately buttoning up his jacket. It had all happened so fast.

He had only met Anna at the university this last spring. In the chemistry class, a kind young lady had let him borrow her notes, to make up for what he had missed when he had been out with a very damp cold. They had ended up going to tea together, then a movie, and then the theater. Before Pfirsich knew it, they were keeping company. Anna had a sense of humor and superb taste. And she played such a beautiful game of tennis.

Pfirsich looked around at Erwin. "I was so relieved when I realized I was fond of her. Really, truly fond of her. Like a companion."

"Well, hopefully."

Pfirsich tucked his pearly handkerchief into his breast pocket, and carefully fluffed it. "I've never felt – that way – toward a woman. I thought it was a change. One I could rely on."

"Love at first sight!" crowed Erwin.

"Na, love at first chemistry notes."

"Chemistry, *ganz genau*. I know how that kind of love feels. I remember the very first time I saw my Lucie."

"My brother the ballroom dancer," said Pfirsich. "You fell for her, on your head. I remember you and the costume party. What you looked like, in that straw boater and ice-cream suit. And the ukulele!"

"What ukulele?"

"It's on the postcard, Erwin, the one you had snuck to her past her parents, like a spy. She still has it."

"She didn't just kiss the postcard," Erwin sighed.

Lucie and Erwin danced every chance they got, anyplace, anytime, and they won awards in ballroom competitions. His friends in the army knew better than to be anyplace near *Hauptmann* Rommel when he'd got wind of a new dance step. His single-minded eagerness to practice to perfection the latest steps for his darling, his treasure, his longed-for Lucie was almost as ruthless for victims as his notorious cross-country skiing exercises, and sometimes more arduous. A man could stop for a breath on the slopes, then ski to catch up; in Erwin's arms, his comrades were whirled around until they were dizzy, and their ankles hurt. Lucie could keep up with him, and she could command him to stop – she was his fiancée – but what could a man do against his superior officer, who had got hold of the step-diagrams for the Fox-Trot, and wanted to put on the damned record "Just one more time"?

Erwin's blue eyes turned brilliant as sapphires with the memory, and he sighed achingly. "I made a fool of myself for her, and I'd do it again. A fine woman can do that to you. Enjoy it, Pfirsich!"

Pfirsich leaned heavily against the dresser. "I wish I could, Erwin. I wish I were like you, with your Lucie. But I'm – different."

"No, you're not."

"Yes, I am. You know how."

Erwin shot to his feet, torn out of his melting smitten memories. "No!" he commanded. "No you're not. We won't bring that up."

"I have to, Erwin. If I didn't, it wouldn't be fair to Anna."

"You think it would be fair to her if she finds out, or, God forbid, if our families found out? *Bitte,* Pfirsich! *Gott!*"

"No, Erwin, of course not. But --."

"'But' nothing! There's nothing for them to find out now, anyway." Erwin stared at Pfirsich. "Is there?" He took his brother firmly by the elbows. "Look at me. Is there?"

Pfirsich was blushing. He leaned down close, and almost whispered, "I'm still having those dreams, Erwin."

Erwin covered his face. "No...."

"I am."

"Pfirsich, dreams are for children."

"These aren't."

"*Verdammt,* Pfirsich, you're not 'different.' You just haven't grown up yet."

"I grew up in the war," snapped Pfirsich.

"Only as a soldier. This is different." Erwin gently placed his hands on his brother's hunched shoulders. "Look, I'm not I. I can't approve, but I understand. But there's a time in life for everything."

"Bitte."

"I know of other young men who have – 'experimented'." This time, Erwin looked away and blushed.

Pfirsich picked up his hat and gloves. "I wasn't 'experimenting,' Erwin. Not with my affections."

"All right, all right. Let's say you were – side-tracked."

"Erwin!"

"All right, fine, wrong word."

Erwin almost backed out of the flat, and Pfirsich lagged behind. Erwin gestured him forward, out into the hall, and lowered his voice to almost a whisper.

"Those same young men, the ones who tried – what you tried. They're now happily married. They're husbands, and fathers."

He let Pfirsich pass him on the stairs, and put a hand on his shoulder. "The family is delighted with Anna, Pfirsich. She's a pretty girl, and she's firm-willed. She'll help you to find the right way."

"She is that."

"What?"

"'Firm-willed'. I keep having the horrible feeling that none of this was my idea."

The people on the sidewalk jumped when Erwin's raised voice preceded him out of the stairwell: "You proposed to her!"

"Yes, but I felt as though I were being coaxed."

"We're all 'coaxed,' Pfirsich!" Erwin was grinning as the bus pulled up. "Do you think any of us would have the courage if the girls didn't prod us?"

"But I can't help feeling – na – that this is all under false pretences."

"It's a little late for this, isn't it? Get on the bus."

Once they'd settled into their seats, Pfirsich said, "I wouldn't hurt her for the world, Erwin, but --."

"But what? You want out of this? Tell her the truth! It's *lies* that hurt women."

"Oh, *Gott,* Erwin, I wish you hadn't worn your uniform."

"What's wrong with my uniform?"

"When you wear it, you're pushy. I can only talk to you when you're wearing your civilian clothes. Which reminds me; do you even own any? Are you planning to come to the wedding in boots?"

"Of course not. I'll be in walking-out dress. Best dress uniform, with polished black shoes. I'll be lovely."

"Honestly, it's like being related to a *Doppelgänger,*" complained Pfirsich. "Out of uniform, you're a perfectly reasonable, thoughtful human being. In uniform, all *aufgedonnert in Gala,* you're nothing but a prancing little martinet."

"I wish you still had a uniform to wear," humphed Erwin. "It might lend you some sense of responsibility."

* * * * *

At the party, the eldest Rommel child, Helene, spotted her little brother across the drawing-room and hurried over to where he was bouncing his own giggling baby son on his knee. Erwin had finally caught up to his sister in height, but that didn't make either of them very tall.

Helene was elegant and reserved in a plain black dress and ironed white collar of appliquéd lace. Erwin looked up at her in respect. He took little Manfred in his arms and stood up. They all exchanged kisses on the cheek, and Helene tickled the baby.

"Hello, Bantz," said Helene, using little Manfred's nickname, then stood back and regarded her brother approvingly through her spectacles.

"Erwin, thank you for fetching Pfirsich. We were beginning to wonder if he'd ever arrive."

"Oh, it's just butterflies," said Erwin. "You know how shy our baby brother can be."

The housemaid approached, carrying a tray with a wine-bottle and two glasses.

"More wine, dear?" said Helene.

Erwin pointed at the glass of claret he'd left on a side-table and shook his head. "Thank you. I'm content."

"I wish Pfirsich would say the same," said Helene.

"He's not content?"

"He's been drinking more wine tonight than I'm used to seeing him enjoy. We're not good with drink; he really shouldn't. Would you speak to him?"

"Just butterflies. Come." Erwin drew Helene to the window that faced on the trellised back garden "Look out there in the garden. See?"

Pfirsich and Anna were sitting close to one another, their heads bent together, sharing sweet nothings on a bench under the lilacs. White lilacs, so warm in the sunshine their perfume spread in through the window. Erwin drew a deep infusing breath. If that wasn't the Perfect Couple, in the perfect setting, he'd eat his best gloves and swallow the wrist-buttons like pills. He hugged Bantz up close to him and smooched him on the neck.

The Lady of the Perfect Couple suddenly sat up straight, and gasped. In the next moment, she'd thrown her glass of white Moselle wine right in the Perfect Gentleman's face, hard enough to sting. This was of course quite horrifying in a girl of her breeding. Especially to her. Erwin would have shouted out the window in protest if Helene hadn't gripped his arm and reminded him not to yell in the baby's ear.

"Oh, Pfirsich!" said Anna. "Oh, I'm sorry."

"No," he mumbled, applying his handkerchief to his dripping face. "I'm sorry. I should have been more circumspect. Anna?"

Anna had risen suddenly to her feet, and was making for the house, her own handkerchief clutched to her mouth.

At the window, Helene frowned. "Whatever did she do that for?"

"I'll bet I know," growled Erwin.

"Erwin? What's happened? What's he done?"

She was giving him that piercing schoolteacher look that was the family inheritance. There wasn't any use trying to put her off; in a moment she'd be Demanding An Explanation. Erwin quickly turned to the page of social tactics marked Family Affection, with its footnote of Respect For Elder Siblings.

"Poor Anna. Quick, Helene, dear, go to her. She needs you."

"Of course." Helene knew her duty.

"I'll talk to Pfirsich."

"Not too rough." Helene grabbed her brother again. "The heart can't be commanded. Have some sense. And give Bantz to Mama, first."

"I will, I will, don't worry."

Helene swooped out to put her arm around Anna as the girl stalked in the doorway. Erwin retreated into the kitchen and handed Bantz to his grandmother and dashed back out the other door before Mama had a chance to ask what was going on. She knew something was; these kids were liable to be up to anything. Helene and Erwin were Rommels, and teaching children and young soldiers gave them both the perfect sense of tactical timing to keep Anna out of the line of sight while Erwin ducked out the back door and cornered Pfirsich in the garden.

"All right, what's coming off here?"

"Oh, *Gott.*" Pfirsich was still wiping his face. "You saw that."

"I keep seeing you, don't I?" Erwin snapped. "What did you do? Did you tell her? You didn't tell her, did you? Not a girl like that. You didn't, did you?"

"I was very delicate."

"Delicate? How could you be delicate?"

"Na, you know Anna wants to teach German history; it's her major at the university."

"Yes, yes, yes. --."

"I said I didn't want to make her unhappy, like Friedrich the Great's wife."

Friedrich's father had imprisoned him and made him watch while they beheaded the young *Leutnant* he had planned to run away with. When he'd been forced to marry in Prussia's political interests, he had said his wife had become "Just another unhappy European princess."

The unfortunate liaison between the young officer and the prince may have meant only that Friedrich dreaded his shackled fate as a king, that the *Leutnant* had just been his understanding and faithful companion, willing to risk everything in the name of loyalty and friendship, that the prince would have preferred composing sonnets to running a kingdom or contracting mutually impersonal royal alliances. But it had never been interpreted that way. The sexually suspicious middle-class mind could never have interpreted it that way.

"Friedrich? You referred to Friedrich?"

"It required subtlety." Pfirsich had begun to play with the mole on his jaw. "That's why I quoted him."

"You quoted him? You quoted that? To her?"

"Dear, you told me to tell the truth."

Erwin Rommel hit himself right across the forehead. "The first time he listens to me!"

"I'm sorry, Erwin."

"Get your hands off that mole."

"Yes, Erwin."

Erwin was going in tight little circles like a circus pony.

"Oh, *mein Gott,* if this gets out – the family – my men – my career – oh, *Gott!*"

Pfirsich rose up to his full slender height, and glared down at his brother. "Don't worry. Give Anna some credit. Did you think I would have taken up with a fool?"

"You did before."

"I never did."

"What about your loose-lipped friend, Peter?"

"Anna is not Peter."

"I can see that," Erwin groaned and put his little hand to his forehead. "I'm sorry, Pfirsich. This could be such a *mess.*"

"I know, Erwin. I understand. You don't have it easy, having to keep a secret like this."

"As a secret it was such a strain, and I didn't think I'd have to worry about keeping it any more." Erwin glared right back up at Pfirsich. "Do I have to worry?"

"It's really none of your business."

"It must be Anna's business. You had to tell her."

"I only told her – I only hinted to her – that I've had these feelings. I never said I would have them again, for anyone but her. I wasn't trying to hand her a basket, to get rid of her. I was trying to be honest with her, to reveal everything about myself. There should be no secrets between husband and wife, not even a secret like this."

"Oh, *wunderschön!* You tell her you're dropping her because you know what you like?"

"I am not 'dropping' her, as you so bluntly express it. And I am certainly not breaking my sworn engagement with her because I'm in love with someone else." If Pfirsich could have drawn himself up any taller, he would have. "If that's what you're thinking --."

"I don't care who you're seeing, Pfirsich," Erwin said coldly. "As you said, it is none of my business."

"That is a nasty thing to even think, much less say," snapped Pfirsich. "I always thought you had an unusually clean mind. I'm amazed, and I'm hurt, that such a thing could ever have occurred to you. What could I have done that you would think I would ever go behind Anna's back? About anything? I would never have hurt her for another woman, why should I hurt her for another man? Explain the difference to me."

It was Erwin's turn to use the schoolteacher look. "You would never have dropped her because you might have been tempted by another woman; why don't you trust yourself not to be tempted by a man?"

Pfirsich was startled. He put a fingertip to his mole and murmured, *"Mein Gott,* is that what I think?"

"Is it?"

"I'd never thought of it that way." He looked down at his brother. "Are you right? Am I making a distinction? Oh, Erwin, love for a woman, or for a man, it's the same thing, isn't it? It's the loyalty that counts. Erwin, you're right."

"I am?"

"I should go right to Anna and offer myself to her. It's my duty; I can't leave her thinking I don't think she's good enough for me."

"Don't you dare! You pinhead, you've hurt her enough already."

"Erwin," Pfirsich said, loftily. "I have to do the right thing."

"You wouldn't know 'the right thing' for a woman if it was printed in the Bible in red letters lined with gold."

"I beg your pardon!"

Erwin poked him right in his upright cringing belly. "Take an elder brother's advice; stay away from the women. They're not the fragile poetic flowers you seem to think they are and they're not going to swallow your 'loyalty' in place of love. Forget your 'loyalty' and just stay the way you are."

"Erwin?"

"You might as well. You obviously can't get along with women anyway."

"Oh, Erwin."

The members of the party who happened to be looking into the garden saw the tallest of the Rommel boys joyfully hugging the eldest, repeating "Thank you, thank you, thank you!" while the little uniformed captain sputtered and struggled in his arms.

"Stop it! You're getting wine on my dress uniform. Just keep it up if you want to get the cleaning bill."

"It's white wine --." Here a kiss in the face. "It won't show."

"It will *bleach*." Struggles successful, Erwin pulled loose. "If you ruin this uniform you will pay for it. I imagine you'll have the money, now."

"What?"

"The money that was to go to the wedding and the honeymoon."

"Oh, that's cruel, Erwin. It's only free now because I've been forced to be so heartless to Anna."

"I'd suggest you send her on a sea-cruise in compensation."

"I don't dare. She'd ask me along so she could drown me off the taff-rail. Just look at her, there in the window; the look she's giving me would strip wood."

"Here," Erwin returned Pfirsich's handkerchief. "Go apologize. Tell her you're sorry you hurt her, but you can't help it."

"Yes, you're right." Pfirsich lifted his head. "I should have that much grace."

"And for God's sake try not to look so happy you're getting rid of her."

"I'm not. I'm only happy that you understand. I'm very fond of Anna; I just can't marry her, not and be honest to her, or myself."

"Then do us all a favor, and don't tell anybody else what went on, if you can help it."

Pfirsich rolled up his eyes. "Don't worry, Erwin. I won't embarrass you, or the family."

"Not me, ant-brain. Do you think Anna wants everybody else to find out? Think of her feelings, if you won't think of us."

"I'll try to think of everyone, Erwin."

"Just keep it to Anna for now, will you? One maneuver at a time; fighting too many armies is what got Napoleon in trouble. Just take on this one small battle, and you won't have to face a Waterloo."

Erwin turned Pfirsich toward the door and shoved him between the shoulders. He was relieved and encouraged to feel no resistance; Pfirsich had never needed much pressure to make him do his duty.

The taller brother lurched forward, at first because the smaller had forced him, and then more gracefully, under his own power. Without hesitation, he headed straight for Anna, who was wiping her fingers with a handkerchief, but carefully and surreptitiously, while she smiled and nodded at the family. She'd kept it all to herself, and her self-control was so strong and sure that when Pfirsich came up to her she smiled at him, put her arm through the one he offered her, and let him lead her off back into the garden, purely for kindness, not for the appearance of it.

Erwin was leaning against the hallway wall, pretending his mind was somewhere else. Since he usually stood firmly upright on his two feet, and was about as unfocused as a falcon, he might as well have been whistling nonchalantly like a cabaret character. That's when sharp-eyed Helene came up beside him and gave him a glass of wine. He thanked her, and downed it in a gulp, not usual in a man of such sober habits, but he needed it. He took a deep breath and started on a second pull.

"He hasn't worked it out yet?" Helene said bluntly. "I wish he would make up his mind, before he marries the girl, and makes them both miserable."

Erwin choked on the wine. Once Helene was done slapping him on the back, he had the excuse of his coughing fit to explain his red face. Helene picked up his handkerchief, and dabbed his chin, as a big sister should.

"Let me guess," said Helene. "You've only just discovered it, and you thought none of the family knew."

"Oh, God," groaned Erwin.

"Don't worry," Helene soothed him. "Half the young men in the world start out confused. I teach children; it's not unusual when they start trying to find themselves. Schoolteachers and officers all know that, if they're any good at what they do. Nobody will hold it against you, even if they do find out about him. It's the one thing that men won't gossip about. I would have thought you knew that."

"I do know it," muttered Erwin. "But not with my own brother."

"What makes us any different than the rest of the human race? It would have been odd if we didn't have at least one like Pfirsich."

"Who knows?" muttered Erwin, looking into the living room, where the family was chatting and complimenting the cake. Their mother turned and looked sharply at them, and Erwin looked away.

"Do you mean, 'Does Lucie know?'" said Helene. "Of course Lucie knows. You can't think a woman as clever as your wife would ever miss something like that, could you?"

"When did she find out?"

"We've all had our little difficult moments with Pfirsich," said Helene. "All the boys in our family are difficult, and if they're not wanting to be opera singers or pilots or – " She pushed Erwin's chest. "—little generals, they're confused about who they like to look at. If the family can put up with you, the family can put up with Pfirsich. We put up with Karl. You knew about Karl."

"Karl," said Erwin. "Karl is discreet."

"So is Pfirsich, in his own way."

Erwin glared out into the garden. "Does he know that you know?"

"Of course he knows," says Helene.

"Oh," said Erwin. "He had me thinking --."

"That it was your little secret," said Helene. "Pfirsich adores you. If he can have secrets with you, all to himself, he'll do it."

Erwin's jaw dropped. "I'll kill him."

"You should be flattered."

"I'll still kill him. I must look a complete fool."

"Of course you don't. It's endearing, how much Pfirsich looks up to you."

"Why didn't you tell me?" Erwin sputtered. "Or is this more of the womenfolk keeping their own council? I swear, in this family we poor little males don't even have a chance. The women run everything, and now and then they just give us a pat on the head. It's like a Hitchcock movie. Spies we've got in this family, and Republicans and actors and --."

"Love-children," smiled Helene.

"*Ich bitte!*" bridled Erwin, glancing at Lucie, over by the desert-table.

"Oh, stop. We all know *everything*. And we know who knows."

Erwin swallowed and got control of himself. "You just do this to amuse yourselves, don't you?"

"Don't exaggerate, dear," Helene admonished. "Now leave those two in the garden to talk out their troubles, and come in here and sit down and have some cake. If you don't have at least two slices, and plenty of praise, you'll insult every woman in the house."

Erwin wiped his forehead with the handkerchief, then nodded and followed meekly. He'd had his moment of rebellion and was pretty well relieved it hadn't come off. If there was one thing you didn't do in the Rommel family, it was cross the Rommel women.

8. Harm's Way

After all the trouble Pfirsich had taken to obtain a degree in practical engineering, the bottom dropped out of the economy and made off with all his job opportunities.

The only position he could land was teaching basic mathematics part-time to elementary-school students, in a tiny one-cow German farm town. And he'd seen the cow, harnessed to a wagon, tied to a tree in the village square. It was quite a comedown from Berlin, barely more than a crossroads, and the out-lying houses kept competitive dung heaps in front of their houses. But they were neat dung heaps, regularly drained for their fertilizing *Jauche,* and their owners' children still had to be taught their numbers, plain adding and subtracting and long division, if only to keep the farm accounts.

Pfirsich was patient with children but only to a point. He didn't have the Rommel feel for long-term teaching. So he combed the engineering trade journals -- from Germany, France, and on desperate days, from England -- line-by-line in hopes of putting his degree into full practice, for a better salary, and in a town large enough to have its own movie theater. And no long hours of squinting *Buberls* reciting the multiplication tables.

He consoled himself at the movie theater in the next town. He had seen dozens of the short films of the dashing comedian Max Linder, never growing tired of The Master's sparkling good looks and divine sense of nonsense.

Mr. and Mrs. Linder's unnerving double suicide had been a blow. Pfirsich couldn't believe it had been suicide. *Aber Lieber,* the man had been in the middle of making a full-length Hollywood film! Why shoot himself, and his lovely young wife, and be found in a bed soaked in blood?

Pfirsich had never thought he would see another comedian who would appeal to him like *L' Homme au Chapeau de Soie.* Then he had treated himself to an evening with the films of a comedy team from America, who billed themselves as The Marx Brothers. They translated beautifully. Zeppo was adorable. When Pfirsich read that one of their new films would be playing, he didn't mind saving up for a train ticket as well as a theater-pass. He enjoyed trains, and made the trip part of a pleasant Saturday-afternoon jaunt.

On his way back from lunch one wet afternoon he'd stopped at the post-office and then the library to read the trade journals. After jotting down a few addresses he headed back to work, turning up his coat collar and shaking out his good English-style umbrella, a heavy black brolly with a steel handle ending in a broad steel knob. It wasn't his usual style but it was such good quality for such a good price his careful Swabian soul couldn't resist it. After the trenches he liked anything that kept him dry.

As he passed an alleyway he heard a man's voice, raised in a bawl of fury. It was a commanding voice, a voice that had seen military service, and it was as much appalled and shocked as it was angry.

"No, go on, just get near me! See whose head gets broken. I was in the war, same as you, and I know all the tricks!"

Somebody was badly outnumbered, and wasn't going down easy.

Pfirsich knew that voice. It was a friend of his.

He began to roll up his umbrella even as he dashed into the alleyway, where he found the blocky veteran backed up against the rough brick wall, a sturdy maple cane held upright in two hands. The man meant to swing it like the Mauser carbine he'd carried in the trenches.

He was facing off, five against one, four young men and a man with a bad scar on his jaw that looked like he'd taken a trench-shovel in the face. They were all dressed in brown, with cloth puttees around their calves and ski-caps on their heads; some sort of quasi-military political gang that couldn't afford its uniforms and had to make do. Pfirsich at first thought they might be members of *Stahlhelm,* The Steel Helmet Brigade, made up of hungry, frustrated veterans from the war. Then he saw the home- made red armband tied around the arm of the scarred man.

Communists!

"Harm!" cried Pfirsich.

Cashiered Sergeant Harm Schaffinder didn't answer. He took the opportunity of Pfirsich's sudden distracting arrival to bring the thick end of the cane around like a rifle-butt into the face of one of the younger antagonists, and his aim cracked a nose and sent the blood spurting across the wet cobblestones.

In the war, Pfirsich hadn't remained a frightened boy for long. Whether he liked it or not, he'd come out of combat a seasoned predator. Now he dove in without hesitation, ducking right through the younger pups to get at the old scarred hyena. He'd spotted the wobble of weakness in Scar-Face's nearest leg -- probably from a bullet-wound or a cold caught in a joint, while standing long hours of duty in the trenches -- and popped him right across the knee-cap with the broad steel hilt of his rolled umbrella. The man howled in pain and went down and backwards into the arms and the confusion of his comrades. Beneath their feet the blood was washing away in the rain.

"What are you doing?" demanded one of the young men in brown. "He's a Jew!"

That's when Pfirsich saw the hand-sewn hooked cross on the red armband. Not Communists at all -- National Socialists. The latest gang of head-breakers, Jew-baiters and promisers of bread to the starving and desperate.

"He's a German soldier!" snapped Pfirsich. He didn't love the army, but Harm was a comrade.

"He's a traitor!" snarled one of the younger toughs. "He stabbed us in the back, he sold out our soldiers to the international industrialists!"

"Young man, that is rhetoric," said Pfirsich, setting his feet more firmly on the slick stones, blinking past the rain dripping off his hat. "If you know he's Jewish, then you must know he was a soldier in the war, and he never sold out anybody to anything."

"That's what he claims."

"We know him by his nose -- and his tail!"

Schwanz. Tail. As in turning tail – or the little tail all men carried in front, and the way the Jews were different there.

Pfirsich glanced at Harm, who just glared. Pfirsich shook his head.

"All Jews are liars --."

"Please," said Pfirsich.

"Don't argue with 'em, Pfirsich," Harm snarled right back. "Reason isn't what you use with these pieces of shit." He feinted at the toughs.

"Harm," said Pfirsich, restraining him.

"I was in the war, same as your ugly friend!" he roared. "Lemme

105

at 'em, Pfirsich, let these baby-shits see what it's like to take on two trench-dogs at the same time, without an old cripple to help 'em."

He and Harm were the only ones with anything like weapons. The four younger roughs had come out to cause trouble with nothing but their fists and feet, and they were hesitant about taking on a real live four-limbed war-veteran, let alone an unleashed pair of 'em. But there were more brownshirts in the alley than Pfirsich thought he and Harm could handle alone, and he began to lower himself down into his hip joints, steadying himself like a troupe ape. The roughs did the same, while the rain beat down on them all. Everybody knew what would happen if they lost their footing on the wet cobbles in a brawl.

Before the roughs could jump Pfirsich and Harm, the scarred man, rubbing his aching knee, spoke for the first time, to Pfirsich alone, in broken-hearted wonder.

"How can a German soldier defend one of them? Do you know what they did to us?"

"Yes," snarled Harm, "We kept the Tommys from shooting you through the back, when you ran for the rear."

"Harm," said Pfirsich. "He was a soldier, too, just look at his face."

"The Jewish bankers stabbed us in the back," pleaded the old soldier. "They sold us out, they sold out the German future for money."

"Do I look like a banker?" demanded Harm, showing a shiny coat-cuff. "Do I look like I have a cent more than you?"

"Please, please!" said Pfirsich. "This isn't right, either of you. *Sind wir denn keine Kameraden?*"

Before Pfirsich could fail to talk anyone into recognizing their comradeship, a window above the alley slammed open, and a woman's strong white clothes-washing arms pounced their damp hands down onto the sill. She leaned out and hollered like the broad-beamed work-eating *Hausfrau* she was.

"You'd better run, all of you, you street trash! I've sent my daughter for the police! You'd better move it -- that girl moves fast!"

Police! The local breed of *Polyp* didn't put up with people spitting on the sidewalk, let alone having their very own little bloody-nosed free-for-alls in the public thoroughfares. This was their beat, and nobody did violence upon human flesh but them. Regardless of a roughneck's political affiliations, they would beat him flat, beat him until he learned what his knees were for, 'till his ashes wouldn't fit a cremation box. Even now the steel whistles were shrieking down the streets.

The pups and their old hyena knew what would happen if even one of the town's territorial leather-visored leather-booted *Polenten* spotted them. They didn't even stop to snap threats back over their shoulders; they were off down the alleyway in a pack before the police could even show their truncheons around the corner. Harm grabbed Pfirsich's arm and pulled him after their persecutors down the alley.

"Harm, what are you doing? We didn't do anything wrong."

"Everybody's in the wrong caught street-fighting these days," said Harm, and kept his grip on Pfirsich's arm. "And you and I are the last people in this country who dare to get caught."

Pfirsich would have hauled back and forced Harm to stand still with him, but the whistles came up behind him and the deep bawling voice of the angry informer, in all the indignity of roused decency, and all the children and stray dogs who had showed up to get in the way, and all the rubber-neckers of propriety who had come to their windows to scream and roar, just as Germans had always leaped to their windows to get an eyeful of the ruckus, and all of it echoing off the narrow-set rough brick walls.

Harm gave Pfirsich another yank, and Pfirsich spooked like a started hare in the hedge with the dogs on the ridge, and the two of them shot off down the alleyway as fast as they'd ever run down the trenches, slipping and sliding, water flying, the tall officer and the steady sergeant, both knowing that what came with noise could kill, and wanting out of it before a head got blown open or ribs got sprung, or a face pounced open with a policeman's billy-club.

Splashing on through street after street, the two comrades finally outran the police and their share of the dogs, and stood panting up against the wall of the house they'd ducked behind for shelter, their collars pulled up against the rain.

"Think we got away?" gasped Harm.

"Oh, *Gott,* I hope so," groaned Pfirsich. "I'm out of a job if we didn't."

"Nice one with the umbrella."

"Thank you. " Pfirsich took a deep breath. "Good Lord, Harm,

107

how did you let those people get you in an alleyway?"

"This is my town. I can walk down any alleyways I like."

"Alleyways are traps," said Pfirsich, and wiped his face. "What a run; I must be out of shape. I need a cup of tea."

"Me too. My place is just around the corner. Want to come up?"

Pfirsich looked at his watch. "I don't have to get back to the school quite yet. Please."

As they walked along the sidewalk at a far more sedate pace, Pfirsich shook out his umbrella, and held it over their heads. They were already wet through, but he preferred not to have the rain pelting right in his face.

"Well, that was disgusting," said Harm.

"That's the sort of thing that goes on in the big cities, now." said Pfirsich, and snorted. "Politics all over the place."

"It's spreading," said Harm. "I've been in places where there are snipers on the roofs; God knows where they're getting the rifles and ammunition. We might as well have stayed in France."

"This isn't what we fought for."

"I fought because I was drafted. What about you?"

"I had a brother."

"Oh, right. Him."

"Na, he won't be getting away with it again; I'm never putting on a uniform again."

Harm nudged Pfirsich into a doorway, then put an arm in front of him as he opened the door to his building..

"Wipe your feet; this is real coconut matting, and *Frau* Frannk will throw me out in a high curve if we wear it down with grit and wet before its time."

Pfirsich sniffed at the odor of disinfectant. Even the leaves of the rubber tree in the blue crackleware pot on the landing looked as though somebody had taken furniture polish to them. The pipes and cocks of the sprinkling system overhead were rubbed to defiant proprietarial cleanliness. Everything in the place said "Mine," in the landlady's deep-waxed object language.

"Nice," said Pfirsich. "Is your place like this?" he asked, following Harm up the stairs.

"No. I pay the *Putzfrau* a stipend on the rent not to come in and clean."

"Why?

"Because if I didn't, I couldn't have any privacy at all."

Harm didn't add that she'd probably report it to *Frau* Frannk, and the old lady would have a heart attack, unable to live knowing there was a possible speck of dust in her building, and her heirs would throw him out for a Dirty Jew. They weren't a nice family, except perhaps *Frau* Frannk's niece, but the girl was too shy to be anything else, certainly not help.

"Here we are," Harm said, coming to a landing on the second floor. "Messy but homey."

Pfirsich had never been to Harm's flat before. A man's home was the one place he could be alone, and former soldiers, treasuring privacy after years of crowding, preferred to meet and socialize in clubs and taverns, and keep their digs to themselves. In a reaction against the army's enforced neatness, old trench-dogs could be infamously filthy. Pfirsich put his head in at the door with dread, but after looking around he entered happily, pulling off his hat and coat and smiling at his friend.

Harm's place was anything but dirty. Bookcases, radio cabinet, table, what Pfirsich could see of the little yellow-painted kitchen through its open doorway, all of it as neat as a polished boot. Even the newspaper in the bullfinch's cage was freshly changed, and hand-tatted antimacassars were carefully centered on the backs and arms of the dark-blue overstuffed furniture. The few well-read newspapers and magazines scattered about the scene must have been what Harm defined as a "mess."

"Oh, Harm," Pfirsich protested. "There's nothing wrong with this. How comfortable."

"That's my training," Harm said cryptically, in a code he knew Pfirsich would understand. Harm had been an airplane mechanic, once he'd made it out of the trenches, and those young pilots could be as dainty as a great-aunt about their machines. The ground-crew had to be scrubbing dirt out of those open rotary engines all the time to keep them running. It was clean as you go, or not go at all. Harm got used to it, and he'd kept the habit.

"I don't need some nosey old woman with a feather-duster in here going through my things. That cleaning lady is like her mistress's first sergeant. But I'd never let my mother see it, she'd have a heart attack," said Harm, and added, in a high woman's voice, "Oh horrors! Yesterday's newspapers!" He pointed at a neat pile of newsprint and cheap magazines on a flowered crewel footstool. "She'd never even notice I was using her doilies on the chairs. Well, siddown already. You're a guest. I'll go make tea. Seen this yet?"

Harm tossed a magazine onto the coffee table, and ducked into the kitchen.

Pfirsich settled happily into the big armchair. Soldiers appreciate comfort, and he was too soon out of the trenches not to comfort his behind. He picked up the magazine, and frowned. Spicy stuff. A wrestling magazine, from the looks of it, and not delicate about the costuming, either. Good heavens. Under the leotards -- were those nipples?

"Good Heavens," said Pfirsich.

"What's wrong?" said Harm from the kitchen.

"Your reading material. The physical culture magazine."

"Sweet, eh?"

"The spiciest thing I've read lately is that new book by Thomas Mann."

"Which one?"

"Death In Venice."

"Tad-zio!" said Harm, repeating the name of the boy in the book. "Not to my taste. A little young."

Pfirsich didn't answer. The way Harm had bawled the name nudged his memory, but he couldn't place it. After setting the teapot on to boil, Harm came in to find Pfirsich still trying to think. He plopped down on the sofa and put his feet up on the coffee table.

"How about this?" he said, and held up a book."

Pfirsich squinted at the title. *The Homosexuality of Men and Women.* By Magnus Hirschfeld. Oh," he said. *"Urnings."*

"The Third Sex," said Harm "As he defines them. The natural deviation from the norm. I see you've read it."

"I've flipped through it."

"And?"

"Interesting."

"Well, it's nicer reading than the novels that have been coming out lately."

"Which ones?" said Pfirsich.

"Oh, those nasty anti-Communist things." Harm made a face.

"Where the proper manly street-goons are always shaving women's heads and giving them laxatives before -- "

"Bitte," said Pfirsich. "We're going to be having tea. Have you been reading those things?"

"I picked one up in a bookstore last week, and just took a look." Harm shuddered. "It was like a train-wreck. I couldn't stop looking. *Gott,* but they do hate women. It makes you wonder why they hate us."

"They think we're like women," said Pfirsich. "They're part of the Find-Your-Sex-In-The-Barracks school, and women interfere with their fun."

Harm made a face. "So, how's life as a schoolmaster?"

"Your mother doesn't live in this town, does she?" asked Pfirsich.

"Hell, no. You know how it is; none of us -- " He arched his eyebrows at Pfirsich. "Can live in the same towns as Mama."

"Well, I could, if I wanted to," said Pfirsich. "But the job was here."

"You could?"

Pfirsich lowered his eyes.

Harm stared at him. "She knows? You've told her?"

"Oh, Harm." protested Pfirsich. "As though I could hide anything from my mother."

"And she didn't have a heart attack?"

"All the women you know seem prone to chest ailments."

Harm slapped his own cheek and rolled up his eyes.

"My mother is a very level-headed and sensible person," said Pfirsich. "A very strong person," he added, thinking of his mother at the failed engagement party. If anybody had looked like a soldier that day, it had been Mama Rommel. Erwin certainly hadn't; the joyful ferocity of battle wasn't in him. He had kept trying to hide in the kitchen, pretending he was more interested in the cake, choking desperately on the one or two bites he managed to get down his throat.

"Well, I suppose you can get away with it," sniffed Harm. "As the boys in the alleyway pointed out -- I'm a Jew."

"Oh, that," said Pfirsich.

"Yes, that."

"You're never been very religious about it."

"Ha! I'm like most people in this country these days."

111

"Well, like most people in our set," corrected Pfirsich. "Most people still regularly attend services. I admit I've been lax."

"Let's just admit it all, Pfirsich. Both of us have been lax for the same reason. Neither your religion nor mine have much use for us the way we are."

"They share the Old Testament," Pfirsich said dryly. "Where men do not lie together."

"And I for one couldn't stand the hypocrisy. And the questions-- where have I been, why don't I come home for *Yom Kippur,* God knows I could use it, considering what I probably have on my conscience, God knows what I'd been up to, why haven't I met a nice Jewish girl."

"I'm not nice?" pouted Pfirsich. "No wonder you never took me home."

"I said a nice *Jewish* girl."

"Well, if they're going to be prejudiced --."

"The girl, if you get my meaning, would have to be circumcised. You can see why I've been out of touch with the family."

"I know," said Pfirsich. "I'm fortunate there. I'm closest to my brother Erwin, though."

"Does he know?"

"Well, he was the last to know --."

"Has he blabbed it to anyone?"

Pfirsich held up his hands. "That man can keep a secret like a woman."

Oiled cotton set on fire between his fingers wouldn't have forced Erwin to blab. Erwin could talk your head off about tactics or cameras or stamps or the best sort of rosin to use on your violin-bow, even if he really couldn't play anything but dance tunes, but a sincere secret, a dangerous security, couldn't have been dragged out of him with hooks up his nostrils. It was something else he'd inherited from their bold and noble mother.

Harm snorted. The teakettle began to sing, and the bullfinch answered it. Harm jumped up and went in to finish the tea. In a few minutes he returned with a pink-and-gold French teapot and two matching cups on a pewter tray, which he set down on the Biedermeier coffee table.

"Oh!" said Pfirsich. "Raspberry-jam cookies. Did you get these at the pastry-shop by the train-station?"

"Yes. I treated myself. Before the price went up again. Since when can a woman keep a secret?"

"When she thinks it's important, she will; you could pull out her teeth, and she wouldn't talk." Pfirsich nibbled a cookie.

"You have a high opinion of women."

"The women in my family are spun steel. Erwin got his secretiveness from our mother. He's man enough to know what's important to men. And woman enough to keep his mouth shut about it."

"That's unusual," said Harm. "The couple of times I met him, he seemed All Man to me."

"Oh, every proper man has his female side, and a real man doesn't try to hide it." Pfirsich smiled. "He's all man when it comes to complaining, at least with family. You should hear him whining to Lucie when things go wrong."

"Well, if a man can't complain to his wife, to whom can he complain?"

Pfirsich took a sip of his tea. "And he's opinionated, and likes to get his own way. He's very outgoing."

"Well, then, thank God he knows enough not to be outgoing about you."

"I wish he could be," said Pfirsich. "Keeping things secret is dangerous; once something isn't a secret any more, then it isn't dangerous. Once my whole family knew about me, there was nothing that could be done to me any more."

"That's not my family," said Harm. "Maybe that's how you Germans do it, but we're Jewish."

"'You Germans?'" said Pfirsich. "What do you mean, 'you Germans?' Since when are you not German?"

"You were in that alleyway with me." Harm pointed angrily at the window. "You heard what they were saying."

"Oh, those people --."

"Try living with it. Don't tell me how your family does things. I'd swap for your family any day. Germans have no idea what Jews go through."

"Live with my family for awhile and see how you like it."

"I'm not talking about family."

Pfirsich put down his tea and put his hand on Harm's.

113

"I'm sorry, Harm. Those people out there really got to you, didn't they?"

"Oh, no -- why should they?" Harm said bitterly.

"I don't blame you for being upset. But those sort of people -- the war."

"I'm supposed to feel sorry for them?" snapped Harm.

"No, but realize that I'm not one of them. I'd never hurt you. And you've seen today I'll stand by you. Remember that."

Harm put his other hand on Pfirsich's. "I know, I know. I don't hold it against you, or people like you. But lately there's been more of that kind of thing. I don't know how to take it."

"That kind of thing has always been there, among people with evil minds."

People just wanted to live and let live. They wanted peace and quiet. The two comrades had seen today what would happen; a woman had brought down the police at the first sign of disturbance. Life was hard enough for the people as it was, without the bannered politicians trying to run everybody's life.

"Nobody likes the street politicals," said Pfirsich. "Look what they did after the war. They uprooted everything."

"I remember," grumbled Harm. "Goddamn Red Socialists."

He'd been afraid to come home in his uniform, because he hadn't known what was waiting for him. He'd fought for his country, and he didn't dare show his face, because he couldn't get a chance to change his clothes, and was afraid the angry crowds on the street would strip him naked.

"I remember," said Pfirsich. "I faced the same thing."

So many soldiers had become this wild cornered pack, who had no work, and knew no other way to help their country but to kill for her. Her enemies had fallen before their guns; their own countries had offered them up. They returned with the blood of their sacrifice upon them, and the belief that the machine-gun and the trench-knife and boot were the only means of enforcing their will. In their desperate ferocity they were strong, like fathers whose strength came only from their own victimship, fathers who feared gentleness and women, terrified of anything that might infringe upon their own bloody self-defense. No one knew where he or she stood because of these false fathers.

"This isn't going to last much longer," said Pfirsich. "Germans don't have that kind of temperament. Germans didn't riot in the streets and demand a new government every other week like the Italians or the French."

"They have in the past!"

"Not in this century," said Pfirsich.

Harm shrugged. "You hope."

"Not any more; we've learned from a hard past; we don't want war and revolutions."

"Don't be so certain."

If anybody was a reasonable people, it was the Germans. Harm had been letting a handful of street-toughs make him forget what this country had been about for so long. *Die lieben Deutschen* was a people of literature and music, and a noble military tradition. Karl Marx had said the Revolution would begin in Germany, but the Germans weren't going to let the kind of thing that was happening in wild dirty Russia happen in their close clean homes.

"I know this much," said Pfirsich. "If I ever had to put on a uniform again, I'd put my hand through a window, and pull."

"Pfirsich," said Harm, and pretended to spit. "Don't paint the devil on the wall."

"Don't be superstitious," said Pfirsich. "I'm not the suicidal type. Nobody in our family is. Not even my younger brother Karl, and he's so badly laid up with malaria from the war that he could at least claim an excuse."

"Just the same, I wouldn't be making such assured pronouncements if I were you. It's just asking for it."

"You think saying something will make it happen."

"Like I said, that's what we Jews have learned; the devil may show up and ask you what you want."

Pfirsich clucked his tongue. "Harm. Don't."

"You gentiles have such a cold idea of God. You're all afraid of Him. We talk to Him. We complain to Him, and ask him Why."

"'Why' – that's Torah, isn't it?" said Pfirsich, with the pride of a gentile with a Little Knowledge.

"Torah is 'How.' 'Why' is Talmud."

"We all pray to the same God," said Pfirsich, guiltily glancing

115

heavenward. "And He's probably listening to us right now."

"He listens to prayer; why shouldn't He listen to conversation, and take action on it when it pleases him?"

"God's an eavesdropper, now?" said Pfirsich. "Sounds a little blasphemous."

"He listens in on sparrows, let alone us; don't ask me if that's our end of the Bible or yours, I said I wasn't very religious. Either way, you have to be very careful what you say. God can get into a mood sometimes."

"God, or the Devil?"

Harm leaned forward and said behind his hand, "Sometimes I think the Devil is just God in a mood."

Pfirsich almost choked on his tea. He wasn't Catholic; he was a good Protestant boy. Catholics grumbled to their god almost as impudently as the Jews; there was a time they had been just a renegade sect of the Jews themselves, and still felt their old privileges with The Most High. But the Protestants had come to him later, in a time of books and rules, and they approached Him in an almost clerkish Fear Of The Lord. They didn't take His name in vain, and they didn't like to hear it done anywhere near them, within reach of a collective lightning strike. Pfirsich put his teacup down on its flowered plate and covered his confusion and his lips with his handkerchief.

"Well, if I don't get along to the school, the principal is going to get into a mood," he said, patting his mouth and folding the handkerchief up neatly before replacing it in his pocket. "I need the money, and these days it's not easy to find a job."

9. But They Won't Let Me Go

Pfirsich had a new job, a good job. Whether he liked it or not.

In 1935, no able-bodied German male, especially with a good record from the First World War, and with the addition of a university education in engineering, could have escaped reactivation.

Pfirsich had been so relieved to leave his job as mathematics teacher and rugby coach to twelve-year-olds, and return to the higher levels of his university training, that he'd never realized he might tempt the swollen appetite of the New German Army, nor that the government was determined to win over, fire or draft every teacher they could get their hands on. The two traditional options that might have been open to Pfirsich to avoid service in the German Army -- telling the draft board he was homosexual, or immigration to America -- were closed to him. The first because it had become a sure ticket to a camp, and the second because America was being difficult about the entry of any German nationals, regardless of creed, who weren't famous or useful.

Besides, Pfirsich didn't want to leave his family or his country; he'd just have to tough out a term of service, and earn the right to stay in his homeland.

So *Leutnant* Rommel, assigned to report for duty with his brother Erwin, kept his mouth shut and boarded a train to his brother's garrison, in Goslar, the Third Reich's agricultural center.

Army Engineer in a farming town. *Oh, ganz prima.*

* * * * *

"God give me strength," he thought to himself, trying to get comfortable, huddling under his long gray army greatcoat as though it were a blanket. He despised traveling by train these days. He could close his eyes, but he couldn't plug up his nostrils. No one could mistake the smell of a train carrying military. Too many bodies, too much tobacco,

117

too much leather and hot wool uniforms, too much sweat, and that hint of urine. And that horrid reek of gun oil on everybody. Did they all have to clean their pistols every morning? Show off that they were all soldiers now?

Pfirsich leaned his head against the cool glass of the window and pulled up the greatcoat around his chin, less for the warmth than the privacy. It was much like the one that had been issued to him in the last war, but the cut was a little looser, a little more modern and fashionable. He'd paid for the tailoring of his tunic and breeches, remembering the comfort of a wool uniform that didn't chafe.

He stretched his booted legs; in the last war, he'd always worn riding boots to travel, because they were warmer and kept his feet dry. And it was much more likely that part of his transportation would be an actual horse, with a saddle it wouldn't take long to get used to. In today's close efficient modern trains, with their links to everywhere in the country, and automobiles and lorries waiting at the end of the line, boots were a mistake. His feet were perspiring and his ankles hurt. He was probably just not used to boots any more. And at the price of them, he'd have to get used to them. He rotated an ankle. He wished he'd just worn his shoes. *They* didn't care what sort of shoes their men wore, as long as they were black. He could have done with a well-fitted pair of English Wellingtons, under a nice loose pair of dress trousers.

Chewing your fingernails about your uniform, he thought. That's what being in the military does to you. All I can think of is starch and blacking and polish polish polish, and whether my seams are straight. In the military, Clothes Make A Man Crazy. Not even the high-class *Junker* pretty boys in the Berlin cabaret scene were as obsessive about their sequined evening regalia.

Pfirsich opened his eyes and peeped over his shoulders at his fellow passengers. They were playing cards all over the compartment and out into the aisle. Most of them were wearing uniforms of some sort or another. Most of them were smoking. The few civilians were trying to get into the soldiers' and sailors' mood, the women smiling while they waved away the smoke; Anything For Our Boys. Once in a while one of the girls would squeal, and go back to smiling; Our Boys were pinching Anything they could reach. The wild young girls in their bright print dresses would pinch right back, and open their berry-colored mouths to casual kisses.

The Nazis spoke to the young people. Without going to war, Hitler had made the country feel as if it had won that war, made it feel superior and safe from ever being invaded again.   Nobody could touch Germany, not now -- they were too afraid of her. She wasn't used to the feeling of not being scared herself, and it made her drunk. She liked it; she felt she deserved it and that everybody else had earned their fear. She was spreading herself out in a jolly giddy licentious spirit of youth.   She couldn't get enough flags and parades. Sure, a few people got knocked on the head -- but if you didn't like the brawling masculine fun of a street-fight, then stay out of the street! Love It Or Leave It. This was Freedom.

Pfirsich sighed. On top of it all, everybody was so excited. That impulsive glow, added to the reek of bulk-cooked, greasy food -- and much too much *Sauerkraut* -- and too much alcohol leaking through their pores. Put it all on a rocking train, and a gentleman was tempted to just get out and walk, so he could give in to his vomiting neatly, in the clean grass by the tracks.

"*Gnädige Herrschaften!*" rang the voice over the public-address system. "There will be a twenty-minute traffic delay before we pull into Goslar! Government cars with priority! Please keep your seats, and keep order!"

Pfirsich groaned.

"Goslar!" whooped a *Luftwaffe* private, and in his eagerness to get to the window, burrowed his blue-clad knee right into the anonymous coat-covered lump that was Pfirsich. He propped his hands against the window, and rubbernecked like a curious goat.

"And government cars! You know the *Führer's* visiting there."

Pfirsich squirmed out from under the knee, and tried to shrink out of the path of the resulting tumult, as everybody on the train came crowding up eagerly to all the street-side windows, including his. With the exception of a few people like himself, who tried to ignore it, and hoped no one would notice. It was just his hard luck he was on a roadside window. He didn't look up to try to catch a glimpse of his country's Chosen Leader. He closed his eyes against the rapid-fire babble of questions and answers.

"Howdja know he's there?"

"It was on the radio."

"Can we see him?"

"I've never seen him -- not in the flesh -- only in the newsreels."

"Do you think I could manage to get his autograph? For my daughter?"

"Ha! Don't get your hopes up, old man," grinned an Army corporal. "There will be Black Pirates -- SS -- in pike man's ranks all around him. He don't set a foot out, without he takes along his private show-window army."

"Do you mind?" Pfirsich finally spoke. "My stomach is not a railway platform."

The corporal looked down. All he could see was a pair of indignant blue eyes, peering up angrily over the collar of a greatcoat, under a neat slick of corn-blond hair. He bent down from the window and thrust his own red beery face at the eyes.

"What's your gripe, stud?" he demanded, his black eyes glinting. "You been under your horse-blanket since we got on -- pretending to be asleep instead of making companionable with us. We ain't good enough for you? And now you don't even wanna get up and see the *Führer. Sie sind nichtärisch, oder?*"

Pfirsich wanted to throw up. He was hot, crowded, unhappy. The man's breath was like a brewery and a cigarette-factory combined. And now he wanted to drag politics into it. "Non-Aryan," indeed. Pfirsich couldn't stand it. With a gagging gasp, he got his legs under him, and levered himself straight up, to his full height, throwing off the greatcoat and revealing his neat sleek officer's uniform.

"Do you mind?" he demanded. "It's too hot."

"Oh!" gasped the corporal, and jumped back. "Forgive me, *mein Herr.*"

The corporal's friends began to rag on him.

"Ha ha! You put your foot in it, Paul."

"Please," begged Paul, bowing like a geisha. "Excuse me, *mein Herr.*"

"Fine, fine," said Pfirsich, rummaging around in the luggage rack. "Where's my cap? Oh, lovely." He'd found it under the seat. "Look at it. Where am I going to find a tailor with a decent steamer?"

"*'Nichtärisch'!*" whooped Paul's friends. "An officer -- a tall officer -- German-blond -- eyes like blue water!"

"Don't rub my nose in it," hissed Paul.

Pfirsich was sadly examining his brand-new visored officer's cap.

Officers were required to buy their own uniforms. If he couldn't find someone who could iron out the creases in this crushed peak, he'd have to buy a new cap. He hadn't been in combat this war yet, and nobody but combat veterans could get away with dashing squashed caps.

"Ouch," he muttered.

"I guess maybe he's actually a dwarf, or a cripple -- or a Jew, isn't he, Paul? He's a Jew, now, is he?" Paul's friends would not quit. "Maybe he's hiding his side locks under a wig?"

Pfirsich had all he could take. Beer, *Sauerkraut,* -- which, Lord help him, he could never stomach without gas -- uniforms, politics, and now brainless low-class racial slurs, the sort that made most of the civilians and even some of the uniforms wince, and made the bright-colored excited girls all shriek and giggle, combined to make the compartment unendurable for him. He took up his greatcoat over one arm, shoved his crushed cap onto his head and grabbed the one piece of luggage he hadn't shipped ahead, because it had his underwear and socks in it.

"Excuse me," he said, pushing past all the eager bodies. "Getting off at Goslar."

"Huh? There's been a delay, *mein Herr.*"

"Need some fresh air," gasped Pfirsich, and finally popped free into the aisle. He thought he was going to choke to death in there.

As he left, the *Luftwaffe* private frowned after him. "That's a very old-fashioned type. Very 'Long-Live-The-Kaiser'."

"No wonder he didn't get excited about the *Führer,*" sniffed Paul.

"Well, he's got it right, you know," said one of Paul's friends. "The army ain't supposed to be all that political. We ain't even allowed the vote."

"Ja, but some of them older officers carry it just a little too far."

"Can't trust 'em," said the *Luftwaffe* private. The Air Force was very political indeed; the Nazis had made airplanes legal again. "Maybe we should report him."

"Oh, don't start," said Paul. "Drag in the SS, and you're likely to get dragged in with him. Those people have no sense of discrimination."

"But --."

"Just cut the cards, will you?"

Pfirsich staggered onto a platform between the cars, where a number of civilians and soldiers were already crowded, braving the threatening sky for a breath of fresh air.

"Oh, excuse me," said Pfirsich, bumping into a helmeted soldier, and apologizing to a woman in a tan coat open over a black dress sprinkled with a print of tiny yellow puppies. "It's too close in there. I needed to get out."

"Understandable," smiled the woman.

"Sorry 'bout the crowd, *Herr Leutnant.*" said the soldier. "We don't have special cars for officers now."

Pfirsich smiled at him. "We never have had, except for staff officers and Generals."

"But you get the idea, *Herr Leutnant.* It's the New Army -- and the New Order. It's all the same for all of us, now. We all live together, and flow together, like the Rhine."

"Melt together," said Pfirsich, wiping his face with his handkerchief.

"Too hot in there for you, *Herr Leutnant?*"

"It's like a hothouse. I can stand heat when it's dry, like the Mediterranean. But not a jungle."

He was thrown off his feet. A helmet-brim clipped him in the teeth. He only just caught the woman, and prevented her being knocked down. A staff car was passing on the road, and everybody on the platform charged over to get a glimpse of it.

"It's a staff car."

"It's the *Führer!*"

"Is that him? Is that him?"

"If you'd get out of my way -- "

Pfirsich gave up struggling to get his feet back down on the platform. He let the little knot of flesh and enthusiasm carry him right over onto the rail. Then he took the opportunity to spin around on the rail on his tailored tailbone, and giving a little kick with both booted feet -- he'd forgotten what a nice convenient levering weight boots could make -- flew off, cap, coat, luggage and all, in a well-judged arc to the rail bedding below.

There he caught himself, set his greatcoat over his shoulders, and with it swinging behind him like a heavy gray cape, started off down along the road. He didn't dare ignore the staff-car, and stopped a moment to toss off a quick salute, then followed its route.

"Where's he going?" said the helmeted soldier.

"*Ja.* What's his problem?"

The woman with the yellow puppies hunched herself into a corner of the platform. She could sympathize with the officer; she wished she were alone and wearing walking shoes. She would have joined him.

Pfirsich didn't have a problem, now. He was happy to be off that train and swinging along muttering to himself.

"Until the *Führer* stops taking up every road and railway and radio frequency and newspaper in Germany, I am going to buy a bicycle. And earplugs."

He soon found a sign: *GOSLAR, 12 KM.* That wasn't bad. He could use pumping the blood, after the public corseting on that train. It was pleasant and cool, too; he would'nt get overheated.

A drop of rain got past his cap-visor and fell onto his warm nose. He looked up and put out his hand.

"Na, a little rain. I lived in sluices of rain during the last war."

In the next moment, he was hunched by the side of the road, in a thundering downpour, miserably trying to hitch a ride.

"And I didn't like it any better back then."

Germany was in a good mood, and acting rich and free. It was easy to get a truck to stop; its owner was just dying to show off. The truck skidded to a spurting halt in the muddy shoulder of the newly-graded road. A window rolled down, and an arm and a voice cheerily raised, flapping in the downpour:

"Heda! C'mon, poor soul. What're you doing, wandering around in the rain like this?"

"Oh, thank you," cried Pfirsich. In relief he thought, I was fearing this country had got into such a fit of self-confidence it had forgotten to be kind. It shows how wrong a little rain can make you.

The door of the cab swung open, and two fresh young soldiers looked out.

"Ha! An officer. Your car break down, *mein Herr?*"

"One of our officers shouldn't be foot-slogging in the mud, not these days."

Pfirsich got in and made himself as comfortable as possible, squeezing his hips into the narrow space left by the greatcoat-bundled young soldiers, trying not to drip.

"I appreciate the lift," he told the elderly civilian driver. "It's terribly kind of you."

"Nothin' too good for Our Boys. I'm extra happy to do it. I'm a veteran; was in the Big One."

"Oh, were you?" Pfirsich brightened. He had taken off his cap, and was wiping his face. "I was in it myself."

"You?" The driver snorted through his red moustache. "Not a young pip like you. A baby ensign, if you were."

"I was. But I was eighteen by the time it ended. By then they were taking them at sixteen."

The driver drove in the clutch and shifted gears. "*Jo,* they did. Just babies. I guess you were pretty much an old man after all, by the time it was over."

Pfirsich nodded sadly. "Yes, sometimes I felt old."

One of the soldiers butted in. "Come on, *Herr Leutnant,* you don't have to pretend to be part of the past. Forget all that -- we're going to wipe out all that old history. Us and Hitler!"

Pfirsich replaced his cap; it was easier to hide your eyes under a visor. Everyone was harping on the same string today, he thought. This Hitler wasn't a politician -- he was a movie star -- and he had a country crammed full of adoring fans.

"What's your name, youngster?" said the driver.

"Youngster," thought Pfirsich. Sometimes it was so inconvenient having such a young face. But he wasn't offended. Oh, dear; he must be getting old.

"My name's Rommel," he said. "*Leutnant* Pfirsich Rommel."

"*Rommel?*" shrieked one of the soldiers. His voice in the small damp cab made Pfirsich cringe.

"Ooooh!" hooted the other soldier. "Not related to the Major in town, are you?"

The first soldier poked him. "If he is, is he going to admit it?"

"What?" Pfirsich looked up in alarm. "What? What's my brother done now?"

"'Brother'?"

"'Now'! He said 'now'! Oh, the Major must have a history."

"It's a scandal!"

"It's a disgrace!"

"It's *delicious!*"

* * * * *

Major Erwin Rommel, the commander of the Army garrison at Goslar, was sitting in his office, arranging and pasting down little bits of colored paper in a big scrapbook. He was intently examining one of the pieces of paper though a magnifying glass, when he heard a familiar voice.

"Erwin?"

He looked up. His brother Pfirsich stood dripping in the office doorway, wearing his brand-new *Leutnant's* uniform. He didn't look pleased.

"Are you working on your stamp collection? In your office? You never mix your hobbies with your duty."

Erwin used the stamp clamped in the tweezers to intimidate his brother. "You're sopping wet. Didn't you get a train ticket? Is this how the New Army expects its young officers to report to duty?"

"I'm not that young, any more," said Pfirsich, and hung up his wet coat and cap on hook on the back of the door. He picked up a ham sandwich from the desk, and fastidiously held it out at arm's length. It had one bite nipped out of it, and the crust was curling.

"Is that all you've eaten?"

"We're not at home," gritted Erwin. "Mama's not here."

"Oh, I see; you're taking your lunch-break in hiding. So you don't have to go out on the street."

"It's raining."

"Oh, it's the rain, is it? You're not made of sugar. I've already heard why you can't go out."

Erwin slapped the tweezers down on the desk. "I can go where I please in peace. I just want to check up on my collection. What's that on your face?"

"You are perfectly aware what 'that' is. Don't try to distract me."

"It's a mole. And it's gone jet-black. You should see to it; it could have become malignant."

"It hasn't changed in three years."

Pfirsich leaned straight over, put his folded arms on the desk, and

125

just looked at his brother. Erwin glared back at him, while all four of their pupils expanded. Suddenly Erwin sat straight up in his chair, his head up like a highbred *Trakehner* stallion. It didn't do any good with Pfirsich; to him he still looked like a Swabian pony who just didn't want to be bridled.

"I am completely within my rights," snapped Erwin, "as a German officer. I was the insulted party."

"'Insulted'?" Pfirsich was taken aback. He stood straight up. "What do you mean to do? Fight a duel?" he said sarcastically.

"Why not? Dueling is legal again."

Pfirsich's jaw dropped. "You can't fight a duel with the *Führer*."

"Oh, you've heard the details, then, have you?"

"The *Führer* insulted you? You don't even know him. How can he have insulted you?"

"He insulted my entire battalion. I won't have it."

"How? He's the leader of a country. You're a Major, and an officer in his army. How?"

"'His army?' The insult is because of *his* army."

"'His' army?" Pfirsich was baffled. "Not this army? Our army? What are you talking about?"

"*We* are this country's army -- Germany's army. I'm talking about --."

"Oh! The SS." Pfirsich put his hand on his breast. "Erwin, what did the SS do? I mean, this time, to you, in particular?"

"Got between us and the *Führer*."

Pfirsich went white. Were they going back to the street battles? Like after the war? Was this another version of The Night of The Long Knives, when the SS used the excuse of homosexuality to slaughter the Storm Troopers? Accusation of homosexuality was a favorite Nazi weapon. Being queer was worse than being a Jew. The Hirschfeld movement died when the Institute for Sexual Research was torched in 1933. Magnus Hirschfeld died himself, in Paris, shortly after he saw the report in a newsreel. The Nazis had a nearly religious fixation upon the Place Of The Penis – whose went where, into whom, and when.

Pfirsich blinked. Who knew what they knew of his own history -- and how they could use it? What could they do to the family?

Erwin barged right into his private moment of projected horror.

"The *Führer's* coming to Goslar to review the troops. Between my troops and him, there will be a line of SS. Guarding him -- instead of us -- and from him."

"That's all?"

"That's enough! So I've refused to turn out the battalion. Until we get an apology -- no parade." Erwin brought his little hand down on the table with a slap.

"That's *all?*" repeated Pfirsich. "That's nothing. Why get upset about it?"

"Well, it's obvious how long you've been out of the army; you've lost your regimental pride."

"It didn't take that long." said Pfirsich.

"That gang of upstart blackbacks is trying to thumb their noses at us -- outright -- in public."

"Oh, it won't be the first time."

"*Stimmt.* And it won't happen here."

Pfirsich threw up his hands and rolled his eyes. "They're just acting as a bodyguard, Erwin. Like Cossacks, or the English Queen's Beefeaters. Every ruler likes to have his special dress-up troops marching nearby. This time, at least, I don't see it matters what the SS is doing."

"No, not 'in this case.' If Adolf Hitler doesn't realize what these people are trying to do, it's up to any conscientious Army officer to alert him. Where have you been? The SS 'just a bodyguard'?"

"I've been studying," said Pfirsich. "To be an engineer. Mostly I've been in school. I didn't have a lot of time for newspapers or newsreels."

* * * * *

It had stopped raining.

Pfirsich stood in the street outside Garrison headquarters. Inside him, it was raining harder than ever. He hadn't even thought about going back to Erwin's office to pick up his suitcase. He didn't want to see his quarters. Right now he didn't want any reminder of his return to the military.

The nightmares had begun within a month of his emancipation from the ranks, right after the last war. Like many former soldiers he dreamt he'd signed up again, and found himself condemned to another tour of duty, against his will, or to his confusion, in barracks he didn't recognize, with soldiers he didn't know. He would jerk awake sweating from a world of trenches and artillery fire and bureaucracy and hunger and stink. He couldn't help but whimper in relief to realize that he need never see any of it again.

Now he would have to go searching to find that real looming unfamiliar barracks, to sign his name on the real company report, and hang his coat in that narrow little closet in that narrow little room where he would be obliged, as a new incoming officer, to stay, until he could finagle some decent private quarters for himself. There would be trenches at the end of it, he knew it, and the noise and stink. It was just hard.

He started down one of the narrow winding streets, looking for a shop or a tavern; someplace that served tea. Hot tea. A place with a liquor license, that could add a little brandy to the cup.

Erwin would remind him that he had forgotten to fetch his luggage. He'd probably hunt him down and accusingly hand it to him. Erwin liked to do things for himself.

10. Seeds

All he'd been able to find was beer, and he'd had three, out of
spite.

He was lying fully-dressed on his narrow little cot in his narrow
little barracks room that evening, diagonally, with his still-booted feet
jutting off one side and his cap on his belly, with his arms tight against
his sides like a scribe's mummy, contemplating the nightmare, when his
brother came to visit. With the suitcase.

"Here," said Erwin, and put it down on the footlocker. "You
forgot this."

"Thank you, Erwin." Pfirsich rolled his head over. "Erwin, are you
going to talk to the people the *Führer* will be sending over?"

"What people?"

"Never mind," said Pfirsich, looking back at the ceiling.

"How did you know about them?"

"Gossip," said Pfirsich.

No way would he tell Erwin what he'd been hearing down at the
tavern. Erwin had been in the army long enough to know that the worst
scuttlebutt always contained a grain of truth. Pfirsich knew the little detail-
minded brute would just pump him for information.

"They'll be meeting us in the hotel attached to the town hall.
Reichsführer Himmler and *Propagandaminister* Goebbels."

"Them? They're pretty high in the government. And you're just a
Major. It's that important to him?"

"Who?" said Erwin.

"Whoever's sending them."

"You must mean the *Führer.*"

"That's it," agreed Pfirsich. "Why go through with a meeting like
this? Why don't you just accept his apology?"

"This is the apology, Pfirsich."

"Oh, good. Then it will be all better, and we can go back to life as usual."

"You don't seem to realize how important this is."

"No, I don't."

"Why don't you get up?"

"This is my bed and my room. I don't have to stand up for anybody."

Erwin snorted. "I thought you were supposed to be the one with the manners."

"I'm being terrible," agreed Pfirsich.

"It doesn't sound like you're sorry for it."

"I'm not."

Erwin leaned forward and sniffed. "Beer."

"Yes, beer," snapped Pfirsich. "Try to get a cup of tea in this town."

"You could have gotten one at the hotel."

"This place has a hotel?"

"Yes, it does. And we have to go there."

"'We'?"

"Us. You and me."

Pfirsich sat straight up. "'Us'? You really mean 'us'?"

"I want you there."

"Now?"

"Yes, now. Get your dress uniform on. And wash your face! You look like you've been riding with your head hanging out the train. What's wrong with you?"

"Just getting over a nightmare, that's all. Or getting used to it."

"And for God's sake brush those boots. Have you been walking in the mud? You haven't even provided yourself with an orderly yet, have you?"

"I just got here," gritted Pfirsich.

"Go get your war paint on. I'll meet you downstairs in 15 minutes. And try to be a credit to the garrison."

Fifteen minutes later Pfirsich was standing in the dayroom ruefully studying himself in a mirror, his white- gloved hands clasped behind his back. He hadn't lost his old knack for getting ready in time for a surprise inspection, even including the moments it took to find the latrine and lose the beer. His boots gleamed black, and his cheeks shone an irritably scrubbed red. In the mirror he looked like a recruiting poster.

A young soldier who came running through the dayroom skidded to a halt, gasped, "Excuse me, *mein Herr!*" and tiptoed respectfully, with a proper artificial display of Military Fear, out the other door. Pfirsich groaned.

"What's wrong now?" said Erwin as he strode into the room.

Major Rommel had pinned on all his medals, full-dress-ribbon style, ranged across his left breast, and his bright enamel blue-white-and-gold *Pour le Mérite* glinted at his throat. He was gorgeous. But he wasn't in dress uniform. He was wearing a field uniform, and in his gray-gloved hand he held a helmet.

Pfirsich knew what that meant. Erwin was going to play Soldier for Serious, and Pfirsich was going to have to take the part of the full-dress diplomatic Master of Ceremonies. The trotting eager amiable Adjutant. The polite young *Leutnant* who ran like a pretty harmless beribboned bitch between the glaring leashed war-dogs of the opposing delegations.

"Oh, hell," he muttered. "Right. I'm 'supposed to be the one with the manners'."

He felt like a fool, gussied up in his pale-teal dress tunic and slightly crushed cap, towering along behind the little helmeted warrior, who was leading him at an urgent march along the city streets, taking the salutes of all the passing soldiers. Pfirsich glanced back to see them whispering and pointing after him and his brother.

"'The Scandal,'" he groaned. "They all know."

"Good," exclaimed Erwin. "Then they know I won't let them be insulted with impunity."

"I think we just look funny."

Erwin didn't even know what he meant.

They passed the Goslar *Rathaus*, and through one of the front hall windows Pfirsich glimpsed an unusual chandelier. It was made entirely of intertwined reindeer antlers. Those wouldn't be only horns locked before this day was over, he mused bitterly.

At the hotel, Erwin sprang up the front stairs without hesitation and took the respectful welcoming gesture of the doorman as his due. Pfirsich followed him through the opened door and into the lobby. At least this wasn't a barracks.

"Himmler!" said Erwin to the man at the desk.

"Of course, *Herr Major,*" said the man, who already knew just what this was about. "I'll ring his room for you." A few moments later he said, *"Herr Reichsführer?* The *Herr Major* is here to see you." Replacing the phone, the man turned to *Major* Rommel. "He'll be right down." He gestured past the lobby. "He asked if you'd mind meeting him in the cafe."

Pfirsich brightened. He was dreading the explosion that would have gone off if Himmler had airily given a room number. Erwin wasn't going to climb any more stairs than he deemed fit. Erwin climbed stairs for superior officers and for glory, not for upstart hoodlums playing at army. Himmler was going to come to him, not the other way around. And in the cafe. Ladies present. Army and SS and Ministry of Propaganda would have to behave themselves. And Pfirsich was finally going to get that cup of tea he'd been dying for.

Pfirsich was relaxing at the table, happily watching the waiter trot off to fetch the prearranged order, when the other guests showed up. He stood up, The One With The Manners, now that he was comfortably at home in a civilian hotel, at a civilian table, and shook hands with Himmler and Goebbels. No party salute from either of them. No doubt they had been instructed to make nice.

The only thing Erwin did was remove his helmet. He slowly stood up, and as slowly held out his hand. No salute. Pfirsich winced. *Reichsführer* Heinrich Himmler flashed *Major* Rommel a cold metallic look through his spectacles, and barely took the tips of those still-gloved fingers

"Cold Fish, that Himmler," Pfirsich thought, and was glad he wasn't offered a hand by the man. What a face. The SS should list a "chin" as one of its duty requirements. How could he possibly wear all that black, and those riding-boots, and still look like a schoolteacher?

Joseph Goebbels, on the other hand, clasped first Erwin's and then Pfirsich's hand in both of his, all smiles and warm brown eyes. Erwin blinked. Goebbels wasn't dressed in that outfit he usually wore in the newsreels; that traffic-warden's-style NSDAP-brown uniform, another of the Nazi party's many cynical attempts to pass themselves off as the Army.

Instead, Goebbels wore a civilian suit, in a beautiful conservative cut, of a light bright camel tan. The wide-legged trousers were a perfect style for him; all that could be seen of what was reported to be a slight clubfoot was the tip of one polished brown shoe. Only Goebbels knew that his short leg was the result of an operation for a childhood illness; "Clubfoot" had been the affliction of Byron, and even in the midst of the *Kulturkampf,* in the struggle of Normal Nature against Effete Education, Goebbels's cherished doctoral degree and two centuries of German Enlightenment wouldn't allow him to limp about among the uneducated classes without showing off his own more cosmopolitan academic background.

Pfirsich didn't his details. He was simply pleased by his friendliness, and his sense of fashionable propriety. Goebbels was making an effort, not trying to be anything but the civilian he was, and Pfirsich warmed to him for it.

"Charmed," exclaimed Goebbels, in his rich mellifluous voice that always sounded so weird coming out of such a weedy little man. Pfirsich had always suspected it might be a stand-in on the radio, or a voice-over in the newsreels. The little man seemed to be full of surprises.

Everyone sat down, and were just getting settled when the waiter returned with the order.

"On my tab," said Goebbels. "Cakes and tea?"

Tea! Pfirsich went pale with longing at the mere smell of the rich narcotic pot. Caffeine is as addictive as any other drug, and he'd been hooked since childhood. He didn't hesitate, and promptly fell back on ceremony as an excuse to grab the pot and pour.

"May I play mother?" he said, filling everyone's cups. This way he'd at least get a full cup in front of him, before anybody decided discussions had to come first. They looked just in the mood to do it, too.

"Sugar?" Pfirsich asked Himmler, who just shook his head and reached for the cup before everybody had been served.

"Barbarian," thought Pfirsich, watching the chinless man in black gulp the strong hot brew. "That, or he has a headache."

He was struck again by Himmler's resemblance to a schoolteacher -- but a bad one. Pfirsich came from a family of good teachers, who prized patience and firmness, and whose knowledge of their subject was the solid first basis of their authority. The man in black looked like the kind of mean ignorant pedant who bossed his classes with raw humiliation and rulers across the hand.

Erwin popped a slice of lemon into his tea. Goebbels reached for the cream, and served himself a pastry. Pfirsich took cream and sugar and a chocolate bisquit; he hadn't eaten since breakfast. Then he poured a second cup for Himmler.

"A headache," Pfirsich thought, when Himmler immediately put his nose into his cup.

Oh, wasn't this going to be lovely? Erwin in a snit, and that man with a headache. Now just pray that Erwin's stomach didn't start up on him, and add to the prevailing nastiness.

"Now what's the problem?" smiled Goebbels, wiping his fingers on a napkin, and turning to Erwin. "The *Reichsführer* said you wouldn't turn out your troops for the parade."

"Not if his people are between my troops and the *Führer,*" growled Erwin.

"Commendable loyalty," exclaimed Goebbels.

"To the integrity of my troops," Erwin said flatly.

"Not to the *Führer?*"

"He is the leader of my country. He must trust his soldiers. The SS is only a quasi-military political organization. The traditional Army must properly take precedence over a mere political organ."

Pfirsich, nibbling his bisquit, was watching Himmler out of the corner of his eyes. If a fish could brood and glower, that's what Himmler was doing. Then he saw Erwin glance at the *Reichsführer.*

"Oh, the little beast!" thought Pfirsich. "He's taunting the man. He's putting him in his place."

Pfirsich quickly addressed himself to the glowering Himmler.

"It's only a matter of regulation precedence, *Herr Reichsführer.* If this were Berlin, of course the SS would come first, but this is Goslar and so the garrison battalion must take precedence. I'm sorry if there's been a misunderstanding; we certainly didn't intend any offence."

He knew Erwin was looking daggers at him. Erwin, of course, had been under no illusion of his intent.

"See, Heinrich?" soothed Goebbels. "Just parade protocol. No mutiny at all."

"Mutiny!" yapped Erwin.

"No, no, Erwin; it's just a colorful turn of phrase." Pfirsich appealed silently to Goebbels.

"Yes," said Goebbels, quickly. "Just a touch of levity."

He knew better. He'd heard Himmler snarl it in all seriousness, only that morning.

"Is that why they insisted on being first?" demanded Erwin. "They were testing our loyalty?"

"Oh, heavens, no," said Goebbels, throwing up his hands. "Of course not."

"They didn't mean it," said Pfirsich. "They just forgot they weren't at home."

"Maybe we could get them a map," spat Erwin.

"We know where to find you," hissed Himmler.

The hair raised on the back of Pfirsich's neck.

"A map!" he tittered, and leaned companionably toward Goebbels. "My brother has such a sense of humor."

"So does Heinrich," said Goebbels. "Very funny, Heinrich."

"No hard feelings?" purred Pfirsich, but his paws were sweating.

"Who goes first at the parade?" gritted Erwin.

"One can always come to a compromise," smiled Goebbels, a little stiffly. It was no fun being caught between Hitler and this uppity little army officer. Himmler wasn't helping.

"What compromise?" said Erwin. "Either we go first, or we don't. Who goes first?"

"Why, the garrison battalion. Your battalion, Major." said Goebbels. "Didn't we say that?"

"No. I wanted to be sure."

"I agree completely; in all matters of protocol or business, one must be exact."

"As long as it's not funny-bus --."

"Thank you, *meine Herren,*" chirped Pfirsich. "See you at the parade?"

* * * * *

At the parade, the perfectly organized and perfectly cordial parade, Pfirsich stood in his parade-gear, helmet and all, sword on his thigh, just like a taller version of his brother.

Now that he'd accepted being here, had marched up to the reviewing stand with his battalion -- without falling out of step, which would have earned him sarcastic comment from Erwin, and an order to

135

show up for early-morning drill practice -- and stood at attention with the men, he remembered the comfort of standing with other soldiers; they all looked alike, and unless they moved against the mass, none of them could be singled out of the herd. He was invisible.

He was pleased with himself; he could still do the *Stechschritt.* Thank God it was forbidden to use except in front of a reviewing stand; booting up like that, kick after kick, like a demented goose, he could have pulled a muscle. When the *Führer* appeared, all he'd have to do was listen to his speech, then salute him when Erwin did. Life was easy.

Speech begun. Pfirsich was happy to discover he could still doze at attention. The helmet- brim shaded and concealed his closed eyes. He drifted off, and didn't hear a word.

Speech finished; happy entertained applause from the townsfolk. Pfirsich woke up, neatly and calmly, with no visible jerk; he just opened his eyes. Here came the *Führer,* with Himmler and Goebbels -- in uniform, this time -- returning the salute and shaking hands with Erwin, congratulating him on a wonderful turnout.

"Lovely," thought Pfirsich. "Almost over."

Adolf Hitler was looking at Pfirsich. Looking right at him, with such an outright intrusive familiarity that Pfirsich's head rose in swan-like indignation. He didn't mind friendliness, but he didn't care for the impudence of a stranger. The eyes were too direct and possessive, and that smile, under that ridiculous little moustache, was insufferable. Pfirsich's face stiffened, and his cheekbones rose clear under the tightened skin.

Mistake.

Adolf Hitler had a photographic memory. That it was only temporary was a secret he kept to himself. As was his habit before making an appearance, he had just that morning been leafing through the pertinent records, with photographs, of Goslar's local army commanders, right down to squad level. His temporary memory would hold for at least a day, lending him the appearance of omniscient knowledge of every detail of his country and her military. It gave him great authority with soldiers; even a general with a bone to pick would step back and swallow his protests, awed by a leader who could name every man in the general's division, even the cooks and orderlies. It was a neat trick and a priceless ability, and it usually worked. Hitler immediately knew the face before him. Then he looked back at Erwin, and at Pfirsich again.

"Twins?" Hitler thought to himself. "I don't remember twins. Is my memory going?" He was irritated and disturbed. "Just when I need it most?" He had to clear this up.

Pfirsich stared at the hand held out to him only a moment, then recovered and took it. As he did, he bent forward slightly, just a hint of a bow, bobbing his face very close toward Hitler's -- and he suddenly felt faint and cold. It was as though the man had an aura, or an odor about him, and it raised the hackles on Pfirsich's neck. His head swam, his eyes blurred. He could have fainted on the spot.

"My brother, *mein Führer!*" barked Erwin, wondering what the hell was the matter with Pfirsich. *"Leutnant* Pfirsich Rommel."

"Delighted," murmured Hitler.

In the same moment that Pfirsich had felt it, Hitler was overcome by such a manifest wave of dislike -- both from Pfirsich and from himself -- that he felt sick. This tall helmeted man didn't like him, and he didn't like him right back. Any chatty niceties Hitler had primed on his tongue choked back down his throat; he took two quick improper steps backwards, just to get away from the icily glaring officer.

He was aware of his own skin, its coldness and its sudden damp; he knew without being able to see himself that he had turned gray. The last time he had felt anything like this overpowering revulsion had been at the end of the last war, when he'd been blinded in a mustard-gas attack, and passed out choking in the slimy mud of a trench. Profound personal dislike always threw Hitler off balance, and this was Hate.

Hitler looked around, desperate for solace, and his eye fell upon the battalion commander. Now there was somebody who liked him; he could always tell. He could take refuge in this man's open, honest affability. He quickly took Erwin's hand in both of his, and smiled at him, with truly relieved affection. Erwin bowed forward, and the same aura that had sickened Pfirsich sucked him in like a warm fleece comforter. He smiled right back.

"A wonderful turnout, *Herr Major,*" gulped Hitler. "Germany can be proud of such soldiers."

"Thank you, *mein Führer.*" said Erwin, grinning broadly, feeling so flattered he could have burst, confused by his own reaction. Not even the Kaiser had made him feel like this. How peculiar.

They saluted, shook hands, and saluted again. Then Hitler and his retinue and his big black car went away. And the band played, and the troops were marched away, and dismissed at the garrison barracks. And Pfirsich had to find a wall to lean up against.

Because if he hadn't, he would have been found out cold on his back on the damp cobblestones. He'd just realized why his stomach hurt. He couldn't stand that man.

"What's wrong with you?" said Erwin, propping him up. He was a fainter himself, because of his stomach, and could recognize the signs in his brother.

"I don't like him," said Pfirsich.

"Who? The *Führer?* Well, that was plainspoken. Why not?"

"I can't say," said Pfirsich, meaning it.

"You're picky, for a newborn junior nobody *Leutnant.* He was nice to you. He shook your hand special."

"Oh, I know he was perfectly pleasant, Erwin. He has manners. And a nice southern accent."

"He's an Austrian, of course he has a southern accent. He's taller than I thought he was." Erwin looked back over his shoulder, his eyes confused. "Good firm handshake. I didn't know he was so good-looking in person."

"Is he?" said Pfirsich.

"What, you didn't notice? I thought you of all people would notice."

"He looked average to me," said Pfirsich. "Short and plain. The moustache doesn't suit him."

"Half the people in Austria wear those English moustaches."

"Including the women?"

"What?"

"That's half the people --."

"Don't start your engineer statistics with me. Are you all right?"

"I don't know. I feel funny."

Pfirsich had never felt anything toward Hitler but the indifferent momentary notice of a face on a screen. The *Führer's* screen speeches were only tedious interruptions in an evening's film entertainment. They made the younger members of the audience restless and silly, too. Newsreels of the frolicking Hitler Youth and German *Bund* Maidens sent them absolutely goofy. Pfirsich had once even heard a teenage girl -- besotted with the sight of camping, marching, exercising and singing youngsters -- turn in the herd instinct of youth to her mother and breathlessly whisper, "Oh, Mama, if I weren't a Jew, I'd be a Nazi, too!"

Now Pfirsich knew more he wanted to find her and shake her. Then he realized that, the way things had been going, somebody else might have already given her all the shaking she could stand -- and her mother, too.

"You'd better go lie down," said Erwin.

"I think so."

"You look gray."

"I feel gray."

He'd heard that Hitler's personal presence could reach out and grab you, that it did things to you, made you hungry for his mere word, that its denial could put you on the edge of tears. Witness Erwin, who never noticed if a man were handsome, and certainly never mentioned if he were tall.

It had certainly done something to Pfirsich. Breathing the same air with the man, after receiving that insincere sneering smile and grasping that limp hand -- how could Erwin give the name of "firm" to that damp oyster, that failing paw? -- Pfirsich knew he had never in his life so immediately, and so corrosively, disliked another human being. It was like a dog taking a dislike to an odor, a purely bestial reaction, nothing human about it. It made him feel like an animal, and deeply ashamed of himself.

He made a mental note that in future that he would keep out of movie theatres. He didn't want to see any more newsreels. They were censoring everything, anyway. And what was the use of going to the movies if the Marx Brothers had been banned.

Bread and Swans

11. Ghost Division

Erwin Rommel became a best-selling author when his autobiography of the First World War, *Infanterie greift an* –- "Infantry On Attack," illustrated with his own naive but lively ink drawings -- went into multiple printings.

His reaction to his own success wasn't very soldierly, if acting like a soldier meant keeping one's emotions to oneself. When he opened the envelope from his publisher, the one with his very first royalties, he flushed with pleasure and showed Lucie. Lucie had her own money -- Lucie had her own diamonds -- and all Erwin really had was his army pay, but she could understand his delight, and watched him, smiling, as he toured around their living room admiring this amazing sumptuous check. When the next payment came, he held it to his breast and whistled.

By the time that third rich missive arrived in the post, he stared at it in pale dread. All these fat checks from a publisher -- the tax people were going to swallow him like a python and spit out his bones. Lucie told him not to worry, that he could afford it, but he was a Swabian and before a *Schwabe* would part with money, he'd part with blood. Even Pfirsich, deep in his own problems, heard his brother's distress.

"They're going to eat me alive," moaned Erwin.

"Oh, Erwin," said Pfirsich. "The solution's simple."

"What? Nothing illegal?"

"Erwin. There's an old author's trick – ah -- accounting process. Completely legal."

"What?"

"Just allow the publisher to keep the funds for you, and have them pay you in increments."

Erwin chewed his lip. "That doesn't sound right. Withholding funds?"

"Well, it wouldn't be like they were making interest on it."

"Where did you learn this -- process?"

141

"Friends in Berlin," snipped Pfirsich.

Erwin blushed. Pfirsich saw it and didn't respond.

That book did more than worry Erwin about his bank account. Former infantrymen recognized its authenticity, and one of those fellow footsloggers was Adolf Hitler.

* * * * *

The *Führer* had plans.

Adolf was the leader of a nation reborn. A deeply persistent man, he'd originally snuck up on society by appearing at parties as the Bohemian eccentric, complete with soft black hat, long black coat and hair, backpack and bright yellow shoes. Everybody thought he was entertaining and ridiculous – which is just how he wanted it. Once he'd found and appropriated the National Socialists, and come out in uniform, he took his political lumps. He had been jailed, and shot at, and lost three major elections before twisting the tally that put him into the Chancellor's office. Now he had his own private railway-car. It was called *Amerika,* and the train that drew it tore down the tracks like the 7th Cavalry, scattering all the other trains before it. A man possessing a train with ultimate switching authority could just as well have his pick of the talent of the country. He threw all the treaty restrictions out the window and began drafting plans, and men.

Hitler was a true son of a suspicious narrow-minded bickeirng farming family. He naturally didn't like rich folks or aristocrats, but he wanted their money and he knew how to bully or pet them or just plain suck up to them to get it. As an erstwhile foot soldier he had something in common with Pfirsich's friend, Peter; he hated officers, and nothing delighted him more than making Generals jump through hoops. He enjoyed watching them grit their teeth while they were doing it.

But it was one of that officer class who had written the book that had spoken directly to Hitler's heart and his own experiences in the war. Neither an aristocrat nor one of a martial family, but the son of a teacher, a plain poor man like himself, a man who had done his time as an enlisted man. Hitler didn't know it was the women who had the money in the Rommel family.

Hitler sent for this simple citizen officer. When he arrived, Hitler recognized him right away. Rommel was that very comforting man he'd met that day at the parade in Goslar, when -- Hitler shook himself. It didn't matter what else had happened at that parade. He liked Rommel, or the shorter Rommel, anyway. He knew he could trust the little officer. He didn't have to like his relatives.

The military that Rommel had helped re-build couldn't be trained and equipped and then just left in peace, stiffening uselessly in its stall. Veterans knew that War is Hell, but once they'd proven themselves in battle even the wisest of them couldn't help demanding the same vindication from the baby troops. The babies couldn't know any better. After the end of the Great War any books against war -- among them photographic records of horrific facial wounds, some of them the worse for the attempted surgical restorations -- had been censored as demoralizing. The greatest anti-war book of the generation had been banned as subversive and emasculating of the courage of the nation. *Im Westen Nichts Neues* had been translated into English as *All Quiet On The Western Front*. The title literally meant "In The West, Nothing New." It was proclaimed to be Bad For Morale.

Hitler re-wrote the oath the Army once took to its country so that instead it was upon his life and self, alone. As an Austrian, from a diplomatic country where words were just words, he knew what oaths meant to the Germans: they'd break their necks before they'd break a vow.

It had taken six busy years to completely wipe out what remained of Germany's stubborn obnoxious urge toward peace, and behind that, two decades of depression and undermining, of carrots and very big sticks. Hitler had been as patient as a comet with an oblique orbit and a toxic tail, constantly circling, retreating, returning, with planetary persistence. Germany was ready at last. She was blinded and deafened, harnessed and armored, terrorized and arrogant as a brutally-trained charger, and pawing the earth for war.

The first thing Hitler did was to try out his new *Luftwaffe* to help his brother dictator Franco in Spain. Bombing from airplanes, as far as he, and everybody who was designing warplanes was concerned, was a natural development. There was no use building an air force if it couldn't be used.

The *Luftwaffe* performed beautifully. The pilots of the Condor

Legion didn't even have proper uniforms, but they came home to medals and parades. The German media blared heroism and glory. It couldn't help it; the journalists had been drafted, and embedded in the military units. In the last century, when Europe had been scrambling for Africa, a bad murderous Governor in German East Africa had shocked the newspaper-reading German public. He'd gotten himself recalled under the weight of their indignation. But this wasn't the last century. Those who could parse out the code that might lie between the lines in the newspapers -- or at this point even wanted to -- had learned it was a lot safer not to talk about it. Not when almost everybody was waving flags and attending rallies. Not when the country was working again, and fed and proud and patriotic. And no one wanted to say anything that could undermine the morale of the soldiers in the field.

Even the people who knew better, knew better than to be seen defaming the flag. When you saw the thugs kicking in proscribed store windows and taking a dump on the goods, you remembered how a Proper German was supposed to act, and looked away, or down at your shoes, and kept your big mouth shut.

The Spanish artist Picasso painted *Guarnica* in grief and outrage at the bombing death of the Spanish town. But Picasso was listed as a Decadent Artist, and Good Germans weren't afforded the opportunity to see his work.

Now it was the Army's turn. When armies are big and strong and well funded, they don't lark around on their borders making faces to keep the Bad Guys out. It's not what they're for.

When the German Army ripped apart Czechoslovakia and handed a few of the bones to Poland, Poland was happy to have them. No other country really did anything but send verbal protests. With that, Germany decided that it was about time it took over its old kingships in the east. She didn't see how the East could possibly protest. After all, many of the old royal families in the Baltic states had been German.

"And where would the Poles be, without us?" everyone in the Reich agreed. Those Polacks wouldn't have a train service. Or be able to read and write. They'd still be out there in dirty smoky little huts and sheepskin jackets. They'd be cornered by the Russians. Everybody knew that.

Poland didn't put up much of a fuss over what that snippy

Germany bitch thought of her. She was happily settling down to carve up and administer the dismembered lands that she considered to have been rightfully handed back to her, and where in the past she had injected a few kings of her own. There were jewels to be had, cities and land and women and serfs, and war has always been how you got them. They didn't realize that Germany wasn't going to treat anybody else like conquered white people. Germany had been denied rich colonies among the colored nations of the world, and she was going to do to the white nations of Europe that which the white nations had spent centuries doing to everyone else. The great colonizers and enslavers were about to reap the whirlwind of their own works.

The Poles got knocked off their spoils by the cat that had shared with them in the first place. The English and French, who had promised the Poles they'd help them, came in snapping and barking. Germany whirled around like a panther and tore across France and smashed the English into the sea. The Soviets, under a separate peace, stood back, waiting as bears wait, for their chance. The beasts of war were abroad in the lands.

Adolf Hitler, who had expected the conquered to vanish or submit in scattered fragments like Red Indians, sat down open-mouthed on his desk in his ornate Chancellery. The foot soldier he used to be turned around with the scaffold memory of war in his eyes and spoke, deeply and genuinely shocked, to his staff.

"Oh, my God, what have we gotten ourselves into?"

Considering who was allied with whom -- he was going to have to change the name of his railroad car.

$$* * * * *$$

Pfirsich accompanied Erwin on the first campaign of the new war. Erwin was right on the front lines, as happy as a pig in hay. He had *carte blanche* for the invasion. Hitler drove up like a warrior king and asked him what he should do. Erwin was as delighted by his leader's presence as he had been the first day he had stood in it.

"The troops would be happy to see their *Führer* in the front lines," said Erwin.

The man with the moustache did exactly as had been suggested.

145

He drove right up and waved at the enemy. He turned around and smiled at his little officer.

"Block the road behind me," he said. "Let none of the entourage follow."

Pfirsich, sitting quietly and unobtrusively amongst the maps in Erwin's *Kübelwagen*, didn't even ask why Hitler might have decided to spite his own people; the man was full of odd quirks and sudden urges, and he always gave way to his inclinations, no matter how they appeared, or how they effected the people around him. Erwin didn't care; he was having so much fun he gleefully stood in the road and waved back Hitler's own cronies.

Pfirsich, still sitting in the car, put his face in his hands, because he knew by now how vindictive and easily insulted those people could be, especially against uppity army officers. But what good would it do him to protest? Hitler's most dangerous weapon wasn't his power to bully. It was his ability to sweet-talk people into doing whatever he wanted, to offer them tea and soft chairs and pastries and ask how the family was – whose birthdays and hobbies he'd learned for the day -- and Erwin was just the sort of fierce little pony that would fall for sugar. Hitler's Nazi cronies gunned their engine and threatened Erwin with their bumper. He reared back and brought up a boot and kicked it.

The Polish campaign was a nightmare. Pfirsich was reeling with disorientation and shock. He thought he remembered what a war was like, but he didn't remember war being like this. The civilians were supposed to be dead by misadventure, not by intent. Lines of refugees were supposed to die only by virtue of sharing the road with military vehicles, not to be deliberately targeted from the air for their own selves. If German tanks ran around a ridge, full-bore, into mounted Polish lancers, the only excuse they could have for the carnage of man- and horseflesh was that the collision was accidental. It was called a hopeless heroic charge of horse against machine, but it was really just a nasty, meaty screw-up.

Like so many of his brother officers, Pfirsich managed to find time to send in report upon report complaining of the obviously intentional brutality practiced, especially by the SS, against the civilian population. Thousands of these reports came in from the east, and were duly filed.

All that these accusations earned the Army was the vindication of the distrust felt toward the Army by the politicals in the government, and the deeper enmity of the SS. The SS took those reports very seriously. They would make sure that the Army wouldn't have any more opportunities for tattling on them.

During the SS free rape of the Polish capitol of Warsaw, German Army troops were forbidden to come within twenty miles of the city limits. The Army protested being denied a legitimate military objective. The SS ignored them. They wanted to pick and choose out of the best loot and housing in the city at their private leisure, and while they were at it, to dismember the Jewish ghetto.

Then the ghetto rose up and slapped the SS right in the face. When the SS yelled for help, the Army refused to leave their positions outside the city. As far as they were concerned, the Warsaw Jews could make *gefilte* fish out of the blackbacks. Then the Army sat back and let the SS get their butts chewed, while they pretended that they were Just Following Orders by not coming to the rescue. Everybody hoped the war would be over soon, at least before the Army and the SS started shooting at each other.

Erwin sent in a few reports of his own, and they seethed with indignation. Part of his protest was personal; Erwin's own dear Lucie's Polish uncle had disappeared during the first weeks of the invasion, and Erwin didn't make himself any more popular with the Nazis by writing rude demanding communiqués to the SS on behalf of his missing in-law. They answered curtly, if at all, pretending to an administrative mistake by addressing their replies to *"Oberst* Frommel."

When the attack on Poland had stabilized, Erwin took command of the 7th Light Panzer Division and dragged Pfirsich across France, pushing the tanks and softer military vehicles up to 100 miles a day. Commander Rommel was grinning like a jackass, and Acting Assistant Executive Officer Rommel was taking ginger pills for motion sickness. Pfirsich got tired of being ill and took over driving the command car, and that gave Erwin more time to stand up and hang onto the windshield and wave his arms and yell commands. Erwin kept smacking Pfirsich in the shoulder and demanding "Faster! Faster!" Pfirsich finally just put his head down and floored the *Kübelwagen*. Erwin didn't go over backwards into the back seat, but it wasn't because Pfirsich wasn't trying.

Pfirsich could drive when he wanted to, and he drove even better when he was angry. They tore into an abandoned village at 150 kph, and Erwin had to hit him hard in the shoulder to make him hit the brakes. The

147

village was full of people who stood and stared at them.

"I thought this village was abandoned," complained Pfirsich.

"Those aren't villagers!" said Erwin.

"Oh, Gott! Are those French troops?"

Erwin looked behind him. "Where are our men?"

"We're alone?" gasped Pfirsich. "We outran our own troops?"

"Turn it around!" yelled Erwin.

Pfirsich whirled the wheel around, flinging gravel, and as the *Kübelwagen* gained traction to fly out of the village, he could have sworn he heard the bolts slamming home in the rifles behind them.

"Go, go, go!" bawled Erwin, and they were heading back down the road, as fast as they'd driven in.

When they saw their own troops ahead of them, Pfirsich just shook his head. They were lucky he could wheel a car around as fast as he could. Otherwise they would both have been holding their hands over the backs of their necks while being searched for weapons. As ticklish as Pfirsich was, he didn't want to think about what Erwin's reaction would have been if he'd started giggling while he was being patted down.

The division drove on and on, day after day, outstripping the cutting edge of the front. Finally their own headquarters lost track of them and began to complain, "Where in God's name did that gang of ghosts go?" and nicknamed them The Ghost Division before they'd reached the sea. Pfirsich still kept an eye on the rear-view mirror to make sure he kept their tanks behind him, until at last he looked ahead and saw the distant waters of the English Channel before him.

Bogged down in a frantic train of refugees and retreating soldiers, Erwin stood up in the car, and at the top of his lungs gave a stubborn old-school French officer a decent chance to surrender.

Erwin's French wasn't any better than it had been in the last war, but he and the old man managed to recognize the convention that if one soldier didn't properly give up by the third request, then the other soldier could very properly shoot him.

"Very good," said the old man, and turned away.

"I am not a joke," said Erwin in bad French. "You are not stop, I do shoot."

"Put down that pistol, Erwin!" Pfirsich tried to snatch away the weapon.

The old officer kept walking, head in the air of the last century, back when an officer rode a horse and wouldn't be run over by a tank. Much less shot in the back. Erwin untangled Pfirsich's grasping fingers from the pistol, then hit him with his elbow and knocked him over headfirst into the back seat. Pfirsich's broad shoulders jammed in the narrow space behind the seat, and the only thing he could present was his wildly waving boots and a stream of muffled cursing.

"Cesser!" said Erwin to the old French officer, using the wrong word.

"Non!" said the officer, who knew what he meant anyway.

"You know -- three time, I shoot. I promise."

Erwin said it as evenly as if the two of them were planning a cross-country riding competition, and working out the rules. He chambered a round.

"Yes, three times, I realize," snapped the old man, over his shoulder, exasperated. "I'm a professional soldier, I don't need this explained to me."

"Stop," commanded Erwin, and took aim.

"No."

The old man turned around, presented his front, and saluted. Erwin switched the pistol to his other hand and returned the salute. And then he flipped back the pistol and shot him.

* * * * *

Pfirsich had managed to unjam himself from the back seat and now he had a protest fit, and Erwin looked at him like he was crazy, which he did look, rather, with his squashed cap down over one ear like that.

"What's wrong with you?" said Erwin, holstering his pistol.

"You shot him!" said Pfirsich.

"Of course I shot him. I told him three times I'd shoot him."

"You shot him!"

Erwin just held up his hands and desperately shook his head; there was no use trying to get his brother to understand an honorable man like the French officer. The French officer, if he'd lived, would have been just as frustrated with such a civilian attitude. Pfirsich straightened his cap with a snort, then put his hands over his eyes and bitterly spat.

149

They roared on until they ran down the hills and against the beaches, where Erwin was photographed with his good leather boots in the salt water of the English Channel. Pfirsich shuddered; as though Erwin could afford another pair of boots if Lucie didn't buy them for him, not boots like those, anyway. Pfirsich hoped, for Erwin's sake, that Lucie never saw the photograph. Then he got such a look on his face, and decided he'd find extra copies to send her. That would fix the little *Truthahn.*

Goebbels saw the photograph, instinct with natural drama, and it gave him an idea. As a good *Propagandaminister,* he knew that Erwin was an enthusiastic amateur photographer and asked him to direct a newsreel-film version of the invasion. Pfirsich was embarrassed; his brother might have been able to take very nice black-and-white photos of soldiers and barns and mares with their colts, but he was no von Stroheim.

Erwin used the French Zouaves who had been taken prisoner as actors, but as relieved as they were to still be alive, Director Rommel couldn't get them to stop grinning and waving at the camera and putting on wild Wagnerian death-scenes. It was a toss-up who was laughing harder, Erwin or the prisoners. Pfirsich shook his head; that was one newsreel that would never get distribution.

And then they were in Paris, marching in *mit Glockenklang und Paukenschlag* through Napoleon's triumphal arch. Erwin and the Ghost Division were all the rage in Paris. The German army, like all conquering armies, thought it could stage parties in a conquered city and expect all the local society to attend. And, such being human nature, its assumption was perfectly correct.

No *Parisianne* will express disdain by absence. The woman of Paris is a social warrior and does not refuse the challenge of the glove. She will not fail to show up in all her finery, and flaunt it to the enemy's face. And if there's a dance-band and champagne, she'll do it to him on the dance-floor, from eight inches away. Young German officers competed like stags for the chance to be sneered at. The ladies of Paris counted coup all over town.

Pfirsich would have enjoyed these parties if it were not for the oppressive tension, that only he seemed to be able to feel, or even acknowledge. He sipped a little glass of watered claret and looked around from under his brows. Regardless of their feelings, whether of arrogance or unease or defiance or guilt or giddiness, everybody else was dancing almost feverishly and gulping down the bubbly with a glass in each hand.

Except Erwin. Erwin wouldn't have been happy at these parties even if he had been welcome. He might have been a practiced dancer, but that was a peacetime accomplishment. Now that there was war, he wanted to be out in the field with his men and his tanks. But no career officer can ignore his social duties, and he dutifully fulfilled his, loitering discontentedly around the city's ballrooms, nursing a glass of claret, trying to focus on small-talk while his mind was out consolidating positions.

His absent stare must have been mistaken for receptiveness. A bold young officer leaned over and whispered to a bold young thing.

"See him?" he said, and pointed, trusting she'd understand. "That's the dashing General Rommel. He's too fast for you."

Here was German arrogance. Here was French pride. Here was a girl of the resistance without any. Wearing one of the flamboyant hats that the woman of France flaunted in defiance of the occupation, she set it, all high sky-blue cylinder and broad watered mauve bow, at the General. She sashayed up right in front of God and everybody, and brazenly propositioned Rommel.

"*Herr General,*" she purred, and reached right out and drew one red-lacquered fingernail ever so softly along his wrist, sending a thrill straight through his body, right down where she meant him to feel it.

Rommel froze at the sensation, locked between the response in his groin and the refusal in his brain; he couldn't jerk back, he had a half-full glass of red wine in that hand, and if it hadn't been for his military dignity he would have squeaked and run. Then his eyes kindled, he smiled, and he purred right back at her. He didn't even bother to hide his response from Pfirsich, who stood there watching this little performance with his mouth hanging open.

"Why, *Mahdmohzell,* how nize you ask," Erwin gleamed. "Wait -- *attendray* -- I go call the wife -- *mahn fehm* – she gives us permission. *Autorization,* eh?" He took the staring girl's hand and kissed it, and patted it. "We wait, she comes on th'train. I'm sure, she thinks you *charmand, Mahdmohzell. Ganz charmand.*"

The girl knew just enough German and Erwin's version of dog French to blush and gasp; a *ménage* was just that much beyond the limits of her sensibilities. She retreated so fast she spilled her champagne. Pfirsich elbowed Erwin, hard, and cut him off in mid-chortle.

"What'd you do that for?" demanded Erwin, rubbing his side. "That hurt! You had hard sharp elbows when we were boys, and they haven't gotten a bit softer."

"Lucie," huffed Pfirsich. "She's not here to defend herself."

"She does the same thing. Just exactly like that," said Erwin, looking injured.

"Lucie?" gasped Pfirsich. "Lucie does that?"

"How do you think she gets rid of suitors?"

"Suitors?"

"Before we were married. She taught the trick to me. She had to use it, in self-defense. They swarmed around her like hornets around a ripe pear." Erwin's eyes lit with yearning. "I should know -- I was one of the hornets."

Pfirsich snapped, "Did she ever offer to jump in bed with you and say, 'Bring a friend'?"

"No," said Erwin wistfully. "I desperately wanted her to."

"And bring a friend?" repeated Pfirsich.

"Oh, stop it," said Erwin, and shook himself. "You're purposely misunderstanding me."

"Damned if I ever have."

"You just don't know your sister-in-law," said Erwin. "Lucie is up to anything."

"Well, you've changed since you got married. No shyness left in you at all."

"I was never the ripe pear, before," Erwin grinned and raised an eyebrow toward one of the elegant silk-sheathed un-resistance girls. "It's kind of fun. If a man wanted to, he could be such a rat."

"But you won't."

Erwin held up a modest hand.

"Oh, please," protested Pfirsich. "Are you bragging? Look at you, you're bragging."

"Lu is a wonderful teacher. She's very talented and oh the brains on that woman."

"She fits right into this family, then. All talent and brains, and more tricks than a goat in a mint-patch."

"Yup," said Erwin, over the rim of his glass. "Lu and I are a team."

"Yes," said Pfirsich. "A demolition team."

He put down his claret glass on an 18th-century cherry-wood lamp-table, considerately setting it on his folded handkerchief, and covered his sensitive exposed wrists by crossing them in front of his crotch. Considering the predatory looks these cat-eyed girls were giving the boys in uniform, Pfirsich thought he'd best protect the mice.

What a hypocrite, he thought. Why have I bothered to protect the finish on that table, when I'm stomping around helping to occupy the place? Pfirsich had never been in a major city during a full-scale occupation, and the cynical spiritual squalor made him queasy. Maybe he owed the girls a try at his wrists. As for the war itself -- he was sick to his teeth of the war, and not for the usual reasons of danger and misery. Danger and misery he knew and could endure. He wanted a break in general from the military and its batty petulant hierarchies.

He requested home leave and he got it, and he took his wrists and his other areas of thin skin along with him.

Bread and Swans

12. New Wine

Pfirsich was sitting on a bench, his feet stretched out before him, his hands jammed in his pockets, his collar turned up around his ears and his shoulders hunched, his mouth sour and his eyes hidden by the visor of a cap tipped forward far out of regulation set.

"Erwin's going to kill me," he muttered.

The bleak little garden behind the cathedral of Notre Dame, with its severely pollarded dwarf trees, stood reflected in the puddles pooling on the over-walked naked earth. Everything was touched with that soft golden Parisian light, reflecting from the clouds even this late in the evening. Pfirsich always felt safe in this garden. Notre Dame is a magnificent monument to out-of-towners, but to the people in the neighborhood, it's just the local church. They go there to quietly pray and light candles to the modest stone saints standing sleepily in their own private niches and their own private shadows. It is always reassuringly, humanly, under repair.

A scaffold here and there threw narrow black shadows like mourning ribbons. Pfirsich pulled his chin down lower into his collar.

Paris was no good for him. Every time he'd come here, something wonderful had happened. He couldn't remember how glasses of wine he'd enjoyed there, when he'd been so overheated by one thing and another, even in the gold-and-gray glow of a Parisian winter. Like it just had his brother, the City of Light always went to his head. But never – never – had he visited it uniform before.

He had been granted the home leave he so badly felt he needed, or at least wanted. To say goodbye to one of his favorite cities, he stopped to have tea in a favorite little teashop on a narrow street around a corner from the Seine. He'd been having wine with it, too. A nice bottle, a peculiarly nice bottle, a *Chassagne-Montrachet*, presented with a flourish by a smiling old friend of a waiter, bought by a new friend. Just the red wine, not the well-known white. Left over, hidden over, from God knows where, or what celebration. An impossible bottle. What christening was it chosen for, in anticipation of a majority-day opening that never happened, because the child had died? Or disappeared? What tears had moistened its dust? Left on the shelf to be bought, just for him, for a foreign officer, for his new friend. Well, put on the tab, anyway -- a new tab, in a teashop peopled by desperately curious romantic gentlemen -- by a New. Good. Friend.

"My life is like a bad play," moaned Pfirsich. "A French bedroom farce." No. An English wrong-door comedy. He pressed one gray-gloved hand against his face.

"If God were a playwright, he could never get a showing. He is such a hack."

Pfirsich knew it wasn't important. The whole world was trying to kill each other, as it had since he could remember, since before he could remember, since long before he was born. That was what was really important. He was perfectly aware of the world's proper proportions.

It was love, again, as usual. Love wouldn't let him pay attention to the world, not full-force, like a man was supposed to be able to pay it. Love chased him around, up and down, all through his life, as though it were important. As though keeping someone hot and happy meant more than killing him. Love wouldn't get off his mind. It unbalanced and confused him. Even when the bullets were flying, Cupid took to wing. It was distracting.

Pfirsich thought of the first time he became aware of the man. Leaning against the shop by a street-side cafe in Paris. Not even a Parisian, but a foreigner like himself. A *Luftwaffe* officer, all taut and sleek in that brand-new cobalt-blue pilot's uniform, boots shining on those long slender legs. All the old armies had known how to make a man in uniform look good, back when soldiers had the right to strut for the girls, before they became drab identical industrial cannon fodder.

The Germans based their military look on the Russian and French cavalry units, and it showed. Rakish and sleek, it showed off the good parts of a man, the neck and wrists and the whole region around the pelvis. *Mann,* what riding boots did for a man's legs.

Pfirsich was a very cold and proper German Army *Hauptmann,* shy and unsocial because it was dangerous to have a social life, at least one like his. The German uniform could be very gray and strict, and Pfirsich's was as strict as he could make it. He was trying not to stand out, and he had

156

failed, quite prettily. A uniform makes a dull man look at least as good as the rest of the men, but it shows off a handsome man like a stallion. A plain gray uniform, with its conscious attempt at modesty, is a lady-killer.

In his attempt to fade into the background, all Pfirsich had managed to do was display his own attributes, his brilliant blue eyes under the black visor, his golden hair and long legs. Not to speak of what was about midway between. He'd sat down all that I'm-Hiding-What-I-Can't meekly in a cane-bottom chair at the cafe and was trying to look unobtrusive over a cup of hot tea.

Pfirsich had many friends in Paris, and hated invading them. The thought of meeting any of them while wearing that uniform made him blush with shame. It wasn't the way to greet your friends. It was decent of the other gentlemen patrons not to stare.

And then along came this man, this pilot. A pilot! A strutting, self-satisfied flyboy, all balls and bullets and brag. The only comfort Pfirsich could take was that he hadn't made the choice. The swaggering *Kriegsflieger,* his own visor cap low and oblique over one dark shining eye, had invaded his table at the teashop -- a table traditional with him since before this war -- as though he'd bought him. Pfirsich's indignation had done nothing to stop the man. Black-haired, black-browed. White teeth. Sharp teeth. That narrow French wolf-look that some Germans have. Painful. Pfirsich hurt sweetly in so many places, just remembering it.

The pilot didn't have a clue what a man like Pfirsich had to live with. He had glanced across the street and seen the shy handsome man oozing modesty and self-effacement, in that irresistible combination of good-looking masculinity and self-control, and he completely lost his head.

Verdammt und zugenäht. That was the most gorgeous hunk of either Adam or Eve that the pilot had ever seen in his life. The pilot liked the women, and the women liked him. To him a man was a comrade or a target, nothing more. Until the blond officer's looks reached right out and shot like hot fingers into the poor unsuspecting pilot's chest and into that part of the human heart that is born a happy free little omnisexual monkey, before it ever gets trained and strapped into a nice Manly cage. The cage fell open before the hot fingers as though it had been held together with thin wax, and the pilot's monkey, full grown with teeth and a pelvis, came hopping out with a joyful liberated shriek.

157

The pilot looked the *Hauptmann* up and down like he was a shop girl, and sat himself with a big stud flourish right down beside him. The *Hauptmann* nearly scalded himself with his tea. The other gentlemen forgot themselves and stared.

The pilot wore the shoulder straps of a mere *Leutnant*, but he assumed the masculine role right then and there. If nothing else marked him as a Man's Man who had been jerked off his straight rails by a crooked thunderbolt of sudden lust, he assumed right away that there had to be a masculine role, as opposed to his opposite's feminine role, and it of course belonged to him.

The pilot snapped his fingers for the waiter. He ordered the wine, in surprisingly good taste and appalling arrogance. He smirked at his conquest. He leered. The gentlemen gasped.

The pilot's name was Melvin. *Leutnant* Melvin Gonville.

"My Dad was English," he admitted to Pfirsich.

Pfirsich was shocked. "You're flying against your relatives?"

"Don't like 'em anyway," said Melvin. Pfirsich was horrified.

"Yorkshire," said Melvin. "All work and no play. 'From clogs t' clogs i'three generations.' Bombing 'em would just bring some excitement into their lives."

If he brought it into theirs the way he'd brought it into Pfirsich's, they were lost. Pfirsich's heart-cage was already open, but his own quietly-closeted monkey, for all its dignified strength and security, was scared nearly out of its wits when the pilot's big hairy heart-ape came and pounced on it in public. He hardly had time to squeak before he surrendered and let the monkeys out to play.

Afterwards -- ach, afterwards. After leaving the teashop, to the gentle cautious applause of the other gentlemen, Pfirsich and his newest conqueror went away to be alone. Even now, he blushed for shame, at the thought of the miserably cheap little hotel to which he'd been dragged. The squeaking wobbly narrow bed upon which the powerful young man had thrown him down. The things they did. The pleasure that was wrested from a protesting, a struggling, a sighing victim.

Had this creature in an unbuttoned shirt no shame of his own? No fear? No knowledge that what they had done could be a death-sentence?

Pfirsich didn't understand. Melvin treated him like a woman. Melvin obviously only knew about women, and not ladies, at that. He'd obviously never been with another man, not even as a young boy, when most men -- and many women -- make their experiments, whether they ever admit it to anyone, even themselves. Or perhaps he'd been with too many men, when he was too young. That happened, too. In either case, Melvin was curious, nostalgic or forgiving enough to reach out for it again. Grab for it again. With hot burrowing tongue and clasping greedy fingers.

Afterwards Melvin assumed that all Pfirsich wanted to hear about was him.

"I'm a pilot in this war," he bragged. "A dive-bomber! Not some clodding infantryman."

Not for him to have to learn to ignore the rain. To him the weather was what could ground him or allow him to him sweep off into the sky to hunt his country's enemies, blood relatives or not, and not what might fall on top of his leather flight-helmet. The only sort of wet that had ever gotten inside his cockpit had been his back crewman's blood and vomit, the man that a *Stuka* pilot referred to as his *Braut*. The word meant a woman on the eve of her marriage, and Melvin had always treated his *Braut* as a sacrificial virgin.

Melvin himself was the kind of pilot would come through this whole war without a scratch. In bed he bragged about joining his fellow pilots in happy brainless games. Kneeling up naked above his wide-eyed conquest, he illustrated wing-play with swooping hands.

"We swung our dive-bombers low, over them French and Belgian wagons, all piled high with hay. The wing-wash keeled 'em over like drunken whores!" Melvin slapped his thighs. "We flew off laughing ourselves into a twist. And my *Braut* complained that he'd get us reprimanded -- again -- and the wagon-drivers jumped up and down and shook their fists at the plane. Their horses and oxen just stood there, blinking in confusion. *Knorke!*"

Melvin was one of those scary magical people who never got hurt and never paid for their sins, invincible enough to produce the kind of envy that invented Hell. Other people can only hope the Wicked Unscatheables will get theirs in the next world.

Melvin had no experience with such inhibitions. He'd spent his life since he'd popped his first pubic hair trying to rub it up against the female equivalent. The last man to absent-mindedly lean across the sink in the barracks latrine too close to the mirror Melvin was using had been punched across the room into the hot radiator and branded for life. One look from Melvin, and the guy didn't report it.

Melvin was a lady's man. Or not a lady. He'd take what he could get. As he expressed it, if it had tits, he was going to be after it like a bombing target.

Pfirsich just looked down at his own chest and shook his head.

* * * * *

Pfirsich looked up at the stark mundane rear wall of the cathedral. He sighed and stood up, resolved.

Well, half the family had things to keep private. If certain independent brothers and sisters and cousins and wives had their cherished secrets — at least one of them running around in short pants and baby skirts -- then he was entitled to his own blackmail fodder.

The family would put up with just about anything. Erwin was just going to have to lump it.

In the meantime, Pfirsich was going home.

13. Coming To Harm

Pfirsich got off the train. He hadn't been authorized to leave it, but he was an officer, and could give himself orders. This was an internal German troop train, but the odors of war were beginning to seep into those of pre-war military cars: vomit, blood, feces, antiseptic and gangrene -- bearable on a field -- compacted on a train into an unbearable miasma. It would be at least an hour before the train would be properly coupled up to the new cars, and ready to move on. He could take his time. It was chill and damp, but he needed to walk and breathe.

He recognized the town; it was the little one-cow burg where he had taught school before he'd been drafted. It hadn't changed much; a place this small would always fall behind the march of history. Unlike so many German towns churning with a wartime economy, the town seemed empty. Most of the young men were probably in the military by now; it was the best guarantee of employment the country had to offer. Pfirsich walked quietly until he reached the town square, and took a turn around it, before his wristwatch told him he should start wandering back.

Ahead of him, in a street he had seldom walked unless on his way to the railway station or the library, Pfirsich saw a blocky man of about his age, wrestling with an unwieldy set of suitcases. The man wasn't helped by the file-papers he held clamped doggedly in his mouth.

Pfirsich hurried forward to lend him a helping hand, and as he approached, the man's hat fell off in the street, and Pfirsich exclaimed in recognition:

"Harm Schaffinder! Stop right there. Let me help you before you hurt yourself."

"Oh. Pfirsich," said Harm, looking up with a start, and mumbling through the papers. "Thank you."

Before doing anything else, Pfirsich first removed the papers from Harm's mouth, snapped them out flat as though they were blueprints, smoothed away the moisture left by teeth, folded them neatly, and filed them away into Harm's coat pocket. Then he began to vigorously brush Harm's coat, where the damp dirt picked up by the suitcases had bumped against the fabric. Harm retrieved his hat, and scrubbed it briskly.

Pfirsich knew how important appearances were to Harm, who despite being a top airplane mechanic during the war had still managed to keep his fatigues starched. He pulled out his own handkerchief, licked it like a careful mother, and began to scrub away at the bright yellow six-pointed star on Harm's coat.

"Hold still," he said. "Yellow shows stains so dreadfully."

"I never travel in yellow, for that very reason," said Harm, readjusting his hat, with the kind of care that the user hopes will control panic. "Never in anything but brown, even in the summer. You'd think they chose yellow for the stars just because it won't stay clean."

"I wouldn't put it past them," said Pfirsich. "Those people are so detail-minded."

Harm hesitated. "You shouldn't be seen with me, Pfirsich. Not a German officer."

Pfirsich stood straight up, eyes indignantly wide. "I'll associate with whom I please. If a German *Hauptmann* can defy the *Führer* and shake that Negro runner's hand at the Olympics, right in front of everybody, then a German *Hauptmann* can help you carry your suitcases."

"So carry already."

Harm bent over to take a firmer grip on the suitcases, and nearly knocked heads with Pfirsich, who had leaned forward to pick up one himself. After a little confused flurry of "Excuse me," they set off down the street, each carrying a heavy suitcase.

"What have you got in here?" said Pfirsich. "Flat-irons?"

"You never realize how much stuff you've accumulated, until you try to travel with it."

"Family visit?"

"Moving," said Harm wryly.

"Really? Oh, you'll have to give me your new address."

"It's orders," said Harm, and patted his suit-pocket. "I got them in the mail yesterday, for travel today. Talk about cutting it close."

"Your company is moving you? I swear, some of these big cartels have no consideration for their employees any more."

"No, not the company, the Government."

"Has your company been assimilated, too?"

"No, the orders say it's because I'm a Jew."

Pfirsich stepped back with his polished black boots, right into a puddle.

"That's what the orders say," said Harm.

"But where are They sending you?"

"Camps," said Harm, and pushed Pfirsich out of the puddle. The spots on the officer's boots offended Harm's innate neatness.

"A concentration camp?"

"Yup."

"They've started on you people now!"

When Pfirsich stamped this time, it was lucky he wasn't standing in the puddle. That was it. First it had been every freethinker and trade unionist and mouthy Catholic priest they could lay their hands on. The crippled -- mentally, physically, politically and what was considered sexually -- were next. Anyone with property who wouldn't voluntarily contribute to the good of the state disappeared as Enemies of that state. Even cabaret singers who sang the wrong songs went into Dachau and came out injured and terrorized.

"There's no one left who dares to protest, and everybody else has had the heart scared out of 'em," said Harm. "They can get away with whatever They want."

"Can't They!"

"As soon as I received my orders, I began to phone around to the family. It occurred to me that they must have received orders, too."

"What did they say?"

Harm's face fell. "Disconnected."

"What? Their phones?"

"Most of them," said Harm. "I could only get through to a couple of cousins, and they were too busy packing to talk. And screaming at the kids! I gave up; I didn't have much time, anyway. Everybody's going; I guess they all got the orders at the last minute."

Harm shook his head. "This is my own fault; I never kept in touch with the family, and I should have, at least for the gossip. You know what Jews are like; we keep whole files of gossip."

"Try being Swabian," sniffed Pfirsich. "There's nothing a Swabian doesn't know about his neighbors."

"It would have come in handy, this time I even had to look up their phone numbers," continued Harm. "I hadn't memorized a one of them. I had to find the notepad first, where I kept the numbers. It was in the kitchen cabinet, under the toast-rack!"

"Surprising where things get to," said Pfirsich.

"And then there was almost nobody on the other end, no matter who I called."

"Nobody?"

Family meant a lot to Pfirsich, and the hollow finality of the word stopped him in his tracks. Harm had really meant that the whole family had received orders.

"Well, the cousins, but they weren't any help. I finally got through to my eldest aunt. Would you believe, she's moving under orders, too? Well, I won't look forward to that. You've never traveled with my aunt, with those huge banging moldy steamer-trunks, and those ancient smelly lapdogs --."

"I need a cup of tea." Pfirsich nudged Harm. "You need a cup of tea."

"I'll get some on the train."

"Oh, please. Railway tea?"

Harm shuddered. "You frighten me."

"Come on," said Pfirsich, and led the way. "I know the schedule. The train's not due in for ever so long, and it's always late these days, anyway. No use standing in the damp and cold. You have time for a cup of tea with me, in a nice warm pastry-shop. While we're at it, we'll get you some decent sandwiches for the train."

They knew the modest shops that would serve anybody, townsfolk, visitors, merchants and trades people, Catholics or Jews, officers or controlled civilians, or people of their own painfully secretive kind.

They found one such place within a few blocks; it was Harm's favorite shop, right near the railway station. Pfirsich could remember after the last war, when the prices had been much steeper. It was a little self-serve cake-shop, and they bought their tea and pastry at the counter, ersatz rum-flavored tarts, not as chemical tasting as the lemon or raspberry. They added some fresh-made sandwiches to go, dropped the obligatory change into the ubiquitous Nazi Winter-Relief can, and settled themselves into a cozy back booth.

Before they sat down, they hung their coats, Harm's brown tweed and Pfirsich's army gray, on the use-polished brass hooks outside the booth, and Pfirsich remarked upon the yellow star that was sewn to the left breast of Harm's suit jacket.

"Now look at that, not just on your coat. Did they make you sew it on your underwear?"

"Not yet," said Harm. "Don't give them any ideas."

"They'll be tattooing it on you next," sniffed Pfirsich, sliding into the booth and getting comfortable.

"They're tattooing themselves."

"What?"

Harm sat down and put his right hand under his arm.

"Here; under the armpit. Their blood-group letter."

"No!"

"Yes!"

"How do you know that?"

"A friend of mine, in the SS -- well, he used to be my friend, before the star -- I saw the letter while we were swimming. He'd just gotten the tattoo, he wasn't supposed to be swimming, but it was so hot and sore." Harm held his left arm out sideways and flapped it stiffly. "It wasn't small, it was done in great big *Fraktur* letters, in dark purple ink. Arm swollen up like a *Bratwurst.*"

"Ow," moaned Pfirsich, and squirmed in sympathy.

"It was huge; it was a great big poisonous-looking Gothic thing. We went to the tavern that night and got drunk, and he got to moaning to me about what else he had to do to join the SS."

Harm took a sip of tea, then hunched forward, and Pfirsich hunched right back at him, gold-blond head against Harm's ash-blond. He recognized a star of gossip on the cusp when he saw it.

"They have to give semen-samples," snickered Harm, and leaned still closer. "Stark naked. *Under guard.*"

"Semen samples?" gasped Pfirsich. "Whatever for?"

"For -- for sperm counts," gurgled Harm, "To prove they're regular purebred stallions."

Pfirsich burst out giggling; he couldn't help it.

"Oh, no," gasped Pfirsich. "Oh, you're making this up!"

"I am not! I told you we were drunk; who lies when he's drunk?

We got to laughing our brains out over the idea. Then we began pouring beer down his shirt, to cool his armpit, until they threw us out."

Pfirsich put his hands over his eyes. It was too too grotesque. All those ebony-clad Black Pirates, strutting in massed thunderous magnificence in the newsreels. Each and every one of them had been required to shave one of his armpits and submit to the disfigurement of the tender pinky flesh, and then walk around with one swollen injured arm carried in crabby crippled misery away from the body, useless, and snappish until it healed. Each one of them, naked, quaking with embarrassment, had been required to shiver alone in a cold clinical examination room, desperately attempting to inject a sample of their manhood into a little hand-warmed specimen-glass, while a guard waited smirking at the door -- he must have been smirking, how could he help it?

Pfirsich tried to stifle his giggles. The woman at the counter looked up at the sound, and at the sight of a marked Jew and a German officer nose-to-nose, snickering their heads off over some private joke, turned around on her heel like a sensible woman who minded her own business.

"Aren't we a couple of cats?" tittered Harm, patting his friend firmly on the back; Pfirsich had started to choke.

"No wonder those people are so grim," gasped Pfirsich. "If that's the way they treat each other."

"It's their own fault." Harm sat back down and smoothed his napkin in his lap." Nobody makes them be so nasty."

"We shouldn't gossip. If there's one thing I learned during the last war, it's don't speak badly of the enemy. It's just asking for a night attack. Maybe that's it; it's the war done this to them; it's turned them mean."

Harm shook his head. "We were in the war, and we're not like that, and there are plenty of guys like us. This bunch didn't seem to have learned that any more than the people who stayed at home. They're as nasty as a postman rejected by the draft boards."

"There were more than limbs shattered in the war," said Pfirsich. "These people were shattered in their minds and hearts. If they were kinder to each other now, perhaps they'd be kinder to other people, too."

"Everywhere you look in this country, there are those red flags with the black crosses."

Pfirsich sipped his tea. "Well, I didn't vote for them, or their flags. I voted for Field Marshal Hindenburg."

"Then you voted for them."

"I didn't vote for *them,*" snorted Pfirsich. "Give me some credit. I voted against them three times before ever I voted for their ticket. No matter how many times they got voted down, they just kept coming back; you wonder where they were getting the finances."

"The big German companies," snapped Harm. "And their buddies, the English and American industrialists. So scared of the Reds, they paid for worse. Lousy cowards."

"Harm, now you sound like Them. I voted for the good old man. I didn't think Hindenburg was going to die in office so soon, or I wouldn't have voted for him. How was I to know that this Hitler person was as good as in the Old Man's will for the Chancellorship?"

"Most people I know never voted for them; most of my family didn't vote for them," said Harm.

"Most of your family? I didn't think any Jews voted for him."

"My uncle, of course. The Field Marshal was the closest thing to the old *Kaiser* that he could get. He's very loyal."

"Yes," nodded Pfirsich. "A very conservative old gentleman."

"And my half-sister. You know the one, I've told you about her. She'd be a Nazi in a moment if she got the chance, if Jews were allowed to be Nazis. But now it looks like she's got her chance; she's now officially not Jewish."

"Did she convert?"

"Better than that. Do you know about these new laws? The ones who say who is a Jew and who isn't?"

"I thought you were just born Jewish. Like being born German, or English. You don't get any choice."

"Well, not any more. Used to be, it was the Rabbi who said who was Jewish. Now it's the government playing Rabbi. They must think they're the Chosen People."

"Master Race," corrected Pfirsich.

Harm rolled up his eyes. "Get this; because my sister's mother was a Christian, she's officially no more a Jew than you are. And because my mother's a Jew, I'm a Jew! Now how does that work? Do Christian women's wombs have Holy Water in them? Does the Jewish sperm get baptized? You explain this to me."

Pfirsich put up his hands. *"Bitte.* I don't pretend to know how those people think."

"Well, now that she's officially -- what's it called? 'Aryan?' -- do you know what she did? Sent out little cards announcing it, on cream-colored deckle paper, with those little hooked crosses embossed into the corners! *Gott,* my family can be so tacky! But she comes by it honestly; I've seen Jews parading around with these yellow stars like they're proud of them. Family!"

"Family?" Pfirsich made a face. "Don't get me started. One of my younger brothers thinks he's an opera-singer. He sings in public. For money."

"Please; your family couldn't do table-service to mine for nuttiness."

"My oldest brother thinks he can play the violin. He'll do it in public, too, even where other officers can see him. It's a punishment, it must be. The Rommels are born stone tone-deaf, and refuse to admit it."

"At least your family isn't snobs."

"I beg to differ," snorted Pfirsich.

"They're school-teachers."

"Then you don't know the breed. Their snobbery is all book-snootiness. They judge you by what you know, or what you can recite. And my mother --." Pfirsich threw up his head and made a monocle around one eye with a thumb and forefinger. "Is a *von* Luz. With her own money. Need I say more?"

Harm wouldn't hear of it. "My half-sister, she's the worst, churched Mama or not. She finally found a way to look down on the rest of the family, and hasn't she just!"

"Did you call her, too?"

"Oh!" spat Harm. "Her? Why would she be home when she could be out parading someplace? Catch her being the proper Aryan wife-and-mother, Children, Church and in the Kitchen. I'm glad we lost her."

"She's still your sister."

"Not according to her, she isn't. Especially not to me. I didn't need her to tell me she'd warned me about what would happen to me. If she'd said 'I told you so,' in that way she does, I'd be on a train, yes, but to go strangle her."

"But she might have known something."

"What could she know? The rest of the family didn't speak to her either."

"Maybe they should have tried," said Pfirsich.

"That wasn't my business. The family hardly speaks to me." Harm's eyebrow went up. "You know why. Does your family speak to you?"

Pfirsich looked down at his pastry. "The women do; you can't keep anything from them. But we don't talk about it."

He didn't add that his brother knew, and wished Harm wouldn't talk about it.

"There! Well, I tell you one thing, Pfirsich," Harm looked over his shoulder. "If they are splitting us up into groups, I admit I'd rather go away under orders as a Jew, than as -- well, one of our kind."

Pfirsich made a face. "I've heard. They don't like us any better than our own people do."

"They might as well be my own Orthodox relatives. I wouldn't want either group to find out about you and me, Pfirsich. If I've got to be part of an identified group, then better a yellow star than a pink triangle."

"A what?" It took a few moments for Pfirsich to get it. "A pink --? You mean, like the star, but --."

"Pink, yes."

"For 'our kind'?" demanded Pfirsich. "No, you are joking."

"No, I'm not." Harm held up his hand in oath. "Where have you been?"

"In the army," Pfirsich said dryly. "Pink triangles." He shook his head and demanded, "Who makes up these things?"

"The insignia mania," said Harm. "I'll tell you right now that no virgin pilot with his first kill was ever so crazy about signs and symbols as this bunch. And who made up 'Nazi" out of *Nationalsozilistiche deutsche Arbeiterspartei?* It should have been 'NadA --."

"Perfect. 'Nothing' in Spanish."

"And in Hebrew? The Hebrew word for 'German Jew' is 'Aske-*nazi*-m'." Surely somebody was conscious of that."

"Isn't that stretching it a bit, Harm?"

"I think they should just call themselves National Shitheads and be done with it."

Pfirsich looked down at his cup. "Harm, where do you think

they're sending you?"

"I told you. Ever since they declared the National Emergency, they usually send people to the camps."

"But Jews – aren't they going to Palestine?"

"Oh, you've heard that rumor?"

"That's an old one," said Pfirsich. "The Jews have wanted to go to Palestine since the last century. I thought the government was talking about sending them there."

"That's the Zionists," said Harm.

"Well, there are Jews who want to leave the country, and the Zionists are helping them."

"Not this Jew," moaned Harm. "Please, no; I hate the heat. I despised the family's summer vacations in Italy; I'd get heat-rash every year."

"You don't like Italy? Germans love Italy. 'Wo die Zitronen blühn.' "

"Not me. I like Germany. All green and cool, with rain and good home cooking. Sweet white wine. Italy -- all that olive oil! That acid red wine. What do they cook with in Palestine? Palm oil, isn't it?" Harm shuddered. "I need my good sweet butter. I was happy to come home after we left Flanders, back to my own country; they cook like the French in Belgium. All sauce and chopped things. Try to get a good potato dumpling on the other side of the border."

"Last time I was there, it was the only place you could get something to eat."

"Not now," said Harm. "We have jobs, we can buy anything we want; most people are treating this war like Old Romans on a holiday, pillaging Gaul and lining up for the Triumphs."

"Too true," sighed Pfirsich.

"I don't want to leave, just when things are really good. I want to stay in the fatherland -- I'd fight for my country if they'd let me -- not end up in some desert that nobody's lived in since the days of the Pharaohs. We don't live there any more. We live here! Gott, Pfirsich --." Harm dug his fingers into his ash-blond hair. "I don't want to live with camels, under a blistering sun, subsisting on dates and fried mutton. I'm a civilized man, Pfirsich, a modern normal German, not some miserable primitive African Blackman!"

Pfirsich reached out and took his hand. "They won't send you to

Palestine. The National Emergency can't last forever. When everything has settled down -- when things are better, and back to normal -- you'll come home."

"*Ja,* but when?"

"The camps can't be that bad," Pfirsich said reassuringly. "You've seen the magazine articles. Compare them to those terrible places the British ran during the Boer war."

"I know, I know," said Harm. "Internment camps can't be any worse than the barracks we lived in during the war. It won't kill me."

"They can't keep you forever," said Pfirsich. "They'd have to feed you forever."

Harm brightened. "That's true. They'd be stuck playing jailers forever. And where's the profit in that?"

Pfirsich rolled his eyes. "And have you ever seen them do anything that wasn't profitable?"

"They want to be the Roman army, and they're nothing but cloth-dealers," sniffed Harm. "I've never met such a bunch of mean cheap bureaucrats in my life. Scratch any one of them, and there's a petty shop man underneath. They wouldn't pay for a dance, if it cost a bad penny. All those marches and movies, and now this war -- you know we're the ones paying for all that, with our taxes. Soldiers don't come cheap."

"Not today's soldiers," said Pfirsich. "All we had in the last war were our backpacks and our rifles. This gang likes toys; everybody's got the latest equipment. Tanks, airplanes, motorcycles by the battalion. Everywhere you go, you have to stop for military or a land-service convoy. And look how they're using the air force."

"Anybody who defies them can expect a bomb on their capitol city," said Harm.

"I wonder how the country can pay for it all."

"Well, let's hope they get their war over with pretty soon. If I can't fight in it, I don't want to sit it out for long."

Pfirsich looked at his watch. "We'd better get going."

The two men returned to the counter to pick up their sandwiches and pay their bill. The woman at the counter was very polite, as though they were just two damp over-coated men, instead of a Jew and an officer in public congress. No reason to be more than unusually pleasant to them, no reason at all.

171

"Well, she was certainly nice," said Harm, when they'd left the shop.

"The owner probably instructed her to be nice to all the customers," said Pfirsich. "There are some people these days who are still just trying to stay out of it. You know what happens if you don't keep to yourself. You go away and you come back with a limp. Even the people who used to speak up are terrified, when they see the people who have been Re-educated."

"Nobody will be able to stay out of it," said Harm. "Even with everybody else making a little Visit Out Of Town, I still thought I could be an exception, and look how wrong I was."

"It's not Russia," said Pfirsich. "We don't have Cossacks in the streets."

"We might as well have," said Harm. "We had a revolution in this country, too. And if we didn't have Cossacks, we're inventing our own kind, as fast as we can."

* * * * *

At the railway station Pfirsich discovered that his own military train had been shunted onto a side track.

"Odd," he said. "Military trains usually get priority."

"Maybe there's a bigger military train coming," said Harm.

They found the platform full of people standing patiently in a knot exchanging body-warmth around their own little stacks of suitcases and baskets and parcels of food. Some of them wore the yellow star, some of them didn't. There were a number of children, some with the stars. A few of the townspeople exchanged smiles and nods with Pfirsich, whom they recognized from his time teaching their smaller children. A couple of the men shook hands and said he made a fine-looking officer. He smiled tightly, and stood aside with Harm.

"Look at that," said Harm. "That must be all the Jews in town. I didn't know there were even that many."

"Neither did I. I only knew about our kind of people," said Pfirsich.

"You only ever do," agreed Harm. "That will show you which I've been closer to, in the last years."

"Well, our kind of people tends to stay together. Sometimes it's the only society they can enjoy, and be themselves in."

"That sounds so sad, now," said Harm.

"Everybody's like that, when you come to look at it," said Pfirsich. "We've no reason to complain, not really."

"I guess so," said Harm. "It can't be so bad. I guess you're right, Pfirsich. It's just for a few months, or until things get better."

Pfirsich didn't answer. He was frowning, watching the train that was pulling into the station. Right schedule. Wrong train.

It was a small station, appropriate for a small town, and the train was pulling the usual three cars. The people began to nudge their suitcases into neater stacks, patting pockets and poking into purses. Everybody was looking for their identification papers, whether they wore stars or not. No travel these days without the proper papers.

As the train pulled up, Pfirsich took off his peaked cap to scratch his head.

"It's not your train, Harm. It's boxcars."

"Stopping here?"

"They'll switch into the side-spur with my train," said Pfirsich. "They'll have to, if they want to let the passenger train through on time."

"They don't seem to be backing anywhere," said Harm.

"Then they'll have to hold up the passenger train."

"Great. We could have stopped and had another cup of tea, if they're going to get this far behind in the schedule."

Pfirsich was so busy watching he forgot to replace his cap. As the train halted, a soldier stood in the cab, clipboard in hand.

"Jews?" he said.

The crowd wondered what he meant. They were all annoyed that their own passenger train was late. Everybody was muttering.

"All the Jews get on board," he said.

Pfirsich, who was taller than Harm, was peering over the crowd into an open boxcar. He'd still forgotten to put on his cap.

"It's a horse car," he said. "Like they put us into during the last war."

"What?" said Harm. "I'm not a soldier, any more. Do they expect us to ride on straw?"

"It looks like it," said Pfirsich.

173

"In this suit? I didn't mind it when I was in uniform, with a backpack and boots. But in a nice coat? And suitcases? *Ich bitte!*"

"Hey! You!" barked the soldier, and pointed right at Harm. "What's your problem? Get over here."

"Watch your mouth, *Knabe!*" retorted Harm. "Who do you think you are?"

Pfirsich winced. He hated playing soldier, and wished Harm wouldn't do it.

"I'm the guy in charge of making sure you people get on these boxcars," retorted the soldier. "God help me, I don't know how I got stuck with this job."

"We're supposed to get into boxcars?" said one of the women in the crowd. She was a flat- faced, hard-mouthed woman who looked like she didn't put up with much. Certainly nothing from lone young soldiers who showed up out of nowhere without her comfortable accustomed local train.

"*Nein, gnädige Dame,*" said the soldier. "Just the Jews."

"Since when do people ride in boxcars? Especially children?" The hard woman pointed accusingly at the straw. "Do you expect children to ride in boxcars?"

"They could have told us we'd need blankets," complained a starred woman. "I wouldn't complain, if we had blankets. Tschah!"

"Those are my orders," said the soldier. "Don't argue with me. Do you want this to get ugly?"

"Who's going to make it ugly?" snapped the hard woman. "You? Young man, I was a nurse in the last war. I've seen uglier than you can get."

A younger man wearing a star touched her on the arm. "Please; I don't think it's going to do any good to argue."

"Young man, I'll argue how I please!" asserted, the woman, clutching her pocket book as though she meant to swing it.

"Get those *ITZIGS* on the train! We don't want the likes of them polluting our town any more!"

Everybody froze. It had been a young voice; much too young to be talking about grown-ups and little children like that. Everyone wheeled slowly around, to find, standing at their backs, hands on his hips, one small, stiff skinny kid, dressed in the Boy Scout uniform of the Hitler

Youth. There was another Hitler Youth with him, a little older, with a hand over his mouth and his eyes wide. As a former schoolmaster, Pfirsich felt his hackles go up.

"That's right!" squeaked the skinny kid. "Let's get this town Jew-free! Let's show the rest of Germany who's going to --."

He didn't get a chance to finish his sentence. A crooked liver-spotted old hand caught him right across the mouth and knocked him flat on his back into the wet street. The older kid jumped back, and took off his cap. The skinny kid stared up to find glowering down at him -- his own grandfather.

"*Opa!*" he gasped.

"What have I told you?" snarled the old man. "If your parents aren't going to teach you respect, then I will!"

He took a kick at the boy, who didn't stay to argue; he took off down the street as fast as he could move. A silent glare of approval for the treatment he'd earned followed after him. The older kid bowed, once, embarrassed, murmuring apologies, then ran after his companion.

"Brat!" snapped the old man. "That's where the kids are going these days. And his parents are no better. Kids didn't talk about grown-ups like that when I was young. The whole younger generation is going straight to hell!"

Pfirsich nodded. Such a rude boy.

"So are the Jews gonna get on the train?" moaned the soldier. "We got a schedule to keep!"

Somebody threw a pebble at him. "Don't talk to us about schedules! Get your damn troop train out of the way!

The soldier wiped his forehead. He'd been stuck with the full responsibility for all three cars, and collecting up the people who were supposed to be on it, and if it was always going to be this difficult, at every single town along the line, he wanted out of the job. He waved his clipboard at the crowd. See? He had a list. That meant he had everybody's names.

He shouted, "We can't move it until the Jews get on board!"

"Are you the only soldier on board?" said one of the Jews, in a tone that made it obvious he'd been an officer in the last war.

"*Ja, mein Herr,*" said the soldier, before he could think.

"There's just you?"

175

"Yes, just me," said the soldier, and then appealed to the crowd. "Me, three boxcars, an engine and a list. For three towns!"

The crowd chuckled knowingly. *Mann,* didn't that sound like the government. Five hundred men for a newsreel parade, and one man sent off to do real duty. Did they even issue the poor *Macker* ration cards for the trip?

"Rotten detail," sympathized another man, no star, in a tone that made it obvious he had not been an officer in the last war. "They sent us out in threes to collect horses, in France. You should file a report of complaint."

"I'll complain," snapped the soldier. "You can bet I will, but they'll complain right back to me if I don't get this job done. Now all you Jews get on this train!"

"What if they don't?" demanded Pfirsich, and in that moment he remembered to put on his cap, and saw the soldier flinch as he realized he'd been completely ignoring an officer.

"Excuse me, *mein Herr,*" exclaimed the soldier, and saluted. "I'm sorry, I didn't see you."

"What are you doing here?" demanded Pfirsich, saluting in return. This officer business could come in handy.

The soldier, craning his neck, spotted the *Hauptmann's* bars on Pfirsich's shoulders. Ah -- not a very big bug after all.

"Orders, *mein Herr,*" explained the soldier, and held up the clipboard.

"Let me see them," said Pfirsich, and held out his hand.

The soldier hesitated. This small-town crowd didn't know him, didn't like him, and they certainly didn't like his business among them. They seemed to know the *Hauptmann.*

The mathematics teacher they had all liked was now a proper German officer, and while *Herr* Rommel had always had an odd high-class version of a Swabian lisp, he had more right to open his mouth around here than some pushy stranger of a soldier who wasn't even assigned to the local garrison.

Pfirsich took a breath for another remark, when Harm punched him in the ribs. Everybody saw that peaked cap switch 'round and duck down to the man beside it; the soldier, who had been reaching the clipboard out toward the officer's hand, snatched it back to his bosom.

"What are you trying to start?" demanded Harm.

"You don't want to get on that train," hissed Pfirsich. "Look at it!"

"It's no worse than when we both rode as soldiers, and I don't want any trouble."

"You don't – "

"No trouble. And you know *why*. Just shut up."

"Harm."

"I'm coming back. We all are! Now shut the hell up."

Harm straightened his hat on his head, picked up his suitcases, and walked right up to the growling soldier.

"Hey!" he said, and dropped the suitcases. "You want to see my papers or not?"

"Thank God somebody's going to be reasonable," said the soldier, pointedly not looking at The Officer. He jumped down from the cab and took the papers that Harm held out to him.

That was all it took. One man who knew what he was doing, who knew who was taking the paperwork, and where to go. The official Germans stepped back, and let the official Jews go forward. Everybody would get on the right train, and get where they were supposed to be going, on time. The soldier moved down the train, taking papers, as the boxcars filled up. The old man with the liver spots on his hands shook hands with another old man, who was wearing a star, and helped him lift his suitcases into the train.

Pfirsich had followed Harm, and as the soldier returned his friend's papers, he waited while he folded them and put them back into his pocket. Then he helped him throw his suitcases on board. The soldier made a point of ignoring them both; he didn't want to see it.

"C'mon, c'mon," said the soldier to the people boarding, sharply tapping his watch. "We're late."

"You're already late," Pfirsich corrected him, his hand on Harm's arm.

"Jawohl, mein Herr," said the soldier, and looked away from them both.

Then Pfirsich put his arms around Harm, and hugged him. The soldier absolutely closed his eyes to them, and got busy with the other people. The tall blond officer was right, thought the soldier; they were already late. To hell with giving himself a stomachache about it. If they got in late he could just shrug and blame the engineer. And the engineer could blame the weather. Or cattle on the tracks. Or a military convoy, taking precedence over everybody and everything else. And he could always blame a tall busybody *Hautpmann,* if nothing else. The soldier shrugged; he was Flemish on his mother's side. He didn't care.

Harm at last withdrew from Pfirsich's embrace.

"You don't want to make trouble, Harm?" whispered Pfirsich.

"I'll be back, Pfirsich. But not if I go to the wrong place, with the wrong people."

He rubbed Pfirsich's shoulder, then turned and jumped up into the boxcar, the last Jew of this town to board, and made himself as comfortable as possible in the straw. Then he leaned out and said to his friend:

"You won't be able to stay out of it, Pfirsich. It will come and get you, too. So just wait, and be prepared."

Harm threw a hank of the straw back out at him, just before the soldier closed the door, and said, much to the soldier's shock:

"Tell 'em you're Jewish! Maybe they'll give us a hut together!"

The soldier was happier than hell; everybody on the list had been in the station, nobody would pressure him about the missing bodies, and he could get away from this officer. He made sure the boxcar doors were all secured, then gave a little delighted hop and ran up to the engine cab. He jumped up and signaled to the engineer, saluting the officer as the train lurched forward, just in case. Pfirsich numbly saluted back. The passenger train was just coming down the track. The liver-spotted old man sniffed, and growled.

"It would have been late, anyway."

Most of the crowd got on board the second train, and the train pulled out, slightly behind schedule. Then what was left of the people gave a collective shiver, turned around and walked back into town. All the good-byes had been said, and it was cold and damp. There was nobody left but the ticket-clerk, and he put up the sign that said "Out To Lunch." Then he left, because he didn't live far, and could get hot food at home, which was more comforting on a cold damp day. The station was nearly empty. It began to rain.

The troop train lurched back into motion and rumbledback onto the main line, halting for final preparations before leaving the station. Before it stood one lone officer, staring as though he couldn't see the train or anything else, his hands hanging regulation alongside his pockets, his eyes on the ground, the rain on his shoulders and the straw on his tall peaked cap.

Bread and Swans

14. New Ground

When Rommel received his latest orders, he wrote to Lucie, *"I'm finally going to get that rheumatism cure!"* And she knew what he meant.

No one else could know that his doctor had told him that he could only cure his rheumatism if he went to Africa, other than the doctor himself, and he wouldn't have been reading Rommel's private mail.

* * * * *

With his brand-new state-of-the-art camera held in focus with one hand, and a cup of fresh hot tea with lemon in the other, he was just asking for a scalded mouth. And when he took a thoughtless hasty suck at the cup brim, that's just what he got.

"Oh, no, Erwin, don't spit!"

General Erwin Rommel wasn't listening; he was sputtering hot tea all over his boots and the sand under them. Burnt pink mouth stretched wide open, he stood blowing until the pain went away. He ignored the spots on his tropical uniform, spots quickly sucked up by the hot North African sun; he was busy burnishing the tea off his gleaming black camera. It was a genuine *Leica,* and he prized it like his mother's heirloom diamonds. He squinted into its viewfinder, his stubby little fingers wrapped stiffly around its polished black-plastic edges, holding it exactly as he would a pair of field glasses.

His exasperated brother, barely contriving to sit at his ease in an uncomfortable camp chair while tending a tea service on a camp table, frowned up at him.

"Can't you even sit yourself down to drink your tea?"

"Just pour me another cup, Pfirsich," said Rommel.

To everybody who ever saw a newsreel, he wasn't "General Rommel" any more. He was simply *Rommel,* the sharp-faced little terror of the sands, who didn't have any use for the rules. He buried Germany's

181

deadly accurate .88 anti-aircraft gun in pits deep enough to change them into anti-tank weapons, and the British squalled "No fair!" He pounced out of nowhere upon the enemy, until they shouted with pain and admiration, and "doing a Rommel" became their highest praise. He didn't care how his soldiers looked, so long as they kept their chins smooth, and could shoot straight. Only his family still called him "Erwin."

Pfirsich had always suspected that Erwin's own outspokenness about the treatment of civilians in Poland had contributed to getting him dumped out here in the desert. Rommel might have been The Desert Fox in all the English newspapers, but he hadn't forgotten the insults at the hands of the SS. Lucie certainly hadn't forgotten her uncle. It probably hadn't slipped the minds of the SS, either; their grudges were as black as their parade uniforms.

Just now Rommel was too deeply preoccupied with his new toy to think of all that. He was so fascinated by photography that whenever he saw people with cameras, he turned and walked straight toward them, just to see what sort of lenses they might have, and perhaps to be allowed to look through the viewfinder, just once. He didn't mind posing for photos, either; he happily indulged in the early twentieth-century's fascination with the little black box, smiling with as much unabashed foolish delight as any young soldier waving "Hi, mom!" His enemies never guessed that an assassin with the newest Kodak could have used the offer of a snapshot to drop him like a stag.

"Don't gulp you tea," said Pfirsich. "You know how touchy your stomach is. You'll give yourself hiccups."

Rommel indulged young people, especially young soldiers, but this was his brother. He snorted at him. Pfirsich just sat and looked impeccable.

Pfirsich liked the desert. He didn't like Melvin not being here, but there were ways of getting the right transfer papers. There were plenty of other pilots; one more would fit right in. The desert seemed to have given Pfirsich a personal freedom he would never have thought of exercising back home. He could imagine what Melvin would do with it.

The Irish and the Germans share a weather oppression. If an Irishman escaping from his dreary home island bubbles over in a champagne-froth of poetry, the German blooms like a tropical flower in the heat. The introspective Teuton comes out in bright colors and big grins against deep red-brown suntans.

The newsreels of the desert troops showed their teeth flashing white against their darkened skins. They were satisfied to burn, and delighted to be running around wearing little more than a cap and their desert boots -- and sometimes nothing else, at most putting on a jacket as the evening turned cool. They seemed to be made happy by the bright light, less desperate and depressed. They took off all their clothes, and all their envy, and they shared. They gave water to their enemies. They dared things. They got away with things. They stole things, sometimes all together as battalions, happy as Cherokee boys sneaking up on the pony herd. They thumbed their noses at the camera and at their officers, if they deserved it, and worshiped their heroes. German blood under the sun of Texas had fermented into Cowboys. In Africa it became the *Afrika Korps*.

Pfirsich was having such fun being a clotheshorse. His boots shone softly in the sun, not from shoe-crème, but from his orderly's loving and diligent rubbing. He never yelled at his orderly, and it showed; the personally dirty little man, a Corporal Udo Schmidt, would have crawled on broken glass -- and then through sugar and gasoline -- if Pfirsich had asked him to. And Pfirsich would never have done more than simply ask him. That's how hungry Udo was for simple politeness and kindness. Udo's own blossoming grew out of a background in the sort of German/Jewish family -- all legal Germans now -- that equated cleanliness with points with God. He had been so sick and tired of the constant washdays and seasonal cleanings at home that he had bloomed out under the sun into a mess of dirty, shaggy hair and unshaven chin. Pfirsich politely kept upwind of him, and let him go his sloppy contented way.

Pfirsich put down his own teacup. "Ever since *Propagandaminister* Goebbels gave you that camera, you've thought of nothing but F-stops."

"Joseph was just being nice," crooned Rommel.

"He's trying to make up to you," sniffed Pfirsich. He'd had a closer look at Joseph Goebbels since that day in the hotel. Joseph could smile at him all he wanted, and Pfirsich wasn't falling for it any more. He could keep his tea-pastries and his phony smile to himself. And his limp, wherever it came from.

"The whole Berlin gang is envious of you," Pfirsich added.

Rommel, focusing on a hawk on the horizon, completely forgot his tea cup. He let it fall onto the table, and the hot tea spattered right at the lap of Pfirsich's elegant breeches. Pfirsich was on his feet, neatly up out of the way of all but a few drops, and glared down at Rommel, this time from his full height.

"You could have burnt me! You did that on purpose."

Rommel never looked away from the viewfinder. "Pfui, Pfirsich, I'd never burn my own brother. Mama would come back after me with a wooden spoon."

Pfirsich gulped. Their mother's funeral had been so recent, within the last year. He distracted himself, dabbing away at the tea-drops with the end of his scarf. The brothers shared a taste for unmilitary neck scarves -- Erwin a plain wool brown plaid, Pfirsich's a length of pure strong peach-colored silk. Erwin's was tucked firmly into the breast of his tunic; Pfirsich's floated on the hot desert breeze. The scarf and Pfirsich's ornate schooled gestures – which had become downright theatrical in the desert -- irritated the hell out of his brother.

"*Pfirsich, bitte.* We may be half a continent away from Germany, but do us all a favor and moderate that effeminate style of yours."

"*Ich bitte,* Erwin. 'Effeminate.' Examine the word. It is an insult to both the sexes."

"Na, when applied to you --."

"There's nothing wrong with me. There is a long military tradition of the elegant officer. There was a time when it was perfectly proper to describe a gentleman of a certain high reserve as 'ladylike.' "

"'Ladylike,' "snorted Erwin, packing away his camera in its leather case. If tea were going to be thrown about now, it didn't need to get into the lens. "You're certainly ladylike, I'll give you that."

"The English called men of exquisite taste and class 'dandies,' or 'cavaliers.'"

"Or *fops.*"

"You have other 'fops,' as you call them, in your army, and you never say a thing against them. As long as they do their duty, and are as brave as you require -- and shave -- you never breathe a word."

"Whatever you want to say about them, they're men. They're not my brothers."

"Brother," corrected Pfirsich. "Unless you mean Karl."

"Karl is discreet," said Rommel. "Karl is quiet and respectable. I

184

never worry about Karl."

"Karl is very ill," said Pfirsich. "Africa ruined him."

"Karl isn't shocking."

"*Oh, bitte.* You used up all your shock on me. If you'd discovered Karl first -- oh, dear." Pfirsich pressed his fingers to his mouth. "It's just as well I was your first victim. All that panic and vapouring. Thank you at least for the respect you have for my fortitude."

"I just wish you'd show it, in the way you act."

"At least I was never a Sissy -- or a Girl."

Erwin fixed his famous glare on Pfirsich. The whole family knew that arrogant stallion stare and that it had nothing to do with pride of spirit, that it was just a prosaic weakness. Rommel had grown nearsighted in one eye, and farsighted in the other, and he was just trying to focus. And he wouldn't wear glasses. The day would come when he mistook camel-thorn bushes for Allied trucks. But right then he knew his brother when he saw him up close.

"I'm sorry, *Lieber,*" said Pfirsich. "We were just children. And you were so very mild and gentle and patient."

"I was a quiet kid," gritted Erwin.

"I wasn't."

Pfirsich convinced him to at least sit down to drink his tea, pouring him a fresh cup, though he couldn't get him to put down the camera. Erwin was still doing two things at once, drinking tea and studying a map, and when Pfirsich solicitously handed him a sandwich, he absently took three big bites out it and then forgot to chew, the wad of food bulging in his cheek as he read.

Pfirsich said, "Do you remember the first time I joined you in the field?"

"Last war," mumbled Erwin around the wad.

"It was supposed to be 'The War To End All Wars,' as our British friends called it."

Erwin shrugged, champed hard twice and gulped. *"In der Tat?"*

"Italy," mused Pfirsich. "I was only seventeen, and I was longing for romance."

"Romance?"

"Italy," repeated Pfirsich. *"Wo die Zitronen blühn.'"*

"You know Goethe rolls over in his grave every time somebody

185

says that," said Erwin, and blew on his tea. "I wonder how many people who were there that week still hear that woman puffing up and down through their memories, calling 'Dahtzyo, Dahtzyo'. "

Pfirsich raised his eyebrows. "I remember that. I hadn't thought about that boy in years."

Erwin sniffed with distaste. "If that's your recollection of Italy, I'm surprised to hear you were so delighted to get orders for another visit."

"I couldn't help it, dear. I was hoping for a taste of the countryside, now that you mention it, unsullied by 'Dahtzyo'. Who of us doesn't want to go see the chestnut forests and the little white houses? And eat dry salted olives and buffalo-milk cheese?"

"Not where we were stationed; up there they ate buttered corn mush, when they could get butter." Erwin made a face. "Not that we got to share with 'em very often. White houses they have here in Africa. But you'd better be prepared to eat dates in Africa -- or sardines."

Pfirsich wasn't listening. He was remembering his first visit to Italy, and the fun he and his brothers had, being chased along the canals by half the incensed fruit-vendors in Venice. Except Erwin, of course. Erwin had been soothing the vendors and telling on his siblings to their parents.

Pfirsich was remembering another country, in the same war. And another Italian. Such a dear fierce young man. Pfirsich's fear and disgust had turned into a treasure of memory. Young love in a war was like sweet oil sweated out of a bitter leaf. Pfirsich almost licked his lips, he even slipped the tip out, then put his tongue right back into his head; as much as he relished the recollection, he didn't want Erwin sharing a private moment. He snorted. What had he done wrong? He'd been no worse than any healthy young animal.

"Worse," he puffed. What a wrong-headed use of the word. It dismayed him.

"Eh?" said Erwin, without looking up, still intent on the map.

Pfirsich had been around since then, he'd traveled and grown rich in affection. No experience of love had since been as fresh and piercing — he intended the pun -- as the time he lost his virginity.

What a moment that had been, right there in the middle of a war. No one had been hurt. He hadn't killed anybody. Guilt for love was ridiculous; the only guilt he felt should be reserved for the times he'd pierced the flesh of other young men with bullets and shrapnel, young men whom he'd never met. Or when he'd helped triangulate artillery targets, too many of them in towns. He remembered dead bodies being used to give substance to the sliding mud, so that dirt trench walls could be raised against the next round of mortars. For that he should reserve his guilt.

Look at Erwin over there, he thought. What a realist, tanned and dirty, covered with fresh sweat and fresh dust, poking into the bottom of his tea-cup and bringing up grains of sand that clung to his finger like undissolved sugar. That was a man who never seemed to have any qualms about anything.

It wasn't because he was stupid. He was just such a consummate soldier, with everything else pared away like fat. He was aimed like a gun for war, the one thing he was supremely good at.

"What a thing to be good at," said Pfirsich.

"What?" said Erwin.

"You know, you never pay me any mind while I'm talking to you, not if I repeat myself a dozen times. But when I'm talking to myself, every syllable I mutter gets your immediate attention. I'm not talking about you, you know."

"Then stop twitching and making noises."

Pfirsich almost put his tongue out, again, to stick it out at Erwin. Well, that was fine, he thought, here he was coming back at him as he had when they were boys. Erwin probably never felt guilt for shooting people. War was Erwin's game, with very specific mediaeval rules, a game he took deadly serious. Erwin liked it best when nobody was shot, but that didn't stop him making points when the rules called for it.

"I'm tired of playing."

"Good." Erwin slapped the map down on the table. "I've found a job for you."

Pfirsich started, and then covered his confusion by delicately poking the end of a little finger into his ear. "Other than playing artificial adjutant and chauffeur to a General who is too dangerous to be let loose with his own car?"

"I'll get another driver. You can do what you were trained to do."

"Construction engineer?" Pfirsich took his finger out of his head and whirled his hand, taking in the whole flat landscape. "Building bridges where there are no rivers -- or buildings for an army that never spends a night in the same place?"

"There's a battalion that needs a commander." Erwin tapped the map. "Feel up for it?"

"A battalion?"

"Yes. You know -- four or more companies?"

"Thank you, I hadn't forgotten."

"You want the job or not?"

"You don't want me on your staff?"

"You want to stay a *Hauptmann* forever?"

"Oh." Pfirsich nodded. "Field promotion."

"You haven't been in a command capacity since the last war. You'll need some command time if you want to advance above company grade. I can get you a brevet rank of *Oberst.*"

"I'm perfectly content as a *Hauptmann.* I don't need to be a make-believe Colonel."

"You want a decent pension?"

"I won't get it unless I retire at a higher rank. And I doubt that will ever happen."

Erwin glared at him. "Why not?"

"I plan to retire as an engineer – a real one -- if I get the chance."

"This is a small battalion. Not many people."

"How small?"

"Two and a half companies."

"Good heavens. That's tiny. Three companies could have been absorbed by other battalions, easily."

"You want more companies?"

"I'd really rather not drag even that many young men into combat," said Pfirsich, with an edge in his voice.

"Don't worry," retorted Erwin. "It's not a combat unit."

"Erwin, is there something about this unit I should know?"

"What should you know?" Erwin shrugged and raised his eyebrows like a peddler's wife.

"What's wrong with this unit?"

"Nothing's wrong. You're the best man for these people."

"I really don't like how you're putting that."

Erwin leaned back his head and talked upwards into the air. "You're -- steady. You're good with people. You're very good with staff work."

"I'm doing staff work now. How am I going to continue to do staff work if I'm doing command duty?" Pfirsich paused. "Erwin, what are you up to? Stop looking at the sky and look at me."

For the first time, Pfirsich saw his brother perform the *Deutscher Blick*, "The German Glance," thrown backwards over the shoulder before speaking in private. Pfirsich looked around, too. They were in the middle of the desert; who did his brother think could hear them? Erwin leaned forward, not so close he'd be mistaken for whispering, but close enough to keep his voice low.

"I've got some information, that I'd like you to keep organized. Just as part of the personnel files for the battalion."

"Do I get to find out what you're hiding?"

Erwin sat right back up. "Who's hiding anything?"

"*Lieber Gott,* Erwin. You sound like an amateur spy."

"We might as well be."

"I thought you despised spies. Mama was a spy, you know."

"Mama wasn't a spy!" said Erwin, all aghast. "Mama had influence, that was all."

"If you're going to play around with --." Pfirsich made a little twirly defining motion with a forefinger. " -- the kind of things that end up in files, well, then you're even more like our mother than I thought you were. If that's possible."

"What do you mean?" demanded Erwin, and lunged forward in his chair, putting his nose almost in Pfirsich's face.

Pfirsich didn't flinch. He didn't even blink. He remembered a peculiar moment back home. He'd passed by a door, where his mother, Lucie and Erwin were sitting in close communication with Field Marshal von Rundstedt, the Commander In Chief West. They were deeply interested in something, and Pfirsich suspected it wasn't about the tea and cake. He'd never seen anything -- not even a military staff meeting -- that looked so much like a military staff meeting. He was about to tiptoe back and listen in on the sly, then decided when he just didn't want to know. Somebody in this family had to be able to claim honest ignorance.

He was about to lose his immunity. Erwin wanted him to do

something with people. With files and people's names. And an odd sort of people. Pfirsich's brows arched; something occurred to him. He could track down and slip transfer papers for Melvin right into the pile, and no one in any overloaded staff office would ask him why any list of personnel was one name too long. It wouldn't be the first time he'd shuffled papers on a desk. If Erwin found out, Pfirsich could haggle with him as needs must.

"I'll tell you what, dear," said Pfirsich, and suddenly lifted a hand and touched his brother on his projected nose. "You just give me that battalion, and we'll take it from there."

* * * * *

When *Oberst* Pfirsich Rommel was introduced to his new command the first thing he did was to unintentionally nickname them.

He was reviewing his half-a-battalion, that stood at blank-faced attention under the date palms; only three companies, swept together from bits left over from other new units formed in the heady yeasty buildup and reconstitution of the New Army, and the first weeding-out of the Polish campaign.

"I can actually tell them apart," Pfirsich smiled to himself.

They were all dressed in the new Desert Tan, and wearing pith helmets. Very proper. But that didn't make up for their numbers, nor for their noticeably conservative records. An ambitious career officer would have been insulted and unnerved to be given this skeleton-crew of unremarkable oddballs. *Oberst* Rommel had looked through their records, and he liked what he read; malleable minds, with civilian experience and expertise, gardeners, cooks, horse-trainers, telegraph operators, even small-plane pilots and circus sharpshooters. And a handful of real oddities, that didn't seem to be much more than civilians, that didn't even have the right record or background for any sort of service. A magician, for heaven's sake. A postcard painter. Some of them didn't even seem old enough; probably just a mistake on the files. Just the kind of things that Ended Up In Files. Not a fire-eater in the lot. Pfirsich warmed to their very record-cards. He kissed one of the little squares of paper, right on its pink-lined top margin.

I'll be able to do something with them, he told himself. Teach

190

them to build. Even teach them to think on their own. Like a new litter of --. And out loud he murmured, "Stray puppies."

For self-preservation, soldiers are intent upon the words of a new commander. Though he'd said it under his breath, in his own tent, he'd been overheard through the canvas, and the 469th Halftrack, Support and Grave-digging Battalion was branded "The Stray Puppies" from their Colonel's own mouth.

What he didn't know, at least at first, was that the Puppies had returned the favor. When Pfirsich's brother so impressed and frightened the British that they gave him the nickname of The Desert Fox, the 469th had taken one of Pfirsich's own names and translated it into *Der Wüstenpfirsich* -- The Desert Peach.

* * * * *

As soon as he was alone with the Puppies in the desert, Pfirsich took shameless advantage and went out of his way to single-handedly dig his own oasis of calm in the desert war.

When no one in authority was looking, he extended invitations to the Allied commanders to come to supper. More intrigued than shocked, they showed up to taste the German field rations and compare them to their own. They found the 469th's commander to be urbane and honest, and in the words of one usually reticent Welsh Major, "Quite sweet, actually." If this German wanted to recognize the danger of the desert and organize a spot of hospitality that would prevent all their wandering troops from dying of thirst, it was one more item off their list. They went away happy with agreements to a separate peace.

The word spread quickly but quietly that no weapons would be tolerated within the environs of Pfirsich Rommel's battalion, and that men of either side could come to him with impunity, for a little water and food and rest, or even a little gasoline before they went their way. He did draw the line, however, when the Australians thought they could get away with using the 469th's limited fueling facilities as a filling station.

An American Captain, Jeff Holz, who had been flying with the British, crash-landed near Pfirsich's unit. He was safely taken prisoner against the threat of the desert that made being captivity not just desirable but a desperate necessity. A man couldn't be left alone to wander panting

191

and thick-tongued over the burning stone and sand. Germans and British and Italians and later Americans would beg to be taken in by captors who often could only point vaguely at the horizon and say, sometimes haltingly in the other man's language, more often only through hand-signals, "Go away -- your people are over there."

Even Erwin Rommel himself, sitting in the turret of his tank, could only impatiently wave away begging prisoners and finally threaten them with a pistol, because he knew he didn't have the food or water or accommodations for them, and that they'd be better off trying to find their own people than riding as an extra burden with his. They went grumbling off into the desert after he finally threw them a canteen of water. Once Pfirsich instituted his private recovery zone, Rommel could at least point in a more likely direction.

Pfirsich worked very hard to provide for his own people as well as his occasional prisoner, and the 469th being a support unit made this very convenient. He even found a way to keep Jeff safe with him in Africa and out of the prison camps. He made the American the editor of the camp newspaper, getting around the Nazi ban on typewriters by applying for publishing status. Jeff made a very good editor; like so many non-native speakers, who have only learned a language with its proper grid of genders and declensions, and are taught no slang until they get away from the classroom, he spoke a purer and more literary German than anybody else in the camp. Except Pfirsich, who was descended from schoolteachers and knew all the rules.

Jeff could have applied for repatriation to any of the Allied units that tore past the 469th in the course of the campaign. Instead he chose to stay and edit the paper. Jeff was an idealist. The same beliefs that made him join the war before he needed to persuaded him that he could actually sneak out the theater secrets of the *Afrika Korps,* concealed between the lines of his hand-printed broadsheet. He never managed to tell the Allies anything more useful than the 469th's camp gossip; Pfirsich could proofread like the schoolmaster he'd once been, and censored Jeff until the poor man was pulling his hair. After awhile, Pfirsich found he didn't have to put a guard on the American prisoner. The man was so obsessed with getting something past his censor that he stayed on, putting out issues of *Der Kauz* long after anybody else would have escaped.

Der Kauz meant "The Screech-Owl," and Jeff intended it to

demonstrate the paper's goal of making an irrepressible noise in the darkness. It also meant "odd guy," or "queer fish," and that's how most of its *Afrika Korps* readers thought of it – and after awhile, of the 469th and its weird expansive commander. Crazy people can get away with anything.

Jeff wasn't the only American in the unit. Arnold Makepeace was an Indian half-breed, but he wasn't a prisoner. He'd grown up near Chicago, the son of a German woman who had come over to America to stay with her Illinois relatives. While his mother was working for a bus company, she met and fell in love with Arnold's father, an off-reservation Indian who didn't talk about his tribe. She married him before she could think about it. Neither of them had done much thinking, and they paid for it. Arnold's mother was called an Injun-lover and a Kraut slut; his father got grief from his reservation family for marrying a yellow-hair, and the nicest thing Arnold was called was The 'Breed. He took and gave a lot of black eyes in school

When Arnold was twelve, his mother finally went back to Germany to think about it and cool off. She did continue to write, to promise she really did intend to return. Instead she sent Arnold a ticket as a birthday present, and his father sent him to his motherland with his blessing, kind of hoping the kid would bring his Ol' Lady back.

When Arnold walked down the gangplank in Germany, he discovered he wasn't who he thought he was. He was no low-class mixed blood, no half-breed woods-colt who didn't even know the name of his tribe. Not now. Now, he was a Warrior Of The Plains, an educated Indian Chief who could speak English and German – and the Germans were all just agog about him.

They came by it honestly. In the nineteenth century, German princes had sent over their finest artists to paint the locals in full regalia, sometimes accompanying the expedition. German royalty slept under buffalo robes and ate delicacies like bear-fat and biscuit-root-and-duck stew. The exhibitions and publications that came back from the New World awed Europe. Karl May's *Old Shatterhand* series of novels about the American frontier started a generation of young Germans dreaming about tipis and painted ponies and buffalo hunts. Adolf Hitler had the whole series.

The Germans loved Cowboys and Indians, with the emphasis

on the Indians. Back when the Germans were the barbarians whooping around the walls of Rome, they'd *been* the Indians – and they'd won. Their modern descendants couldn't help but identify with another tribal people. The Nazi government may have branded everybody else on the planet as *Untermenschen,* but they couldn't blacken the Red Man in the eyes of the Germans.

In one night, Arnold went from Prairie Nigger to Noble Savage. His family showed him off like a visiting prince. His new friends took him to the opera, to the movies, to church, to party rallies, to taverns, everywhere. They hung on his every word, hoping for the saga of his Western adventures. Who else could boast their very own Red Brother? His mother beamed; her outcast son was suddenly a star, with the potential to be a war-hero.

Arnold didn't know anything more about living as a native American than his German worshipers. His father had been a tile-setter, and Arnold had grown up in a third-floor city apartment. But he'd read all of James Fenimore Cooper, and seen dozens of the cowboy movies, including a pre-war *Lone Ranger* movie in which Tonto had worn swastikas around his headband. Arnold mined the movies and pulp fiction, and, lubricated with German beer, began to expound on his life on the wide open plains. He was so giddy playing Red Warrior that he greeted the blood-red *Hakenkreuz* banners hanging in the narrow German streets as the war-flags of his people.

Arnold wasn't thinking, but forethought wasn't something he'd inherited from either parent. The excitement of rallies and parties sent his new friends off into the military, and Arnold signed up as fast as his parents had married, full of the same sort of happy dreams. He didn't wake up until he was marching around drill-fields, diving into the mud of combat-exercise fields, disassembling rifles and peeling more potatoes than he'd ever seen in his life.

And then he was in Africa, and praying that America wouldn't get into the war. He had never planned to follow his ancestors' warpath against that people. The Germans counted a man's maternal bloodline to make him a German or a Jew, but the Americans accepted only the blood of the father. To them the seed was everything, the vessel nothing. Even though Arnold was as much German as he was Indian, and the Indians didn't have American citizenship, Arnold had still been born in America.

And Americans don't easily give anything away.

Arnold used tiny red, white and blue African beads to outline the eagle-and-swastika design on his *Afrika Korps* cap insignia. It looked like the Navajo and Hopi thunderbird and sun-swastika. He hung shed feathers from an African Lanner falcon off the back of the cap. His motives weren't clear, even to himself. He might have been showing off for his German cousins, or camouflaging himself as having the right to be an enemy to the American relatives.

He didn't go as far as war paint.

Bread and Swans

15. Mercy

"Mine He*rr!*" cried a soldier, running up the sand dune, waving a scrap of paper in one dark hand. "Eet message for *Monsieur Oberst!*"

"Thank you, Abdhul. Who's it from?"

Abdhul was The Stray Puppies' Moroccan volunteer, originally a member of the *Afrika Korp's* African auxiliaries. He'd discarded the pith helmet and leg-wraps, and now wore comfortable loose trousers and desert boots and a *Stahlhelm*. The 469th, like the rest of the *Afrika Korps,* had taken to wearing anything it pleased, including some uniform parts from opposing armies. Abdhul's choice of a helmet, worn even out of combat, when almost everybody else preferred the comfort of a faded tan bill-cap, marked more than the color of his skin. The "Steel Helmet" had been the militant ex-servicemen's organization after the last war. Abdhul wore his helmet to fit in, but it only made him stand out. The other men said he was just trying to out-German the Germans.

Abdhul's black face was proof that race in the Third Reich was often a matter of convenience; anybody could be *Ehrenarier,* an "Honorary Aryan." The government had even usurped rabbinical function in designation of religious status. In the confusion and twitchy mythology that would continue for decades after the war, some people would think they were Jewish because the Third Reich had for its own greedy convenience designated their ancestors as Jews.

Neither Pfirsich Rommel nor Abdhul himself found anything odd about a black man wearing a German helmet. As far as Abdhul's pay records were concerned, he might as well have come from Hamburg. Although perhaps that wasn't the best comparison; Hamburg was a northern port city, whose lively harbor-side red light district had a long careless history of transient colorful fatherhood.

Pfirsich unfolded the thin paper of the message, and poked into his pocket after his *pince nez.* They weren't there; he must have left them in the administrations tent. He held the message out at arm's length, and squinted at it. Then he handed it to Abdhul.

"Hold that up for me, will you, *Lieber?* I can't see it without my glasses."

Abdhul was pleased to help; The Stray Puppies liked their Colonel. He never gave orders; he only made polite requests. The Colonel was stringently proper with everyone, and the men hadn't trusted that approach at first. They were used to being roared at, and thought anything else was a sign of weakness. Like the German totem animal, the horse, they didn't think you were serious unless you were yelling and kicking. But horses can come around with kindness and sugar, and so had they.

Like all the rest of the 469th, Abdhul knew how far-sighted Pfirsich Rommel was getting; the Colonel didn't make any attempt to hide it, or anything else, for that matter. His men had all made a guess about his personal life, and had wisely adopted his attitude that it was none of their business. You could be put in a camp for knowing a queer, much less being one. Best not to know.

The Moroccan, with the sense of social delicacy native to his people, dutifully took the paper and stood back another arm's length from his commander, holding up the message steadily so the older man could focus on the scribbled message.

Pfirsich sighed. "Kristof's handwriting isn't getting any better. Could you remind him to print?"

Kristof had been the civilian telegraph clerk, and was the 469th's radio operator. Pfirsich had only recently discovered that Kristof had a hearing problem, and was deeply aphasic. He couldn't spit out a word to save his shy little life. Kristof had been terrified of discovery, but Pfirsich, as part of his own policy to save what he could from the war, patted him on the head and told him to go back to work. Kristof hugged him.

Abdhul looked at the note. "Theese ees preent. Kristof -- la -- not write screept so preety." He held out the message again.

Pfirsich squinted at the lines. *"Dear Brother -- ',"* he read.

"Thee General?" said Abdhul.

"Yes, dear." Pfirsich read out loud. *"What are you doing to your eyes? Coming to see for myself. Rommel.'* "

"Thee General! *Per dieux!* He comes?" gleamed Abdhul.

Like all the *Afrika Korps,* he worshiped his General, and was excited

198

as a cub at the prospect of greeting the Alpha wolf. *"Unser Rommel,"* as the soldiers called him. "Our Rommel."

"Yes, dear. Time for dress tunic and war paint for me, and shaving for all of you." Pfirsich retrieved the message, and fluttered a hand at Abdhul. "Go run tell everybody shave. You know what he says about smooth chins; 'Shaving makes you feel younger.'"

"Javole, mon Colonel!" saluted Abdhul, and ran.

"He's come to look at my records," sniffed Pfirsich, studying the message, and recognizing his brother's personal code. "Doesn't he have anything better to do?"

* * * * *

Pfirsich was tucking his best dress scarf into his cleanest tunic when he heard the shots -- and then the screaming.

He didn't ask. He grabbed his cap from his startled orderly's hands and shot off across the camp, running as fast a his long booted legs would take him. They brought him to the base of a cliff in time to hear one of the men milling there snarl:

"Scheiße! Here He comes. Shoot the little bastard before He gets here!"

"Hör' auf!" shouted Pfirsich, in a voice as loud and raw as his brother's.

He didn't know what they were up to, but whatever it was, it involved bullets going into flesh, and he wasn't having it -- not here, not in his battalion area, where he'd gone to the trouble of secretly breaking bread with the English and Australian commanders, and obtaining a separate and quite illegal cease-fire with them.

He'd never been violent, but he was big, and when he flew in amongst his men they jumped out of the way from pure instinct. By the time he could stop he found himself in their midst, and at his feet lay a cowering dark boy, probably an Arab or part Arab, his thin dusty arms held trembling across his head. He'd been beaten all to blood.

Pfirsich was appalled. He stood straight up and spun around upon his men, a head taller than any of them. Rather then looking up at him, they looked at their feet.

"Lieber Himmel!" he cried. "What are you doing, abusing a young

199

lad like this?"

"They're worst when they're young." protested a soldier.

"Like snakes," said another. "And this little snake bites." He pointed away across the crowd, and they moved back to show his example. *"Mein Herr,* look! That's all that's left of Ehrlichman."

One of the battalion's corporals, Friedo Ehrlichman, lay at the base of the cliff, compressed into an inert bloody pile that looked even smaller than the little trembling boy. Pfirsich had seen war in Rumania, Italy, Poland and France, and he recognized a dead man when he saw one. It was obvious the man had fallen off that cliff, and hit hard.

"Oh dear," Pfirsich said, bending over the little broken bolus. "I can see why no one called a medic."

"He didn't just fall, he was shot," said a soldier.

"By that kid." snapped another, pointing at the culprit. "A sneaking civilian. If he wants to fight, let him get into a uniform."

"Ja, we have to do it. He can't have the fun without he joins the club."

"Shot by this child?" said Pfirsich. He'd seen young snipers before, but this was only a boy, and a thin little thing at that.

"Here's his rifle!" A soldier displayed the weapon. "British. He's a sniper for the Tommys for sure."

"An Enfield?" frowned Pfirsich. "How could this little fellow pick up that heavy thing? It's as tall as he is."

"He did it!" they insisted.

"We saw him."

"We should do him."

"Make an example of him; hang him up in his own village."

"Hang up his whole village!"

"I beg your pardon!"

Everybody shut up. The Colonel's eyes changed color when he was angry, and right now they were the strangest iridescent purple-gray. He looked like he'd gone engine inside.

"These sand-rats won't learn," insisted one of the men. "Not unless we teach 'em good, *mein Herr.* You remember what it was like in Poland."

"Yes, I do," gritted Pfirsich.

"They're tough and stupid," insisted the soldier, making a kick at the Arab boy. "They need brutal lessons."

"That will be enough!" said Pfirsich.

"We should," murmured the soldiers.

"Enough! Punishment where it's due -- but only where it's due."

"Then we can punish the kid?"

"No you may not!" said Pfirsich, and bent his tall form like a jackknife to examine the frightened bleeding boy. "Beating a child. Go back to duty. I'll deal with this."

They glared at the boy; they'd have eaten him raw in pieces if left to it. Pfirsich glared at them.

"I know how much you hate snipers. But he's only a baby. Take poor Ehrlichman away; don't leave him lying under the flies like that. And send me the medic."

The men left reluctantly, driven by their officer's repeated gray glances, to bury the dead man and fetch the 469th's only medic. Pfirsich put a hand on the shivering child's head.

"Herr Oberst, The General's here."

Pfirsich stood straight up, so fast he got a stabbing pain between the eyes. He blinked in agony.

"Oh, no -- now?"

The soldier who had brought the report nodded eagerly. Pfirsich's vision cleared. He looked at the child, and cried out to two of the loitering soldiers. "Hide him! Take him someplace safe, and --." He saw the look on the men's faces. "Don't take any pieces out of him."

Rommel was only a half-a-hill behind his own report. He was in the camp in his neat little armored car, the one he called *"Greif,"* or Griffin, almost before the sand could be kicked over the blood of Ehrlichman and the boy. Rommel hopped out of the vehicle and zeroed in on his brother.

"Guten Morgen, Herr General," crowed Pfirsich, and saluted.

"Guten Morgen, Herr --." Rommel stopped in mid-salute. *"Moment,* little brother, you never salute me any more, much less call me 'Herr General.' "

"How impolite; I will in future."

"I don't know why I come see you; what is supposed to be a mere dutiful inspection always turns out to be a difference over *Weltanschauung.* Since you've come to the desert, you've got the bit in your teeth."

"'Inspection'?" said Pfirsich. "Your message said --."

"I didn't say what I was inspecting. Where are your files?"

"In the administrative tent, of course. And since when do you look at papers? Those papers are my business, now. Why don't you do something more interesting -- go break down an engine, or lay some landmines?"

"What's going on around here?" Rommel interrupted him.

"What are you talking about? You haven't even looked at the records."

"No, I mean around here, right now. What are you up to this time?"

"*Oh, bitte.* We're just getting ready for the inspection."

Rommel's head swiveled on his stocky body like the turret of a tank. He turned on his heel and headed into the camp.

"There's something going on under the surface, here," he growled. "Don't think I don't know this little lunatic asylum you're running here, by now. You'd better tell me, before I find out!"

"This 'asylum' was your idea --."

High-pitched screams came rocketing out of a nearby tent.

"Stop that!" shouted Pfirsich.

Rommel turned on his heel and pounced right at the tent, cutting through the men standing about it like a wolf through sheep. Before Pfirsich could move, Rommel had thrown back one whole wall of the canvas, popping the tent pegs loose to do it. The men all tried to look surprised. Rommel took one look and rounded on Pfirsich. The men flinched when he roared:

"What is my word on torturing prisoners?"

"My men are not torturing prisoners," protested Pfirsich.

"What's that?" insisted Rommel, pointing at the little boy, who was curled up in an even tighter ball, if that was possible, and was trussed much too tightly with a rope.

"Well, it is a prisoner," said Pfirsich. "But he won't be tortured. I can guarantee you that."

"Can't you see how they've tied him?" demanded Rommel.

He whipped out his hunting knife and dropped onto his haunches. In a moment, he'd sawn loose the knots and pulled away the ropes, at least the ones on the boy's wrists. The boy didn't uncurl. When Rommel saw the red rasped skin on the wrists his head snapped up, and he really did look like a wolf, and one with a hurt pup.

"This child's been beaten. Who's done it?"

Nobody knew.

"I haven't found out yet," said Pfirsich.

"Then find out! And punish him! I won't have it. Don't you move!" he roared at the men, who had begun to slide away from the tent. He turned upon his brother.

"And what are you doing with an Arab, and a mere child, for a prisoner?"

"Na, it seems he's killed one of my men."

"Why?"

"I don't know, dear, I hadn't been able to ask him, just yet."

"How did he kill him?"

Pfirsich took the Enfield from one of the men, and mutely offered it.

Rommel stared. "That's an Enfield! It must weigh as much as that kid does."

"You think so?" said Pfirsich.

"He must have propped it up to aim it," said Rommel. "And dragged it to get it here."

"He was too little to outrun my men."

"Determined little fart." Rommel was bending over the boy. "*Mein Gott,* he is young. What's a brat like this doing with a gun?"

"Well, they do mature earlier than we do. It may be the climate."

"If being 'mature' means being let run around with a rifle, then somebody needs to talk to this boy's people."

"Erwin?"

"Get me an Arab translator. Do you have one?"

"Yes, the chaplain."

"Good. Get him out here," said Rommel and headed for *Greif.* "And finish untying that boy."

Rommel was hardly out of hearing before the boy let out a squeal. Pfirsich spun around upon the men, one of whom was kneeling in front of the boy and following the General's orders after his own fashion, as brutally as he thought he could get away with.

"Stop that!" Pfirsich was livid. "Can't you even untie him without taking out your feelings on him? Leave it to me."

As he knelt at the broken child's bound feet, Pfirsich glared at the men. "Get me *Kaplan* Stange, and tell him to prepare himself in his most churchly style."

As they ran to do his bidding, Pfirsich worked carefully at the damp knots, crooning tenderly to the boy, who wasn't listening.

Stange's our best Arab speaker, thought Pfirsich. And his being a religious man won't hurt.

Pfirsich pulled the rope loose just as the medic trotted up. Pfirsich could see he'd received a prejudiced report. He admonished him to be kindly, or else. He was going to warn him not to let the boy escape, but that kid wasn't going anywhere, not with those swollen ankles. Pfirsich stayed to observe the initial medicating, then left to greet the chaplain.

* * * * *

Two hours later, Pfirsich found himself perched next to his brother in a huge German halftrack, gripping the cage-like antenna-assembly to keep his kidneys from being joggled loose.

The Arab boy, wiped down and bandaged, sat beside Rommel. He was so delighted by the big deep German dust-goggles they had given to him to wear he had forgotten his bruises. Rommel was a father himself, and knew how single-minded a child could be, especially a boy child. When his own son had been a small thing, he had often bought off his tears with a toy or coin or a piece of candy. The little fellow beside him now might have been out shooting German soldiers, but to a conditioned father like Rommel he was just a kid with the wrong toys. The goggles seemed to be doing the trick.

All around them towered tanks. Other armored vehicles roared alongside them in a dust storm escort. Pfirsich leaned over and cupped his hands over his mouth, and slipped into the abbreviated forced dialect of full shout, stuttering as the big treads rumbled under him.

"Erwin," he yelled. "Awfu' b-big escort -- just lil' village!"

"What escort?" Rommel yelled back. "Just traffic!"

"Village -- m-mud -- straw; knock walls down!"

"Mud straw s-since Bible days! Won't even crack 'em!"

"Scare 'em!"

"Them? Used to it! Just 'nother army. Like parade!"

"Not tryin' scare 'em?"

"This?" Rommel jerked a thumb back at the rumbling vehicles. "Just everyday hardware!"

Pfirsich sat back and quit trying to argue at the top of his lungs. He'd lose anyway. He realized that Rommel would arrive in the village with no intent to terrorize. He would appear in the little town as if dropping in on a social call, as if blandly accustomed to all this firepower, as though it were so much kitchen furniture. Whether he meant to or not -- whether he meant to horrify the villagers, or he were just on his way to another assault, and dropping the boy off on the way -- either way, they were meant to understand the Naked Power possessed by the Germans, and be convincingly persuaded to keep their little primitive selves out of the way of Our Great Big War.

Pfirsich put his hand over his face. It wouldn't work with the French, or the English, or even the Poles. What made Erwin think it would work with a proud people like the desert Arabs?

When the dust storm drove over the rise into Arab village, everybody stood and watched.

"It's the Britishmen again, isn't it?"

"No, it's the German people."

"The other ones?"

"The old ones?"

"No, no, not the Italians, their new friends."

"Oh, those. The new ones."

"Good. We've never sold them anything before."

Everybody ran back to their houses and yards; in a few minutes they were back out into the street, dragging with them young goats, chickens, jugs and baskets of eggs and tomatoes and dates and lemons. The German vehicles had barely lurched to a halt, when they were being ascended by assault-teams of fruit-sellers and mint-tea-vendors.

In the settling golden dust, the modern tank-men didn't hesitate. The villagers needed merely to poke a rosy orange or a bunch of sweet grapes through the view-ports. The crewmen took one famished sniff and whipped open their hatches, launching into eager domestic haggling, making up in frantic hand-signals what they lacked in words.

Their stomachs and mouths jaded and cankered upon canned

sardines, thick fat Italian canned-meat-rations and pasty boiled spaghetti, these Soldiers And Officers Of The Reich were immediately transformed into roving hungry boys, by the power of their sore gums and loosening teeth, aching for just one little bitter orange or handful of sugary dates hairy from camel-skin bags, or, God be praised, a real true fresh buttery egg.

Pfirsich tapped his brother on the shoulder, and pointed at the impromptu steel-floored marketplaces. The tanks could hardly be seen for the scrambling bodies and swatches of cloth laid out to display the explosion of provender. One raw-gummed soldier had bought a capful of ripe tomatoes and was simply squatted down on his own turret, hungrily devouring them without any further preparation, not even a shirtfront rub to take off the dust. He winced in pain and delight with every acid mouthful.

Pfirsich said, "Erwin, if we mean to impress them, I think we'd best tell the men to close their hatches and not buy out the Friday market."

"Well, they're hungry, and they need the fruit," said Rommel. "But you're right."

The General unwound the boy's hand from his arm, then stood up and roared, "Back in the tanks! Close the hatches!"

A whine like a wronged dog rose up over the tanks. The vendors had only just begun to distribute heady addictive sips of the raw palm-sap toddy called Arrack – "The first one's free" -- and the soldiers absolutely whimpered when they realized they wouldn't be getting any more than that one taste.

"Close them, you icebutts!" howled Rommel.

The hatches whanged closed like the burrows of giant trapdoor spiders. In the moment of silence that followed the fading reverberation, muffled German voices could be heard swearing in desperate frustration.

"What wrong?" said one of the vendors, staring down at the little man who had frightened away her customers. She had already learned enough German to bargain with the new customers.

"Maybe they don't want to haggle," said a vendor, his hands full of preserved lemons. "Sometimes the British people didn't like to. Maybe these people are like them."

"They are sitting silent in their trucks, and not speaking," said a woman cradling a tender young goat in her arms. "I saw their mouths watering; you could see roast kid in their eyes."

"I don't trust people who don't want to bargain. That's not friendly."

"It's not generous."

"I think we'd better run fetch the *Mufti.*"

The whole colorful crowd deserted their places on the tanks, wrapping up their goods without losing a date or cracking an egg. They flowed down off the steel sides and flew back to the village with the practiced ease of the opportunistic merchant, all of them talking as fast as they ran.

"Erwin," murmured Pfirsich, accusingly. "Look how you've terrified the poor creatures."

"Be patient, Pfirsich," grinned Rommel. "Let 'em stew."

"All this just to intimidate a few poor villagers."

"'Intimidate.' In the name of our American cousin Anna - this is just Expediency!"

"'Expediency'" gasped Pfirsich. "Not that word. I heard it too often in Poland."

"So did I."

Pfirsich flinched. Would he have to write a report informing on his own brother?

A bundle of flapping black robes came at them from the village, putting on all the speed it could manage, carrying on a high-pitched female tirade that showed no hint of breathlessness. The Arab lad heard her, saw her, put his goggles on top of his head, and began to gabble delightedly to her, showing off the half-track as though he owned it. Pfirsich recognized the body language between the boy and the shrieking woman

"Oh, dear, Erwin. I think that must be his mother."

"Good," said Rommel. "'bout time she showed up."

"Erwin, you'll have to have mercy on that poor boy, now, certainly, with his mother here."

"Even less."

Pfirsich's mouth dropped open, then closed again, in a hard pale line.

"If you go right ahead with what you intend I'll never speak to you again."

"Yes, you will. I know you."

"I'm not that weak."

"You'll agree with me."

"I'm not staying in this vehicle," huffed Pfirsich.

He knew where this was going. He'd seen this kind of crap in Poland, and he didn't want to see his brother do it. One old French officer had been enough; he wouldn't put up with the same done to a child.

Before he could be restrained, he had leapt down off the steep sides of the half-track. On the ground, he signaled up imperiously to his chaplain:

"Kaplan Stange. To me!"

Stange stared down at him, wild black eyebrows working nervously, then looked sideways at Rommel; he was a brave man, and of an independent and deeply moral mind, but he was a German army chaplain, and in the Third Reich he had been stripped of any special privileges or dignities beyond any secular officer. If anything, German chaplains served as courageous spiritual volunteers, hanging onto their tenuous positions purely upon grudging military sufferance.

On the other hand, he was a good soldier, and chose his battles. And a good soldier, like a good dog, knew who was the real master here.

Pfirsich snapped at his brother, "Well, aren't you going to order me back into the half- track?"

"Nee," drawled Rommel, then flipped a little pointed hand at the chaplain.

"Go ahead, *Kaplan,* jump right down there with him."

Stange hesitated.

"No, I mean it. Jump right down."

If Stange had been a dog, he couldn't have looked any more happy and relieved to find both masters of like mind. He swung right down over the sides of the half-track and came to a springy lithe halt beside his own commander, and stood relaxed and ready, wagging a cheerful notional tail. Pfirsich glared up at his brother.

"Giving me enough rope to hang myself? I promise you, it will be the only rope that's used today."

"I agree!" grinned Rommel.

"And nobody's going to be shot, either."

"Mein Herr?" said Stange.

"Don't worry, Stange," said Rommel. "Just follow orders.

Introduce us to Mama, there."

Pfirsich added his own two cents. *"Kaplan,* do try to translate in a mild and humane manner."

"Just introduce us, Stange," repeated Rommel.

The chaplain did as he was told. The woman stood with crossed arms; she was a desert woman, not a city woman, and veils were a matter of convenience. She was barely wearing one, hooked loosely as she'd run from her kitchen just barely over her nose, and her hostile gleaming eyes didn't veil their meaning at all.

Even as Stange was making apologies, an older man in a green turban appeared out of the crowd, and Stange repeated his greetings to him, the village *Mufti.* The mother bridled, the *Mufti* glared. At the same moment, the two of them turned their eyes upon the boy, who shrank down behind the gun-ports and put his arm around Rommel's dusty booted leg. Rommel looked down at him, sternly, and shook his head.

"Is this your child?" he asked the mother, pointing at the cowering lad.

In German or Arabic, she knew what he was asking. She answered in a fury so vehement that Stange didn't need to translate, while Rommel nodded in agreement.

"Tell her exactly what her child did," ordered Rommel.

Stange finished the whole story to her. Rommel could tell when the chaplain got to the part about the dead German soldier; the whole village erupted into excited talk, and glowered up at the boy. His mother's veil practically puffed off her face, and she had to grab it.

Around the world, a boy caught stealing fruit or breaking windows or otherwise playing the little secret rebel would pretend to carefree rebellion at the threat of retribution. But he would shiver in dread at the prospect of being caught and dragged back to face -- Mama.

The boy buried his face against Rommel's leg; everybody was here, everybody could see what was happening. He wasn't being exposed to a savage unforgiving military tribunal. He wasn't even being delivered into the hands of his kinsmen's leaders, for summary justice. He was being handed over to his mother! In front of the soldiers he had wronged, in front of his whole village, before the eyes of his *Mufti,* he was being given over to his mama. He shriveled in humiliation.

"Good," said Rommel, when the boy's mother had run out of

steam. He frowned down at the boy. "Go to your mother." He pointed at her, in unmistakable direction. "Go on. You've been enough trouble. Go take your medicine."

The boy couldn't have oozed out the halftrack more abjectly if he'd been liquid. Head bowed, his eyes closed, he slunk over to his mother. She didn't even look at his bruises. She reached out and slapped him and told him what she thought of his prank, and the Germans didn't need a translation.

"What is this, camel-calf? Shooting the neighbors? We don't even know these people! Is this our war? Is that manners? Wait 'till your father finds out."

"They beat me," he whined.

"Not hard enough!" snapped his mother. "You can still walk. Praise Allah they caught you before you did worse."

The *Mufti* shook his head and addressed Stange. Stange looked up at Rommel and gestured helplessly.

"His apologies, *Herr General.*"

Rommel nodded graciously. "I'm satisfied, if she'll keep the child at home."

Stange translated, including the reference to 'child'; that was clear, from the way the boy cringed.

Rommel reached down into the halftrack, and brought up the Enfield, which he flung down to the *Mufti*, confident the old desert warrior would catch it. He wasn't disappointed; the old man caught the heavy brutal weapon with the loose-wristed grace he might have used to trap a butterfly.

"Oh!" said the woman, and snatched the rifle away from the *Mufti* and shook it at the boy.

"Your uncle's second-best rifle! How did you plan to pay for the bullets you borrowed? Carrying water to his donkeys? On top of it all, your uncle will be off doing nothing but trading for salt, and will come home to be shot or hanged? Why? Because his silly nephew has a brain of salt?" She slapped the kid again. "Don't you know the rules of war? You stay home and help me clean date-seeds for the camels, like a baby, if you have no more sense."

She'd have had him by the ear if he hadn't had the sense and the timing to duck away and run ahead of her. She took out after him, flailing him with her voice.

"If you think the Germans have beaten you, you will want to go back to them, you will beg for their tender loving fatherly protection, before I am finished with you! I will beat you so you will not fit a grave!"

Everybody laughed -- the *Mufti,* the people, the Germans -- the poor boy could have sworn he heard the hilarious braying of the very donkeys. Even the tanks seemed to tick over in amusement. He bawled his head off all the way home, mama vulturing on his heels.

Rommel dusted his hands. "All right! Let's go home!"

Stange almost bounced back into the half-track. Pfirsich stood riveted, gleaming up at his brother in admiration.

"Pfirsich, come on, will you?"

"Erwin, how superb!"

"Oh, stop it," snapped Rommel. "Get back up here; we don't have all day. And we're in mortal danger. Get up here before they remember to sell us things."

It was too late; the villagers and their dates and chickens were already swarming up the tanks, and the hatches were popping open to welcome them.

* * * * *

"We didn't have a chance," sighed Rommel, peeling an orange.

They were traveling at the head of the caravan line of tanks and half-tracks, now, instead of in the midst of a roaring wedge, and they didn't have to shout. Not even above the bleating of kids and lambs and the cackling of chickens that rode all over vehicles festooned with bunches of fruit and baskets of eggs and jugs of *Arrack.*

"They cleaned us out."

"I'm glad that's all that happened," said Pfirsich. "I was in cold dread at what you meant to do."

"I thought you knew me better," huffed his brother.

"Don't have a hissy-fit," said Pfirsich. "I've seen you shoot people."

"Soldiers," Rommel corrected him. "I'm a soldier. And I only shoot soldiers who've been given a chance to make a decision, or to fight. That," he jerked a thumb over his shoulder "Was a child. Children should get as many chances as possible."

"Not everybody thinks that way."

"Nature doesn't think that way," said Rommel. "The first time a fawn puts a foot wrong, it goes down the throat of a wolf. We're human, we have options. We should do what we can for the young and foolish."

"Thank the good Lord you decided against expediance."

"'Expediance'?" snorted Rommel. "All the 'experts' equate expediance with brutality. Pah! We'd have had a village, or a whole tribal region, really caring that we could be destroyed, and joining this war against us."

"You decided for kindness." Pfirsich patted his brother on the arm.

"No decision," snapped Rommel, and moved over. "Cruelty never came into it. Too short-term. We made our example, and we left."

"What example?" said Pfirsich. "I didn't see you make any example."

"I did," said Erwin. "No boy in any of those villages will think of getting involved with this war. Easy decision, to be kind. Kindness is easy."

Pfirsich just looked at him.

"Don't look at me like that," said Erwin.

"Most people think cruelty is easy."

"Cruelty is just plain bone-laziness masquerading as manhood," said Erwin.

"Spoken as a true Swabian," sniffed Pfirsich. *"Arbait moacht sellig."*

"True Hard Work," gritted Erwin, "Blesses You because it is never cruel; only when it cuts corners, and doesn't look to the future."

"Now you sound like Papa."

"We'd have paid for our mean laziness with a desert full of civilian partisans to chase and to trade bloody deaths with. Nothing but snipers and cutthroats and hangings, like a snake devouring its own tail, 'till nothing was left." Erwin made a move that in anybody else would have been a shudder. "No thank you. I don't want any of the pie we ate in Poland. The experts be damned. I've always found that kindness is far more expediant than cruelty."

"You are a Cynic."

"Yup," grinned Erwin, and offered Pfirsich a section of the peeled orange. "Have some?"

"Bitte," said Pfirsich, and only hesitated for a moment before taking the orange from his brother's fingers and popping it into his mouth. He wasn't immune to the desert hunger for fruit.

"Now," said Erwin, sucking on the rest of the orange. "We didn't get around to looking at your records, did we?"

"Maybe next time," murmured Pfirsich, and pulled his cap down over his eyes. "Right now it isn't expediant."

Bread and Swans

16. Home Again, Home Again

After so long in the desert, civilization had faded right out of Pfirsich's memory. Like a captive girl in the American Indian Wars, he had grown into another tribe and another family, with another way of getting the daily buffalo and succotash into the pot. He didn't think much about what had been home, because now this desert was home. He sheltered in a tent, ate uncooked Iron Rations and overcooked spaghetti, drank local tea heated over jerry-rigged sand stoves. His neighbors were a lot of dirty tired loose-toothed soldiers who had to be fed and kept alive and working, and kept from being shot if their chief could help it. He expected things to be simple, because that's the way it was out here.

Life was simple heat, simple cold, simple light, simple dark. The desert stalked by in hot dervishes of sand, stripping paint and clogging gears, scouring eyes and chafing under the waistbands and collars of form-fitting uniforms whose only concession to the desert was their color. Nobody wanted to look like a New Guy, and the first thing they did to a new recruit was to help him bleach and distress his clothes. Even Pfirsich caved in to the fashion and broke the peak of his cap.

The toughest man has nothing more between him and the universe than his own petal-thin human skin. None of the ointments issued to the soldiers cooled their friction-sores. The only salves they could have bought locally were too strong, meant to ease the harness-burns of camels and donkeys. Desert people weren't crazy enough to wear trousers and boots and underwear in the sandy wind. They gentled the universe in a little pocket around their fragile skins by wearing loose robes, walking in their own cool private tents.

The sand and cliffs shimmered with heat, the air so dry the men of all the armies couldn't recognize how hot it really was. They would faint off the tops of tanks and lie unconscious, the flies crawling in black bunches on their sticky eyes. They revived to be chewed out by their sergeants and told to keep their hats on. Bodies struggling to adjust for survival of the killing heat of the day didn't armor themselves against the cold of the night. When the sun went down the guards around the circles of tanks the Germans called *Lagers* shivered in their greatcoats and caught colds that they tried to bake out when the sun came up. The locals walked by in their own warm private tents. It rarely rained, but it made up for the rarity by coming down hard enough to sweep heavy trucks down hillsides and dump them on their sides in the muck at the bottom. Everybody suffered, Germans, British, Australians, Italians, Americans, anybody who hadn't been raised here and who didn't know better than to stay out of flood-gulfs. The locals walked calmly by, the wet dripping easily down their own dry private tents.

Pfirsich Rommel was sitting in his own command tent, listening to the rain plopping onto the canvas. He was fingering a single file-card, and grinning to himself.

He was happy. Melvin had been with him for over a year, blowing into camp at the most inopportune moments, offering him careless primitive joy. Melvin wasn't emotionally demanding. He wasn't even loyal. Pfirsich was happy that Melvin didn't want anything from him except what he could provide with his eyes closed. It was shallow, but it was refreshing, and perfect for this moment in his life.

He was happy because Melvin had messed up his existence. Out of impure motives, part boredom, part curiosity, Melvin had no sooner hit the Dark Continent than he organized a night between Pfirsich and a girl, half French, half native. It took a native medicine that tasted like moss and iron in Pfirsich's coffee to make him forget himself, or his what he thought of as his firm preference. In Africa, such things aren't so definite, and the herb-women know the simples that will complicate a man's life. The view through the keyhole of the girl's room -- that Melvin had appropriated for his own prurient uses -- had been proof how well the Native Herbs had performed. Afterwards, awash in shame and guilt, Pfirsich didn't talk to Melvin for a month. It took six weeks for Melvin to get back into his tent. After nine months' ill-suppressed bitterness at his pilot's thoughtlessness, Pfirsich was presented with a beautiful lion-colored boy child. He'd never known how happy it would make him. All was forgiven. When Pfirsich's younger brother Gerhard heard about it -- there was no keeping anything from the family -- he smirked, "See? Homosexuals can learn a skill."

Pfirsich was content because he had found a place where he could survive and create his own society. Even his orderly's desert hygiene hadn't prevented the mucky little man from making social connections with the locals. Udo had somehow gotten himself married to a handsome native nomad girl, first in a tribal and then in a Christian rite. Pfirsich couldn't say a thing; he himself had been ceremonially presented with a purebred silver-white Arabian mare, and he didn't dare sell or trade or even gift her ladyship without risking insulting some important local chiefs. He'd given up protesting, and just enjoyed taking her out for evening gallops. If nothing else, he could always say he was displaying appreciation for their gift where the chiefs could see it.

And Pfirsich felt a barely tangible yet constant ache of gratitude, because, finally, after all this time, he had tracked down his friend Harm. He was in a camp called Fliessenburg -- or Flossenberg. Pfirsich couldn't quite read the name on the file-card, but that didn't matter, he'd find that camp, and he'd find a way to get Harm out of it and into Africa. Hair-brained Melvin wouldn't be jealous; he would probably even enjoy the adventure of flying him to the dark continent. They'd figure out where to send him from there. Here there were no border guards. They would find a way. Pfirsich kissed the file-card, and tucked it back into his uniform pocket.

He had given the Officer Of The Day the night off. The man had looked so sick when he showed up for duty. Probably scurvy.

"Heavens, dear," said the *Oberst*. "Look at you. You can hardly stand up. Give me your pistol and go lie down."

"My pistol, *mein Herr?*"

"Oh, mine's been packed away in oilcloth for a month."

"Certainly, *mein Herr,*" said the officer, and coughed miserably.

"Go back to your cot. Do you need any dry blankets?"

The poor man gave him a grateful look, shook his head and staggered off back down the command-tent hill, his teeth chattering and his shoulders hunched. Pfirsich might not have been as hard as his brother, but like him he always put his men first, especially when they were sick or needed rest.

It was nearly evening. Pfirsich sat wrapped up to his ears in his greatcoat, his bill-cap pulled down as low as he could tug it, pouring a muck of thrice-brewed tea-leaves and sand out off the bottom of his teacup. He looked up at the rain dripping off the edge of his tent-flap.

"How do we get sand in our tea, when the sand's all glued down as mud?"

"Gets into everything, *mein Herr*," said his orderly, Udo Schmidt, washing up by scrubbing the pot with mud. If he'd answered that question once, he'd answered it a thousand times. And washed a thousand thousand teacups and pots since he'd come to the desert. He held the pot up and grimaced at it. He'd been hardly out of school when he'd joined the service, and he'd done more housework than shooting.

"Here's Kristof," he said, at the sound of footsteps platsching in through the mud. "What've you got now, Kristof? *Hochwasser?*"

The dumb radio operator came in out of the rain, a stack of wet hat and slicker and hood, and held out the little envelope of oilskin he used to protect paper from the wet. Pfirsich took it, shook off the drip, and opened it. The piece of paper inside had been written on and erased, carefully, more than once.

"*Hochwasser,*" read Pfirsich, and tucked the paper right back into the envelope, then handed it to Kristof, to use again.

The German code word for a sudden British attack meant "flood." When the floodwaters tore down the slopes and the Germans got on the radio yelling "*Hochwasser, Hochwasser!*" whoever they were talking to who wasn't being flooded thought the enemy had come in out of nowhere. There had been a lot of confusion and frustration and screaming over radios until they settled down to prying trucks out of the mud and cursing to themselves, dripping. After about the fifth time, radio operators just rolled their eyes and twiddled their knobs. Nobody in command thought to change the code word.

"More trucks gone," sighed Pfirsich. "Thank you, Kristof."

Kristof nodded.

"They'll need more of ours," said Pfirsich. "How are we ever going to get anybody any supplies if we're always giving our own trucks away like this?"

"Don't know why you brought it," said Udo to Kristof. "Could have stayed where you were, and not come out in the wet."

Kristof shrugged.

"Bored, huh?" said Udo.

"Would you like a cup of hot tea, dear? Udo, be kind and make this poor man a cup of tea." Pfirsich tried to pull his greatcoat collar up even farther around his ears. "And I could use another cup, too."

Kristof flipped back his hood. Udo lit the little jerry-rigged stove, made of a cup of gasoline poured over the sand in a tin can ventilated with perforations in the rim. They had long ago run out of the chemical tablets for the lightweight collapsible *Esbit* cookers. They were getting low on matches, even though the German army packed matches like the Americans packed toilet paper.

"Good," said Udo, and handed Kristof the pot. "Take that and get us some fresh water."

Kristof stepped back into the rain and craned his neck, looking up. He strained up with one hand and pulled on the projecting flap, dumping a stream of rainwater into the pot, then handed it into Udo's waiting hand. Pfirsich looked up.

"I would've thought most of the sand was washed off by now."

Udo looked up. "Always more sand. I'm sure the oil's gone by now. You didn't taste any, did you, *Mein Herr?*"

Pfirsich didn't even shudder. He just absently shook his head. He'd been a Captive White Girl for a long time now, and only cared if his Buffalo Soup were hot, or at least thick enough to conceal the sand on the bottom. Because of the overcast it was getting dark fast, but he wasn't worried about the tea keeping him awake. Falling asleep in a war-zone wasn't a problem. A war-zone wore a man out, even when he wasn't ducking lead.

When Kristof had gulped his tea, wiped his silent mouth and slogged off back down the wet hill, the sun -- at least according to the wristwatches, for it couldn't be seen through the overcast -- had set behind the mountains. Udo had gone to bed, and Pfirsich sat in the dying glow of the sand-stove, slurping at his tea and occasionally spitting out the sand. All he could hear was the low hiss of the rain. He wasn't used to it any more, as he had been at home, and he couldn't press it into the background. He sat there in the dark, entranced with the sound of liquid falling far down out of the sky, with his last mouthful of lukewarm tea held in one cheek.

Pfirsich didn't hear the first shell come in until it hit in the middle of the truck park.

He was out of his camp chair and down the escarpment without a word, silent as a cheetah; it wasn't going to do a lot of good to yell "Attack!" when that was obviously what somebody was already doing. All around him, his people were tumbling out of their tents, and the guards, without their commanders concern for redundancy, were bawling "Attack! Attack!" A guard's helmet bounced under Pfirsich's feet, and he only missed a bad fall by dancing around it and skipping off the top.

Pfirsich could hear German rifles, pistols and machine pistols, with their fast firing-rate like the trill of a cat, in a medley with the slower and more guttural rattle of the enemy's weapons. Without starlight he couldn't see very well; the attackers should have sent up a flare, but there must have been a failure in their command structure, and evidently nobody had been issued torches for the attack, or something, probably, maybe – who knew? All the available light came from explosions and muzzle flashes. Everybody was screaming and charging and retreating and running in circles in the usual three-ring combat circle-jerk, until the first flare went off over the battle-field and turned everything sparkling yellow in the rain.

The first thing Pfirsich saw was two wet soldiers in short bulky jackets and turtle helmets – the recently arrived Americans? -- who had gotten turned around in the dark and came running toward one another, one of them panicking and putting a burst of machine-pistol fire into the belly of his countryman. The survivor didn't seem to realize what he'd done; he ran on into the dark, out of the light of the flare, and somebody out there in the blackness squawked like a stabbed chicken and probably died. Pfirsich couldn't tell if it was an American or a German -- it was an international squawk.

Pfirsich would later feel he'd stood for an hour, at least, looking down in the yellow light at the dying American gurgling and spitting up black blood at his feet, but in the same moment the man had hit the mud, Pfirsich had already spun around and gone slipping and sliding up the muddy escarpment, all thought of that cramping twisting leaking body at the bottom of the hill gone from his mind. He filed it away unconsciously with his nightmares. It would come back later.

As he leapt to the top of the hill, Pfirsich yanked the sick officer's pistol from its holster, bounced it in his palm, and grabbed the grip. He skidded into the radio tent, where Kristof had already powered up the set and held out the microphone to his commander. Pfirsich grabbed it and didn't sit down in the camp-chair Kristof shoved toward him.

He keyed the microphone with no confusion of purpose. He wasn't a 42-year-old *Oberst* who had forsworn war and pledged to keep his men safe for their homeland. He was an 18-year-old *Leutnant* who could triangulate an artillery strike with one eye closed, and didn't recoil when the guns did. He wanted to hit something; he wanted to lean forward with his binoculars and watch all the nondescript broken bits spatter up into the light.

"DAK Unit Code Odal Spade under attack -- request support centered 350 meters eastern perimeter Hill B105. I said, Hill B105," repeated Pfirsich. "I said B105! No, not two hundred, three hundred! Three hundred meters! Can you hear me? Three --."

The microphone crackled with static. Pfirsich didn't mean to glare at Kristof.

"Try again," he gritted.

The little man went back to work on the radio, his whole silent body expressing profanity, and Pfirsich took two long steps back out into the yellow light. There was no use yelling at his men. If they were going to do anything, they were doing it already -- he knew that from the sound of all the gunfire and yelling, the hiss of the flare overhead, and the resounding "brrrrngg!" of brass rotating bands flying loose from exploding shells. When the damn radio finally kicked in, he could get some flares and artillery support of his own.

Where Pfirsich could only hear the rain before, now he heard every last thing as clear as in a fever. He heard someone running up behind him; the man's feet pounded like a heartbeat. Pfirsich whirled around and looked him in the face.

The enemy soldier's eyes were wild with excitement and purpose. His platoon had been commanded by their Lieutenant to bring back a German officer for interrogation, and this tall blue-eyed doll-puss had to be the Herd Stallion. Oh boy, was he gonna grab this kraut bastard and get the hell out of here, toot sweet.

He was in the middle of swinging his short rifle by the muzzle, sweeping it forward right into the German officer's legs, when the officer spun around and looked at him.

The rifle should have caught Pfirsich in the back of the knees, harmlessly buckling his legs and knocking him down into the mud, a bruised captive. But when he turned, the full power of the blow caught him right across the kneecaps, crushing both of them into pieces no bigger than pearls.

The pain was so intense that Pfirsich couldn't even squeak. The blow didn't just shatter his knees; it overloaded the sensory information to the nerves around his joints. Jangling and scrambled, distracted from their normal stabilizing twinges, they were unable to assist the knees in maintaining their balance.

Both legs simply broke grotesquely backwards and pulled all the ligaments out of their sheathes. Pfirsich keeled over right flat into the mud and as he hit he passed out. He lay there with the yellow light glaring down through the rain, the tears running out of the sides of his unconscious eyes into the mud.

The American stood there staring down at an interrogation subject he would have to carry if he wanted to get him back to his Lieutenant. Crap. Well, that was stupid. Goddamnit to hell, I didn't mean to hit him like that, how the hell is he gonna walk? And look how goddamn tall he is. God knows how heavy he must be. I'll have to get one of the guys to help to even pick him up.

The soldier heard a mewing sound and looked up to see the German radio operator staring at him with his earphones around his neck. The German was mouthing at him, but all he was producing was smacking noises with his lips and tongue, and the American's attention locked on him like he was a naked woman doing the Rumba with bananas around her hips.

Then the orderly of the officer that the American had shot came up behind the American and stuck a bayonet into his back, splitting the muscles and slicing right into his left kidney. Uremia toxins and pain gushed into his system.

His eyes rolled up in his head and he flopped facedown in the mud with both eyes still open, beside the officer he would never have had a chance of picking up by himself.

* * * * *

Pfirsich woke up with the yellow light still glaring down in his face, and it took him at least a minute before he realized it wasn't hissing. It wasn't a flare. It was the morning sun, shining high in a hot steamy sky, and he was lying on a stretcher that was being loaded into the back of an ambulance. He was aware of a numbed and distant pain in his legs. He felt very peaceful, but he was curious about where he was, and why he couldn't hear any of his men's voices.

"Oh, wait," he moaned, and tried to lever himself up onto his elbows.

"You lie back," said the medic and put a firm hand on Pfirsich's chest and pushed him back onto the stretcher.

"But my men."

"You haven't got any men, now," snapped the medic. "You're a casualty. You're anonymous. Lie down. Emil, if he doesn't behave himself, knock him out."

"Right," said Emil, who was strapping down another groaning anonymity. "Relax, stud. You're hopped up on morphine. Just enjoy it."

"No, wait," protested Pfirsich, and dredged up enough energy to grab the side of the ambulance, groggily wrangling a view of all that was left of his command.

As far as he could see up the slope of the escarpment, wavering in the sunlight, everything was broken. The earth was pitted, and already dried, and the water in the shell holes was steaming in the new day's heat. There wasn't a tent or a latrine that wasn't flattened. The few trucks and the one car that had been left to the 469th weren't going to do anybody any good any more. They were hollowed out and scattered up and down the landscape, their torn burned fragments mixed with dead gobbets of blistered humanity.

There were as many bodies in *Afrika Korps* tan as there were in American brown. The few figures still up and moving were mostly German, limping around among a few obviously crippled Americans. The only sound was of ambulances as they left crammed with the wounded. There was no sound of human voices, beyond the murmurs and commands of the medics. In the hours since Pfirsich had passed out, the wounded that remained must have screamed and cried and whimpered themselves into exhausted silence.

Pfirsich stopped struggling as the stretcher slid into the ambulance.

"Jesus Gott," he muttered. "What the devil did they hit us with?"

223

"'They' didn't," said Emil, busily buckling his stretcher into the rack.

"What?"

"Our artillery," said Emil.

"Oh, no," mumbled Pfirsich. "Oh, no. I must have called in the wrong coordinates --."

"I doubt it," said Emil. "We've had trouble with those guns before. The bores are all burnt out, and nobody knows where those shells will hit any more. Your men got blown up by the ships that didn't get through for the last six months. Really made a mess here."

"Oh, my poor men."

"Ach, not that many dead. They either got splattered over the hill by direct hits, or got themselves a *Heimatschuß* -- nice little wound to send 'em home. Most of 'em already got trucked off to hospital." Emil patted Pfirsich on the shoulder. "Don't you worry yourself, stud. If we can get 'em back home alive, they'll thank you for having the good luck to call in that artillery unit, bad bores and all."

"Dear God," whispered Pfirsich, and folded his hands.

Emil straightened Pfirsich's useless numbed legs on the stretcher and pulled the last buckle tight with cheerful feelingless competence.

"Have a nice trip!" he said, and jumped down out of the ambulance.

He whipped the tarpaulin over the back compartment of the truck, bringing a deep brown comforting darkness down upon the wounded men.

"Rev 'er up, Max!" he yelled.

The next thing Pfirsich heard was the cab doors of the ambulance being slammed shut, then the engine coming to life. The heat started to rise in the dark compartment. The ambulance lurched into motion and a breath of steamy air puffed in through a rift in the canvas. A distant scream floated in from somewhere up the hill, breathing up and down with the dying lungs, growing weaker as the truck shimmied off down the muddy road. Somebody must have gotten his second wind.

* * * * *

Pfirsich spent a long time in the hospital in Germany. An officer who can't walk, much less run or jump or crawl or carry, isn't much use in a field situation. A soldier is a Beast Of The Foot, after all.

He lay in bed in an open hospital ward, consumed by irritation and boredom, without even the privacy of bed-curtains that an officer might have enjoyed during the last war. No book that had formerly interested him was capable of distracting him. He certainly didn't care to read the newspapers; he had never had any taste for fairy tales, especially in the mendacious and malevolent form that the press had taken of late.

Part of his regret was for the American Captain Holz. Before either the Captain or the 469th was transferred back to Germany, Pfirsich had meant to let the American publish a little snippet of harmless information in *der Kauz*, just to allow him the glow of accomplishment, with no other intent in the world than kindness. It wasn't much of an omission, more a missed opportunity, but Pfirsich still wished he'd had the chance. He would have liked to quietly observe Holz researching around the camp, hugging his little newsprint subterfuge to himself and trying not to grin. Pfirsich had learned a long time ago that making people happy was the most fun on the planet, and he indulged when he could.

Now, lying in bed, when Pfirsich dipped into the papers, it was for information on the most public member of the family, *Feldmarschall* Erwin Rommel. Erwin had finally made it to the desired peak of his career, the one he'd been shooting for — literally — since the Great War. The newspapers followed him as a media darling. He'd become a star. But even then Pfirsich had to sharpen a talent that every German was improving in these days; the ability to read between the lines. The papers had proclaimed the Russian campaign a fearsome success, but an army that needed to send out a beggarly call for donations of blankets from the populace wasn't hiding anything, certainly not its own misery and bad planning.

From what Pfirsich could translate from the papers, Erwin was having his troubles in Africa; it looked like there might be too many Tommies and Aussies and Amis for even him to handle. The papers lauded Rommel's heroic soldiers and brilliant tactics, but he wasn't moving east, toward Egypt, in one straight steady line. His battles raged back and forth across the northern continent, as they seemed to have been doing forever, Tripoli, Egypt, Cyrenaica, Gazala, Alamein, Berlin and back again. Between illness and health and fame and infamy, he fought as his duty demanded, but he didn't keep silence.

The family knew their eldest son moaned and whined about his supply situation. Pfirsich hoped he'd at least stay out of the line of fire. Erwin had the negligent habit of running around the Front, assured that he could direct everything from his tank, like some fiery half-witted *Leutnant* instead of the sly old *Feldmarshall* he had now become. Field Marshall's were supposed to handle their silver-headed Interim Canes – the informal version of their more ornate batons – with reserved dignity, not brandish them over their heads in full charge.

No more sense than he'd shown in the last war, thought Pfirsich. Some of his Staff officers said they wished they had an officer with a little more cowardice, so they could at least keep track of him. If Erwin weren't careful he'd get himself surrounded or lost or run off into the Mediterranean or something. Or captured.

Pfirsich snorted. That would be wonderful, wouldn't it -- Erwin fuming around inside a prison camp, stamping his boots and poking things with his fancy cane, grumbling and snarling, almost gnawing the wires like a freedom-crazed rabbit, making God-knew-what sort of career hell for some poor put-upon prison-camp commander off in Britain, or America, or somewhere. Serve him right if they stuck him out in the desert. Wisconsin, or whatever they called it. They'd put him on the Island of Elba if they thought they could keep him there. Keep him locked up where his hero, Napoleon, had been held in captivity. Who held Elba right now? It didn't matter, wouldn't do 'em any good to put his brother on any island; Erwin could swim like a fish. They'd be lucky if he didn't tunnel his way out with his bare fingers and teeth and take most of the camp population along with him down the beach and out to sea, on whatever small boats he could commandeer. He'd kill the guards who got in his way, just with dirty looks.

Unless the camp commander kept his wits and brought in the newsreel cameras. Erwin would be having so much fun giving interviews that he'd never be able to tear himself away to escape. He'd be signing autographs before it was over. There was a little of the Captain Holz in Erwin

Pfirsich blew out his lips at his newspaper, and his neighbor in the bed to the right didn't even look up; he was used to his left neighbor making noises and muttering to himself. Pfirsich sighed. His brother would end up in Hollywood yet, another German film darling, like Marlene Dietrich or Fritz Lang. All those Hollywood starlets would go mad just to touch his medals. The silly sluts would get a surprise when he threatened to go fetch Lucie.

Pfirsich shook himself. He flipped the newspaper onto the bed of his neighbor, who had been waiting for it, and picked up an engineering periodical. He might as well use his time in bed to do something more constructive, so he spent most of his time brushing up on construction engineering. The best anesthesia was between his ears.

His sister Helene would drop in now and again, when she could take time from her position as a private tutor. Helene had left the public schools when the Nazi gang had gotten their narrow minds and wide paws on the curriculum, but the last time Pfirsich had spoken to her she had been teaching Shakespeare and doing it quite openly. The government had never banned the Bard. One of Shakespeare's earliest and most devoted audiences had been in Germany, and his plays had been translated so soon after their first publication that the Germans couldn't help but think them as native as Goethe or Mann. More German than Heine. Hitler's whole generation wrote assigned essays on the plays and sonnets at school. Banning Shakespeare would never have occurred to them.

Helene occupied her mind right now with other things than poetry four centuries old. She always looked preoccupied these days, and Pfirsich held out his hands to her.

"Hi, sis," he said, as she bent over to kiss him on the cheek. He brushed her hair back from her ear, and she slapped his fingers before he could tickle her.

"You've lost weight," he said.

"Rationing." She smiled. "Helps a girl keep her figure. You're very thin yourself. Are they feeding you well, child?"

"Oh, very well," he lied. "I'm on vacation, after all." He pointed at his knees.

"Do you hurt?"

"Not really. Not like at first. There's no infection, it's all internal. I'm improving daily."

"Do you think you'll walk again?"

"It's not muscle damage. It's the bones, of course, and in the joints and ligaments. It's all mechanics, the cables and cross-ties, braces, hinges." He held up one of his engineering periodicals. "My knees will be a little tight and clumsy, but I'll be able to get around."

"And run?"

He shrugged. "Probably not. I'd need the ligaments for that."

"A pity. You have such a handsome stride."

"I'm still alive. Ah, have you had any luck with Our Friend?"

"Our Friend" was code for Harm Schaffinder. Pfirsich didn't have a private room.

"Have you written him?"

Pfirsich shook his head. They both knew that the postal service -- as drafted and embedded as the journalists and teachers and doctors and mine workers and farmer's unions in the national cause -- would be keeping track of any letters. It wasn't the route to take. And it was doubtful the letters would have been given to Harm, anyway.

"Have you found out if he's all right?

"We're trying," said Helene. "We have to go through channels."

"I know," Pfirsich sighed. "How's the family?"

"It's good." Helene glanced at the ward. "Our brother's back from Africa."

Of course she wouldn't have said "Erwin." The Rommels could be intensely private, now more so than ever.

"Oh, that's good. Our sister will be happy."

In the family code, "our sister" meant Lucie.

"He's not."

"Now what? He's never happy lately."

"Well, That Man --." Helene used the family code for Hitler. "He won't let our brother go back to -- to the front. Our brother is upset."

"What about his command?" Pfirsich meant the *Afrika Korps*.

Helene was digging around in her purse. Very quietly, she said, "Well, the command has been taken over by another officer."

It was an obvious statement, and Helene knew it. She glanced at the patient in the next bed. The tactful man was deeply engrossed in the newspaper. The patient in the other bed lay fast asleep, his yellowish wasted face damp and tremulous, giving way now and again to deep wrenching tics.

"Oh," said Pfirsich. He'd seen how the younger soldiers in Erwin's command had looked at him. Our Rommel, they said. He hoped they'd be all right without Their Rommel.

"This is from Karl," said Helene, and held out something.

Pfirsich took it. It was a little round pot-metal box, just a little larger than the German soldier's belt buckle that had been set into its lid. In North Africa, such things were made on little shop forges, so small that breath blown through bronze tubes would bring the stove up to smelting heat.

"He had it made while he was in Africa, in the last war," said Helene.

Pfirsich rubbed the bowl and counted the tiny oval beads set around the edges of the belt-buckle. Thirty-seven.

Nobody heard much from Karl these days. Karl had always been more private than the other boys, and when he was a man he socialized with a different set of people, even more different than Pfirsich's, who had secrets of their own and were happy not to pry into each other's. Karl had been seen with circulars and newsletters from the Magnus Hirschfeld movement, and he might have attended lectures at their teashops before the Nazis closed them. To Pfirsich, tea was just something you drank. He had never wanted to discuss, much less believe in the *Urning*. Two sexes and all their combinations were enough for him, thank you, without adding a philosophical third.

Karl was more like their father in that he was willing to delve into his own personality and its formation. He was open-minded, and open-ended. Pfirsich was like Erwin and their mother; they knew who they were, they came down flatly on one side or the other, and didn't ask pointless questions. Karl kept his researches -- or more properly his business -- to himself and Pfirsich preferred that he did.

Karl had one protecting advantage; he was a disabled war-veteran. He still suffered from the malaria he'd caught while flying in the first African campaign, all those years ago. He might have retained the power to read newsletters, but he didn't go to parties, he didn't go visiting, he rarely arose from bed. He just stayed home and shivered and sweated and thought as much as he liked. He took sponge baths rather than stand, and dined like a Roman nobleman, lying down.

Looking at the little pot metal box, Pfirsich realized he didn't like to see Karl surrender a souvenir of his youth and health.

"What's this mean?" he said. He held out a tiny yellow-metal spoon that he'd drawn from the box, between three fingers and a thumb.

"He used it after he caught malaria. It's an apothecary's spoon," said Helene. "For measuring drugs -- and poisons."

Pfirsich held it in finger and thumb. "Why does he send it to me?"

"Does anyone ever know why Karl does anything?"

"No," said Pfirsich. "Karl's in pain, and pain puts us in a foreign country."

He didn't like the spoon. He put it back into its box and pushed it under the pillow, then winced in a strange land of his own. Helene put a hand out toward his nearest leg.

"It's bearable," said Pfirsich.

"How long will it take before you heal, do you think?"

Pfirsich shook his head. "Who knows? It's not muscle; it won't knit soon."

"How soon?"

"They say I'll need operations."

"Months?"

Pfirsich shrugged.

Helene took his hand. "It's just as well."

"What? You don't want me to walk?"

"Somebody in this family could use the rest."

"Karl's resting. I won't be."

"Just lie back, and don't worry about anything."

"Worry about what?"

Helene stood up, and pressed a kiss on his forehead. "I'll tell them you won't -- be able to walk -- for a while."

"What? What?"

She turned to go. "One less for the party will make the preparations so much easier. Logistically, you know."

This damn Family Code. Pfirsich glanced nervously at his ward mates, both the conscious and the drugged. He gritted and gulped, and finally spat out his own version of the cipher.

"I can't believe you're throwing -- a party without waiting for me to get well."

"We'll throw what we throw; don't you throw a fit over it. We'll have another one, when you are well, or not, as needed," said Helene, and strode out, waving over her shoulder.

"You never objected to my being at a party before."

"It wouldn't have done any good," said Helene.

"What did you mean by that?" demanded Pfirsich.

If the tall man could have risen and run after his sister as she disappeared, he would have leapt in front of her and blocked her passage by force. As it was, he only disturbed his waiting knees, and their lusty protest made him chirrup like a squeezed bullfinch. The patient with the newspaper dropped it just enough to stare at him over the top of the page, over a black-and-white photograph of Hitler that looked just as startled -- at least That Man had his mouth wide open, but that was nothing new -- and the yellow unconscious patient echoed Pfirsich's shrieking chirp with a breathy rasp of his own. Helene sailed out of the ward as though she had small fascist mouse-demons skittering and biting at her heels.

"How --," gasped Pfirsich, choking on The Code. "How inhospitable!"

The patient with the newspaper slowly shook his head. No wonder the man was always muttering to himself, with relatives as puzzling and vacillating as that.

Bread and Swans

17. Casting The Stones

It was a long time since Africa.

A long time since *Feldmarschall* Rommel had come back to confront his Leader, and had been forbidden to go back to his men, and gnawed his fingernails in fury and grief as his soldiers were forced back to the sea by the British and Americans and were finally captured *en masse* with everything they had: their officers, their equipment, their patriotism and pride. The only thing they'd lacked had been gasoline, and the troop-ships that never came to snatch them away from defeat. They went to prison camps in North Africa and Arizona; the German legions left the deserts for the rest of the century.

They didn't suffer the fate of the soldiers of Stalingrad, whose few survivors went further than even Napoleon, on past Moscow, on to Siberia.

"What a great people," said Charles de Gaulle, among the ruins of the hard-fighting city.

"The Russians?"

"No, the Germans -- look how far they got."

No Frenchman ever forgets Napoleon's Russian campaign. So many of them hadn't come back, or the Germans who had accompanied them. Most of the Germans didn't come back this time either.

Hin ist hin.

* * * * *

Since Africa, Pfirsich hadn't been in a position to act as his brother's unofficial brevet sounding board, whipping boy and maid-of-all-work.

He was too busy being dragged from bed to operating table to bed, losing weight and gaining bits of surgical metal, as overworked doctors tried to pin together his muddled knee-joints. He knew very well that the only reason they were bothering with him was because he had one famous relative and a whole stable of grimly determined ones, and one or two with money. Otherwise the doctors would have whipped off both legs below the knee and sent him home to grow bedsores. For once in his life Pfirsich was content to accept the privilege that comes with convenient bloodlines.

In the meantime, Erwin had gotten assigned up and down Fortress Europe, even commanding the beachheads in France for a time. He frowned and almost stamped when he discovered the state of the coastal defenses. There weren't any. The Fortress didn't even have a wall. *Mein Gott,* it didn't even have a place to pile the bricks. Where the hell had the German Army been? No -- where hadn't it been? Poland, France, Sweden, Spain, Greece, Italy, Africa and Russia. Up and down half the known world. The first German soldier to die in the war had been killed in China, ironically enough defending Chinese civilians from the Japanese while attached to the German Embassy.

When Rommel was done groaning over what he saw -- or didn't see -- on the French coastal maps, the side of him that went out and took hold and made things happen virtually jumped up and down in place and clapped its little hands. *Mann!* Did he have work to do.

As a result he'd been racing up and down the coast in a frenzy of accomplishment, driving staff-cars and armored carriers into the ground, plunging against the harness so hard for such long hours that he sometimes just flopped down asleep face-first onto the planning table, much to the relief of his overworked staff. They quietly wondered if they couldn't bribe his orderly to slip something into the urgent little man's food, nothing lethal -- that dog-like orderly would never stand for lethal -- but just sufficiently nauseating or mildly cathartic. With Rommel, it wouldn't take much. Fortunately for his diffident stomach, duty prevailed.

Since he didn't have enough soldiers for the work, Rommel turned to the French coastal population.

"There aren't enough soldiers left to force the French to work," protested his staff. "Not even as slave laborers."

But to Rommel it was obvious.

"Pay them," he snapped.

The little Field Marshal was nothing if not practical. He knew farmers, and as a practical Swabian himself he recognized kindred spirits in the French, who are an Eminently Practical People. They'd seen a lot of wars, almost as many as the Germans, wars dragging back and forth on their home soil. Particularly on the coast, where they'd never liked the *Isle d' France* anyway, especially not since the Parisian Revolutionary government had come around and beheaded a third of the adult population. They had long memories out there on the coast.

As for the present war, the coastal farmers and fishermen asked themselves who would suffer from a second invasion in five years.

"Paris?" they sniffed. The Paris that rolled over and truckled to the neighbors to the northeast in the first place?

In their opinion, Paris could stand there on its island of sickly yellow dirt and swallow the German occupation and lump it. Them and their *la belle France* attitude, and their snotty accent, and when they weren't surrendering to the Germans, they were killing each other, like back in 1871, while the Germans tapped their toes outside the city gates and waited to conquer the survivors. Guillotines or jackboots -- what was the difference? The Germans could have Paris.

The coastal farmers and fishermen came to work for the Germans and hauled concrete and dug foundations, and were reimbursed for it. At least the Germans paid a man a decent day's wages.

Rommel was tired, and unhappy with the arrangements as they stood, but he was getting more satisfied every time he went out and looked at the progress of the construction. He walked up and down on the foundations of bunkers and along the tidal flats and slapped his boot with his silver-headed Interim Cane.

"*Doch,*" he smiled. "*Wohl.*" This was really beginning to look like something.

And then he received a sudden very urgent message from Lucie to come home.

"Darling, I'm dead busy right now," he protested into the phone, his mind on everything except the conversation. There wasn't a bunker or a bit of barbed wire in enough places on those beaches. They were so short of troops he had to make do with concrete and underwater barbed-wire hedgehogs. My God, the British and Americans would be able to walk right up those bare stretches of sand. He'd have to see how the *Rommelspargel* performed. "Rommel's Asparagus" was the nickname for the big crossbeams standing in the sand, right under tidal level. They'd

235

bust anything the Allies sent into the beaches wide open They'd --.

"Erwin, I would really love to have you home."

"Home? Now?"

"For my birthday."

"Dearest Lu, I don't dare leave right now. It's a complete tangle --."

"Erwin," she rapped out, and he automatically stood up ramrod straight, even though they were only on the phone. "You need to come home for my birthday."

Erwin blinked. He understood, now. He never got so deeply involved in a military problem that Lu couldn't immediately recall him to the realization of a more important agenda.

"Yes, darling," he said.

"And bring me a pair of shoes from Paris, will you?"

Erwin was nodding, briskly, as though she could see him. The shoes would be a perfect cover. A birthday present, of course. Everybody knew how smitten he was with his wife. Why wouldn't he stop off to indulge her with a pair of real Parisian shoes? *Gott,* Lu had a brain on her.

"White ones?" she said, to prompt him to answer.

"White ones!" he agreed. "Oh -- White Ones!" He practically hit himself right across the forehead. Family Code! What had he been thinking?

He was so impressed he completely forgot to be reminded of her shoe size.

Men don't remember personal dates or personal statistics. Any man who has to remember personal dates has no woman to love him, and it hurts; he purposely forgets, just to prove to himself that she really will take care of him. And Rommel was deeply beloved. So he wasn't to blame when he brought his Lu the wrong size shoes. She put the shoes aside on the bedside table and gave him a big happy hug and kiss. Her darling thoughtful man. His fine clever woman.

All the historians were left scratching their heads over why one of the Great War Captains in all of history dropped everything like it was hot *and* ugly and went flibberty-gibbeting off to buy his wife the wrong size shoes -- white shoes, too, in the name of all the Gods of Taste and Fashion -- and was dangerously absent from the coastal defenses at the most spookily inopportune moment he could possibly have chosen.

D-Day just happened to start on Lu's birthday.

* * * * *

Oberst Rommel had to ask. He grabbed his startled brother's elbow, and nearly hauled him out of his saddle.

"Erwin! How can you allow yourself to be seen with Oscar Schindler? He has the worst reputation in the entire capital. And that's saying something!"

Feldmarschal Rommel grinned, and just refrained from patting his mount on the neck. The little bright-bay mare, part of a small livery stable still maintained for the occasional uses of the German High Command, was intently picking her way through the unavoidable tumbling bomb-rubble of Berlin, and interference made her irritable. Rommel preferred her to a car for private excursions for a number of reasons; she could climb handily over the heaps of bricks and broken pipe and wires, she didn't require a drop of petrol, and she couldn't be fitted with a wire.

The bay's whole body was instinct with concentration, and her rider didn't interfere. He could talk with as little distraction as a back-seat rider with a chaffeur.

"Well, he's a bit of a womanizer, if that's what you mean," said Rommel.

"The man's a cold-blooded opportunist," Pfirsich said.

Pfirsich's red chestnut stallion was dancing with his rider's nerves, and at the advantage of the unmistakable weakness of his rider's thighs.

Pfirsich's knee-damage had been inexorably creeping up and down his legs, the ligaments -- that repeated operations had never been able to re-attach -- shrinking around the inserted metal bits, the muscles withering, so that not only could he barely hobble even with the use of a cane, he was gradually losing the strength of leg he needed to maintain a horse's confidence and direction. He had nothing remaining but his arms to control the stallion.

And this stallion hated humans. He was a rare survivor of Germany's thousands of starved, frozen, shot, shrapnel-gutted, butchered and devoured gun-carriage teams. He was a smart horse, he remembered, and he resented.

"Oscar keeps his ear to every rotten wall in the city," said Pfirsich. "There's nobody's dirty hand he won't shake, and nothing he won't get involved in. He can't be trusted. Everybody in Berlin and half of France knows it."

"Everybody does," shrugged the General. "None of us is perfect."

The stallion had a hard mouth and a combat mindset, and no human arm has the iron to force an iron-mouthed horse into its own agenda. Pfirsich fought the brute, curvet by slashing curvet, nearer the mare, so he didn't need to raise his voice to Erwin. The stallion retaliated by trying to savage a citizen who ducked behind one of the few remaining upright lampposts. Pfirsich hauled him away, then smacked the foaming brute, not because he though he could get through to him, but partly as a comfort to himself.

"I'm sorry. He's not happy," he apologized to the citizen, who was backing away from the infuriated horse as fast as the broken bricks would allow.

"Who? Schindler?"

"No," Pfirsich said. "But I still find it very peculiar that you'd even be seen with him, much less try to defend him."

"When was I with him?"

"Right there in the foyer of the Hotel Adlon, watering-hole for half of Berlin. You were blatant."

"I wasn't 'with' him." They'd reached a clear spot. Rommel clucked to the mare and she bounced forward. "I only spoke to him in passing."

Pfirsich urged the stallion right after him, but he was forced to use his crop and handclaps on the neck, and the beast all but exploded under him. He wrestled him to a trot to match Rommel's mare's.

"You passed something to Oscar," said Pfirsich. "I saw it."

"He dropped his handkerchief."

"That was your handkerchief."

"That's what I mean -- he needed one."

An exhausted infantry captain looked up and didn't salute. He had been supervising the search for buried victims after the last American raid, and he wasn't in the mood for the niceties. He glared at his brother officers as they clattered by.

When Rommel pressed his thighs hard around the bay mare this time, she threw up her head and nearly hit him in the face.

"Keep it up, young person," he said, "and you'll be wearing a martingale."

Pfirsich hunched his shoulders. He could feel the infantry officer's eyes drilling him between his shoulder blades.

He didn't envy the burial crews their dirty work. There were too many dead to be hauled away and buried, so they were heaped up in the rubble and set on fire like plague victims. One of the duties of the burial squads was to collect the wedding rings of the dead, and they stripped them off corpses by the clinking tarnished bucketful. The order had been issued in the desperate hope of the besieged that there would be a way to somehow identify heaps of ashes by plain gold bands.

"You had something wrapped up in it," insisted Pfirsich. "In the handkerchief. Something that sparkled."

"This isn't any of your business."

Once again, as so many times of late, Pfirsich saw his brother perform the *Deutscher Blick,* The German Glance. When Rommel looked back, his face was bitter and pinched. Without saying a word, this time he put spurs to the mare, and controlling her sudden impatient hop he galloped away, out of the busy street, forcing Pfirsich to haul the rebellious chestnut into a gallop after him.

People glared at the galloper, then recognized him and cheered. Everybody knew what Rommel looked like; nobody else was that small and fierce. He made even Hitler look tall.

The Field Marshal didn't let the mare rest until they'd clattered off the broken cobbles and onto the soft paths of the *Tiergarten* Park. Only when the comparatively undamaged green trees and the unconscious waters of the river Spree safely surrounded them did Rommel rein in the mare and turn on his brother.

"You of all people should know better than to speak like that with people around, Pfirsich!"

"Don't lecture me, Erwin. I saw what it was, all wadded up in your handkerchief. Lucie's diamonds --."

"Bsst! Bsst! Bsst! Your Sister!" hissed Rommel, and made the quick little hand-signal for the Family Code. "Say 'her,' or 'she,' or even better, 'them,' or 'somebody.' Even gender can be a clue, at this point.

239

Everybody thinks of me as the head soldier in our family."

"I've heard you, whenever you two discuss anything. 'Whatever you say, dear, whatever you want, darling'," Pfirsich mocked. "It's a point of fun with everybody who knows you. She quite leads you around by your nose."

"Yes she does," said Erwin, and his chin rose proudly. "I couldn't have a better commander. She's got a head on her shoulders, and the courage of a trooper. I trust her," he repeated.

Pfirsich nodded impatiently. "Where else would you get diamonds but from her?"

"I'm a Field Marshal," protested Rommel. "Generals get nice things, booty and land and castles. It's traditional, as far back as Rome."

"Egypt," said Pfirsich.

"Cave dwellers, for that matter," said Rommel. "Always gave their chiefs the best hole in the ground,"

"To live in or as a grave?"

"Both. A pension and a state funeral."

Bitte. They may get spoils offered to them, but they don't always take them. The only thing you ever took were those flimsy British sun-shields you used to wear on your hat in Africa." Pfirsich sniffed. "Some booty."

"The photo-boys loved 'em."

"You won't even take the estates in Poland and France that That Man tries to offer you. Even General Guderian takes estates."

"Guderian didn't have a choice; his house was bombed out. He had to have someplace for his family."

"You simply refuse to be beholden to That Man."

"I'm already in his debt; he made me a Field Marshal."

"He got more than his money's worth. And he treats you shamefully. You don't owe him anything."

"I owe him gratitude --."

"Pft --!" spat Pfirsich.

"But not political obligation," finished Rommel.

"If you're that wary of political hooks, let alone wealth, nobody can have been trying to bribe you with diamonds."

"Well, keep it to yourself. You never know."

"Besides, these diamonds went from you to Oscar, not the other way around."

"Pfui. You probably saw some drops of wine glittering in the candlelight."

"Erwin, you've already admitted they were diamonds. And I recognized that one emerald-cut yellow stone."

"Yellow Moselle wine."

"That was Grandma *von* Luz's favorite stone!"

Rommel didn't even try. "How did you see that?"

"There was a mirror behind you. How could I not?"

"You weren't even in the building; you were loitering outside the hotel, looking at the nude statues."

"*Ich bitte*. Those awful white blocky things," Pfirsich shuddered. "You may not care about art, but I have better taste that."

"Can't tell if they're men or women," grumbled Rommel.

"I wasn't looking at them, and I was not in the street."

"I heard your cane tapping around out there."

"I wasn't in the street, I was right in the entry-way, with a clear view of the mirrors."

"Well, we are getting far-sighted in our mature years, aren't we?"

Pfirsich wouldn't relent. "My Sister's family diamonds, her inherited fortune, handed over to that Schindler person!"

"Well, it's not for love."

"I shouldn't think so. The man is trash. Self-indulgent trash."

"Don't think about it."

Pfirsich put his hand to his mouth. "Oh, dear, it's not --."

"Don't get mixed up in what you don't know about."

A half-dozen options ran through Pfirsich's mind, but none of them touched upon his own illegal condition. The thing that Harm had been hiding when he was taken away on the train hadn't yet been discovered in Pfirsich. Pfirsich winced; he still hadn't been able to do anything for Harm, and didn't even know if he was still in the same camp, or even alive, or still listed as a Jew and nothing worse in the eyes of the Reich. A man had to be so careful.

Being homosexual in the Third Reich didn't scare Pfirsich a fraction as much as the horrible prospect of having his whole brave and politically busybody family frog-marched off to the most remote barbed-wire enclosure. Torture and starvation in himself he could take, a lot easier than heartbreak.

"Is he blackmailing us, Erwin? What does he know?"

"He only knows what he needs to know, Pfirsich."

"What's he trying to take?"

Rommel leaned forward in the saddle and fixed his brother with his blue eyes.

"Let me assure you that Your Sister knows exactly what to do with her own wealth. I can't lay a finger on it, even if I wanted to."

"Erwin, don't poor-mouth. Mama left us all with trust funds. None of us would have had to work, if we didn't want to."

"Compared to L -- Your Sister?" Rommel snorted. "If she wants to use me as a go-between to scatter her diamonds around, for her own purposes, then she has only to hand me the jewels and point me in the right direction. I don't question her orders. I trust her," Rommel finished simply, with quiet pride.

"I'll take on Schindler myself. She doesn't have to."

"Don't you fool yourself," warned Erwin. "She's the most formidable member of the family -- after Grandmama -- and she won't take it very well if her pretty little brother-in-law gets in her way. You don't cross the Rommel women. *Mein Gott,* Pfirsich, even Himmler knows that."

"I would never interfere with their wishes," protested Pfirsich. "I respect them deeply."

"Then do as Our Other Sister told you to do. Stay off your feet."

"Who needs us now?" Pfirsich asked bluntly. "Is it a friend of the family?"

"Pfirsich, will you just shut up? I'm not going to brief you out here in the reeds."

"There aren't any microphones out here in the reeds. You said so, yourself."

"Did you check your saddle?"

"They wouldn't fit on a saddle," said Pfirsich.

"Haven't you ever heard; 'The less you know, the better'?"

"I'm not asking for a detailed briefing; I just don't want us to be in Oscar's power."

"Pfirsich, we're not in Oscar's power. He's one of our contacts."

"Oscar?" said Pfirsich. "Oscar? Oscar Schindler?"

"We're not in Africa any more," said Rommel. "We can't do what we could do then, because so many of those earlier resources are simply beyond our reach. If an Oscar Schindler can be a resource, we turn to him."

"Whatever for?"

"He's a Nazi, Pfirsich. A useful Nazi. None of us are Party Members, except Lu, and she's a woman," Rommel reminded his brother. "We need Oscar."

"Oh dear," said Pfirsich. "How did we end up needing Them?"

Rommel leaned on his hands, thinking, then said, "Oscar is on our side. He's running a labor camp, in association with his business."

"Our side?" Pfirsich gasped. "Since when have we been on the side of labor camps?"

"He's using his position to keep his workers alive. But he can't do it alone and he needs to pay off the people he deals with. Some people have even more commercial sense than loyalty or hate or fear. That's where Your Sister comes in. And the diamonds."

"Is it only Oscar she's helping?"

"Everybody needs help, right now. Haven't you seen those bags of mail I get? Everyone is writing to me."

The letters all begged Rommel to do something for the country, to save it, as though he could. Old women and children, trusting him like a crusading knight. Women begging him and promising anything if he could find their missing men-folk, or at least discover how they had died. Soldiers, infuriated at the betrayal of their loyalty and of their oath. The honest, the naive, the purely opportunistic, anyone who was backed into a corner and in their desperation believed Germany's African hero could stretch forth his hand and accomplish miracles for them. Heartbreaking.

Rommel had stopped opening the envelopes, both because he had no time, and in a misery that he wasn't able to do a thing for the people who had written the letters, not even take the time to comfort them. And he could do was instruct his secretary to send a short note for him. He felt helpless, and it wasn't a feeling he was used to bearing. When he took into consideration how many of those letters were censored, how many were simply seized and destroyed, or even kept as evidence, it hurt him just to imagine the full volume of his people's agonized cry for help.

"Erwin, you don't think they censor your mail?"

"There isn't a German alive today who can trust he won't have his mail opened or confiscated. Do you think even I'm allowed to see all my mail?"

"You used to enjoy getting mail."

Rommel sighed. "It used to be fun."

"You used to get marriage proposals. You're lucky Lucie never slapped you."

"Yes," said Rommel, and unconsciously rubbed his chin. "The girl has spunk. But she hasn't had any rivals writing me letters in a long time."

"I hope not."

"I wish I could do something for these poor people, but I can only fulfill my public duty. I don't dare do anything else, not with the way the eyes of the whole country have been on me, especially since I was in Africa."

"Are *they* watching you, Erwin?"

"Of course, 'they' are watching me; there's no one 'they' exempt from surveillance. But since Africa I've become a public figure. Little brother, I have no more privacy any more than a royal princess. If I tried, personally, to do something, I couldn't even do this little any more. That's why I don't ask. The fewer the better," he emphasized again.

"Erwin, you sound so helpless. I've never heard this tone in your voice before."

Erwin shrugged. "I'm not helpless. I just keep my eyes closed, so those who can afford to open their eyes don't get them poked out."

"I'm glad you can still trust someone."

"I do trust you, Pfirsich."

"I know you do. I'm grateful. But --."

"But this time, you stay out of it. You've done all you can do at this point, thank you very much."

"Erwin."

Rommel held up his hand. "You'll do me more service if you don't get involved. Do you want us all thrown into a concentration camp before it's over? Yes, I can see you've thought of it yourself. There's no one who doesn't fear that, and with reason."

"It's as though the whole country has become prisoners," muttered

Pfirsich. "How did this happen?"

"We're not prisoners, Pfirsich. Not unless we chose to let them make us prisoners. We can make decisions, we can find things out if we really want to, we can find a way to do some good."

"So how am I supposed to do some good?"

"By not asking questions."

"Isn't it time I started?"

"You've got to know when to ask questions, and when to keep your mouth shut. I don't expect you to be well informed, anyway. For one thing, you've been in hospital, and even there you didn't read the papers. *Mein Gott,* you don't even listen to the radio, or watch newsreels. Believe me, they made a mistake when they drafted all the journalists into the army; those boys manage to sneak things in between the lines. If you'd been watching, you'd know."

"Well, I haven't been watching newsreels."

"I know, I know, because you don't like That Man's voice."

Rommel motioned back outside the trees, in the direction that Pfirsich knew was toward the gutted Chancellery.

"It's only fair, Erwin. He doesn't like me either."

"He never says a thing to you."

"Of course he doesn't," sniffed Pfirsich. "He despises me. He sweats poison at the sight of me."

"Don't put on airs. That Man doesn't even see you."

"Of course he doesn't; he makes a point not to see me or speak to me. Which I'm perfectly happy with; do you think I want his notice? He's hated me since the first time he saw me, 'way back in '35."

"When did you ever see Hitler in 1935?"

"In Goslar, *Herr* Absent-Mind. When Himmler and Goebbels came to the hotel."

"Oh." Rommel's brow wrinkled. "That wasn't '35, that was '34, wasn't it? Were you there?"

"Yes, I was there. How could you forget? I practically kept you from having a fistfight with Himmler."

"I never did."

"You probably don't remember, you were so busy showing your teeth at him. That's another thing, Erwin. That man is out for your blood."

245

Rommel started so strongly that the mare danced under him.

"No, not *him*. Himmler."

"Oh," grinned Rommel. "I know that."

"He's hated you ever since."

Erwin waved a hand dismissively. "No, no, let's not go so far. It's only that I disagree with his actions."

"Erwin, I was there. You were rude to him. You dug your own grave that day. He's been just dying for a chance to get back at you, ever since."

Erwin squinted.

"Erwin, that is an extremely petty man."

"He's detail-minded."

"A little man, a man who doesn't forget a word of sleight or insult in a lifetime. And with an unfathomable capacity for detail. Have you ever seen what he has in his office?"

"You mean The Wheel?"

"Yes, The Wheel." Pfirsich shuddered.

The Wheel; Himmler's mechanized card-file. He strongly implied that it recorded the name of every single German on the planet. There were probably Germans, or even Austrians, in Java or maybe Tibet, whose names he had on file. He was so proud of it that there wasn't anyone, even the scullery maid, in Number 8 *Prinz-Albrechtstraße* that hadn't seen him demonstrate it. People had been known to duck back into file-rooms when they saw him coming down the hallway.

Rommel nodded. "I know. He's demonstrated the damned thing to me at least three times. You'd think it was a new kind of chicken-feeder."

"And I'll bet on your card -- which you know very well he's got, and in red ink -- it says: 'Memo: Get back at that little *Knirps* for incident at Goslar. Soonest'."

"Oh, pft," said Rommel. "None of our family is on The Wheel."

"Aren't they? Didn't you hear what he'd said?"

Rommel cocked his head at his brother.

"He said that he's got at least one member of every single German family in a concentration camp, so he can fetch anybody, or make anybody dance, any way he likes."

"He's bragging," said Rommel.

"He's not. Himmler doesn't brag. Have you ever looked into his face? If you don't count that uniform he wears, he is almost neurotically modest."

"Don't be paranoid."

"Don't tell me not to be paranoid. Who's the one dragged me out into this swamp, because he was afraid people are walking down the street with microphones in their hats?"

"Well, they usually are. At least the SS hats."

"Who else did you think I meant?"

"Could be anybody, these days," said Rommel.

The mare had been getting more and more restless; her internal clock was going off like an air-raid siren. Rommel noticed the disturbance going on under him and looked at his wristwatch.

"Hopp-la. Right you are, girl. Come on, Pfirsich. We'd better get these horses back to the stables. Going to be time for the afternoon bombing, pretty soon."

"Oh, Pfui," said Pfirsich. "And I meant to pick up some soap, to save my orderly a trip. Udo gets as irritable as this horse if I overload him. He's mad enough that he's back home in Berlin and has to bathe."

"You've still got Udo?"

"He's one of a handful of my people who wasn't wounded in Africa. I don't know where any of the others went, not their units, not even the countries they've been assigned to. Poor Udo, once he'd recovered from the shrapnel wounds, he hunted me down and begged to stay with me, looking over his shoulder the whole time."

"Battle fatigue."

"More than that. Erwin, I think he's got Family Code of some kind, too. I have my suspicions, but I don't ask."

"Wise."

"I couldn't very well turn the poor little guy away. God knows he's the least suitable man to ever serve in the military. To be absolutely charitable, the man's a lousy soldier, Erwin."

"The country needs all its men."

"Like you haven't got an orderly."

"Do you really need an orderly? You're hardly on duty!" snapped Rommel, pointing at his brother's thigh, the one on his side of Pfirsich's stallion.

"I would just as soon at least one man doesn't end up shot through

247

the guts if I can help it."

"Fine. But if he's overworked now, wait 'till tomorrow. Tonight there will probably be a heavy night bombing, and everybody will have to help dig out in the mornings. You'll probably be able to get something done in the afternoon, before tomorrow's bombing," said Rommel, turning his horse and setting off at a trot.

"*Ja* -- if the shop is still there," said Pfirsich, and bent his protesting mount into a canter after his brother's mare.

18. Backstage

On July 20th, 1944, the German army made an *Attentat* upon the life of Adolf Hitler. It was their fifteenth attempted assassination.

After that, no one tried any more. In the first place Hitler really seemed to be the invincible child of fate, and Fate was always the strongest of the old Germanic gods. In the second, the SS caught up with and destroyed the conspirators and their families. The commander of Paris, General von Stülpnagel, attempted to commit suicide with a pistol held to his own temple and only succeeded in blowing out his eyes. On the operating table to save his life for trial and execution two weeks later, he muttered the name "Rommel."

On July 17th, in France, a fighter-plane, some said British, some said American -- some would later even say German -- had strafed Rommel's car, killing his driver and throwing the Field Marshal out of his seat. He was hurled against a tree that stood green and oblivious of human fate even as a man's skull crumpled against its bark. The little man was found fac e down in the ditch, bubbling in his own blood. On the way to the hospital, a French pharmacist saved the German officer's fading life by injecting him with two ampoules of camphorated oil, a moderate dose that slowed and strengthened his stuttering heart. A less conscientious or more political man would have used more, and brought on convulsions.

Everybody in the family, and so many of the people of Germany, were amazed and overjoyed to hear that Rommel could have survived such an accident. When Pfirsich managed -- he hoped nobody asked how -- to get to the hospital in Paris, he was amazed to find his brother was more than conscious. He was sitting up in bed, with a bandage over his one destroyed eye, trying to swat the inevitable summer flies with a slipper. The nursing staff was convinced the Field Marshal must have lost his mind along with the eye.

"No," said Pfirsich. "He's only practicing to retain his aim, to retrain himself to hit a small swift mark with only one eye and no depth perception."

"Ahhh," said the nurses, impressed.

"And he hates flies," said Pfirsich, remembering Africa. "They drive him out of his skin."

"Oh," said the nurses, looking askance at the Field Marshal's room.

When Pfirsich had first seen Erwin without the bandages, he stopped breathing for a moment himself from the image of sentient death that presented itself to him. He'd seen men with smaller holes in their heads rotting in the trenches. How could his brother be up assaulting insects? After a few days, how could he be walking around? In fact, how could he be stalking around the hospital, demanding he be released for duty?

Nobody could talk him back into his bed, not with the country groaning with war out there beyond the hospital. Rommel was convinced that he had to talk to Hitler, that only he could persuade his leader to bring the war to an end. It was evidence of the damage that had been done to him that he still clung to the belief that at this point Hitler was capable of listening to anybody, to anybody at all but his own deranged voice. Hitler had become a grievously sick man, in some ways far more incapacitated than Rommel, but he was an invalid who held the power of life and death over his own doctors.

Rommel wouldn't get back into bed, and he was was going to pace himself into a stroke. Pfirsich was there when a doctor who was weary of trying to cajole the defiant patient back into bed lost his professional patience.

"Wer hört nicht, muß fühlen," Pfirsich heard the doctor mutter, and flinched.

The German Dharmic chant -- listen or get hurt. Pay attention, or pay for it. Hear me, or suffer the consequences.

Be it on your own head.

Too angry to send an orderly, the doctor whipped down among the wards himself, fetching back an anonymous skull from pathology and a hammer from the hospital carpentry shop. By the time he returned, he had walked himself into a frustrated muttering rage. He felt no shyness about staging a noisy little forensic demonstration for the Field Marshal's personal education.

"*Herr Feldmarschall,*" he snapped, to get the patient's attention, then whacked the yellow-brown skull twice, hard, with the hammer, caving in the left temple and cheek-bone, sending the white eggshell shards of the bone in little projectiles from around the left eye-socket. He thrust the mutilated skull into Rommel's face, and barked:

"That's what your skull looks like! Go back to bed!"

All the teachers in Rommel's ancestry immediately recognized a classroom demonstration, and his trench experience understood the meaning of that much cranial damage. People with skulls that looked like that should be dead and buried. Underground for the past week. Communing with the worms and their ancestors. *Ganz klar.* Rommel even gasped. He almost squeaked. Pfirsich was as much grieved as relieved to see him shrink back and turn pale, and hold out an arm to be led tottering back to bed.

It didn't last.

* * * * *

Rommel was out of the hospital far before anyone expected it, certainly before the doctor wanted to release him. He had himself driven right back home to his native Swabia. So much for the pathology lesson.

When the Field Marshal strode into his villa in Herrlingen, on his own wavery feet and with his bandaged head, and saw the look on his Lucie's face, he managed as much grin as he could with his crushed temple muscles. Her look just got worse. He took the hint and stopped smiling.

"At least I'm not carrying my head under my arm," he said. "Can't be that bad."

He had the constitution of one of his own tanks. Now and again he could be seen in full uniform again, chugging along doing what duty he was capable of, head up, chin out. The only thing that anyone noticed was that, rather than happily standing to be photographed full-face and smiling, he would turn his face to the side and sit or prop himself against something, so that no camera could get a record of his smashed cheek and drooping eyelid, or catch the slight instability in his stance.

* * * * *

Nobody but his doctor and his family knew about the strokes. No one else knew about the weakening heart.

Pieces of his broken brain would let go, something would burst, and down he would go. His straining heart gasped and skipped and knocked him flat. But not for long; he was always right back on his feet. His doctor watched him struggle and finally made the decision for him. He put his foot down and put the Field Marshal on home leave.

"I'm not that bad," said Rommel, keeping the good side of his face toward the doctor.

"You're as gray as your uniform," said the doctor.

"I can't afford to be off duty now."

"Do you want me to tell your wife?"

Once he was out of the public eye Rommel spent a lot of time in loose-fitting mufti, sitting on the couch with his eyes closed, his brow tense with every breath. But his uniform and boots stood ready for him, for the day when he felt up to full battle harness. The first phone call would buckle him right back into it.

* * * * *

On the wet evening of October 13th, Pfirsich showed up at the villa in Herrlingen. Seven days before the Field Marshal had received orders to report to Berlin. This evening Rommel wasn't home, but his manservant, Rudolf Loistl, was. He no sooner let Pfirsich in at the front door than the phone rang.

"Go ahead, Rudolf," said Pfirsich, limping into the doorway on his cane. "I can take care of my own hat and coat."

As Pfirsich stood in the doorway, shaking the water out of his coat, he heard Rudolf answer the phone.

"No, I'm sorry, *mein Herr,* the Field Marshal is still out. Oh! General Burgdorf. Tomorrow? I'll be sure to tell him, *mein Herr.*"

"General Burgdorf?" said Pfirsich, gimping into the room as Rudolf put down the receiver. "Wilhelm Burgdorf? That's an old friend of Erwin's. It will do him good to see old friends. Where is he?"

"Out," said Rudolf enigmatically. Pfirsich raised his eyebrows, but didn't pry.

Loistl reported the phone call to Rommel when he returned that evening. The Field Marshal looked terribly drawn and pale and preoccupied, but he smiled.

"Thought they wanted me back," he said through white lips. "They couldn't get along without me. Probably want me to defend East Prussia. I haven't fought the Russians since last war; be interesting to see what they're like now. Rudolf, get my uniform ready."

* * * * *

Pfirsich tried to stay out of the way the next day. He got up early, before anybody else had risen and struggled downstairs and out to the garage to have a look at the little converted wood-burning car that Erwin had been complaining about.

"I'm a Field Marshal," he grumbled. "I deserve better than that little crate. For the look of it, if nothing else."

"Of course," said Pfirsich. "But think how much more fun this one will be to tinker with."

Erwin loved to fuss around with engines; years ago, he'd completely disassembled a new motorcycle in the living room -- Lucie had yelled at him -- and put it back together again, just because he'd never worked on that particular machine before. If he wasn't going to be allowed out on long-term active duty, maybe the little wood-burner would keep him occupied. Pfirsich was curious about the machine himself.

Pfirsich was up to his elbows in the engine, doing more tinkering than he'd intended, when he looked up and saw Erwin taking a turn out in the garden, wearing his favorite brown jacket and leaning on his son's arm. Manfred was home from service with the *Luftwaffe* Auxiliary. Wasn't it amazing how the boy had grown? He was a whole head taller than his famous father, and supported him with ease. Pfirsich shook his head. Erwin would probably never go running or swimming or skiing as he used to. That made three brothers crippled now, by disease, and mistake, and tree. Only Gerhard was still up and singing.

When Pfirsich hobbled back in to breakfast, trying to juggle his cane and a rag to wipe his greasy hands, he found Erwin actually sitting at the table and pouring himself a cup of coffee. Good sign. If he was willing to attempt to put something into his pouty touchy stomach, a stomach even more petulant than usual, to actually take something into his mouth and chew without nausea, then he must be over the worst of it. And it meant that the swelling had gone down in his jaw-joint.

Rommel finished a roll and the cup of hot coffee, showing every sign of enjoying it, and rose from the table with every sign of life.

"Well! Guess I'd better get back into harness," he almost chirped, and went upstairs, all by himself, to put on his uniform.

When he came downstairs, he looked like he might have been whistling. He was brushing the sleeve of his *Afrika Korps* tunic and his face was radiant; even his cheeks were pink. He looked better than he had in months. As he reached the bottom of the stairs, he put out his face toward Lucie, with warm happy intent to kiss her.

That was as far as he got.

He stood frozen, turning a livid clay-white; even his ear lobes were blue. Lucie had only time to put out a hand before he suddenly went down on his knees, genuflecting like a beautifully shot roebuck, to collapse flat on his face in the hallway. Lucie dropped onto her knees and turned him over. His one functioning eye was rolled up in his gray straining face. She loosened his tie and unbuttoned his shirt, while Pfirsich limped off to call for the doctor.

Rommel had been struck down by another stroke, or perhaps a heart attack, one of the worst he had yet suffered since his head had been crushed during the attack. It was a killing stroke, nearly a death-stroke, and though he soon came to himself, they all knew what it meant.

He was dragged staggering to the couch and there could only sprawl backwards on the Navajo blankets, unable to hold up his head, trying to recover from the feeling that his brain had been stripped, that his soul was sinking and shrinking inwards from his skin, back up along the channels of his physical body like ebb tide from an estuary. His fingers and hands were so numb and cold that he kept flexing and glancing at them, as though not believing they were still there.

"Not now," was all he could moan.

Pfirsich came limping back. "Doctor's on his way, but I don't know when he can get here."

"It's the infection," said Lucie.

"I thought he was healing."

"No," she said, and traced a line over the side of her head.

"Infection in the brain under the temple, and the back of the head. He's just getting worse."

Pfirsich put an arm around her, even though he knew how strong she would be. He looked down at her, still cradling her as protectively as his cane would allow.

"I thought you'd gotten a -- a strong modern medicine for him?"

Lucie nodded. "Yes, Penicillin. From the British."

"From the British?" said Pfirsich.

Lucie gave him a look and he didn't question how she'd done it. He'd come to think that Lucie could have gotten anything she wanted, short of peace, on the earth, and the glimpses he'd had of the machinery of her contacts so startled and disoriented him that he had come to accept that she was capable of anything. The Spanish say the brave bull's fighting heart comes from mama – and the Rommel boys proved the proverb. Since Mama Rommel had passed on, Lucie had inherited the position of *la vaca principal.*

"Oh yes," Lucie assured him. "There's nothing they won't do for him. You don't know how fond of him they are."

"The British love a good enemy," said Pfirsich. "I'm glad you could contact them."

"Through the Portuguese Mailbox," said Lucie.

"Thank God," said Pfirsich.

From what Lucie had told him, the British had originally set up the Mailbox to catch German spies in England. With all the efficient clarity of the military mind, the British secret service knew that anyone who sent letters through neutral Portugal to anyone in an enemy country must be a spy. With the military mind's closed-in insular world-view, it never realized that everybody has relatives.

Spies might have been using the Mailbox, but they would never be recognized, not through all the epistolary noise. The price of its use was only a shilling or a mark. The Mailbox began trickling with letters from the English writing to their German cousins, to uncles, mothers-in-law, old business partners and school chums, keeping cautious tabs on the well-being of their absent loved ones. The Germans wrote back. As the word spread, more and more letters came in, composed with great caution and sent with reckless relief. That might have been manageable, but when the Americans, with all their German blood connections, entered the war and found out about the Mailbox, the little hopeful creek became a flood.

Americans wrote letters like *"Dear Uncle Heinrich; We can't tell you where your Milwaukee cousin Harry is serving in the Air Force, but please be careful of the planes with the following markings..."*

In response a German *Luftwaffe* Major nervously told his men, *"My cousin Harry from Milwaukee might be flying around here; don't shoot down any planes with the following markings..."*

Of course most of the letters hadn't been so brazenly composed; most of them were made up of deeply personal and completely incomprehensible family codes. Military codes, no matter how involved or arcane, are always breakable. The Enigma machine was a simple concept; a bunch of lettered and numbered wheels and keys, the code-technology equivalent of a wooden pull-toy. The only thing that made it workable for the Allies was an inside military contact in Berlin sneaking out the numbered codes, every single day. Even the pride of the Americans, the Navajo "code-talkers," would have been useless if the Japanese had only known a few well-disposed Navajo. Or bought a dictionary.

But a true family code is indestructible. It is the most insular language of all, with the most peculiar and private references, and can't be defeated.

The Rommels had gotten a lot of practice with their own code, but von Stülpnagel hadn't been in on it, and even if he had, his blown-out eyes and the anesthetic made him blind and numb to all discretion.

19. Harvest

Later that morning Rommel began to shiver, on and off, and his teeth began to chatter. He knew what that was; he'd seen it before. Lucie came and sat beside him and put her head on his shoulder, because she knew it was all over. The days of courting, the days of dancing, the long days of loving, of an eventful and later precarious married life, all over. Even if the doctor came now, he couldn't have done a thing for the hurt creature, the helpless hurt animal that is all a man becomes when his soul begins to imagine another home.

The family was pulling into itself, like the life of their chieftain. Now they found themselves again having to face outward against an infringement of life and death, one they'd lately not so much feared as expected. With some of the underground finagling they'd been involved in, the obscure movements made by Lucie's jewelry and money, Pfirsich doing magic tricks with a lot of peculiar paperwork, and the theatrically-experienced Gerhard helping to disguise people the way he'd once disguised the love-struck Erwin, the family had lived with the expectation of the knock at the door. And here was the knock -- not the one they'd expected, but a knock nevertheless -- at last.

A parachute brigade stationed nearby wondered why the SS was surrounding Rommel's house. A Special Escort, they decided, a Signal Honor of some kind.

"Those blackbacks always seem to have enough people for ceremonies," said one of the paratroopers.

"Catch them on the front lines," growled another.

"Maybe if we convinced them it's a parade-ground."

If they had thought that their favorite General was in danger, so close as that, they'd have done something about it. They would have plowed through the middle of the Black Pirates like so much heavy cannon shot. But nobody suspected that anyone in Germany could threaten Rommel.

Everyone knew how much Hitler loved him.

It was Pfirsich who opened the door at the knock. He hoped this would be good news, a call from the country for Erwin to return to duty. It might give him the strength to fight through for a few more days. But when Pfirsich saw the two generals standing there -- one a friend, the other a stranger -- with their blank eyes and drawn jaw-muscles, he almost slammed the door in their faces. Their expressions said it all; those were firing-squad faces. But Pfirsich had no choice: they were here to see the Field Marshal. He had to let them into the house and bow politely.

"Is the Field Marshal at home?" said the taller of the two.

"Yes," hazarded Pfirsich, recognizing Burgdorf. "Could you gentlemen wait here in the living room? I'll have some coffee brought in."

Rommel wasn't on the couch now; he'd stumped slowly upstairs to one of the bedrooms, leaning again, but so much more heavily, on his son's arm, and had been dozing on the bed for most of the morning, stretched out fully dressed, coat and hat and all, against the internal chill from which he could not defend himself. He looked disturbingly as though he were laid out for burial. The family and Rudolf and his faithful aide-de-camp, *Hautpmann* Aldinger, had been checking in on him, turn and turn again, every few minutes, and had been very relieved to see some of the color begin to rise like a spring seep to retouch the cold bluish white of his damaged face. Now he looked like the undertaker had brushed a little rouge onto his cheeks.

Pfirsich met Lucie in the hallway outside her sleeping husband's room, and she knew from her brother-in-law's face that something was wrong. Pfirsich always looked exactly like his brother when something was wrong. Her own expression, the flash of her dark eyes in the dark hallway, told him that she knew there was trouble.

"Downstairs," he whispered. "They're here. The two generals, Burgdorf and a General Maisel. Come to see --," he pointed his chin up toward the room.

She frowned. "They'll have to come back. He can't even sit up."

"I've given them some coffee. I'll ask them to return later."

"Ask who?"

Both Pfirsich and Lucie jumped; in their own minds, they would have been surprised to see the profoundly stricken Rommel ever walk again, much less creep up behind them and hiss a question at them, and with such demanding authority.

"Erwin!" they both said at the same moment.

"Who's here?"

"Two generals," said Lucie. "Wilhelm Burgdorf and another one, a General Maisel. Pfirsich says they look as though they have bad news."

"They look like bad news," revised Pfirsich.

"No, no. That's not what they said last night. I'll go talk to them," said Erwin, removing his cap and coat.

"You go lie down," said Lucie. "I'll tell them to come back."

"No, I won't be here," said Rommel.

Neither Lucie nor Pfirsich said a thing. Her dark fierce eyes blurred and she lowered them. Pfirsich felt a cold needle pinch under the eyes, right against both sides of the nose.

The family crept carefully down the stairs, Lucie going ahead of them as reconnaissance and point-man, Erwin sagging against his son -- a son now so much taller than he -- not even attempting to control the trembling all along his limbs. He needed his strength when he appeared before the generals, not here with his family, who didn't need or want it, and like a wise and experienced soldier took the opportunity of his son's protection to rest and save his soon-to-be-required energy and courage. He pressed his face up into his son's neck, like a kitten nuzzling for warmth against its mother, and Manfred could feel the little man's shallow thready breath against the skin of his throat. He cupped his chin over his father's clammy forehead, willing the warm blood into the veins of his throat, as though he could revive all his father's failing circulation. He didn't even think about tears; all he could think of were those tiny cold hands and fading lips. He lifted up his father's free hand and blew his warm breath upon the stubby pale fingers.

At the bottom of the stairs, without even looking back, Lucie strode into the living room, dark head up, a beacon of welcoming hospitality. She recognized General Burgdorf and introduced herself to Maisel.

"Gentlemen!" she said. "My husband will be right with you."

The two generals had risen to their feet, and in the same movement, as though connected to them by a transmission cog, Erwin straightened up. The energy he had been saving by leaning on his son shot back into him. His life and color returned, the breath in his nostrils was warm. He no longer looked like a painted corpse. He pulled away from Manfred and stood up on his own power. Like an actor he strode out with ease and grace onto his stage. He had only to act as though he were brave and well, and he would be brave and well, just as he'd always believed.

He took his cue. He hit his mark.

"Gentlemen!" he said. "Please, come into my study. Thank you, my dear," he said to Lucie.

He took her hand and gave her the little peck on the cheek that was the heart-warming requirement of a brave military man with his wife, and that was genuine between them. The generals nodded approvingly, and sat down with their Field Marshal. Then the door closed, and Lucie and Manfred went back upstairs to wait.

A gentle tap came at the Lucie's bedroom door.

"Come," she said.

Pfirsich peeped in.

"What is it?" he asked. "What did they want?"

"I don't know," she said. "Where's Aldinger?"

"He's gone to get the Normandy dossier," said Pfirsich, and ducked his head. "Erwin thought he would need it, if they didn't send him to Prussia."

"Normandy?" said Lucie.

"I think Erwin thought it was just possible somebody would think he could be reassigned to the western defenses."

"I doubt it," said Lucie. "With that head-wound, he would collapse faster than France."

Footsteps came up the stairs behind them; they had only a moment to stand back from the door, so they wouldn't be seen when it opened. It swung open and in strode Rommel. He went right up to Lucie and put his arms around her, and put his face in her neck. He didn't collapse, but stood up strongly against her, pressing his body against hers, feeling as much of it and its warmth and curves as he could. Then he stepped back.

"In fifteen minutes I will be dead," he said.

"What --,"she gasped.

"It's poison or the People's Court," he said. "I've been implicated in the *Attentat.*"

"You? How?" Lucie was incredulous.

"General von Stülpnagel said a name, on the operating table;

he tried to shoot himself. When they had him under the gas, he said 'Rommel'."

"'Rommel!'" said Pfirsich. "Why would he have said that? You weren't implicated in the assassination --."

"He meant me," said Lucie, her face white with suppression.

Pfirsich looked into that formidable pale face, and knew it was true, and that nothing in the world could have made his brother happier than that fatal mistake.

Rommel grinned. "They all thought it was me. They'll never know -- they won't even try to look for anyone else!" He held out his hand -- it was beginning to tremble -- to Lucie, who took it and held it to her face.

"And, among other things, it seems I'd been nominated as the new *Reich* President -- and the *Gestapo* found the nomination."

"You were never part of that!" gasped Pfirsich. "They can't blame you for that!"

Rommel gave a wheezy giggle. "I know -- me! A politician! Could you see that? Somebody wasn't thinking." He put his hand to his heart. "Oh dear."

"But you never would have tried to assassinate anyone."

"It doesn't matter. I was part of the plot to have the *Führer* deposed --."

"But never to assassinate him." Pfirsich was on the edge of tears.

"You'd never be part of anything so dishonorable as assassination, " said Lucie. "They need to be convinced of that --."

"Not me," said Rommel, his voice weakening. "But they're painting everyone with the same brush. A general housecleaning."

Rommel raised his head and turned it toward Lucie, and the look between them, the sudden realization, was almost something that could be touched.

"Yes," gasped the dying man. "That's what you have to tell them -- afterwards. For the boy's sake." He looked at this brother. "Pfirsich. When the war ends, the enemies will still be there, and not just Nazis. You have to do whatever Lu tells you to. And the story you've just discovered -- you have to support it. No matter what. Lu?"

The dark woman leaned over her little man. The others in the room turned and pulled away from their private moment of last affections. But what Lucie had to say had nothing to do with love.

"Himmler," she whispered.

"No. He couldn't stop it," muttered Rommel. "He tried, but That Man is frantic, and not listening. Heinrich's scared."

Lucie's eyes narrowed. "He'd better be scared of me."

"No --."

"You be quiet. You need to rest. Heinrich owes me."

Rommel's hand tightened weakly in hers, but he wouldn't have had the strength to oppose her on his best days. He's have to leave her behind to fight any way she saw fit, and hope that her anger and grief wouldn't charge her off a cliff. For all he knew, his dark woman could do as she threatened; for all they had shared, so deeply, in such detail, he knew there were strange worlds where she had gone and closed the door behind her, to protect him and the boy. His own mother had been that sort of woman, with the keys to doors of Bluebeard's Chambers that no one else could have held. Lucie had a ring of the same kind of keys, he knew that -- and he hoped the right people were afraid of her, or would stand allied with her, when the keys fit and the doors came open across the bloody floor. He closed his eyes and hoped for the best.

Pfirsich was standing in the corner, his hand to his forehead, his other hand trembling on his cane. He didn't say anything. He couldn't. Those two brave people were still whispering, still fighting, the only way they knew how to fight. Pfirsich would help in the fight, any way he could, but he couldn't be part of their last moments together. He did his best and just tried to be part of the wallpaper. Rudolf, who had come up to the door, stood silently just trying to be part of the air.

"But I'll beat them," said Rommel, at last, loudly enough for Pfirsich to hear as well. "I'm dying anyway. And they don't know I'm dying."

He wouldn't have brought it up, except as a true statement of the situation.

"Rudi, where's Manfred?" said Rommel.

"Downstairs listening, *Herr Feldmarschall.*"

"Fetch him."

When Rudolf had gone Rommel said, "They think they're threatening me. They've made me an offer."

"What?" said Pfirsich and Lucie together.

"A bargain. A show-trial and my family into a camp -- or a

quick death, a state funeral, and my family protected from all further prosecution."

Lucie pulled away. She must have had warrior blood in her. Roman barons and Polish Lancers. Her dark eyes shone like a charger's.

"Then go to trial. We owe it to our country."

"No," said Rommel. "I won't risk any of you. Not like I am now."

Brother and wife started to protest, and when Rommel shook his head at them, it was a mistake. He went gray and put his hands to his head. Pfirsich stepped forward at last and put his hands under his brother's elbows.

"Oh, *Mann,*" groaned Rommel. "I feel like my brains are jellied. I can't tell if it's a stroke or a heart attack or both. That's one reason I can't go to trial. You all saw me this morning; I'd never survive to actually stand trial. I wouldn't survive to make any more bargains for your safety. And if they know I'm this sick, there will be no bargains."

"I don't want any bargains," said Lucie, in a predatory tone. "I have my own ways of dealing with those people."

"I know you don't need to bargain, dear Lu," said Rommel, and kissed her hand. "But we have a son."

"Yes," said the cornered tigress. "We do."

"I have a sister, and brothers. The war will be over soon, and I want you all to survive. Your country will need you. And the decision's been made. I simply won't live to make it to a trial. I won't, Lu, you know it."

"I know."

Rommel put his hand to his head and gulped with nausea. "Lu, I'll tell you right now, if these strokes and infection are what I have to look forward to -- until they finally beat me down into my grave, then -- then I'll take That Man's little white pill, and welcome."

"A pill?" said Lucie, her hands clasped. She had never so much as heard her husband talk about, much less anticipate, giving up. It was a new experience. She hated it.

"Cyanide," said Rommel. "When I told I couldn't bring myself to use a pistol -- let them murder me if they're going to do it!"

"*Oh, Gott.*"

"They informed me they'd kindly brought me a 'special preparation.' Gone like that." He snapped his fingers. "Better than being bludgeoned down by a series of strokes, I'll tell you that. Oh, get me a chair."

His knees were buckling out from under him. Pfirsich pulled out a chair, and Lucie swung her weakening husband into the seat, and his whole upper body flowed in one febrile movement over onto the bed.

His head lay down on the blanket without his least attempt to exhibit any strength. From where he lay, getting his breath, he spoke up to them, his eyes bright and alert, as though he were standing up lecturing his eager troops. His body had failed him, like a motorcycle with a broken frame. It was useless to ask it to give more than its very least, to do more than save its strength for the coming crisis. So he ignored it, leaving it lie there like the discarded unimportant puppet that was all it had become, and with his last remaining spark of power used no more than its eyes and lips to speak to the ones who loved him.

"Lu -- Get Manfred." Rommel's teeth were beginning to chatter. "I want him out of all this. I don't want them to come at him without any warning."

Lucie was bending over her fading man, stroking his sinking temples, her great dark eyes burning.

"He's coming," she said.

"Get him away. Make him go to the English, if you have to. To the English. They'll take him. One more refugee."

"Of course."

"That Man will respect you, as the widow."

Lucie closed her eyes at the word.

"He'll have to," insisted Rommel. "He'll never ask what you've done. That Man could never suspect a woman of being able to do what you've done, so you're safe."

"Don't worry," soothed Lucie, as he failed before her eyes. "I'm safe."

"But Manfred is the son," he stuttered. "And you know what happens to sons. The Romans didn't let them grow up to seek revenge. Blood-guilt!"

"I know."

"The English were always my good enemies; I know they'll be my son's good friends."

When Manfred came in, Rommel, trembling with rigor, quietly explained through his clattering teeth what would happen, then sent him to fetch Aldinger. The aide hurried up the stairs, the Normandy dossier in hand, but when he heard it wouldn't be needed, and why, he nearly dropped it.

"We can shoot our way out!" blurted Aldinger. "There are paratroopers stationed near the house, right outside the SS positions. All we have to do is get to them."

Rommel waved a hand -- he didn't dare shake his head -- and refused the sacrifice again, because it didn't need to be made.

* * * * *

Fifty years later, one of the old paratroopers, now a moderately successful businessman, would ask, "Whatever really did happen to Rommel?" In the course of a leisurely conversation over drinks at a professional meeting, he would discover that, no, Rommel did not die of his wounds, that he had actually been poisoned. The old businessman would be surprised. But he couldn't have known; all of Germany had thought that Rommel had died of his wounds, and after the end of the war, the paratrooper, no longer a soldier, would be too busy trying to remake his own life, to think of a dead officer he knew only by fame.

Fifty years too late, talking to the wrong person, just in passing and in the coincidence of a chat, and finally supplied with all the details of that long-ago day, he would make the connection between the day Rommel died and the SS he had seen around the Field Marshal's house, and would realize that his paratroop unit could have attacked the SS and saved the Field Marshal.

The worst thing about cruel information is that it can be made up of such little gray dull bits, and can lie in wait, distantly scattered and buried in your head for years, and it only takes that last piece of the puzzle -- or that last unaware constructing hand -- to make you want to shoot yourself, or at least kick yourself around the room. The old businessman was on the moment the young paratrooper, and almost leapt to his feet in a young soldier's fury and indignation. Then his knees protested, and he was his -- literally -- old self again. He collapsed back in his chair, and in his regret could only order another whiskey-and-soda.

Only the Rommels themselves knew that they didn't want any help.

* * * * *

While the lethal emissaries waited in the villa garden, the Rommels and their friends wrote their final script, the one they would stick to for years and years, because they would never know when or if any of the wolves would still be out there in the woods.

Erwin's wife and his son didn't want him to go through a death of long slow suffering, either, and so when the car took him away, these brave people kept their mouths shut and pretended to be too afraid to protest. They pretended he was strong and hearty, and he played his role to the end.

Two people who loved him stayed in the kitchen, because they couldn't keep up the Rommels' brave and long-cultivated front. *Hauptmann* Aldinger because he couldn't help his twitching fingers and grinding teeth, Pfirsich because he couldn't help his tears, and was hiding Aldinger's pistol by sitting on it. He'd sneak the pistol back into the *Hauptmann's* holster once he was able to get to the coat-closet, and provided he could talk Aldinger into returning to the living room with the grieving family. He'd be lucky if he could keep him from waving a handkerchief and whistling at the paratroopers across the field.

No one was in the car with Rommel when he took the cyanide from the pad of cotton in the tiny case his brother had given him, the little pot-metal box with the German soldier's belt-buckle in the lid, and tucked the box back into his pocket. He almost grinned at that little white pill lying in the palm of his gray glove, sharing with it in connivance as with a friend, at the thought of what he was putting over on those stupid Nazi bastards. Even as he stared down at the pill, his hands shaking with the chill of rigor, he must have known how he had managed to cheat them, all of them, at last.

And in the end, they couldn't even force him to kill himself. A last stroke knocked him backwards against the seat, and the pill was retrieved from under his writhing body, with much grumbling and picking off of lint, and then pressed manually by another man's gloved fingers through his working wet jaws and down his constricting throat. The man got his fingers bitten -- badly -- for his trouble. Rommel passed from the convulsions and sobbing of the stroke to the sobbing of the poisoning without missing a heartbeat, punctual as the stroke of a drum.

It was as though his body wasn't going to acquiesce to its own self-destruction, even now, when it was dying anyway, and the sacrifice had to be made for country and family. It passed out of its consciousness forever, out of any ability to do itself or any others harm, and forced its most high-ranking murderers to finally do the murdering for themselves.

Bread and Swans

20. Oblivious

The Third Reich liked titles, and the Germans like nicknames. The Herman Meier cap was a khaki-colored mobcap with a visor. It was named after Herman Goering, who had said, "If they ever bomb Berlin, you can call me Meier!"

The American planes had been after the city centers again, vindictive as swans, intent on raising the kill-count of living human beings, and dropping phosphorous thermite bombs onto cities. Thermite doesn't burn brick or asphalt; it bubbles and cooks its way through living flesh. It has no other purpose.

No one in Germany could know the cheery obscenity of a pre-bombing briefing among the Allied pilots, but they could see the results. The trick of turning their enemies into non-humans had been raised to a high journalistic art by the Americans. With their history of Indian wars and slavery, union busting, invasion and gunboat diplomacy, they were past masters at turning anybody from inconvenient aboriginals to whole modern nations into mere beasts whose sufferings were unimportant or even desirable. The Nazis were Johnny-come-lately amateurs in comparison. But then, there was very little the Nazis did that was original. They got all their best ideas from somebody else, and polished them up for modern use.

The results kept Pfirsich on his feet, leaning trembling on his cane, almost useless except for the duty he had been assigned to.

He had been stationed in Berlin. There he'd been put to supervising the burning of the dead victims in great heaps in the midst of the rubble. This used to be the duty of the Punishment Battalions, but now Regular Army had to chip in. The flesh-grease ran over the bricks, and the soot and stink from the burning human beings blackened the sky. Pfirsich stood there and tried not to throw up more than five times a day.

He was sick to death of shooting the screaming victims he could

269

not save. First but least, the Phosphorous Units were required to start the day by gulping down cheap white liquor, to numb their minds and their scruples. Pfirsich was one of the group that had earned the nickname of *Köter.* It meant "Mutt," literally "Vomiter," because of the nasty things street-dogs would eat, then haulk back up.

Pfirsich was by preference a wine-drinker. He didn't mind getting a little tipsy, but the one time he'd gotten stinking white-lipped drunk, in college, he'd awakened to a violent sick headache. Now he could never smell *Schnaps* much less stomach the stuff. To give his stomach-lining the opportunity to absorb the alcohol before he threw it back up, he was compelled to consume twice the assigned amount, trying desperately to hold down the sickening mouthfuls long enough to do some bad.

When he was so hammered everything looked like it was under water, he took his cane and hobbled off slow and weak through the rubble, one hand holding him up like an old man, the other gripping his loaded pistol, listening for those despairing panting screams that were the mark of the conscious burning Thermite victim. Time and again, the ones who still had eyes would see him coming, and reach out with what limbs they could move, begging, begging that he use that pistol, just as fast as he could.

The American planes kept droning over, and somehow the use of Thermite never quite made it into their newspapers.

The Americans, like all people, were a decent people. And like all decent people, if they had found out they would have taken a long time talking themselves into believing it was for the best. Not much longer than they'd ever done it in their history, any of the hundreds of times. But they'd have done it in the end. It was something they were very good at. They'd had a lot of practice.

Pfirsich had been very upstanding and soldierly of late, almost traditionally Prussian in his dutiful enlightened self-effacing humanity, and despite the difficulties of standing up to a regime that had poisoned his brother, his brother's army and the concept of his nation along with everything else in his life, he had managed not to be involved in any massacres. He'd seen his share of them, but he'd protested. He knew he wouldn't do any good, but at least he could say he'd done it; morality isn't often about what a man can do, but what he can try to do, and Pfirsich had tried.

After awhile he looked around him and realized he was just another of the same sort of honorable German officer who chewed up his own stomach-lining with unresolved questions at night and spun ineffectually in circles in the daytime, hobbled by his own antiquated humanity and sense of honor, unable to tear loose and do any real good because he just didn't know where "good" was any more.

Now that he was forced by that very humanity to massacre his own people, he was wondering if he shouldn't have just started shooting people when he was told to. Everybody was going to be dead, anyway, and it might have helped his stomach. For the umpteenth time, he told himself he felt like an overworked sword, All Temper And No Edge. Unless it was the edge of cutting somebody, hard and deep, down to and through the gristle and charn, so they'd remember it. Temper, temper.

He didn't wear a sword. His army wasn't in the last century, and his country certainly wasn't in the present one. Not an excuse, of course, only an attempt at a reason, but sometimes, very rarely, in a moment of sightlessness, it saved mirrors.

Now and again Pfirsich discovered a mirror, somehow surviving in all its fragility no matter how the city shook. Likely the silver backing provided just tension enough to hold the glass together, like the metal that can keep a country, or a soul, from shattering, so that it can hang ready for its final destruction.

When Pfirsich found a mirror still whole, most often in the back of a bombed-out apartment building, he staggered back in the smoking shadows from what he at first drunkenly thought was a ghost. He always saw something worse, the face he was just beyond bearing any more, and he had a tendency to punch the glass right out of the frames, hitting it again and again, until his gloves and his knuckles shredded red.

Jesu Christu, this is what his brother had fought and died for. This was the Honor of Country. This was the Science of War. This was The Defense Of The Homeland. This was Acts of Patriotism. These were the petty demanding shams, the little monsters always under the bed, forever keeping everyone awake so they couldn't drift into the healing sleep of decency. The more he remembered his brother, so profoundly, so finally asleep -- the little modest corpse, lying there with its hands crossed so peacefully, so helplessly on its medal-besprinkled breast, all the lines of pain brushed away by the pitiful hand of death, but with such a look

271

of pressed disgust around the locked lips -- the harder Pfirsich hit those mirrors.

"God damn you," he said. "God damn you, God damn you, God damn you!"

He wanted to be doing what he was doing. He hated every moment of it, but it balanced him, overloading him with such anguish that it all but cancelled out his own, and his last nerve went numb. Then he could lie down in the dripping caverns of basements orphaned of their buildings, and sleep without twitching, without dreaming, even drooling a little. Dead to the world.

His didn't blame the family, he certainly did not. He didn't blame his country, not even the poisoners. No, he didn't, he truly didn't. He didn't even blame the planes that droned over day and night and their frightened oblivious crews. Someplace in the smoking ruins of Berlin, while the papers from files and libraries floated down from the gutted floors above, like white doves sailing to earth, Pfirsich took Karl's little round pot-metal box, with its tiny yellow apothecary's spoon, out of his pocket.

Helene had given the box to him after the funeral. He'd asked her where she'd gotten it, but she just shook her head. "Karl's," she said. "It goes to the brothers. You keep it – for now."

Pfirsich threw the box down into the choking brick-dust, and stirred it under with the tip of his cane. He didn't turn away; he kept his head very still. He closed his eyes, determined to retain his skull's rigid immobility.

When he finally opened his sticky eyes and looked down, the tiny dimpled burial plot had not changed or disappeared. It was still at the same distance from the toe of his right boot. When he bent over, very stiffly, from the hips, and poked in the dust with his dirty gloves, there was the brassy glint of the belt-buckle in the lid. If it hadn't been there, he would have turned and stalked away and never looked back. But there it was, winking remorselessly, and he had to take it up and brush it off with his ragged glove, and put it back into his pocket, with all the revulsion of the princess forced to let the frog eat from her plate.

He needed his fingers whole and unswollen, or he wouldn't be able to fit them around the pistol grip and through the trigger housing. So instead of smashing his own image he began to carry an extra flask with him, and whenever he was surprised by a mirror, he forced himself to stop and take another deep swig from the pocket-flask. Then he hobbled off to put a charitable bullet into whoever wanted it. Humanity required it. The code of his addictions demanded it.

A woman who lived near one of the last working water-pipes in the smoking city offered him a cup of tea -- and a wet rag to wash his face -- and the realization that he was noticeably dirty, on top of everything else, was the well-bred man's last straw. He was grateful for the tea, but he looked like a bum, and he knew it.

He felt like an abused overworked cart-horse sucking down that tea, knowing that his harness was all askew and that his flanks and hooves were plastered with dung, but thirsty, my God how thirsty. He was thirsty right down to his soul. He didn't have any will any more for anything beyond thirst.

And all that *Schnaps* wasn't going to cut it.

Bread and Swans

21. Nothing Lasts Forever

Pfirsich was rubbing his dirty face and yawning. He was filthy, exhausted, so hungry he couldn't face food when it was actually offered him, and hadn't had enough sleep to keep an old woman alive, except for the time he had spent snoring in a lax sordid bundle in the puddled mud inside the front gate of the camp. But at least he wasn't thirsty.

His captors hadn't been thinking when they told *Oberst* Rommel and his men that the war was over for them. After years of war, the German prisoners who had been combat soldiers were so bone-sore wrung-out tired that they had simply collapsed on the spot, and the American soldiers couldn't get them to wake up, no matter how they punched or kicked or cursed them. The prisoners were going to have their sleep out, if it killed them. Rather than run the arriving trucks over them, the Americans had at last ordered the earlier prisoners to haul them to the side of the gate.

They'd been left there, in sun and rain, for two days, like a pile of dirty corpses. Pfirsich had awakened with his face in somebody's blood-stained armpit, and the familiar smell -- not decay, but the indescribable piteous smell of a faded soul -- told him that the man had passed away in his sleep. Pfirsich had envied him his look of sallow pinch-faced peace.

* * * * *

He was sitting in front of a desk, in a small room, under a very bright light, and he still wasn't fully awake. He was trying to decide if he was hungry or not, but his stomach hadn't talked to him in over a week, so he wasn't sure. Nobody had fed him, and when he'd awakened he'd simply rolled over and sucked the water out of the pool he was lying in, with no more fastidiousness than a cow.

Since then he'd risen and taken his water from the cleaner pools in back of the prison barracks; the ones farthest removed from the latrine-

275

trenches, paddling in the water of earth for his drinking and his washing, like a wild swan. Some of the earlier prisoners, hearing what his own men had said about him, and seeing their respect for him, had offered him from their own store of the earthworms they'd dug from the mud. But he wasn't capable of digesting bread soaked in water, much less raw meat, so he'd thanked them and declined. Politely, of course; one didn't insult one's hosts, but after all the diligent mining by starving prisoners, a healthy fat earthworm wasn't that easy to come by.

His soul as much as his stomach would have lurched to deprive others of their little store of food. This wasn't so much a proof of his own morality, as proof of the strength of his pity; Pfirsich had such a weakness for feeling sorry for other people that it hurt him more than hunger. He could never have taken so much as a mouthful from such gray hollow-eyed skeletons, because his own heart would have twisted like an ulcer within him, and he couldn't take the pain. He knew the difference between this and true magnanimity, and didn't try to do himself any honor over it.

It was fortunate for the men who had tried to feed him that he hadn't seen a mirror in over a month; one look at his own skull-faced self, and he would have been so frightened by the pity for his own emergent skeleton that he would have bitten off their fingertips along with the earthworms.

* * * * *

When the American guards came to fetch him, they pointed their guns at him and laughed and threatened him. He just looked at them, too worn down to care. It embarrassed them. They grabbed him and dragged him across the compound, each of them jerking an elbow in so many different directions and yelling in accents he didn't understand that he just gave up in confusion and just let them haul him into this room.

They'd been forced to allow him to sit, because their little scuffle had so worn him out that when he stood in one place for any length of time, his legs, never very recovered, collapsed out from under him. You can't question somebody in a fetal position at your feet; you might as well try to question a rag doll. They had to keep hauling him to his feet, and it wore them out. They dropped him into a chair and he almost slid out of it.

The man behind the desk had begun to yell at him, as though it were going to make what he was saying any more comprehensible. It had all gone wrong when Pfirsich stated that his last name was Rommel, and the man almost blew a blood vessel and accused him of trying to curry favor. It took Pfirsich's rumpled stained ID papers to convince his captor that he really did have the same last name as the respected famous Field Marshal. The man blinked at him; he thought of Rommel as a kind of movie star, shimmering in a newsreel or sending a chill up the spine during radio reports, but the thought that he might have flesh-and-blood relatives, that he was a womb-born breathing eating shitting human being, with nipples and a belly button and nose hair and snot and a scrotum and semen just like everybody else, came as an almost supernatural shock. The man felt as though he were speaking to the first cousin of the Monster Under The Bed.

Then everything got bogged down while Pfirsich had himself an impotent little cry, because he remembered that his brother was dead.

Unlike the man at the desk, Pfirsich knew how his brother had died. The family was keeping that to itself as long as it could. God only knew who in the British government would consider Rommel's rumored participation in the attempt on Hitler's life to be the act of a traitor upon his own national leader; better safe than even sorrier. For the present, it still didn't make the questions the American asked Pfirsich any easier, or more understandable.

"What about Auschwitz?" the sergeant demanded, in rather good German, but with a sibilance that sounded as though he'd taken language courses from a Rhinelander.

Pfirsich blinked, and wiped his tired red eyes. Had he heard right? "Aus-schwitz?" he repeated.

"Auschwitz!" sneered the American.

"Oh, how nice, thank you." said Pfirsich; no matter how tired one was, manners never went astray. They could save your life. "I could use it, I really could."

The man was still bent over the desk, still in the posture of assault, but there was no sound issuing from his open mouth.

277

"It's very kind of you," prompted Pfirsich. "I'll take you up on it."

"What?" the American finally said.

"It's a kind of sauna, isn't it? I could use a wash. Oh, and thank you for the delousing, this morning. It was a great comfort." Pfirsich scrubbed a dirty long-nailed finger through his half- long, mucky hair. "I haven't even tried to comb out the powder, I thought I'd leave it there, until it did some good. But a sauna, now that --."

"What the hell are you talking about?" said the American sergeant, and his Rhenish accent hissed like rain on a hot rock.

"'Aus-schwitz' --'Aus-schwitzen' -- 'sweat out'?" tendered Pfirsich. "A sauna? A hot bath? Is that what you mean? Sometimes, when foreigners use German cognates --."

"It's a name!" snapped the sergeant.

"Polish?" hazarded Pfirsich. It sounded Polish; the "witz" ending.

"I knew you knew what it was, Nazi."

Pfirsich just blinked; he wasn't going to argue with his captors. He hadn't allowed his prisoners to talk without reason, either. Prisoners who talked too much could lead to trouble. The proprieties were the same everywhere.

"Don't pretend you don't know!"

Pfirsich swallowed. Maybe he did know it, whatever it was. The American was terrible in his assurance. Pfirsich himself had been confused past dread these last few weeks; there had been so much going on. He had a foggy impression of ghostly thousands -- perhaps millions -- of people, in all sorts of uniforms or dark civilian clothes, running every which way, without knowing where they were going to settle, and just trying not to die on the way. They'd been talking all sorts of languages; it had been the Tower Of Babel in Hell. Pfirsich wasn't sure what he knew or didn't know, any more. He was too tired.

"It's a name!" prompted the sergeant again.

"I'm sorry," Pfirsich said, meekly. "Are you looking for someone? I don't recall anyone by that name in any of my units --."

The American slammed his fist onto the desk. Pfirsich didn't jump. He did blink; that was as close to jumping as he could come.

"This is nothing to be clever about!"

"I'm so tired I'm stupid. My apologies."

"Bergen-Belsen!" yelled the man, and brought down his fist.

"Treblinke!" The fist again.

"Sergeant," said Pfirsich. "The German army kept precise personnel lists. If you can't find them, perhaps they were civilians."

"Don't get smart with me, Nazi. You'll learn we don't put up with that any more than you did! We're just a lot more decent about it than you were."

Pfirsich looked up. "'Nazi'? Do you need a party member to find these people? Long-time party members often have deeper access to files."

"Ohhh," sneered the American. "So you're not a Nazi? Another one, huh? You're an officer. Only Nazis could be officers!"

"I received my commission during the last war. If only someone with party connections can help you, then I'd be of little help."

"And you ain't a Nazi now, huh? Sure you're not. A Social Democrat, huh?"

"No, I never had affiliation with but one political party. I am P. G. – *Parteigenosse* -- now. But I became one late in the war, so my connections are rather useless. Certainly for file-access."

"Lousy timing, huh?"

"Yes." Pfirsich nodded. "I should have joined earlier, if I'd wanted to do any good."

The American looked so blank that the schoolteacher in Pfirsich's blood sat up wearily in response. It wouldn't let him leave it alone, not until the American understood. He leaned forward, marshaling his remaining concentration, and spoke slowly and clearly.

"If I wanted to help anyone, I had to become a Nazi."

"You didn't have to do nothing!" snapped the sergeant.

Pfirsich put his hand to his forehead; it ached. He was going to have to explain. These Americans were like people from behind the moon; they didn't seem to know anything. You had to clarify everything to them. Why couldn't he have been taken prisoner by the British? They lived on an island, too, surrounded by a moat like the Americans, but it was closer, and smaller, and they had some contact with the outside world. And the British were an educated people. Bizarre as it might seem, as hard to believe or to explain, he'd gotten the impression that the Americans looked down on an education; he couldn't understand why they didn't think they needed one.

279

"If you weren't a Nazi," he began patiently. "You were suspect. It was easy to join. And cheap; sixty *Pfennige* a month. A bargain."

"That's your excuse, huh?"

"It was just how we lived."

"So what did you do once you were -- *'P.G.'*"

"Me? Stopped looking over my shoulder so much."

"You did it for your own good."

"I did it for my own nerves."

"Well, that's honest."

Pfirsich shrugged. It had done very little good. By the time Pfirsich had joined the Party, the Party didn't trust anybody who wasn't an Old Fighter.

The American glared at him. Smart-ass snotty Kraut bastard. Always some kind of line, always had some excuse. Looked like an aristocrat, too, some kind of purebred; blonde and tall. Probably still had a monocle on him someplace. Just another wealthy aristocrat in boots. He'd show this guy. He'd put him in his place. Germans still hadn't learned -- he'd teach 'em!

He yanked open a desk drawer, and pulled out a photograph album.

"All right, Nazi, you wanna be stubborn --." he said, and slapped it onto the desk.

He shoved it toward Pfirsich.

"Open it!"

Pfirsich complied, gingerly. The album was covered in very smooth brown leather, and he didn't want to soil it, or smear it with delousing powder. Almost daintily, he turned to the first page.

He peered intently at the first photograph, then reared back.

"Pretty stomach-turning, ain't they?" said the sergeant.

"I broke my spectacles."

Pfirsich drew his head back further, then finally picked up the book and slid it far out on the desk, at the distant end of arm's length.

"Hm," he said at last, squinting. "Nasty photos."

"They make you want to vomit!"

"Yes," said Pfirsich. "They will 'till you're used to it."

"Used to it!" gasped the sergeant.

Pfirsich examined the photo. "This looks like the clean-up after a bombing."

"That's not a bombing," snapped the American.

Pfirsich looked up. "The way the corpses have been stripped -- and their condition. All the quicklime. It was hard to get to everyone before decomposition."

"That's -- you know what that is," insisted the American.

Pfirsich rubbed his face. All right; the man wanted to play guessing games. He wasn't in a position to demure.

"Artillery casualties? Battlefield?"

"Don't try that! There have never been such pictures."

Pfirsich was rotating the album, and turning pages, still trying to focus.

"I don't know. They really look a lot like Goya; the Peninsular War. But that may be a matter of personal eye, something I may be seeing that you aren't --."

"Educated, are you?" sneered the American.

There it was again. Very odd. In response, Pfirsich nodded, oblivious of the American's hurt feelings, still examining the photos.

"You're right about one thing; they usually kept things this extreme out of the papers. We all knew what the our dead looked like after the bombers had been over, especially when we stacked them up to burn, but newspapers are more circumspect."

"Your dead?" gasped the American.

Pfirsich winced. "Are these your people? It's hard to tell when they get this bad. We all look alike when we're dead."

The American was shaking. He grabbed the album, flipped through the pages, and thrust it back into Pfirsich's grubby hands. Pfirsich observed him solicitously for a few moments before focusing on the page.

This time he really did have to work to focus. Naked dwarves? Little old men? What were those little white bigheaded black-eyed things? They looked like living skeletons. Oh dear.

"Look at the poor starved children," he murmured.

"Now you'll admit it," hissed the American.

He wasn't prepared for the look Pfirsich gave him. The German's exhausted blue glare hit him like a lance.

"What purpose does it serve you now, to gloat over our children to me?"

"Your children?" stammered the American.

"Are you trying to break me? I've nothing left to break."

Pfirsich yawned, shivering. The American was wearing him to a string.

"This is the way they looked when we got back to Germany. All that fighting, and back home, our own children were starving."

The album slid out of his grasp and onto the floor. Pfirsich looked down and groaned, knowing he'd have to pick it up, but he'd have to get past his own spiritless body to reach down. The American was sitting there, very silently, leaning back in his chair, staring at him.

"They're -- they're not German children," he said at last.

Pfirsich was still concentrating on getting together the energy to bend over for the book.

"Probably. Most of the children on two continents probably look like this right now," he said.

With a sudden jerk, he leaned over, snatched up the book, and flipped it up onto the desk. The American jumped and almost went for his pistol, but Pfirsich was settling back into the chair, completely drained. To the worn-out German hoisting the book had been like lifting a block of concrete. He needed to think hard to go on with what he'd been saying.

"We started a war, and the children are starving. God's going to get us for that."

"Well, yes --." began the American.

He wasn't used to the soldiers he'd interrogated volunteering anything, at least not an admission of responsibility. This one was odd. The American had the uncomfortable feeling that the German wasn't so candid because he was honest, as that he was fearless, either by choice or inability to be anything else, and that his captors, and what his captors could do to him, meant nothing to him.

The American was used to seeing trembling abject Germans, and believing they trembled from guilt. He couldn't begin to imagine, he had no experience of reference to imagine the ordeal they had been through. He couldn't comprehend that they saw him as just another part of that ordeal; no novelty, but just another part of the old old threat. To them the invaders were nothing new. They were just a new wave of the French, or the Swedish, or the Russians, or the Polish, or the Golden Horde, century after century of marauders and invaders, military and religious conquerors, forcibly conscripted Hessians and Prussians, angry crazy Brownshirts, or whoever got drafted into the war of the moment, and had no loyalty in a fragmented time to turn them aside from cutting their own people's throats.

When the time came for this war, this people had learned, as before, to look over their shoulders without being caught looking -- *der deutsche Blick* -- and to clamp their mouths shut in determined duty, as always, and not to look aside from their daily goals, if it would help one more generation survive.

The movies and newsreels that had portrayed them in martial celebration had never recorded the grim silent life that had become reality and normalcy. The clenched loyalty to work and duty and honor that were, in the end, the only religions you could hold onto, the only prayers that let you stay sane, or at least allowed you to act sane. No one said a thing against the war, nobody dared. If your government wanted to invade and bomb its neighbors, if your government came and took your neighbors away, for whatever law it made up and decided had been broken, there wasn't anything you could do to stop it. You could only wait, and endure, and hope the invasion wouldn't come back, not this time. And in the name of God never look out the window, past the drawn curtains, when you heard the screaming in the streets.

The Germans were getting down to their ancestral business, now. They didn't expect help, they didn't expect hope. No one would come to save them, not ever, they told each other, the invaders would occupy them forever, like American Red Indians, and they believed in their bones that they were staring at decades of starvation and exhaustion, and possibly extinction. They had seen their country steeped in death before; it was no use whining for their dead. It had happened so often in their turbulent surrounded history that they knew the bitter details, and they did as they had always done, just thrust down their heads and gritted their teeth and got ready to work their way back up out of another bitter pinched black hole. At least it was nothing new. They'd get over it, they always did. They weren't called "stubborn" for nothing.

The American was still trying to reckon up Pfirsich against the other prisoners. They had been skittish, like horses made shy by long years of unpredictable abuse; this tall dirty blond brute just didn't seem to care. It was either exhaustion or arrogance, and the American wasn't going to stand for either.

"I'm sorry," said Pfirsich. "Didn't mean to drop your book; I'm fumble-fingered right now. If you need to ask me any more questions, I'm sure I'll be more clear-headed, when I've had some more sleep. Please excuse me."

"Oh, sure."

"This war's been tough on you, too," Pfirsich said suddenly. "I can feel for what we put you through. I was there for the Normandy defense, and my bro -- Field Marshal Rommel didn't make it very easy for you."

"What?" said the American.

"Rough," said the German, and looked at the other soldier with washed-out comradely pity in his eyes. "Really rough."

The American was covering his eyes. He couldn't take it; this German was feeling sorry for him. He was astounded. This filthy pile of lice and starvation was looking at him with such brotherly concern it hurt.

"Don't," he said.

He had thought he would have been the one in charge of the pity rations. He thought he knew how it was done; knock 'em out, teach 'em a lesson, show 'em what's what, starve 'em, scare 'em, keep 'em awake -- then do what they'd never expect. Raise 'em up, feed 'em, and make 'em grateful to be like us Americans. Like a woman who got out of line; knock her down, shut her up, have a little fun with her, if it would teach her her place, then make an Honest Woman of her. All nice and friendly, on Our Terms. The victim penitent and Oh So Grateful for a little kindness. We Hurt You because we Had To. Your Own Fault; You Made Me Do It.

It wasn't supposed to be the other way around. The Indians weren't supposed to be feeding beef to the Cowboys. Wretched beaten Germans weren't supposed to be extending lordly pity to their conquerors.

The American uncovered his eyes. "I wasn't at Normandy. I came up through Italy."

"That was rough, too," said Pfirsich. "Everybody fought so damn' hard. So many people died." He muttered. "If only we could have stayed home."

The American's hands came down; he couldn't stand this Nazi bastard's kindly superiority one more moment.

"Now you will. You lost."

"We all lost."

"You lost worst!"

Pfirsich shrugged. "We came in second."

"Yeah -- and you started it!"

"Oh, please," groaned Pfirsich. Not the playground, again.

The American was furious; he scooped up the album, leafed through it, and slammed it back on the desk in front of the prisoner.

"You know what these are, don't you? You know because you helped kill them!"

"I killed soldiers," said Pfirsich.

What was this man trying to tell him? Was he accusing him of specific deaths? Of course they were hunting down people to prosecute. Pfirsich scratched his nose; maybe he was one of them. The war had become so terrible, and he'd done some terrible things.

"Are these soldiers?" demanded the American, and pointed to a picture of a pile of dead children.

"I didn't kill --." Pfirsich stopped, and then sat and ached. "Yes, I killed children."

The American shuddered at the admission. "You killed these children!"

"No. No, the children we killed, we didn't leave in a heap like that. And we never stripped them, the poor little things. We properly burned them, nice and clean, in their own poor clothes."

"You burned them!"

"It was all we could do for them." Pfirsich looked up, his eyes dull. "They were dying. And we had no means of stopping their pain. We had to shoot them."

"You shot them."

"Not shot --."

"Don't deny it!"

"I couldn't," muttered Pfirsich. "Forgive me."

"Forgive you?" gasped the American.

Were the German values so twisted that they were ashamed when they couldn't kill children? What kind of monsters were these? What kind

285

of unearthly alien unpredictable creatures? The American stared at the German in terror.

"I couldn't. Not even when it was the only way. I -- I smothered them." Pfirsich looked at his hands, and shuddered. "I smothered them to death with my hands. I still have the burns."

He held out his scarred hands, with the chemical stigmata still plain to see on their palms.

The American was so confused he simply pointed shaking at the photo.

"These children were starved to death -- in a concentration camp!"

"No. Thermite bombs."

"Thermite --!"

"You dropped phosphorous. Your bombers were dropping white phosphorous on the cities."

"Huh?"

"It killed men, women, children, animals, everything. It doesn't kill right away; it eats. We had no painkillers for the dying; what little we had just wasn't strong enough. We had to get drunk every morning and every night before we could go out to shoot them."

"What?"

"I'm not accusing you, yourself. You're just a soldier. How could you know?" Pfirsich shook his head in sympathy with the sergeant. "You couldn't stop a thing like that. You're not to blame; you're just a soldier. Not even your pilots are to blame. They were only doing their duty, following their orders. They didn't even know what was in the bombs."

Pfirsich hoped they hadn't known what was in the bombs.

"No no no," insisted the American, thoroughly disturbed by the turn this had taken.

He was supposed to be making the accusations, and if there was any forgiving to be done, that was his job! Americans burning children? He didn't want to know. It had to be a lie. The knowledge of it hurt, and still more the German's forgiveness for it. How could the Americans have committed a crime for which a German could forgive them?

The sergeant pushed his brain around until it found the door that so many Americans would go through at the end of the war.

If the Americans did it, he told himself, then the Germans deserved it! German children were just worms, the vicious offspring of vicious parents. They were all guilty, no matter their age or sex or what they had actually done. They started this war; no American had to feel any pity for them. No American had to take any responsibility for anything that had been done to them. Any softening of an American's heart was a betrayal of dead American soldiers.

Yes, he remembered, that was it; he wouldn't let it get out of his mind, again. No American pity equaled no American responsibility; he had to remember what he'd been told.

"These children weren't bombed," he said. "They're Jewish children. They died in your camps! Don't claim you don't know!"

"I know now," said Pfirsich. He remembered when he'd found out. He'd thrown up. For days.

"Now?"

"I know now."

"Didn't you even try to think about it before?"

Pfirsich closed his eyes. Thinking. It used to be his shield and his comfort. Thinking had been the jewel of the human soul. Thinking set you above the animals.

Thinking had become so dangerous. And so uncertain. And so untrustworthy. Thinking whistled over the top of your head like bullets. You stuffed the rooms of your mind with cotton-wool, to keep out pain and grief and fear and death and those crazy deathly stories you could do nothing about, until you couldn't think, and it failed you.

Maybe the Americans were right to despise thinking. Maybe someday, when the time came for the Americans not to ask questions, to be silent and grim and dutiful, because they knew nothing could be done, then the capacity the Americans possessed to close their minds would become a comfort, if nothing else, that would allow them to survive, if only day by day, if only as living creatures, without need for a dangerous conscience. Nothing is completely evil in this beautifully balanced world; maybe a locked mind let you survive.

"You sure had an idea what was going on in there, and you made no effort to stop it!"

"Stop it?"

"You could have stopped it!"

287

Pfirsich stared blankly at the American. Back-Of-The-Moon wasn't the place at all; it had to be even farther out of the real world than that. What planet was this man from?

"No," he said. "I couldn't."

"That's what you're telling yourself!" snarled the American. "Didn't any of you care?"

"Care?"

He remembered his friend Harm Schaffinder, and closed his eyes, and brushed his forehead, as though brushing away straw. Harm had never come back. Poor hopeful brave Harm. So afraid to be officially identified as a *Wärmer,* he probably died as an *Itzig.*

You didn't have to do much to end up in a camp. Write some books; sing the wrong songs. Tell the wrong jokes. Have the wrong parents. Love the wrong love. Come from the wrong country. Pray to the wrong God. Call the wrong person the wrong name in the wrong place. Try to help someone else. Especially try to help someone else.

"You've heard of the Culture War?" Pfirsich said. *"The Kulturkampf?"*

The American shook his head. "Culture Fight?" Sometimes he wished he'd received a better briefing. Or they'd stuck to giving him the dumb trembling soldier krauts. These upper-class officers, with their fancy educations, were out of his league. They were more than he could handle without yelling, or hitting. Give 'em half a chance, and they'd start Latin on him, showing off their culture. No, not showing off. Just using it, like it was everyday talk. The worst thing about it was they didn't do it like they thought he was a nincompoop; they did it like they thought he'd understand, on their level. It pissed him off, but reet.

Pfirsich wondered, what if he and Harm had known what would happen? That day at the railroad station. It's said that you can always see the fruit in the seed. But when had such blood-red fruit ever grown before?

Harm might just as well have not showed up for the train that day. He could have forced them to come and get him. He could have waited in his flat, been warm and comfortable, made himself toast and tea, while the soldier went and tattled on him. When the SS came to get him, he could have stood up and laughed in their faces about their sperm samples and armpit tattoos. He might have been able to make them blush. He could

288

have made them kick down his door, he could have thrown the toast-rack at them before they shot him. If he was going to die anyway, he might as well have done it at home.

Pfirsich wished Harm could have contacted him so that they could have been having tea together when the door crashed in. A German officer drinking tea with a proscribed Jew! The blackbacks would have gone crazy with protocol, just trying to figure out what to do with the bodies.

"Culture lost," he said at last out loud.

"Huh?"

"It just lost. It got scared."

"I don't get it."

The American wanted all the definitions; how could he, an outsider, ask about what happened, if the people who lived through it didn't have all the details themselves, and couldn't understand how it had come about? How could he explain how years of creeping fear, of one little ugly loss after another, had finally made a whole culture at first fight, fight hard for its life and its world, then begin to cringe and back away, then become too afraid to raise its eyes when it heard screams? How could he explain how the very poison it had struggled not to swallow had in the end become so sweet and addictive? And that those who couldn't swallow it could only choke?

It made no sense, no sense whatever, even when you'd lived through it, when you tried to sort it out, and see how and why and where it had all happened; how did the sergeant expect him to try to explain it to a man from another planet? Why didn't the sergeant wait for the books? Somebody would write them, somebody would try to make some kind of sense of it, true or not, and then the sergeant could know what to think, what to properly think, so he'd fit in and not be a Outcast For The Truth. A pariah is still a dog, and kicked.

"Don't try to put me off the track," said the American. "You know they came and took the Jews away in trains."

Pfirsich moaned and put his hands to his face; poor Harm had gone away and he'd never see him again.

The American was very pleased with himself. That's what all the Germans should be doing, feeling sorry for just breathing, for just being on the planet with human beings.

289

Then the German turned his hands around, rubbing his eyes with his knuckles, and the American saw the chemical burns on the dirty white palms, and he gulped and looked down, quickly, and waited for the German to make the decision to speak. At last Pfirsich took that decision, bringing down his hands, so that the American could look up and meet his eye.

Pfirsich said suddenly, "Do you have a cigarette?"

The American just nodded.

"Could I have one? You know, I haven't smoked in years; not steadily, anyway, since the first war. And sometimes during college examinations. But I could use one right now." He rubbed his face. "I keep seeing – a friend of mine."

The American handed him a pack. He wasn't supposed to offer the people he interrogated any kind of comfort; it was part of the process. But the German made him nervous.

Pfirsich daintily withdrew a cigarette, so as not to dirty it, and handed the pack back. The American lit the cigarette for him. Pfirsich took a draw, and sat back, and blew the white smoke out his nose. As the drug went to work, stilling pain, alerting his heart, he felt his strength flowing back into him, and sat up and focused.

"Oh, that's nice," said Pfirsich in a stronger voice. "Mild and strong. But this is your native plant, isn't it?"

The American nodded, mutely. He looked at the pack, up at the prisoner, and back at the pack. Then he pulled a cigarette and lit it for himself.

"No wonder it's so good," said Pfirsich. "Native-grown is always best."

"Well, what you grew here in Germany is pretty native."

Pfirsich shrugged. "We do things our own way."

"You won't any more, y'know," said the American, almost confidingly. "Not when we're through with you."

"Well, I suppose that's up to you," said Pfirsich, and drew greedily on the cigarettes. "You won."

"Yeah, we won, you won't forget we won." The American leaned forward on his elbows. "Take it from me, you're going to learn to hate Nazism --."

"We don't need you to teach us that," snorted Pfirsich. "We learned to hate it first-hand."

"You people are going to learn democracy."

"We tried Democracy. It got us Hitler."

"What?" The German had messed up the American's script. For the moment he was stymied. How the hell could The Voice Of The People have produced Hitler?

Pfirsich took a drag like he was trying to replace his lungs. These cigarettes were really good. They made the schoolteacher in his blood get up on its hind legs and look around for an argument.

"My people helped to form some of the original tenants of democracy, back when it was nothing more than Mob Rule."

"Oh yeah? Uh – so when was that?"

"During the Civil War."

The American heard the word *"Bürgerkrieg."* Literally "Citizen's War." The only translation he could think of – "Civil War" – didn't make sense from his viewpoint of history. He almost raised a hand to scratch his head.

"But democracy, as you term it," continued Pfirsich, in a manner that comforted him with the memory of a family of teachers and peaceful schoolrooms. Quite beside what effect it might have on the American, a man who hadn't gotten good grades in history, and spent a lot of time in schoolroom corners.

"Or the ancestral idea of democracy. Really just the hope for a less restraining feudalism, with fewer masters for the farmers and no overlords for the masters. Even that was wrong for that time. Revolutionary ideas must come when their time is ripe."

"What the hell has the Civil War got to do with your country?"

Pfirsich drew in a great revivifying draft of the burning drug. Really good, this stuff.

"Our Civil War, our *Bürgerkrieg,* in the 1500's."

"Oh," blinked the American. "You had a Civil War, too?"

"More than one. But this one was The Peasant's War. The peasants fought for their freedom, and ended up hanging from the trees, and the knights who had sided with them were slaughtered. It was a modern impulse, but not a modern time. But you see --."

Pfirsich took another thoughtful puff. "This time, in a modern time, Germany went conquering, instead. Now, conquest is a primitive impulse. Ach!"

Pfirsich put his dirty fingers to his mouth in the tingling rush of intellectual surprise. "Were we being modern -- or did we just get it backwards? We did then what we should have done now -- and now we --." Pfirsich stared up at the ceiling. *"Main Gott,* and then everybody just followed us into it."

"You're just saying that because you didn't win!" squawked the sergeant.

"Then maybe that's our blessing, and your curse --."

The American hit his feet. Pfirsich covered his head, almost giggling. He was going to get a beating, and he knew just the best sort of mud in the camp to plaster on the bruises.

But the American didn't go for him. Instead he charged to the door. He threw it open and yelled into the hallway.

"Come get this guy! He's giving me history lessons!"

"But — but you have to listen," said Pfirsich, uncovering his head in amazement. He wasn't going to get hit? Evidently not. "You have to hear – "

"And I think he's drunk!" said the sergeant. "Find out where he got it!"

Pfirsich stared. What a nice man. These Americans seemed to be really very gentle people, if you gave them a chance, and Pfirsich was in the mood to give everybody a chance, now that he had the opportunity.

Wouldn't it be nice if he could be sweet again? Wouldn't it be nice if being made of sugar wouldn't get big dripping syrupy bites bitten out of you?

Pfirsich beamed up at the sergeant, feeling a deep affection for him, and for the renewed prospects of peace and endearment, for the trivial and silly, the banal and childish. Wouldn't it be wonderful to live again like nothing was serious? Like nothing was important? As though there were no self-important sneering gravity to weigh a man down?

The sergeant turned around and saw the sweet, pale, transparently loving expression shining up at him, and the hair went up on the back of his neck. He jumped right out into the corridor. Backwards.

Pfirsich gaped; how could the sergeant possibly know? And if he did, how could he think that someone like himself could have survived? Didn't he have any idea how much the Nazis had hated people like him? Pfirsich put his grubby hand to his lips and this time the giggle got out. Was it possible that such ridiculous peaceful misunderstandings would be in fashion again? And that instead of it leading to a vicious beating or a bullet in the back of the neck, all you got was a shocked look?

Could there ever be people who could be capable of being shocked, again? People who were delicate. And tender. And joyful and careless, foolish without the penalty of death, relaxed, with the luxury of petty irritability over nothing. Someday there would be tea again, and silk pillows and peach-colored wallpaper. In little peaceful villages along and across the borders of France and Germany. And kisses. Oh delight.

Seeing the guard outside the door beckon to him, Pfirsich took another rejuvenating drag on the cigarette, then raised himself shakily to his feet. As he hobbled out the door, with the guard on his arm, he paused and looked back at the photo album again. He petted it in passing. Poor babies. Poor people.

"Poor Harm," he said, and left the room.

The American sergeant sat back down in his chair. He didn't move. He was pressing both hands over his mouth, fingers steepled up over the end of his nose. He was looking at the notes he'd been taking, from all these German prisoners, for the last month and a half. He was looking at them with his eyes bulged out wide, and he was unable to breathe.

Goddamn queer know-it-all Nazi fucker. Made a pass at him. Fucking queers, the bunch of 'em. Everybody knew that's how they were. Everybody knew that's what made them so crooked.

That's what he got for letting one of 'em talk.

Doubt.

Doubt in what he'd been told and what he believed, about what other people knew or believed. He knew better. He knew with whom he'd been dealing, and he'd still let the sommabitch get away with it. Goddamn bastard faggoty Nazi aristocrat Prussian kraut. That was what he believed, and he was sticking with it; by God, no matter what happened, he was sticking with it!

Bread and Swans

22. What Goes Around

The combat squad herded their little lot of filthy prisoners into the front gate. Their freckled corporal pointed at the gang of confused losers.

"The war's over for you guys, so you can settle down and not try fightin' anybody any more. Okay? Relax, awready."

A one-legged German on a crutch made out of a broken cut-down window-sill, who spoke better English than the usual "Hants Up!" or "Don' Sschoot!" depending on the fortunes of the moment -- though he didn't yet understand the ubiquitous "okay" -- gawked, and translated to his wondering fellows:

"He says the war is finished for us."

"This is it," said something that looked like it might have been an officer at one time, but probably not now. No officer had shoes like that.

The prisoners all raised their weary heads, shoulders drooping in submission. This was the end of the road. They'd be shot, now, and it really would be over. They sank their heads back down between their shoulders, clenching their fists with the chill, closing their eyes and waiting like sick horses for the final bullet that they were beyond fearing or even knowing. They could Rest.

Their weapons had been taken from them, along with whatever personal goods they possessed; they didn't protest, because the last man to do that, a *Leutnant* who refused an American corporal his wedding ring, got his brains blown out for his trouble.

The Amis ran out of control the moment their officers were out of sight. Even sullen or unfriendly children could end up as just more dead Enemies. Profound personal dislike seemed to throw Americans off balance. They wanted more than unconditional surrender – they wanted unconditional love.

Their headquarters realized this wasn't newsreel material, not for the American people, anyway, not yet, and films of the dead bodies were sequestered with other distasteful and incriminating records.

Their prisoners just ducked their heads and waited for their own ends. Good soldiers can't afford mercy – the captives knew that.

"No," said the one-legged prisoner who could speak English. "Not this time. He said to rest ourselves. He means that we won't be killed."

"What?" said a German corporal who had a bad case of jaundice. His eyes were as yellow as lemons.

"You ain't in the army no more," said the American corporal, who could see he wasn't getting across to these guys.

The interpreter quickly interpreted. The prisoners stared at him, then stared at their captors.

"We're out of the army?" said the officer thing.

"Really out?" said the yellow corporal.

"We don't have to follow orders," said the one-legged interpreter. "We can rest."

"Rest," gasped the yellow corporal, and blinked his yellow eyes.

It took him a moment, but then the full import of the interpretation got through to him. His body -- that had been held upright for months purely from the need not to be left behind and die -- suddenly dislocated from the neck downwards; the knees let loose in sovereign grateful relaxation, and he fell flat forward from his full height, onto his yellow stubbled face in the slimy gray mud.

When he went down, his comrades went down with him, like so many dominoes or a stack of rifles when one has been pulled out of the pile. The squad of Americans had to jump out of the way to keep from being pulled down into the muck. The one-legged man's crutch hopped up over the top of the heap of bodies with the force of his collapse and hit one of the escorts in the chin.

"Fucking Krauts!" the man growled.

He was still rubbing his stubble and grousing when a no-necked American sergeant showed up and started chewing out the soldiers who were supposed to be in charge of the heap.

"Damnit! You stupid fuckers know better than to let the Krauts go at the gate."

"Hey, Sarge, don't look at us," said a skinny private, just as filthy as any of the prisoners on the ground, and looking like he envied them their rest. "We ain't prison-camp guards. We don't know th' manners 'round here."

"Don't gimme any of your 'manners,' " yelled the no-neck sergeant. "The Krauts haven't had any real sleep in weeks -- sometimes in months. The minute you tell 'em they're free, they go to sleep on you."

"We got 'em here," grumbled the freckled corporal.

"And you can wake 'em up!" snapped the no-neck sergeant.

"Those guys?" said the corporal, and slung his carbine back over his shoulder. "We got a schedule. We'd miss it a month by next Sunday if we stayed around long enough for them guys to wake up. We gotta get back in the line."

"What good are you?" said the sergeant.

He saw one of his own men, who had seen the new prisoners collapse from clear across the camp, came running up like a dog at a turkey shoot. The new arrival was a tomahawk-faced guy, with big bitter brown eyes. He didn't hesitate, channeling the momentum of his arrival into an eager kick, straight into the belly of one of the gray corpse-like prisoners, lifting the body, that was limp and unresponsive as any genuine corpse, right up into the air. The combat squad just wrinkled their noses and left him and his camp to their business.

"Come on, Nazi!" the little guy snarled at the bobbling bundle. "Get up!"

"Oh, give it a rest, Greenbaum," said the no-neck sergeant. "You could kick 'em 'till your feet fell off. These guys are like they're full of chloroform when they're like this."

"Some Supermen," said Greenbaum, who was circling for another hit.

"You wouldn't say so if you'd been at the Bulge," said No-neck. "These guys can fight when you'd be reeling. They must be wore to strings to be like this."

"They don't look like much now," said Greenbaum.

"No, they don't, but you'd be a fool to underestimate 'em," said No-Neck. "We did, and we paid for it."

"That why you always call 'em 'Krauts,' and not 'Nazis?'" sneered the little man.

"Shove it, Greenbaum. I ain't gonna discuss your personal problems." No-neck pointed across the camp with his chin like an

297

Indian. "Just go fetch some of the other prisoners and get this new gang outta the gate, or we'll have 'em piling up here like shot buffalo. This shit is catching."

Greenbaum took off like a hunting dog when one of the turkeys has got up and flown. He steered right around the back of the temporary barracks, knowing where he'd find the biggest herd of German prisoners. They were always hanging around back there where the sun hit, standing stupid and useless under the eaves, and if he ran fast enough, and light enough, he could catch a few of the slower horses.

Most of them heard him coming and ducked free behind the buildings, slipping in a combat-crouch around along the fence, but a little knot of them just stood and stared at him from under their caps. Look at 'em, thought Greenbaum, they even stood like horses, hipshot with their hands in their pockets, he could have sworn he saw them swivel their ears around at him.

"You! Come on, Nazis! You got work to do!"

The tallest one, right in the middle, was even flaring his nostrils at him, and blinking those big pale mad-looking blue eyes.

Oh, hell, thought Greenbaum. There's that big blond stud in amongst 'em again. He's always trouble.

Greenbaum didn't so much fear tangling with the big stallion, who was in himself one of the most inoffensive people he'd ever met; and lame in both legs to boot. It was the attitude that spread abroad about him, whenever he was standing there in the sun by himself. The other Germans would come herding up to be close to him, and the more of them there were with him, the more like bucking they got. They went from being a sad knackery clump of overworked cart-horses, to a band of nervy mustangs. Anybody coming up on them suddenly was liable to get a wall-eyed stampede, or a hoof where it hurt.

Greenbaum slowed down and worked slowly toward them, like a coyote after a colt, and they heeled around to face him and follow his every move, just like the colt's herd.

"*Scheiße*," sniffed one of the herd. "Here comes Grünbaum, running calling us names again."

"I'd like to catch that sneaky mouthy *Itzig* without his pistol," snarled a prisoner who was gray-green as a lizard with eating over-preserved Iron Rations. "Hitler didn't go far enough, and I'd like to do some catching up for him."

"That's enough, Rueßletz," said a man in a Hermann Meier cap, "It's crap like that lost us this war."

"My dears," protested Pfirsich, and it was indeed he, totally innocent of the fact that Greenbaum incongruously thought of him as The Big Blond Stud, God Damn Him. "We don't have to snarl at each other any more. Shouldn't we try to be charitable toward one another again?"

"Greenbaum isn't." snapped the Lizard.

"That's Greenbaum's problem. And you can understand his viewpoint."

"I can't."

"Try." Pfirsich turned to Greenbaum, who had finally moved in close enough to be addressed. "Yess, Corporal Greenbaum?"

"Don't do that," complained the little American.

"Vhat, dear?" smiled Pfirsich, with genuine sweetness. He was so happy to be able to be sweet to people again that he couldn't help overdoing it.

"Don't pretend to be polite to me," sneered Greenbaum. "You don't like me -- so don't pretend you do."

"Dear, I vas taught manners," said Pfirsich. "Und manners mean no'ting, if ve are polite only to peeple ve like."

"I knew you didn't like me."

"Ve shure do not," agreed the Lizard.

"You shaddup, Nazi!" commanded Greenbaum.

"I am Nazi by choice," hissed the Lizard. "You ist born a *Itzig!*"

"I'll choice you!" said Greenbaum.

He didn't know what *Itzig* meant, but he suspected it was the native German for "Kike." The sound of it didn't offend him like the American word, but he knew the intent when he heard it. He jumped the Lizard, pawing at his service pistol, and the prisoner came right back at him, leaping closer to grab Greenbaum's pistol hand before he could get off a shot. They scuffled and kicked and spat foam in each other's faces. It was plain to see that the two of them had just been awaiting their chances, with no authorities around to tell them to get their hands off each other.

"STOP IT!"

They found themselves suspended in the air, shaken back and

forth like a couple of bad puppies, gasping. The tall blond inoffensive stallion had grasped them each by the scruffs of their necks, one in each dirty gray-gloved hand, and was shaking them, hard, until he suddenly let them hang. They were astounded -- the man was a cripple! Yet he'd picked the both of them right up off their feet, as though they were all standing in water. In amazement, they hung in his hands and let him do as he would with them. They both suddenly realized how tall he was.

"I swear," said Pfirsich, with an exasperated smack of his lips. "The two of you are like a couple of snapping mongrels. I'll have to hit you with cold water, next."

He gave them one more hard shake and set them down on their feet. Then he bent over for his cane and motioned sharply toward an officer, a man with his left arm missing to the elbow.

"Hauptmann Kroener!" said *Oberst* Rommel. "Come get Heiner. He's baiting Corporal Greenbaum again."

The mutilated officer hadn't lost any of his sense of authority. He lurched forward and herded Heiner away, with the furious prisoner trying to glare back around the officer's.

"Heiner, how many times do we have to deal with you two?" said the officer.

"It's his fault," said Heiner, herding with great reluctance back into the depths of the camp.

At the same moment, Pfirsich was backing Greenbaum back toward the fence. For a cripple, he had a very intimidating limp.

"Und you do not be zo ready to pull de pistol."

"It's his fault!" said Greenbaum.

"I vill report you to Sercheant Hilty," threatened Pfirsich.

"Yeah? I was in the right."

"Greenbaum!" snapped No-Neck Hilty, coming around the side of the building. He had heard the grumbling and squabbling, and figured that Greenbaum must have been stirring up the prisoners again. He wished someone would transfer Greenbaum to a combat unit, and let him get his brains blown out to his heart's content, while there were still Germans willing to do it.

"I told you to fetch some prisoners, not start a fight."

"Yes, Sergeant, be right there, Sergeant," said Greenbaum, and then, under his breath to Pfirsich, "Don't tell him. He'll have me walking the wire in a full pack all night."

"Na, don't gife me anyt'ing to report to him, und you vill not hafe to ask," sniffed Pfirsich. "Hello, Sercheant Hilty," he said affably.

"Hi, Colonel," said Hilty, and saluted. "Got bodies in the gate, again."

Pfirsich nodded and saluted back. He didn't do it with anybody else, but it always made Hilty happy.

Hilty grinned. He liked getting a swift bold salute from a real old-fashioned Kraut officer, especially one that was so nice and friendly, without any of the sucking up some of them tried to do. This one was still a soldier.

"Come," said Pfirsich to the men standing around him, and pointed toward the gate. "Let's help the Sergeant get our men up out of the mud."

The mustangs almost wheeled around in a body toward the gate. Nobody protested; nobody even thought of fussing, but just trotted off to help shift bodies.

Hilty beamed as he watched them go. The Colonel was so helpful, without being condescending or sullen, without the blank broken look that hung over so many of these people. The Colonel, as always, was a model of good manners, even standing in a mud hole with his face like pale death. A real soldier.

Pfirsich herded his horses off toward the gate. He would be so happy when he could finally stop being a soldier, and get back to the proper business of life.

23. It's My Party

In the autumn of 1990, an old man -- a comfortably successful dealer in second-provenance better-grade French, Spanish and Italian furniture, porcelain and enamel-ware, with the occasional sideline in presentation Italian armor or weapons, and possessor of a small but much-admired pop-culture doll collection -- went to Amsterdam to drink Champagne.

He'd had a very nice party right in his hotel suite the night before, and all his family had been there, and some old comrades from the war. They'd stayed awake until the sun came up, popping bottle after bottle, until they were kicking corks all over the hotel suite floor, and the children were asleep in the bedroom, under the coats and purses.

His great-granddaughter was there, the granddaughter of that lion-colored boy-child he'd sired in the desert, and everyone else of his bloodline, and their in-laws. The differently gendered are often forced to build their own tribes from scratch, and their adopted or surrogate children can depend on more than their share of bloodline or volunteer aunts and uncles, cousins, friends and associates. The Others seldom have latchkey children.

Pfirsich's former orderly, Udo Schmidt, was there. He'd come back from the Russian lead-mines twenty-five years before. He spoke mostly Russian now, and on good days he thought he was back in Africa. He was missing an eye. He'd come home with the help of Pfirsich's son Manfred -- who was working for the U.N. -- and as soon as he could stand up straight, Pfirsich set him up in a tavern in Berlin. It was called *Udos kleine Kneipe* -- Udo's Little Pub. Udo spent most of his time sitting at the bar, while his two waitresses ran the place and did the books and reported on a quarterly basis back to *Herr* Rommel. Udo usually had a glass of beer in front of him on the bar. When he went to the toilet, he dropped his glass eye into the beer to keep other people from nipping from his glass.

Herr Kjars Winzig was there. Winzig had been a *Leutnant* in the *Afrika Korps* days, and there wasn't a day that hadn't passed without his cavilling about having to share his tent with the unit's American prisoner and newspaper editor – especially when the prisoner used his tentmate's cot for doing layout. As it turned out, Winzig was responsible for having Udo sent to Siberia under *Operation Keelhaul,* part of the American Bribe to allow the Soviets to grab and hold anybody they wanted from the conquered territories, including soldiers and their families if the Russians could catch them. Right after the war Pfirsich wanted to wring Winzig's neck, but they were all old now, and tired, and Udo had come home. Kjars was a retired manager for T.W.A., with a wife and daughter. He flew into the United States once a year, around the holidays, to visit an old friend.

Jeff Holz, the 469th's former American prisoner, owned ½-interest in a hotel in Chicago, where Kjars spent a lot of time in the bar playing old '30's jazz on the upright piano while their wives went shopping or to the opera. Kjars and Jeff had flown into Amsterdam on the same plane to attend Pfirsich's party. Jeff brought a research file with him that he had been promising Pfirsich for years.

Jeff had a very personal hobby. He spent his spare time hunting down evidence of what had happened to some of the old 469th. Pfirsich didn't expect much; most of the 469th had been re-assigned to other units, and were probably final casualties of the war. So much for the filing system. There wasn't much Jeff could trace, and oddly enough it was from the Russian theater, where records were especially thin on the ground.

In the freezing winter retreats, the dumb radio-operator Kristof had both legs blown off. He couldn't scream, and then he couldn't walk. None of the wounded could be left for the Russians to kill. He was thrown, leaking plasma and matter, into the back of an overloaded ambulance that was latched closed and taken out on the slushy road and into the line of vehicles on the retreat.

Those retreats were a hell of mixed soft- and hard-shelled vehicles -- tanks, armored cars, staff cars, ambulances -- all without lights in the night for fear of YAK bombers. Tank commanders screamed at officers in staff-cars to get their crap-hole *Klapperkasten* out of the way. The officers screamed back, and sometimes had to jump out of their cars when the tank drivers hit the gas. They had their orders, everybody was out to get from point A to point B, and nothing would get in the way of the tanks, that lurched over the waves of frozen mud like battle-cruisers. The little ambulances crawled between them, up and down, little bouncing mud-dories, and their latches had been secured in a hurry.

Kristof must have slipped out of the back of the ambulance into the road, right into the blacked-out traffic. He couldn't run, he couldn't scream, and what crushed fragments of him were left must still be in the road. No amount of reconciliation between Russia and Germany was ever going to tweezer him up out of the dirt and send him home again. Russian sunflowers would have to be his only monument.

Chaplin Stange, who couldn't hide his decency any more than a cruel man could hide his cruelty, had gone on comforting people in Russia. He took his comforting right up to the front line -- in fact, right over the line. The frontier guards warned him. It was the usual warning, that the Hyena Squads -- the SS -- had been through the area like the plague on wheels and that the *Partizani* had retaliated by hanging stray German soldiers upside down with wire in the trees, first stripping them naked to freeze, sometimes disemboweling them, and suspending them low enough so the wolves could get at them.

Stange didn't listen; there was a Russian family out there, all that remained of a crossroads village, a woman and two kids, cold and hungry. Pfirsich could imagine the conversation. The Chaplin himself had been such an unimaginative man, with no ability to picture the world other than by the duty he owed its children.

"What if the Ivans find out you helped them?" asked one of the guards. "They could get shot, or shipped to Siberia."

"Not if they starve or freeze first."

"You ain't going, *Herr Kaplan*," said the other guard, doubtless lowering his rifle on the chaplain.

Stange gave up and went back into the lines, that much was known. The guards, who knew him, warned the night guard to watch out for him trying to sneak past them in the dark. But the chaplain was a resourceful man. He wasn't with his unit the next morning. No one knew if he got to feed or pray for the Russian family, before the Partisans had their way with him. But there was no one alive in the village the next day, and the chaplain never came back.

The 469th had enjoyed more social contact with the Africans than was usual for an *Afrika Korps* unit. Pfirsich and his descendants had spent long years looking for their African connections, including Udo's wife and Pfirsich's Arab mare. But the girl was a nomad and her people didn't object if a woman took a second husband if the first disappeared. The pretty white mare was only a horse. Africa was a big place and wars move people around. No matter how Pfirsich's clan had searched, the two females seem to have blown away, unfindable, somewhere in the drifting sands of the vast continent.

Arnold Makepeace, the Indian half-breed, had been captured in France. He wasn't wearing beads or feathers, just German uniform and a German helmet. When the Americans found out he was an Indian, they judged him as a man from their proprietary lands. Americans have no sense of irony. Arnold was given a quick drumhead court-martial -- a courtesy they weren't extending to everybody -- then shot as a traitor.

* * * * *

In the first silver morning light, Pfirsich stood on the balcony that opened upon his hotel room, leaning out from under the railing and past the awning, letting the delicate misty rain patter down on his balding blue-veined old skull and dampen the shoulders and upper arms of his gold-brocade Viennese bed robe.

"What a beautiful town, especially in the rain," he murmured, and held his glass out into the soft mizzle. "Champagne with rainwater; what a cocktail." He sipped at the glass. "What a digestive."

"Where's that old fool?" came a voice from inside the room. "Out on the balcony again? He'll catch his death!"

His companion and comrade for longer than the last half century came bustling and grumbling out onto the balcony. Melvin Gonville, as he now preferred to be called, in deference to his father's English blood, was twenty years younger than his jolly old friend. He could even get away with dyeing his hair back to its original jet-black, with a concession to reality in the form of one sweep of silver back from above his left temple. He wore color contacts – today's were green -- and narrow shoes and still did push-ups, but he had been bucking for Grumpy Old Man since he was fifty, and on some days he made it all the way to Curmudgeon.

Melvin led with his face out into the rain and was stopped in his tracks by the first touch of water on an eyelash. He blinked and sneezed and ducked right back under the awning.

"Pfirsich? Pfirsich -- out of your wheelchair -- and in the rain!"

"Come out on the balcony, Melvin," purred Pfirsich. "It's a wonderful morning."

The old man was standing up on the bottom rung of the balcony guardrail and was waving his slowly diluting glass out over the street, making a wide gesture of salute to the mist-cloaked red roofs. The watery Champagne swirled out and joined the raindrops and showered down, a cool touch of the fire of alcohol through the air and water to the earth below.

"I love this city!"

"You are drunk," snapped Melvin. "This city is gray and soggy, like always. Try landing a dive-bomber in the fields around here. You might as well be landing in chocolate mousse."

"Mousse! Chocolate mousse *am feinsten.* Did you order any for breakfast?"

"Mein Gott, you rickety old fool, come in here; you're just asking for trouble with your lungs."

"This city is wonderful. My lungs are wonderful, too! They're springing like a lamb."

"How much champagne did you have last night? Your kidneys are going to boil up and dribble out your ass."

Melvin still had a pilot's vocabulary, and when annoyed, he used it.

"Kidneys! Yes, kidneys. I want a lamb's fry for breakfast."

"Chocolate? And kidneys? You'll throw up."

Pfirsich just climbed up one more rung on the railing and proclaimed his freedom and joy to the city.

"My kidneys -- my knees -- my back -- my joints -- *none* of them are ever going to trouble me again -- not after today!"

Pfirsich fell down off the railing so gracefully it was almost a hop, and if he could have, he would have skipped back into the hotel room. But when he turned he found that Melvin had retreated back into the room before him, and was sitting sobbing in the wheelchair. Pfirsich shuffled in and hugged his shoulders, nuzzling him with his soft-haired old man's muzzle.

"Oh, Melvin, my darling, my dear, my dearest; don't cry. It's not sad. We owe a death."

"*Oh, Gott,*" groaned Melvin. "Why couldn't you have gone in for treatment? I would have given you a kidney. Hell, I'd have given you both of them. Right out of my back, with a kitchen-knife. You know I would."

"Darling, it's not just the kidneys, now. It's the whole machine; it's just falling apart. I'm tired of hurting, and I just want to leave."

"Don't you love me any more?"

Pfirsich poked him. "You know better than to ask that. Do you want to keep watch over me when I'm lying in bed with tubes in me? When the only choices I have include pulling out the tubes? When I'm lying there, all blue, even the white of my eyes, and my breath like a bad engine, do you want to end up tempted to do the pulling yourself?"

Melvin just gasped and covered his eyes.

"Room service!" came the knock at the door, and Melvin jumped up out of the wheelchair.

"Breakfast!" said Pfirsich. "Let's eat."

In came the server, pushing that little white-covered table covered with silver dishes that has always symbolized effortless luxury, on the stage, on the movie-screen, even in fairy-tales, where it appeared as the magical tablecloth that set itself, or the bewitched goat or calf that that spat out a banquet. Or, thought Pfirsich, following the idea, in Africa it was the magical bird that shat yogurt. He lifted a cover and smacked his lips delicately while the server floated the beautiful breakfast over to the table.

"Braised endive with Gruyere cheese," Pfirsich cooed. "And perfect hot coffee, and cream you could stand a spoon in. Is there anything like Dutch butter? Oh, look, those lovely caramel-filled wafers you warm on top of your coffee cup. What's under this cover?" he said, and lifted it.

"Don't you touch those!" snuffed Melvin. "You don't dare eat that brined herring."

"I do, and I will."

"Not with the chopped raw onion."

"With the chopped raw onion. Young man," he said to the server, who understood, if he did not speak, perfectly good German, French, English, Spanish, some Arabic and Russian and even a little Swahili.

"Here's a little something for your trouble. And if you bring me a hot lamb's fry -- simply spitting with hot bacon and more onions -- there's be a little more for you again. And the coldest chocolate mousse for desert."

"Desert for breakfast?" wailed Melvin.

"Feelen Tank," said the young man, took the proffered tip, and left the two old gentlemen to enjoy their first -- and in Pfirsich's case his only -- meal of the day.

"Glutton," muttered Melvin, as Pfirsich snapped his napkin before laying it over his lap and tucking in with gusto. Melvin didn't even touch the cup of black coffee the server had poured for him, and after Pfirsich had taken the first edge off his hunger he noticed that his friend's usually hearty appetite was gone.

"Oh, you," said Pfirsich and kissed him on the cheek. "My delicate boy."

Melvin didn't even try. He just teared up and choked, "Why?"

"I hurt," said Pfirsich. "And I'm tired."

"And you're going to make me watch."

"I want you to be there."

"Why me?"

"I sent away the rest of my family," said Pfirsich, buttering a hot bun. "Even my darling great-granddaughter, poor child. It was enough they were at the wake."

"Thanks. They're going to resent me, being the only one who gets to be there with you when you --."

Melvin couldn't finish. He pressed the heels of his hands against his forehead and squinted back the tears. Pfirsich put down his bun, and took his old lover's hand in his.

"I didn't want to hurt them."

"You think this doesn't hurt them, not being allowed to say goodbye to you?"

"I said goodbye to them last night. Before I absolutely passed out from too much Champagne. I might as well have been dead and on my bier, for all I knew. I don't imagine I looked much better than dead."

"You didn't look good. You didn't even respond when they all kissed you, one after another."

"Did you kiss me?"

Melvin snorted. " 'course I did."

"And my face wasn't cold, was it? You remember how cold a dead man's face could be."

"How would I know that?"

"In the war --."

"I didn't go around kissing dead bodies!"

Pfirsich ignored him. "I would rather my family kissed a face that was still warm."

"I'm going to be the one who kisses you when you're cold," gritted Melvin.

"I trusted you, and your old warrior heart, not to be hurt, but to understand."

"I'm not a warrior!" wailed Melvin. "I haven't flown a plane in years!"

"Not even in your sleep?"

Melvin hung his head. "Every night."

Pfirsich squeezed his hand and said, "You were beautiful as a pilot."

Pfirsich never lost his terror that they would end up in the blackest of the black camps, even after the war ended, when the Allies made the homosexuals they found starving and broken in the camps serve out their sentences right there where the Nazis had left them. But Melvin had still managed to get away with it; at least he knew better than to kiss in the middle of an army parade ground or a P.O.W. camp. Not much better, but that at least.

"I was, wasn't I?" agreed Melvin. He had opened the bottle of thick icy *jenever* gin and poured himself one *borrel,* one little shot-glass, right to the rim as it should be, knocked it back and poured another. "Beautiful."

"You were a stunner. I was helpless." Pfirsich put his hand upon Melvin's cheek. "And we met in Paris, City of Light, and Romance."

"Paris!" snorted Melvin. "That city -- 'romantic.' It shaved its women's heads and painted swastikas on their tits. Paraded 'em through the streets."

Pfirsich patted his cheek. "That was a long time ago."

"A few poor bints," said Melvin. "Whose greatest crime was sleeping with us *Boche.* The whole town had been sleeping with us, one way or another, and they took it out on those poor bitches. Rotten froggy hypocrites."

Pfirsich had never heard Melvin express pity for anyone, hardly for himself. With Melvin's record of womanizing, his bitterness was surprising. Maybe he was feeling guilty for screwing those women and running off and leaving them to their vengeful compatriots. Maybe he had really liked women as people. Maybe he could sympathize with that class of woman. In his way, he was one of them.

"I want you with me today," said Pfirsich. "You're still the closest of all to me, closer even than my own flesh and blood. We're heart-cousins, even if we aren't related by blood. I adore you. I couldn't send you away. Pour me a *Kopstoot.*"

"Eh?"

"It's Dutch. Means a Kick In The Head. Go on."

Melvin poured him a shot of the *jenever* and handed it to him. He took it, pinkie cocked in the air, swallowed it, and coughed.

"Hmf! That's raw," said Pfirsich.

"Jong," said Melvin. "The young stuff's rougher. Did you want the old mellow stuff?"

"No. No, this is perfect." Pfirsich held out the glass. "Top me up again."

Melvin did, and Pfirsich followed the shot with a couple of strips of smoked eel. After he'd downed a third brisk shot, he ran a finger around the inside of the glass, rubbed the drops of gin over his fingers to cut the fishiness, then wiped them on his napkin and leaned back in the chair. He put both hands on the edge of the table and carefully levered himself to his feet.

"So, are you going to help me get ready for my flight?"

"Your flight?"

"I'm flying away. You know where we have to go. You might try to lend a flavor of celebration to such a joyful occasion."

"Joyful! You're about to allow yourself to be poisoned. Like a stray cat!"

"Poisoned? I'm about to be transported -- etherealized -- raised up to -- to --."

"Oh, for God's sake, Pfirsich." Melvin took more of the gin.

"Well, transported, anyway. Get my suit, will you?"

Melvin stared at him, quickly poured and gulped another glass of gin, slapped his napkin onto the table and got to his feet. While Pfirsich was limping over to his wheelchair, Melvin pulled the suit and the matching Italian calf grain shoes out of the closet.

"It's your best New York suit. You'll -- you'll look handsome in it."

He helped Pfirsich lower himself into the chair, then laid the suit in his lap. He sat down on the bed and broke the new crisp cotton Oxford shirt out of its plastic.

Pfirsich brushed the suit's rich lapels and sighed. "I wish it were my wedding dress."

"Your what?"

"What I was wearing when we met, Melville," Pfirsich said dreamily. "I think of that as our wedding day. Do you remember?"

"Yes," said Melvin. "I said 'Hi, handsome,' and all you could think was, 'How the hell does he know?' "

"Well, I don't suppose I would have phrased it like that. Get me the little gold paper box out of my suitcase."

"I do remember what you were wearing," snapped Melvin, digging round in the case until he found the box. He handed it over, too upset to ask what was in it, assuming it was cufflinks or a tiepin. "Here. I don't think a wartime German officer's uniform would be quite appropriate these days for a stroll through downtown Amsterdam."

Pfirsich took the little box and held it to his cheek. "It would make them happy." He set the little box on the side-table by the bed, but kept glancing at it. Melvin didn't notice.

"How the hell would it make them happy?"

"I could tell people I was on my way to be killed -- and burnt -- in it. They would weep with delight."

"You can be so morbid sometimes."

"I know what makes people happy! Can I possibly make clear to you how happy I am this day is here?"

"You couldn't wear your uniform, anyway, it would just hang on you. You've gotten so thin, like you were at the end of the war."

"Nonsense. If I still had it, I'd have had it tailored."

"And you would have to lose the sword."

"The last time I saw my uniform, it didn't have a sword. It had a burnt-out pistol. It was a filthy threadbare rag. And that was over fifty years ago."

Melvin dressed on in silence, maneuvering Pfirsich's stiff bony arms and legs into the suit, tying his tie, straightening his vest. He knelt down and pulled on the French silk stockings, over the horny old feet, gently, so they wouldn't catch on the brittle skin. He carefully slipped on the shoes and tied the laces, not too tight, because sometimes Pfirsich's feet would swell.

While Melvin was busy rearranging the old man's legs on the foot supports, Pfirsich opened the little gold box and from it took a small package of crisp waxy gold-shot pink paper, old paper, but still beautiful. He unwrapped it to reveal the round pot-metal box with the German soldier's belt-buckle in the lid, the one his sister Helene had retrieved before Erwin's funeral, drawing it tenderly from their dead brother's breast pocket and kissing it before giving it to Pfirsich.

Pfirsich had carried it for the rest of the war, and then put it away for fifty-six years. The yellow spoon was still in it, and he wedged it in place with the pink paper, so it wouldn't rattle. Then he wrapped it carefully in his handkerchief and tucked it into his own inside breast pocket. From his toiletries box he took a package of violet breath pastilles. Melvin stood up, and Pfirsich looked up at him.

"Ready?"

"No."

"Well, I am."

"This is murder."

"You can't murder yourself," said Pfirsich, and tapped a pastille onto his tongue.

"It ain't legal."

"No, but it is *gedogen.*"

"Eh?"

"It's the Dutch for 'allowed.' When one makes one own decision in Holland, one is allowed to act upon it. It's an adult country."

"You're going to be a teacher to the end, aren't you?"

Pfirsich put his hand over his shoulder and tapped one of his wheelchair handles.

"Push," he said.

* * * * *

313

Out in the rain on the street Melvin stumped reluctantly along pushing the wheelchair. Pfirsich sat stoically in his Paris-tailored black trench coat under a British umbrella much like the one he'd carried as a teacher after the end of the First World War, but with the head of a hound instead of the original steel ball. He carried his gold-headed Irish blackthorn cane across his lap, just in case. It was raining so hard that very few people were out, not even the hurdy-gurdy players trying to earn a few coins with *On The Streets Of Amsterdam*.

"Some combat pilot you are," grumbled Pfirsich. "Are you going to snivel all the way to the doctor's office?"

Melvin didn't say anything; he just stopped walking and stood helplessly with his head down, dripping rain off his hat and tears off his chin. Pfirsich took his cane up off his lap and poked him with it.

"Oh, go away! Give me my rolling gloves. I will get myself there."

"No, please -- please -- Let me go with you -- be with you --."

"Oh, so now you've changed your mind." Pfirsich held out a hand sheathed in rubbed Spanish kid. They would never have survived hard contact with his wheel frames. "My rolling gloves. Now."

"No." Melvin stepped backwards. "No."

"I have to go there sooner or later. And I really don't want my kidneys to catch up with me this morning, not the way I've been abusing them. Come on," he said, tapping his Swiss watch. "We're on a schedule here."

Melvin stood and shook his head. He put his face in his hands.

"Now!" barked Pfirsich. "My gloves or your hands on this chair!"

Several passersby jumped at the sound of the rough old voice.

"Quit yelling in German," hissed Melvin. "You're frightening the Dutch people."

The people walked by, trying not to stare, and wondering what was the matter with the old guys. Pfirsich twisted around in his chair, and lanced them with those pale blue eyes of his, that had faded with age until they always looked icy, and when he widened them with feeling they could scalp a person standing.

"Do you mind?" he snapped. "This is private."

The Dutch people hurried off down the sidewalk and left the two crazy old Germans alone. Those people weren't predictable when they were young, let alone when their brains were starting to wear out. They didn't need their big bad boots to make them touchy and given to kicking.

Taken as individual animals, the Germans still could get very intense and gabby and pushy, especially when you didn't agree with them or you butted into their own arguments. Best leave them to squabble in the rain in their wheelchair, if it made them happy.

"Nosey neighbors," grumbled Pfirsich. "I can't stand nosey neighbors."

"You can at least try to die with dignity."

Pfirsich crossed his arms. "It's my party, and I'll die like I want to."

"Oh," said Melvin. "Oh, you are the worst."

"Come on. I don't want to sober up. If that gin gets through my system before I'm gone, I'm going to blame you."

"Oh!" said Melvin. And then, "You!"

* * * * *

They finally made it to their destination, but not before they'd frightened more people, including five on bicycles, and a large dog hitched to a cart. If they'd been younger or didn't have the wheelchair, they'd have ended up at a station house as a public nuisance. Possibly deported.

The people on the bicycles got out of their way without comment, all but one of them. She remembered how her grandfather used to grumble about the bicycles the Germans had seized in the last war, and what he liked to mumble at German tourists.

She stopped for just a moment, long enough to hoot, "I want my bike back!"

That was ill-timed. This wasn't a tourist. This was one of the Germans who had actually stolen one of the bicycles. Not officially seized it under order, but come upon the owner outside a bakery and snatched the blue bicycle right off the curb from behind him.

Back then Melvin whooped off down the street with the owner and his dog running and barking furiously behind him, while the *Leutnant* sat up straight on the seat and kept pedaling and double-thumbed his nose at the man. The owner reported the theft to the German occupation authorities, and they not only reprimanded *Leutnant* Gonville for behavior unbecoming an officer, they gave the man his bicycle back. Then they gave him a receipt and seized it properly.

The old man Melvin had never really become whirled around on the modern girl and if Pfirsich hadn't stuck his cane between his legs and almost tripped him, he would have chased her down the street. She wasn't used to seeing old men get so angry, not even the most crotchety old Dutch Uncle. She stood right up on the pedals of her bicycle and skidded off into the rain.

"Behave!" Pfirsich snapped and hauled Melvin back by his sleeve. "I can't take you anywhere."

In the square called *het Spui*, they were held up in front of the statue of *'t Lieverdje*, the little boy who stood there grinning like he thought the world was funny. They had to untangle the chair from a dog-harness worn by a big work-dog that was pulling a cart full of cheese and milk. Melvin took down the owner's name, so that he could pay for the spilled milk-cans and the Edam cheeses that flipped out and rolled into the gutter. Or at least he tried. He was shaking so hard that he couldn't write it down on the hotel breakfast receipt that he found in his pocket, so Pfirsich took it and his pen away from him. There was no use trying to write on the damp crumpled scrap. Pfirsich took out his wallet and handed the dog's owner a dark-green card, embossed in bronze.

"Just contact that number," he said. "You'll be reimbursed. Do you understand?"

The man nodded. He understood enough. Business cards always meant responsibility.

"Oh!" gasped Melvin. "You won't be there."

Pfirsich shot him such a look. "You'll be there. It's the business number."

"I couldn't, I couldn't," choked Melvin.

"Call him," Pfirsich said to the owner, and pointed at Melvin. "He'll pay you."

"He's not really a dairy-man," protested Melvin. "He's mostly a tourist attraction."

"Do you mind?" said Pfirsich. "He's a business-man, he has a

316

living to make. Don't listen to him, *Mynheer.* Ask to speak to my grandson. This man is useless."

The dog stood there and grinned. Melvin started to steer the wheelchair away down the street, but Pfirsich stuck his cane in the wheel.

"What now?" groaned Melvin.

"We're going in here," said Pfirsich, pointing at the *bruine,* one of the Brown Cafes, the old smoky beer-and-gin joints of Amsterdam, a little corner of a place called the Hoppe.

"Haven't you had enough to drink already?"

"I want some *gezelligheid. "*

"What the hell is that?"

"It's like *Gemütlichheit,* but without the sense of humor."

"Don't talk Dutch to me! You know I don't understand it."

"It's almost German."

"It's not," Melvin drawled. "And you don't speak it."

"I like to learn new things."

"Now? You want to learn new things now? Where are you going to use them?"

"Well, there will be Dutch people in the afterlife."

Melvin shoved the chair forward into the doorway.

"The only thing I like about the Dutch is what they drink."

"I'm buying," said Pfirsich, as the door closed behind them.

* * * * *

When the doctor had received Pfirsich's phone call, he said, "Are you sure you want to do this?"

Euthanasia, or assisted suicide, wasn't legal in the Netherlands, only *gedogen.* In Holland voluntary death was less a medical procedure than a litmus test of personal freedom. In 1990 it had no academic background, and was left in the hands of doctors necessarily uninstructed in the proper ending of life. Historically doctors were only trained to heal, not to accept the futility of a treatment. But if self-destruction was the intent, then it followed logically that death must be a successful cure.

This doctor had no training in A.S. but he knew that what he was being asked to do was illegal. The courts were willing to accept *force majeure* as an argument, with proper proof of consultations, and this left any doctor as much concerned with the courtroom as with the treatment room. It didn't help when the patient called from a foreign country expressly to take advantage of the amorphous Dutch legal position toward self-destruction.

Herr Rommel had not been ambivalent. *Herr* Rommel stated firmly and decisively that he hurt, that he was tired, and that he had made the choice, not from fear, but with clear purpose.

"Are you sure you want this?" the doctor said again.

"I have lived long enough," Pfirsich said, calmly, over the telephone. "I know it will upset some people, but I'm very close to failing."

"You've had medical evidence of this?"

"I have the evidence of my organs," said the voice. "I'm frittering away. I'm not going to last another month."

"Has your own doctor said --?"

"My own body has said."

"What sort of medication has your physician prescribed?"

"There isn't any. I'm a dead man."

"Now before we discuss this --."

"I would like to make an appointment."

"I would really need documentation from your own physician."

"I shall bring it."

"I would like to speak to your physician."

"I shall have him call you."

"You have to understand that I shall have to call in colleagues for consultation."

"I am perfectly aware," said the infinitely patient German voice. "That you have legal considerations. Everything will be seen to, in the event of prosecution. The worst you may have to suffer is *berisping.*"

Reprimand by the Amsterdam medical tribunal. The doctor was taken aback that the patient knew the term. What the man said next made him nearly drop the phone.

"I won't be needing *Vesparax,* or anything like it," said the strong old voice. "That's too slow. I would prefer injection. You shall have full cooperation, of course. My partner shall see to all the particular. Won't you, Melvin?"

The doctor didn't answer for several moments. This wasn't like dealing with the usual bags of fear or misery, of unbearable physical pain or psychological agony, or both, or sometimes neither except by untraceable perception, looking up at him with moist trust, begging for a decision, just wanting the suffering to end, and devastated that there was no other choice. No family was standing by to make sure that it was done. No exhausted wife, no over-wrung adult children. Just an unstable angry life-long lover who had no control over his very self-assured old mate. The doctor could hear him sputtering bitterly in the background.

All the doctor had was the man's voice on the other end of the telephone, the call from Germany, but it was the voice of confidence, of a man sure of himself, sure of his mission. A commanding voice. The doctor could only think it was like the voice of an officer. My God, he thought, he was dealing with a German officer, one of the old ones, like his grandmother had told him about. The man was giving orders, and the doctor would just have to go along and follow them. He was almost afraid to meet him. The man was *force majeure* personified.

"Are -- are you sure this is what you want?" said the doctor again.

* * * * *

"Herr Doktor."

"Mynheer Rommel," said the little bald man with the horn-rimmed glasses and the prominent chin, coming from his clinic with his hands out. He looked relieved. "Welcome!"

Pfirsich took his hand, "You're cheerful today."

"Of course he is," growled Melvin, angrily kneading Pfirsich's shoulder. "He's Dutch. He gets to kill a German."

"Ech! The war's been over for years," said Pfirsich. "You have to forgive him, *Herr Doktor.* His generation grew up smack in the middle of the war. I don't think they ever got past it."

"Of course, of course," said the doctor, nervously patting Pfirsich's other shoulder. "Sounds like my father."

He had almost expected an image from his grandmother's stories to come in through that door, and it shook him to find that in everything but costume he hadn't been far off.

"Do you mind?" said Melvin and swept the doctor's hand off his friend's shoulder.

"He's hurting, *Herr Doktor,"* said Pfirsich, and patted Melvin's

319

other hand, that was grimly maintaining its place on his back. "He doesn't want me to go."

"I know, I know. It hurts the family .the worst," the doctor finished lamely.

Melvin shot him an evil look. In his younger days, when he went heeled, it might have been the last thing the doctor ever saw.

"Where is the rest of the family?" said the doctor.

Pfirsich removed his hat and umbrella and handed them to the receptionist. "I couldn't stand it, *Herr Doktor.* I know it's weak of me not to let them be here, but I couldn't bear it."

"Are you sure?"

"I have a very strong family," said Pfirsich. "They understand, this is for me." He gestured toward Melvin. "And him. Melvin?" he said, and held out his hand.

Melvin jerked like he'd been stabbed.

"Come on. It's time. Help me go in and get up on the table."

"Oh," said Melvin. "No."

"Be a soldier again, for me."

Melvin just looked at him. "I was a pilot."

"Pilots don't do lifting?"

The clinic nurse made to take the handles of the wheelchair, but Melvin beat him to it, grabbing the handles as though they were the pistol grips on a cockpit machine-gun. The look he gave the nurse made the man step back. Did they allow such looks in peacetime? Pfirsich gave a cracking snort and shocked everyone when he slammed the tip of his cane to the floor and levered himself right up onto his feet.

"*Mynheer* Rommel!" said the doctor, hard-put to modulate his voice. "We don't take kangaroos in this clinic."

"I will walk," said Pfirsich.

The nurse made a motion to support his elbow, but Melvin got there first. Pfirsich didn't pull away, but he made it clear he would do it himself. He limped slowly, with great upright dignity, into the operating room, with nurse, doctor and lover herding him carefully like three sheep dogs behind a dog-butting old ram. The doctor was busily polishing his glasses on his sleeve.

In the room the door was closed, and Pfirsich put out his hand to Melvin, who automatically helped him take off his coat and hat. The nurse stood aside, waiting for a signal from the doctor, who watched carefully. These last moments were important; the patient must be left to direct them himself. The court would want proof. And witnesses.

Pfirsich pressed his hip against the table, facing toward the foot, and consciously lightened himself, giving himself all the spring he could manage on his toes. At the same moment, Melvin, who had put an arm around his shoulders and behind his knees, rolled his old friend's shoulders onto the table while smoothly swinging up the legs. Years of levering Pfirsich up into his high bed had prepared them both for dignifying a moment that could have been an ill-timed struggle. Especially considering Pfirsich's knees, that had been replaced with steel twenty years before but had never stopped hurting.

Pfirsich lay back easily and Melvin arranged the pillow under his head. The nurse raised his blond-white eyebrows, impressed. The old man was thin -- the meat on him wouldn't have filled a hat -- but he was tall, with a big knobby old skeleton, and made a heavy awkward burden. Nothing for amateurs.

"Comfy?" said the doctor. "Thank you, *Mynheer* Gonville."

"Yes, he's comfortable," Melvin snapped.

"Shhh," Pfirsich comforted. "This is lovely. I'm chock-full of Champagne and gin, you know."

"I thought you seemed very relaxed," said the doctor, maneuvering carefully to a position beside his shoulders, next to the supply cabinet. Melvin was following the doctor with guard-dog eyes.

"Very."

The nurse said tentatively, "Shall I get his -- his sleeve?"

"I'll get it," snarled Melvin. A little more and he'd bite.

"Thank you," said the doctor, motioning surreptitiously at the nurse, who stepped back, as Melvin rolled up that sleeve with proprietorial efficiency.

"Now you know," said the doctor, "There will be two injections --."

"One to put me to sleep, and one to send me on. Yes, I know."

"Good. Good, I'm glad you know."

"You know, Doctor," mused Pfirsich. "I've heard chickens are more tender if you give them beer before they're beheaded."

"It relaxes their muscles," said the doctor, very carefully arranging

321

his instruments, so that they wouldn't make a sound as he laid them out on the cloth on the steel stand. These weren't people who wanted to hear noise, not the least scrape or clink. The old man was ready to attack, and the older man was in a state of near bliss that it would have been criminal at this moment to disturb.

"It's the same thing if you drop lobsters into white wine before boiling," said the doctor. "It anesthetizes them."

"Lobster!" said Pfirsich. "We could have had lobster."

"Glutton," said Melvin.

"Put a lobster in my coffin, will you, dear?"

"Do you know what that will smell like?"

"Roast lobster," smiled Pfirsich. "Delicious."

Melvin snorted.

"Smile," said Pfirsich to him. "You have a lovely smile."

Melvin smiled like a guard-dog. Pfirsich looked up at the doctor, who was still quietly engaged.

"*Herr Doktor,* do they allow beheading for this -- in Holland?"

The doctor didn't start. People at this point in their lives were liable to ask all sorts of questions.

"No, they don't," he said. "Though it's not supposed to be a very painless method, either."

"Thank God!" said Melvin. "Or he'd ask for it."

"Pity," purred Pfirsich. "It would have been dramatic."

"Ham," said Melvin.

"What better time for theatricality?" agreed Pfirsich. "And I'd have done it in my uniform. With my medals."

"What medals? You did everything all your life to avoid awards." Melvin looked up at the doctor. "He gave to charities for years, and all of it anonymously. I never got to go to a charity banquet the whole time we were together."

"Beef boiled to rags," shuddered Pfirsich. "Once was enough."

"*Mynheer* Rommel," said the doctor. "Are you ready?"

"I'm ready, *Herr Doktor.* Do it before I sober up. Melvin, hold me."

Melvin froze.

"Melvin." Pfirsich took his hand, hard. He still had strong hands. "Hold me. I'm going, and I want you with me."

Melvin's face pulled up into a white knot. "I wish I could be with you. I wish I could go with you." He put his head right down on Pfirsich's chest. "Why can't I go with you?"

Pfirsich pushed him off. Melvin sat back and crossed his arms and sulked.

The doctor wasn't startled, but he still winced. It wasn't the first time a friend or family member had voiced that wish in particular. He'd heard of suicide pacts. But this unpredictable person was not just saying it because he hurt. He meant it. He yearned to follow his beloved as a swan wings after his mate. These two loved one another as did the black swans of Australia, the powerful avian homosexual couples that fought and guarded their surrogate young like red-winged black angels.

The doctor would not have been surprised now if the old man had crawled up onto his ancient friend's bier and demanded to be allowed to commit technological *suttee* right there. The doctor wouldn't have allowed it, of course. Suicide pacts were one area he did not want to approach. And this wasn't how civilized people acted. This was savage love, and bitter, and more difficult than it needed to be. This wasn't normal.

"Melvin, hold me," said the ancient friend in a tone of command that made the old man blink. He unwound his crossed arms and slid them around his friend, and pressed his face into his neck. He wasn't going to look.

Pfirsich put his hand to Melvin's head and slid his fingers into his hair. Gently massaging the black-dyed scalp, he spoke.

"All right, doctor."

Pfirsich closed his eyes and pressed his own face into the top of his friend's head, breathing the odor of his hair and skin. Sweet, musky, milky, beating hot with the blood that warmed the thoughts, it came to him as a memory. If the dead had memories, he wanted it to be this one. The two of them didn't say one more word to each other, they just lay still and pulsed and waited.

The doctor was shaking as he filled the first syringe; he hadn't expected this. The very few times he had performed this treatment, it had been dubious and wearying. Love foundered in despair and impatience, compromises struggled through discretion, liberation and loss. He and the patient and the relatives had wrestled each time in a ferment of bitterness and blame. It was like navigating the very estuary of the afterlife, pilotless

323

on the cold side of eternity's river.

None of those times had prepared the doctor for what lay on the table before him now. This double bundle of disagreement and hellish intention was like a pair of mating porcupines, or wolverines indignant and lascivious over a carcass. They breathed up a warm draft of violets, sweet as the odor of blood, as the old man's breath quickened. The doctor didn't know if he dared lay hand on either one of them.

Then the patient turned his lean old head and focused upon the doctor those exacting water-blue eyes.

"It's October 14th, *Herr* Doctor. I'd like to have it done today."

The doctor's mouth tightened. He wasn't used to patients giving him orders, and this one had never done anything else. If there's one thing a doctor can't endure, it's infringement upon his competence or his mastery of his discipline.

The doctor applied the first needle with complete authority. The scent of violets rose up and perfumed the room.

* * * * *

When the funeral home staff drew the heavy steel tray back out of the crematory chamber and began to collect the gritty dust to place into the gold-and-pink porcelain urn that the old man had chosen, they found, mounded over with the human detritus, four inorganic objects.

Two stainless-steel knee joints. The staff had expected those. They carefully brushed and polished the joints and placed them in the gleaming ebony wood box-stand that would support the urn.

One blackened lump of what had been pink plastic, which was to be placed in the urn itself. This was the remains of a rare original 1950's black-haired *Barbie* doll, the best loved of the personal collection. It had been the slightly damaged one of a pair; the other, which was in mint condition and pressed from an earlier mold, had gone to the Manhattan great-granddaughter. She had helped to dress the sacrificial plastic virgin in a blue sequined dress and fur hat she had minutely cut and stitched with her own hands, and laid it in the coffin herself under her great-grandfather's arm. At the funeral, the surviving doll had appeared in a dress of a matching cut, in black, with a broad flat black straw hat and Chantilly lace veil, a miniature version, of course, of the granddaughter's

324

outfit. Perfect.

And found last, near where the heart had been, a fused lump of yellow and gray metal. The staff thought it might have originally been two objects, one brass, the other pot-metal.

When they had cleaned it they showed it to Melvin. He had no idea what it was. He put it in the box with the knee joints.

Bread and Swans

Epilogue

It was a year and a day after the funeral that Melvin was discovered in his bed with a silent heart.

Pfirsich's son supposed that he'd just received his flight orders late.

Donna Barr is best known as the author and artist of the drawn book series *The Desert Peach* and *STINZ*. Her books have won San Diego Comicon International's *Inkpot Award*, the *Xeric Grant* and the *Arch and Bruce Brown Foundation Grant*.

She lives on Washington State's Olympic Peninsula with her husband and former army buddy, Dan Barr.

She would like to come back as one of her cats.